J.T. NICHOLAS

RE·COIL

J.T. NICHOLAS

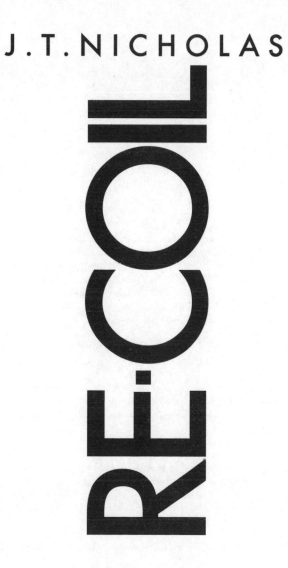

RE-COIL

TITAN BOOKS

Re-Coil
Print edition ISBN: 9781789093131
E-book edition ISBN: 9781789093148

Published by Titan Books
A division of Titan Publishing Group Ltd
144 Southwark Street, London, SE1 0UP
www.titanbooks.com

First edition: March 2020
10 9 8 7 6 5 4 3 2 1

A CIP catalogue record for this title is available from the British Library.

Printed and bound in the United States.

For Julie, who encouraged
(and still encourages) me to keep going
no matter how many rejections poured in.

To die, to sleep—
To sleep, perchance to dream—ay, there's the rub;
For in that sleep of death what dreams may come
When we have shuffled off this mortal coil,
Must give us pause: there's the respect
That makes calamity of so long life.

HAMLET

1

The derelict vessel drifted against endless darkness.

I made no sound as I walked along the ship's surface in the sliding shuffle forced by magnetic boots, nothing but electrical charge and the ferrous content of the hull keeping me from spinning away into the deep. My ship was out there, too, of course, a hundred meters away and matching vectors with the wreck. Not that it mattered. If something went wrong while I was EVA, they might as well be back on Earth.

I kept the slow, steady shuffle, making sure one boot latched firmly before sending the mental command through my personal Net that deactivated the electromagnet in the second and sliding it forward in turn. Rinse. Repeat. Slow and steady and, most importantly, survivable.

It took almost fifteen minutes, but I found myself before the airlock door. With a thought, the miniature spotlight mounted on the shoulder of my suit blazed to life, bathing the door in harsh white light. The beam revealed pocking along the hull, not unexpected given that the ship could have been drifting through the system for decades. But it also caught the edges of three almost perfectly circular holes, two centimeters in diameter, and arrayed in a neat triangle, near the door's center.

Analysis, Sarah, I thought.

My agent's voice—a contralto programmed to be calm, soothing, and always well modulated—came back at once, resonating in the depths of my mind, from the place that I always associated with my Net implant. *Diameter, twenty-two millimeters. The smoothness suggests a cutting laser, though there are no signs of metal fatigue. Certain drills would also be possible, though it would be difficult to maneuver them into position outside of a shipyard. The holes are equidistant from one another and placed to form a perfect isosceles triangle measuring thirty point four-eight centimeters per side.*

"Did it come from the inside, or the outside?" I asked aloud, my voice hollow and tinny in the vacc suit's helmet.

"Say again, Langston."

This voice didn't sound from the depths of my own mind, but rather crackled to life over the vacc suit's speakers. "Wait one, Miller," I replied, staving off the issue for the moment. *Sarah?*

Insufficient data, the agent responded.

"Great," I muttered. "You getting this, *Persephone*?"

Miller's voice came back. "Roger that, Langston. Got three holes punched in the side. We've been running the data through the *Persephone*, but we've got nothing."

"Yeah. Sarah's coming up dry, too."

"Your call."

It wasn't much of a choice, really. The *Persephone* was a small ship, outfitted for salvage operations, with a crew of just four souls. Miller piloted, Harper ran the heavy equipment, Chan was our techno-wiz, and I was the lucky SOB who got to play EVA specialist. When we could get close to space junk, it was normally Harper's show—they drove the mechanical arms and cutters that could crack open any debris that didn't need the finer touch of a direct human hand and bring it aboard the *Persephone*, leaving Chan and me to pull off the small bits in relative comfort. But when the junk went tumbling and spinning, it was my job to get over to it, try to stabilize it for the *Persephone* to approach, and if that wasn't possible, grab whatever was worth the most creds.

We'd been working together for a few years now, going out a couple of months at a time and laying claim to what salvage we could find. Lately, we'd been finding a lot of nothing. Scrap metal that barely kept fuel in the *Persephone*'s tanks and flavorless synth-soy in her larders. I couldn't speak for my crewmates—when we left the ship, we tended to go our separate ways until the next mission—but I could certainly use the creds. Coil premiums were coming due, and as things stood, I had enough in my free balance to cover them, but only just. I really didn't want to go into arrears. A derelict vessel on a ballistic trajectory into Sol was too good a find to pass up.

"Roger that, *Persephone*. I'm going in."

"Be safe. And keep the video streaming."

"Will do."

I turned my attention back to the airlock door. The exterior of the ship didn't tell us much. Starship design hadn't changed significantly over the past hundred years or so. They say that technology used to change much faster, growing and expanding at an almost logarithmic rate, but those days were long gone.

Humanity may not have peaked, but it had, at the very least, stabilized. The vessel wasn't broadcasting any transponder codes. That wasn't unusual on older salvage—no power source could last forever. Our visual inspection hadn't yielded any exterior registration on the hull, either. Not that all ports of call required one. Earth and the domes of Luna and Mars did, but that was mostly a hallmark of the days of ocean-borne vessels. Ships in space seldom got close enough to one another to make something as pedestrian as numbers and letters painted on the hull useful. Without any way to identify it, the ship could have been years, decades, maybe even a century old.

However old the ship might have been, airlocks hadn't changed much. Two things on the left side of the slightly-larger-than-man-sized door caught my attention. The first was an eye bolt, and I pulled the safety line from my harness and clamped it in place, tethering me to the ship. Surviving open space was about being careful, consistent, methodical… and taking advantage of every redundant system and safety feature available. I wasn't about to go drifting endlessly through the deep while some branching proto-me picked up my life where I left off.

The second thing was a small access panel. I depressed it slightly, and it popped open, revealing the controls for the airlock door. Unfortunately, those controls were nothing more than a blank screen. I cursed under my breath.

"Looks like we've got a true ghost ship, here," I said. "No power to the airlock controls." In most ships, the exterior airlock controls were slaved to the same power systems that handled life support. If trouble arose, you knew that the rescuers could reach you quickly for as long as you had air and heat. After that, it didn't much matter, since cutting through hulls took time that an asphyxiating crew probably didn't have. It happened more than most people thought; no matter how stable the tech or smart the AI, neither human error nor the uncaring hand of entropy could be completely mitigated. When you had thousands upon thousands of vessels plying the space of Sol, even a small percentage of vessels suffering catastrophic mishaps still added up to a lot of missing ships. Multiply that over all the years humans had been active in space, and you realized just how much junk was really out there. It sucked, but it kept us in business.

"Can you cut it?" The voice belonged to Chan, and even over the radio interference, she managed to sound sultry.

The harness I wore over my vacc suit bristled with tools. In anything other than microgravity, I probably wouldn't have been able to carry it. Even with that, I had to be careful about mass and inertia, so as not to inadvertently smash myself into surfaces at speeds that my coil couldn't take. But it did give me a few options.

"Probably," I replied. "Wait one." *Sarah, do I have enough plasma cutters to get in?*

In answer, a web of glowing dashed lines appeared on the airlock door, transfixing two of the three holes already bored through the composites and tracing a path that would result in an opening big enough—if only just—to pass me and my equipment. As if to drive the point home, an arrow pointed at the dotted line and the words, "Cut here" appeared beside it. Agents like Sarah may not have had the full personalities and cognitive abilities of Alpha AIs, but she'd certainly managed to pick up a bad sense of humor somewhere.

"Okay, *Persephone*," I said. "Looks like Sarah thinks I can cut through. Estimated time is…" I paused, and, without prompting, Sarah added a digital clock display to my view. "One hour, twenty-seven minutes."

"Roger that, Langston." It was Miller's voice again, a deep bass. "Be advised, we estimate eight hours—that's zero-eight hours—until we'll be close enough to Sol that heat and radiation are going to become problems."

"Gotcha," I replied. "No dawdling."

With that, I grabbed the first metal cylinder from my belt, tightened my safety tether, and brought the nozzle close to the hull, right beside one of the holes and on top of the line Sarah had overlaid. I pressed the firing stud, and a cone of blue-hot plasma belched from the torch. The cutter functioned by sending an electric arc through a flow of argon, exciting it into the fourth state of matter. It didn't require an oxidizer, which was just as well. Oxygen was precious enough without wasting it on cutting. My vacc-suit facescreen automatically polarized, darkening before the intense light could damage my eyes. I drew slow, even breaths, moving the torch at a barely perceptible rate as the metal of the door began to glow a brilliant cherry red.

The countdown on the digital display in my view read 1:38 and I was on my second-to-last plasma cutter when I finished slicing through the composite airlock door. I grabbed an electro-magnetic grip—little more than a power source, some wire, and a handle—from my harness and pressed it against the piece of metal still seated in the door. A mental command activated the magnet, locking the handle to the door. I shifted my feet, sliding them around until they were both planted just under the hole and activated the magnetic locks in them as well. By bending at the knees and hips, I slid down into a crouch, and wrapped both hands around the handle of the magnetic grips.

I drew a deep breath and stood, keeping the motion smooth and the force constant. The door section pulled free and rather than trying to fight its inertia, I held on long enough to guide it safely past my head, and then let go. The chunk of metal drifted off into space, another bit of junk that would, eventually, be pulled into the sun.

"I'm through."

"Roger that. Be careful."

Maneuvering through the hole required unclipping the safety tether and deactivating the magnets in my boots. For just an instant, I hung next to the derelict vessel, only Newton and Keppler keeping me in place relative to the ship. Then I grabbed the edges of the hole I'd just cut and swam my way into the airlock.

My boots clicked back onto the deck, and I swept the beam of the flashlight around me. The unadorned gray of the bulkheads drank in the light, making the room seem somehow darker than the blackness outside. The light passed over a lump, positioned before the hatch leading deeper into the vessel.

I focused the beam on it and froze. "Damn," I muttered. "You guys seeing this?"

There was a long moment of silence on the other end of the

comm. "Yeah, Langston," Miller's voice came back. "We've got it. Is that what I think it is?"

It was a body. A body that had succumbed to a combination of asphyxiation and decompression. It had been male, once, though the features were distorted enough that it was nearly impossible to tell much beyond that. "It is," I replied to Miller's question while simultaneously sending mental instructions to Sarah to take several deep scans of the scene from the suit's external sensors.

Already done, Langston.

"You know what you've gotta do, Langston," Miller said. "This just turned into a retrieval."

"Roger that, *Persephone*." I steeled myself for what came next. "You guys might want to turn off the displays for a minute." I received an affirmative click back and swallowed hard.

One of the tools on my harness was a small laser cutter. Not powerful enough to slice through bulkheads, it was the perfect tool for salvaging electronics or other equipment that was bolted rather than welded in place. It also made a fair utility knife if the need arose... and an excellent field scalpel.

The corpse sat with its back against the door as if the person had simply sat down to die. There was no expression on the face—it's hard to have an expression when your features have been twisted by asphyxiation and decompression—in fact, it barely looked like a face at all. Which was good, considering what I was about to do.

I reached out one hand and placed it on the corpse's shoulder. In the microgravity, it was easy enough to turn the body over. It spun, maintaining its seated stance, frozen in position by the near absolute-zero temperatures of the holed and depressurized ship. I braced the body between the deck and bulkhead, relying on my boots to keep me in place as I pressed down against the corpse. It wasn't pretty; it wasn't fun; it wasn't dignified. It was, however, necessary.

I found the hollow at the back of the corpse's skull and pressed the laser cutter close. Then, I began to cut. Flesh, blood, and bone all sublimated under the heat of the laser, creating thin trails of smoke that dissipated almost instantly. It didn't take long. I reattached the laser cutter to my harness and pulled an old-fashioned, fixed-blade knife from its sheath at my hip. Another steadying breath, and then I fed the tip of the blade into the incision I'd made, probing until I felt the faint click of metal on metal. I traced the object with the blade, freeing it from the surrounding tissue, and then used the knife as a lever, slowly working it to the surface.

What emerged from the wound was a ceramic-metallic cube, less than two centimeters on a side. Hard to believe that something so small could contain all of a person that *was* the person, the ego, the id, the psyche... the soul. Whatever you wanted to call it, it was the sum total of what made you... you, and the miracle of modern medicine meant that it could all be backed up and slated into a new coil. Provided it didn't go careening into the sun anyway.

"Got the core," I said.

"Roger that. Are you going deeper?"

It was a good question. Retrievals always brought creds, since most people were willing to give just about everything they had to keep on living and to keep their memories intact.

Better yet, payouts for retrievals were built in to even the most basic of coil insurance policies, so the creds were guaranteed. But we hadn't even cracked the doors on the main vessel, and there was no telling what treasures might await us within. *Sarah, how much time do we have left?*

Radiation levels will approach detrimental limits in five hours, fifty-eight minutes, and twenty-one seconds.

"We've got time, *Persephone*. I'm going to try and go deeper."

I got another click in acknowledgment, but I knew my fellow crewmates. A retrieval was good, but a retrieval and salvage were better. I turned my attention back to the interior airlock, playing the flashlight over it, looking for the manual overrides. I found the panel and slid it open. And then stared at the mess that had been made of the controls.

Both the standard and manual controls looked like they had been hit with a plasma torch. They were melted into slag, and I doubted the door could have been easily opened… from either side. Which raised more than a few questions.

"*Persephone*, your monitors back on?"

"We're seeing it, Langston."

"Is it me, or does it look like this guy locked himself in the airlock and then slagged the controls?"

Harper's voice. "Did you check the interior controls to the outer door?"

"On it." I shuffled back to the hole I'd cut in the airlock and found the panel to the outer door. Sure enough, the controls behind it had been melted, too. "Looks like our retrieval didn't want anyone else getting to him… at least not without some cutting. From inside the ship or from the outside."

"But why lock yourself in the airlock?" Harper asked, their voice perplexed.

I grunted. "I don't know, but I've still got a couple of plasma cutters left, so maybe we can find out." I moved back to the interior door and examined the half-melted controls. *Sarah, can I cut my way in?* In response, a window popped up in my vision, showing a standard airlock schematic. It scrolled and zoomed, focusing in on the manual door release. Sarah highlighted the pertinent section, and I nodded. "I don't have to cut all the way through the door. Looks like I might be able to disengage the interior lock. Won't work if the rest of the ship is pressurized, but it's worth a shot."

"Be careful."

"Roger that, *Persephone*."

It took both of my remaining plasma cutters, but, following Sarah's silent directions, I managed to burn through to the hydraulics. The fluid that bubbled sluggishly from the lines when I cut them was a hybrid synthetic far removed from anything that had once been called "oil" and designed specifically to remain liquid at the near absolute-zero temperatures that would claim any derelict vessel. I played the last of the flame from the torch gently over the surrounding metal, heating it and encouraging the flow of the fluid. After only a moment, the cutter sputtered and died.

"Okay, *Persephone*. Moment of truth." I shuffled back to the door and grabbed the wheel. Once again, I made sure to apply force as smoothly and constantly as possible, slowly increasing the amount of strength I was putting into it, until it finally began to turn. More hydraulic fluid flowed from cut lines, droplets drifting around me in the microgravity. The wheel spun, and I felt the *thunk* of the bolts releasing. I pulled, and though the door resisted, it finally gave, swinging open and beckoning me into the darkness beyond.

2

The airlock opened into a short hallway, ending at another hatch at either end. The flashlight mounted on my shoulder provided the only illumination, casting odd shadows as I swept it through the hall. The beam caught the edge of letters, where the bulkhead met the overhead, and I focused the light there. Three lines of standard text, and a pair of arrows. The top row read, "Airlock." The second row read, "Control" and an arrow beside it pointed off to the right. The third read, "Passenger Cabin" with an arrow pointing off to the left.

Sarah, have you identified this vessel, yet?

Insufficient data. The vessel has no active Net transponder. General physical characteristics are consistent with a mid-range passenger shuttle, of the type used for moving between planetary masses and their moons. Most commonly found around Jupiter.

We're a long way from Jupiter, Sarah.

Current estimated position puts us approximately seven hundred and fifty-four million kilometers from Jupiter.

Thanks. Super helpful.

You're welcome, Langston.

I swear she sounded smug. "Well, I guess one way's as good as another. How much time do we have left?"

Miller's voice came back at once. "Four hours, Langston. You need to be on your way back here in four hours, latest."

Passengers or crew? I thought about the bloated corpse in the airlock and shuddered. So far, I hadn't found any evidence of the ship being holed—other than the outer door to the airlock. But something had depressurized the vessel, and the thought of a passenger cabin filled with the decompressed dead sent a shiver running down my spine. I turned to the right and made my way to the door.

The manual controls presented no problem, since no one had attempted to melt them. I opened the door and panned the light across. Another corridor stretched before me, and I followed it. It branched off twice, but I ignored the side corridors, moving steadily forward to—I hoped—the bridge. My hopes bore out when I reached another hatch, this one with the words, "Control" and "Authorized Personnel Only" stenciled across it.

The hatch was shut, but whatever had caused the person in the airlock to seal themselves in must not have bothered the command crew, since the door wasn't sealed. The latch spun freely and the door swung inward. I braced myself, mentally gearing up for what I expected to find—the distended coils of the pilot, captain, and astrogator.

Instead, the light revealed an empty chamber. The boards and screens were dark, the chairs, empty. Nothing seemed out of place. It was as if the crew had simply got up and left, shutting the door behind them on their way out. The only problem was, every regulation of every merchant and military vessel required that the bridge be manned at all times. Sure, you could maybe get away with a Net link for a minute or two, but any spacer who lived long enough to claim the title knew better than to tempt fate too much. I'd been aboard more than one vessel that had been evacuated. No one ever took the time to close the doors behind them, all nice and tidy. And if they hadn't had the time to evacuate… in that case, the bridge shouldn't have been abandoned. Finding bodies was never fun, but sometimes finding nothing was worse. "I've got a whole lot of nothing on the bridge, *Persephone*."

"We're seeing it, Langston," Miller said.

"And it's creepy as hell," Harper chimed in.

"Can you get the box?" Chan that time, stepping on top of Harper's words almost before they got them out.

"Wait one." I moved to the captain's console and found the access panel. A little work with a screwdriver, and the panel came free. I pushed it away, letting it drift. There wasn't much harm it could do at this point.

I shone the light into the cavity, revealing a mix of cubes, boards, and dark fiber optics. Amidst the various electronics, there should have been the box, the successor to the antiquated flight recorder that logged the ship's position, astrogation data, and ship's logs. Instead, there was an empty place in a circuit board.

"It's gone," I muttered.

"Say again?"

"It's gone, *Persephone*. Removed." Which didn't make a whole lot of sense.

"Did they evac?" Miller asked.

"And leave a crew member or passenger sealed in the airlock?" That thought sent a little tingle of fear coursing up and down my spine. What would it be like, to remain sealed away, while you heard the evacuation pods firing, one by one from the other side of the ship? "I'll check the passenger cabin."

"Roger that, Langston. But hurry. Clock's ticking."

I made my way back through the corridor, past the airlock and toward the main cabin of the ship, ignoring the side passages that led to engineering and, presumably, the escape pods. As I approached the final hatch, my feet slowed. What would I find on the other side? Empty chairs and mystery, like on the bridge? Or distended corpses? I drew a steadying breath and spun the manual hatch release.

The door swung inward in silence, on hinges so smooth that I barely felt the faint resistance. My light swept over the chamber, illuminating row after row of what my tired mind first took to be sleeping people. They sat in the acceleration chairs, eyes closed, lips slightly parted, row upon row of perfectly still bodies. It took a moment to process—to realize that the stillness was *too* perfect, that the faces were not composed in sleep, but slack in death. It took a moment to remember that the ship was airless, depressurized, drifting through space. In that moment, I felt suddenly, completely, and utterly alone.

"You still there, *Persephone*?" I asked the empty space, forcing the words to calm despite the panic I felt crawling up my esophagus.

"We're here, Langston," Chan said. Her voice was soft, perhaps overwhelmed by the images coming back to the ship over the Net, but it was somehow soothing.

"I…" I cleared my throat. "I'm not sure we have enough time to do the retrievals." That was a lie—or at least, not the whole truth. Maybe there was time, maybe there wasn't. I'd been working salvage long enough that retrievals were an inevitability. But there was something so… dehumanizing about cutting into an empty coil and prying out the little bit of storage that held most of what a person was. If they were smart, they were backed up, anyway. If not… But, damn it, they *were* lucrative, and all of us could use the creds.

"Understood, Langston." Miller this time, cutting into my reverie. "We make twenty-seven, that's two-seven, coils." There was a long, long pause. "How many do you think you can get? Estimate time remaining at… approximately three hours."

Shit. Miller was trying to be subtle, trying to be nice. There was plenty of time to harvest the cores from the coils. And there was plenty of reason, too. I had a job to do. Best to be about it.

"Message received, *Persephone*. You may want to blank the vids again."

"We'll keep them running. It's the least we can do."

I didn't respond to that, instead stepping into the passenger cabin. I moved to the first row of acceleration chairs and turned my attention to the first corpse. The coil was bio-female, young, and, at least when imagined with the full flush of life, attractive. It showed no signs of decompression or trauma, and the eyes remained, thankfully, closed. I tried to stop thinking of the coil as a person—what made it a person was safely locked away in the core, anyway. It was just a shell, and one that had outlived its usefulness.

The rational part of my mind knew that to be true. It didn't stop the twisting in my guts as I pulled the frozen body forward, and moved the auburn hair out of the way, baring the hollow in the base of the skull. The laser cutter and the knife did their work, and in a few minutes, I was sliding another core into the bag on my harness.

The work was grisly, but not particularly difficult. The entire coil and core were engineered so that it took only a passing familiarity with anatomy to affect the retrieval. It wasn't the sort of task that required my full attention—in fact, it was the sort of task that begged for that attention to be turned elsewhere. *Sarah, why are the coils not showing signs of decompression?*

Insufficient data at this time.

I ground my teeth together. *Guess.*

As you wish, Langston. The first and most likely cause is sufficient time during decompression for the fluids and gasses in the body to adapt to the changing pressures. Other possible causes decrease greatly in probability and include flash freezing, absence of fluids or gasses in the system to begin with, or administration of outside agents to prevent decompression.

I knew Sarah was right—no one spent long in space without garnering a basic understanding of how decompression sickness and sudden decompression worked. Yet, at the same time, none of her answers made any sense. Who would sit idly in their acceleration chairs while the pressure in the cabin slowly went from one atmosphere down to vacuum, presumably taking with it all the breathable air? The coils showed no signs of flash freezing or desiccation, and the only outside agent I knew of that could prevent decompression was a vacc suit. What had happened to these people?

I moved down the line of chairs, the laser cutter doing its gruesome work, and the little pouch of cores at my hip slowly filled. I was down to three rows when I felt a slight shiver course through the derelict's hull.

I paused in my work and waited for a moment. The shiver came again, and then grew into a steady vibration. I felt the faintest tug pulling me toward the back of the cabin. The ship was accelerating.

"*Persephone?*" I asked aloud. At the same time directing a mental, *Status?* at Sarah.

"What the hell's going on over there, Langston?" Miller demanded. "Our sensors show that the derelict's engines just came online."

The vessel is powering up and accelerating toward Sol, Sarah confirmed.

"Shit," I swore. "I don't know, *Persephone*. The damn engines just fired. By themselves. Are you sure no one's aboard?"

"Sensors aren't showing anything living over there except you, Langston." There was a momentary pause. "Time to get off that boat."

"Yeah, that's a big roger. Heading to the airlock, now." I panned my light across the last three rows. Nine souls lost, at least for a few months. I turned to go, but something stopped me in my tracks. Something had been different on those last bodies. I swept the flashlight back, panning it over the coils, looking for whatever had caught my attention.

One of the corpses, its pale, lifeless eyes wide open, stared back at me.

3

I jerked back from the sight, my entire body lurching away, which in microgravity was a stupid idea. The motion, sudden and sharp, tore my magnetic boots free of the deck, and sent me drifting, tumbling toward the front of the cabin. The beam of the light spun with me, panning across the bulkhead and overhead, losing focus on the open-eyed coil.

My heart raced as I reached out, using my arms like shock absorbers against the bulkheads, pulling my knees to my stomach and working to reorient myself so that down was, once again, the deck beneath my feet. I'd spent enough time in freefall that the move was instinctual. The boots touched down on the deck, electromagnets engaging, and I swept the flashlight back toward the far end of the cabin.

The rational part of my mind insisted on telling me that residual electrical energy in the brain could stimulate the ocular muscles and make the eyes of the corpse snap open. It had less explanation for the fact that the same coil, which had until that moment been firmly strapped into its acceleration couch, had pulled itself up and was floating in the microgravity. It moved gracelessly toward me, limbs that should have been long frozen reaching out to pull it past the seated heads of its fellow corpses, still locked into their own acceleration chairs. Its hands closed on the back of one of those chairs, and it pulled, launching itself forward, arms stretched out before it, fingers reaching.

The coil flew at me like a missile, the steadily increasing tug of the engines hardly slowing it. My conscious mind was still trying to catch up, to process what was happening. That didn't stop instinct from kicking in, and my hands came up, even as I twisted my body at the hips and shoulders and knees, presenting as thin a profile as possible while my feet remained locked to the deck. The outstretched hands missed me by inches, and the rest of the coil continued to float past.

I dropped my hands down, slamming my suited forearms into the coil's back as it passed, imparting a new vector that sent it careening first to the deck, and then bouncing off toward the overhead. The force jarred me, not just my arms, but put a terrible pulling strain on my ankles as the boot magnets competed with the action/reaction force of the strike. I once again pulled free from the deck, but only just, floating a few inches off the ground.

"*Persephone*," I gasped. "Are you seeing this?"

I received no response.

"*Persephone*, do you copy?"

Silence.

Sarah, where the hell is Persephone?

My agent's voice echoed in my mind. *The* Persephone*'s Net has gone offline. Insufficient signal strength to ascertain any additional information.*

What?

The Persephone*'s Net has…*

I interrupted the agent with a quick *Cancel* query. I managed to reorient myself back toward the front of the cabin, using the chairs to pull myself back down to the floor. The... coil... was still flailing up near the overhead, its movements too jerky and spasmodic for microgravity. Which was alarming in and of itself—the blow to the back would have incapacitated a normal person. Of course, so would being suitless in vacuum. Normal had gone right out the airlock.

To further complicate things, the force of our acceleration was now a noticeable pull toward the aft of the cabin, like being on an incline in normal G. The struggling corpse began to slide along the overhead, drifting toward me. Whatever was driving it, it seemed to have at least some degree of rudimentary intelligence, because it stopped its flailing and curled into a gently spinning ball. It rotated with enough speed that it would have made me motion sick, but it also all but guaranteed another opportunity to grab at me as it drifted past, unless I took action.

I was cut off from my ship, alone in a derelict vessel, accelerating into the sun, with what should have been a corpse trying to grab hold of me for what, I could only assume, were nefarious purposes. Taking action sounded like a damn fine idea.

I'd been holding the knife and laser cutter, but I let them drop. Scavenging could be a dangerous business, and the smart play was to be prepared for the certain unpleasantness that came up from time to time. Which was why, in addition to the various tools and equipment, a small Gauss pistol hung from my harness.

I tore the weapon from its holster, pulling it up along the center of my body and pushing out from there to minimize the reactive force. My heart thudded against my ribs, and my breathing came in short, staccato bursts as I brought the sights to bear on the tumbling corpse. As they intersected the drifting shape, I squeezed the trigger.

The pistol made no noise, though I felt the vibration as it fired, and the force of the heavy ferrous bearings leaving the barrel drove my arms up with recoil. Only my suit boots, still struggling against the pull of acceleration, kept the additional force imparted by the weapon discharge from moving me backward.

The projectiles that flew from the barrel moved more slowly than pulsors or other military-grade weapons and were much more massive, more in line with an ancient bullet, though without all the smoke of a chemical propellant. The relative slow speed and high mass kept the Gauss pistol safe to use in the confines of a ship, with a very small chance of the burst breaching the hull. It wouldn't have mattered much aboard the already derelict vessel, but not all our salvage operations took place on airless hulks.

The three rounds that belched from the barrel may not have been able to penetrate a ship hull, but against an unarmored, unsuited coil, they worked just fine. The first round only grazed the monstrosity tumbling toward me, opening a narrow line along its shoulder. The second struck more solidly, tracing a deep furrow down the back of the tightly curled body. The third punched through the torso, eliciting a sudden series of spasmodic jerks that disrupted the graceful roll and turned it into a macabre puppet dance. The corpse—once more behaving as expected for a corpse—flashed past me, hitting the rear bulkhead and staying there, pinned by the thrust of the engines.

That thrust was rapidly becoming a problem for me. *Sarah, estimate current acceleration.*

Passing 0.4 G, Langston.

The boots wouldn't hold past half a G or so. In fact, if I uncoupled one to take a step, they would probably fail. "*Persephone?*"

Still no answer.

Shit.

I shoved the pistol back into its holster and turned to the nearest acceleration chair. The coil in it was middle-aged, graying, but fit, distinguished-looking. An "elder statesman" kind of look. Or had been, before I'd used the cutter to pull out his core. I braced one arm on the couch and, making sure my boots were secure, used the other arm to pull the body from the chair. We were nearing half gravity, and the coil probably weighed close to eighty kilograms. I grunted, and heaved, keeping my feet firmly planted. The coil drifted upward, clearing the top of the acceleration couch, and then gravity— or rather acceleration, did its part.

I pulled myself into the chair, using my arms more than my legs, releasing the magnets and, for just a moment, dangling precariously. But I managed to seat myself firmly, the thrust pushing me back against the gel seat. "*Persephone?*"

The Persephone*'s Net is still offline, Langston.*

What the hell had happened? Why was the ship's Net down? We were too far from any habitat or station for me to connect to any other network. The derelict's bridge might have enough power with the engines up and running to broadcast farther, but the only ship that could get me off this wreck before it fell into the sun was the *Persephone*.

How much time, Sarah?

Please be more specific.

How much time until this ship falls into the fucking sun? Or until the heat and radiation get so intense that they microwave me?

Sarah's voice, calm as always, responded, *At current rate of acceleration, the edge of survivability will be reached in approximately seventeen minutes. Total destruction of the ship will occur approximately twelve minutes after that.*

Fifteen minutes to live. I'd backed up, of course. I did before every run. But that was weeks ago. Time that would be lost, gone never to return. I had questions, so many questions. How had all these people died? Why had the engines suddenly fired? What had caused the coil to animate and attack me?

Most importantly, where the hell was the *Persephone*?

"Dammit," I swore aloud. I didn't have any answers, but it was worse than that. When it was over, when they re-coiled me, I wouldn't even remember the fucking *questions*.

I felt a bead of sweat trickle down my forehead. It wasn't the stress, or adrenaline, or anything else. I had started to sweat because of the temperature. I brought up the suit diagnostics, splashing them across my vision. External temperature was rising. The suit's enviro-suite was trying to compensate, engaging cooling units, but it was a losing battle. In about—I queried Sarah—sixteen more minutes, the sun was going to cook me. And things would likely get very unpleasant before that.

So, what? Give up? My fingers twitched toward the Gauss

gun at my hip. It would penetrate the suit's helmet easily enough, and end things before they got too bad. But even knowing that the branch from a few weeks ago would be shoved into another coil, I couldn't bring myself to do it. So, what? Wait for the end?

Fuck that.

Sarah? Estimate current acceleration.

Approximately one point oh-one G and climbing.

Just slightly heavier than normal. I flexed my fingers. I could deal with that.

I maneuvered on the acceleration chair, getting my feet beneath me. I forced my mind to reorient itself, to think of the direction of the chairs, the bulkhead behind me as "down." It took some concentration, but when I opened my eyes, I was no longer being pressed back into an acceleration chair. Instead, I was *standing* on that chair. Above me was the back of another chair. More chairs descended below me, more above, forming a ladder. I reached out, and began to climb, moving over the discarded coils, pulling my body weight up against the increasing force of acceleration as I climbed "higher" into the ship. With the engines live and power coursing back into the derelict vessel, there was a chance the communications systems would be working. I doubted I could call for help—the *Persephone* wouldn't be ignoring my calls if there wasn't *something* interfering with the broader signals. But it was damn hard to stop comm laser from pinging a relay. *I* wasn't getting out of this in one piece, but if I could make it as far as the bridge, maybe I could send some kind of message.

The odds sucked, but that was the life of a scavenger.

4

I hated waking up in the body shop.

Consciousness and acclimation were slow processes, and the first thing I became aware of was that I was aware. Which felt odd, and somehow wrong. Next came the sensation of lying on something hard and cool. But the sense was muted, faint, more of a memory of what it felt like to rest upon something hard and cool than doing so. That was the extent of sensation, and I knew that, for a while at least, it was all I was going to feel.

An ancient poet from Earth's past had once written of shuffling off the mortal coil as an analogy for death. Humanity had taken it a step further, though. Technological advances theorized that the mind, the essence, some said the soul, of a person could be digitized and preserved, given that a large enough reservoir of storage space was available. The advent of quantum computing provided the raw storage and processing needed to turn that theory into a reality, taking humanity one giant leap closer to immortality. The rest was easy.

Cloned tissue produced new shells, new coils, in which the

mind could be inserted. Genetic engineering ensured that those coils were as perfect and purpose-built as any machine. They had to be slow-grown, as something in the chemistry of the brain required a certain degree of aged stability before accepting a core and by law, no one could be re-coiled into a body younger than sixteen years of age. That created any number of issues, particularly in those tragic instances when children died, but the ramifications of stuffing people with multiple decades of life into, say, a five-year-old body were too much for society to accept. And so, humanity, still unable to break the boundaries of our own solar system, effectively obtained immortality. Of course, it was never that easy, not with people being people. In the early years, with every aspiring biotech company trying to pump out home-grown coils as fast as possible to make a quick credit, the quality control had been nothing short of abysmal. And the issues went beyond the simple cosmetics and capabilities of a given coil. Improperly grown coils suffered from... call them wiring problems. The wetware of the brain, if not grown slowly over years to very specific and demanding standards, caused compatibility issues with the cores. The results weren't that different from any number of violent psychoses.

That's when the various polities stepped in. Most of the megacorps had a certain degree of extraterritoriality, but they were at least nominally subject to the will of the governments of Earth, Mars, Luna, and the various habitats and stations scattered throughout the system. When those governments acted in concert, even the corporations had to bow to their will. A set of standards was established and a new corporate entity, a new monopoly, was formed. BioStar was given the sole rights to create coils and held to the exacting standards. There were still errors of course, coils that didn't quite meet spec, but most were built as solid as the human form could be. Of course, limiting the supply to a single company, coupled with the growth time required for stable coils, meant that there was always a queue for getting put into a new coil and that, unless you had the top-of-the-line insurance policies, you pretty much had to take whatever body they stuffed you into.

Which brought its fair share of problems, but they weren't really the ones I was concerned about at the moment. Getting a backup of your mind shoved into new flesh had its own drawbacks. It took a while to acclimate, to really feel like the new coil was yours. But, more importantly, you accepted a certain data loss, as some termed it, between the time you had last backed up and the time you were re-coiled. For the ultra-rich who changed coils like the rest of us changed clothes, that might only be a few minutes. Pop into your local coil center, pick a new body, do a quick backup, and be inserted on the spot. For those of us who could only afford the most basic backup insurance, which provided for new coils only in the event of advanced age or death, that lost time normally measured in weeks, and in rare cases, sometimes as long as years.

How long, Sarah?

Agents were backed up in almost the exact same way as people, storing a copy of the AI at the point in time when the person was having their backup done. But AIs didn't have the shock of adaptation to a new coil, or the emotional baggage of realizing that, somewhere, some-*when*, a version of them had just been wiped out of existence. The question was vague, but since it was the question asked by most people when waking up in the body shop, AIs were programmed to handle it.

It has been sixty-three days since this instantiation was created.

I was still too new to my coil to register the physiological responses to surprise. My stomach didn't drop. My heart didn't race. My mouth didn't go dry and no sweat broke out on my body. Nonetheless, a cold, numbing sense of surprise flooded my mind, and for a moment all I could do was try to mutter, "Sixty-three days?"

The words were unintelligible, barely sounds at all, since I still had little control over my new vocal cords or lips. But they were, apparently, loud enough to catch someone's attention.

"Awake, then, are we?" The words were cheerful, almost chipper, and full of a brisk professionalism that just screamed medtech. They had a crisp, vaguely British edge to them. "Well, you've no doubt already queried your agent and learned that your re-coiling was just a bit, how should I put this… unusual? We'll give you all the details once you're a bit more, well… you. In the meantime, I need you to open your eyes. Do you think you could do that for me?"

I'd been through this a half-dozen times before—salvage was a dangerous business, after all, and it wasn't the most dangerous business I'd ever been involved in. The question should have been perfunctory, but there was a note of actual concern behind those words. What had happened to me?

I drew a deep breath—at which point, I suddenly became aggressively aware of the fact that I *was* breathing. That resulted in a brief, panicked moment where my conscious mind struggled with the autonomic responses of its new coil. It was a lot like I imagined suitless exposure to vacuum would be—wanting to breathe, struggling to take in precious, life-giving oxygen, but at the same time, being somehow unable to make your lungs work, despite seeing and feeling nothing that should prevent it. It passed quickly, leaving me momentarily panting.

I concentrated on my eyes, on opening the lids. They felt heavy, not from lack of sleep, but physically challenging, requiring an effort of muscle and will to manipulate. Slowly, ever so slowly, they parted, revealing a blurry and bleary world about me.

"Well, that's good, then," the British voice said. A slightly darker oval appeared in the generally bleary light that was my current field of view. A brighter light swept past my eyes, once, twice, a third time. "This may sting just a bit."

Something warm and wet poured into my eyes, and I blinked rapidly in response to the mild irritation that came with the fluid. It had the desired effect—with each blink, the blurriness eased, and my new eyes finally came into focus. The man leaning over me was fine-boned, dark-skinned, and, as was the case with almost every coil, physically attractive. He held a plastic squeeze bottle in one long-fingered hand and was dabbing at my face with a cloth held in the other.

"Are you back with us, then? Can you talk?"

Again, there was that edge of worry in his words.

"Where?" I forced the single word out in a strangled croak. It was deeper than it should have been, or at least, deeper than my old coil would have produced. It was definitely a bio-male voice though. Re-coiling facilities tried to put people back in the gender with which they identified, unless they specifically requested otherwise, but coils were in short supply. It wasn't unheard of to be re-coiled into whatever was available. If you did end up in the wrong body, your options were somewhat limited. You couldn't simply ask for a new one—the demand for coils always outstripped the supply and only the very, very wealthy could get a new coil at whim. The rest of us were stuck with whatever meat our cores got pushed into. If you ended up with the wrong plumbing, you could still try for reassignment surgery, but most people had to put all their spare cash into paying their re-coiling insurance premiums, with not enough left to buy the kind of medical policy that would cover reassignment surgery.

After three hundred plus years and several coils due to the perils of my profession, I fell into what had come to be called the gender-pragmatic portion of the spectrum. All things being equal, I felt most at home as a bio-male but the one time I'd been re-coiled into a bio-female shell, I hadn't felt any particular distress. Sure, I missed some of the muscle mass, but the smaller frame had been helpful for some of my salvage ops. And I'd still been me—thought the same way, liked the same things, been attracted to the same types of people. That wasn't how it went for everyone, of course. Some people were gender-adaptive. Their behaviors changed fluidly along with their biology, and they could find happiness regardless of the plumbing. Others were more gender-adamant. They had a firm mental image of who and what they were, and when they ended up in the wrong bio-shell, they suffered from mental and physical distress. Many of those folks had clauses in their policies requesting to stay archived until a bio-sex appropriate coil became available. The thought of volunteering to be archived made me shiver.

"Where are you?"

I tried to focus my mind back on the present, remembering the medtech trying to make sure that all my mental faculties were functioning. I nodded.

"Prospect station, in the medical facility. Do you know where that is?"

Stupid question. And still that edge. Not much to do but answer though, since my limbs still weren't responding. "Near Venus."

"And do you know *who* you are?"

Of course I knew who I was. What kind of question was that? "What... is... going... on?" I forced the words out, a low breath on each.

"Please answer the question. I'll explain everything once I'm sure you are undamaged."

Undamaged? I was in a brand-new coil, my old body, my old mind, dead and gone in a way that was, quite literally, unfathomable to the new me. What kind of damage could I possibly have suffered? Had something gone wrong during the re-coiling? I wanted to sit up, to pace, to express the frustration I was feeling with action. But my body still refused to respond to the signals from my brain, so instead, I grated, "Carter Langston."

"Good, Mr. Langston. That's very, very good." His voice nearly sang with relief. "One final question, Mr. Langston, I promise, and then we'll answer some of yours. Do you remember coming in here for backup?"

"Yeah." I coughed, and it seemed to loosen something in my throat, since words began to flow easier. "More than *two months ago*, according to my agent. We were going out on a salvage run, so I made sure to back up. Now, what the hell happened? I should have been back in action after thirty days, max. It was in my policy, after all. And why all the questions? And where is my crew?" I tried to shout the last few words, but the muscle control failed me, and instead they came out as a strangled gasp.

"I'm afraid I don't have any information on your shipmates, Mr. Langston. I'm sure if they are here for re-coiling, your agent will be able to assist you in that." Too right, she could. I sent Sarah a mental command to track down Chan, Miller, and Harper if they were on station. "My name is Dr. Johnathan Parsons. I was assigned your case only a week or so ago, when the technicians had repaired as much of the damage as possible."

"Damage to what?" I spat out. "I died, right? Isn't that why I'm here?" Prospect had been the last station I'd backed up on, before venturing out with the *Persephone*. It was theoretically possible for a person to be re-coiled anywhere, regardless of where their last backup had taken place, but no one wanted to risk any kind of data loss in blasting petabytes of information across the cosmos.

"Forgive me, Mr. Langston," Parsons said, and he actually sounded contrite. "I work in biology and genetics, but I do not do software well. Perhaps I chose my words poorly. When I say damage, I mean corruption."

That word sent a spike of fear straight into the pit of my belly, and icy tendrils of it coursed up my spine. "Corruption? Are you telling me my fucking *backup* was corrupted?" A jolt of adrenaline dumped into my system and I sat bolt upright, throwing my legs over the edge of the table and bracing my arms against it, getting ready to push myself to my feet.

"Slowly, Mr. Langston, slowly," Parsons said. He placed one long-fingered hand against my chest. There was barely any resistance, but it was enough to stop me from standing. "You haven't yet adapted to your new coil. If you insist on throwing yourself about, you might cause yourself injury."

"I don't care about the damned coil. What went wrong with my backup?" Saying the words, even thinking them, twisted the insides of my new body, and I had to choke back the urge to vomit. People were *supposed* to be immortal. Even the poorest, uninsured saps were guaranteed backup and re-coiling. Sure, if you couldn't pay your premiums, the process might take years, but all of the polities of Sol agreed that it was a basic human right to eventually have your core shoved back into a coil. But that only worked when the backups stayed clean, pristine. Which, given all the effort and credits put into perfecting and protecting the storage methods, was supposed to be guaranteed.

"We don't know. It must have been a systems glitch. The techs said they had never seen anything like it before." He paused, long enough for me to briefly consider murdering him—or his coil anyway—for dismissing my near-permanent demise as a *systems glitch*. "But you're okay. Your cognitive functions appear normal. Your adaptation to your new coil is… well, given that you've already started regaining control of primary motor functions, I would say it's astonishing. And you don't seem to be experiencing memory loss… other than the normal lag, of course."

The normal lag. Two months gone. Who knew how close it had come to being permanently gone? "Get out," I muttered. "Get the hell out and leave me alone."

"Of course, Mr. Langston. There are clothes for you in the closet. I understand you've done this before. There will be the usual tests before you can be discharged. In the meantime, I'll have some food and water sent." With a slight nod, he turned and strode from the room, leaving me alone with my new body and an old mind full of dozens of jumbled thoughts.

5

I studied at the mirror, trying to get used to the face staring back at me. The coil was heavier than I was used to, layered with slabs of muscle that felt awkward and ungraceful compared to the body I'd had before. The features were equally thick and heavy, like they'd been carved from rock with a rough chisel and never known the fine finishing hand of a master. The skin tone was a few shades darker than my last body, a fact that in times past might have presented its own set of prejudices and complications. Humanity still had innumerable issues, but at least the process of switching coils had been the death knell of melanin-based discrimination. Thick brow ridges, narrow, deep-set eyes. A chin so square and sharp-edged it looked like it could be used to smash rocks. I suppose it was handsome, in the way that mountains are handsome, but the sheer size would make navigating the tangled wreckage of derelict vessels more difficult.

I scrubbed too-thick hands vigorously over my new face, rubbing away the weariness. The coil was the one I was stuck with, so I might as well get used to it and move on. At least the plumbing was what I, personally, was most comfortable with and the implant seemed to be top-notch. *Sarah*, I thought, *status on the crew of the* Persephone?

No members of the Persephone's *crew, apart from yourself, appear to be aboard Prospect station, Langston. I have broadened the search to nearby habitats, but with the transmission lag, I may not have results for a few hours.*

I grunted, something my new body seemed well designed for. *What about the ship? Any indication what happened to the* Persephone?

The last record I have been able to find is from fifty-two days ago. At that time, the Persephone *transmitted a salvage claim to the Venusian Consortium, tagging a derelict vessel being pulled into Sol. The* Persephone *was granted rights to attempt to bring any salvageable materials and any recoveries from the ship. No other records have been found.*

The Venusian Consortium was a conglomerate of stations in near-Venus orbit. They'd started with the idea of terraforming—a pipe dream given that the temperature on the second rock from the sun averaged a balmy four hundred and sixty degrees Celsius and widespread terraforming had yet to be successful—but had eventually put so many stations in place that they'd hung a flag and called themselves a nation. They lacked the power of Earth or Mars, or even of the Jovian Alliance, but given how big space was, the fact that they were the closest polity to Sol gave them at least a certain level of legal weight when it came to authorizing salvage in the area. No one else was close enough to bother with policing it. So, we'd been going after something close to the sun. That was dangerous, sure, but fairly routine. What could have gone wrong?

The door to the medical bay opened, and I turned,

expecting Dr. Parsons, or one of the medical techs, coming to take me for yet another round of testing. Instead, a slim, athletic man wearing a coil of Asiatic genetic makeup slipped into the room. He wore a neatly pressed suit of deep black silk, black shirt and tie, and a pair of thin black gloves. Something glinted in his right hand, which he held tightly against his leg.

"Who are you?" I asked, stepping into the doorway of the small bathroom to get a better look at him.

His eyes locked onto mine, and something in them made my blood run cold. He didn't say anything, only regarded me with those black, soulless eyes as he raised his right hand, revealing the four-inch mono-blade.

We stood that way for a frozen moment, sudden heart-pounding fear making it impossible for me to think straight. A slow smile curled his lips, as if he were savoring the moment and he took a long, gliding stride forward.

I stepped back and slammed the bathroom door shut, hitting the magnetic lock plate as I did.

Sarah, alert the doctors, or security or someone.

I'm sorry Langston, but the Net access in the area is being disrupted.

"Wonderful," I muttered. An impact shook the door, rocking it in its frame. A shoe or shoulder being put to it, no doubt. And it wasn't exactly going to hold for long. I glanced around the bathroom, looking for anything that could serve as a weapon. Nothing. A different sound came from the door, and I turned my attention back to it just in time to see the point of the mono-knife punch through. The edge, far sharper than any razor, began slicing toward the handle, seeking the circuitry that kept the magnetic lock sealed.

I had scant seconds to make a decision. There was no way out of the bathroom. And, given that the nameless assassin on the other side of the door still hadn't said a single word, negotiation seemed to be out of the question. I was going to have to fight.

I moved, putting my back against the wall beside the doorframe, the side that had the latch, my eyes locked on the steady progress the knife was making along the door. There was a flicker from the magnetic lock, and the display on it went from green to red, indicating that it had disengaged. I had time to draw half a breath, and then the door exploded inward on the power of another well-placed kick.

The assassin came right behind the kick, rushing in with a speed that would have been overwhelming had I been standing in front of it. The knife came first, and I acted on instinct, smashing down with the edge of my right hand, aiming for the small bones of the wrist, and dropping as much of my body weight into the blow as possible. It was a move I'd had to use before, in my old coil, though in far less dangerous circumstances. I hadn't counted on the increased weight and strength of my new body, though.

The jarring impact coursed up my hand and arm, numbing and tingling. But I heard the crack of bone from the assailant's wrist, and the knife flew from it, clattering against the tiled floor and sliding beneath the sink. The man grunted in pain, but never slowed, turning toward me with a short, vicious punch from his uninjured hand.

The blow hit high on my cheek, snapping my head back and making a brief kaleidoscope of light dance before my vision.

I reacted on instinct, bringing both my hands up before my face. More pain blossomed on my left forearm as it intercepted an elbow intended for my head. A knee thudded against my ribs as I staggered back the meter or so left to me, ending up in the corner of the bathroom. The assassin surged forward, relentlessly kneeing and elbowing. I couldn't slip or dodge the onslaught, only cover up as best I could, taking as many of the shots as possible on my arms or legs, protecting my head, ribs, groin, throat, and stomach.

A dozen blows fell in those first few seconds, and I silently thanked whatever chance or fate had put me in a coil protected by thick slabs of muscle and heavy bone. But it couldn't stand against the onslaught forever, and I knew I had to make something happen. I brought my right leg up behind me, planting my foot against the bathroom wall. With a roar, I surged forward, shoving off the wall like I would in microgravity, bowling full force into the much smaller coil and bearing it to the ground.

Even on the way down, he managed to keep throwing those short, heavy elbows, and I grunted as I felt a rib finally give way from the force. But then I was on top of him, punching down with hands much larger and more powerful than they had once been.

The assassin twisted beneath me, somehow managing to free his legs and get them wrapped around my waist, locking his ankles behind me. I had been raised in microgravity, one more hab-rat in the bowels of Selene, where the station admins had scarcely bothered with the power expenditure to run the artificial gravity. I'd had my share of tunnel fights in a place where combatants had little choice but to physically lock together in order to exchange blows, so I ignored his legs and concentrated on driving my fists into his still-expressionless face. He somehow slipped past one of the punches, and lunged upward, wrapping one arm around the back of my neck, and shoving the other under my chin, pushing and pulling, closing my airway.

I wrapped my arms around his shoulders, and surged to my feet, bringing my attacker with me. He kept his grip, and as my vision dimmed, I looked wildly around. The edge of the sink caught my eye and I lunged forward, driving my attacker's back against the ledge. There was an explosive *whoosh* of air as his breath was driven from his lungs, and his grip loosened. Loosened, but did not release. I reared back and smashed him forward again, and then a third time. On the fourth, a resounding *crack* echoed in the small bathroom, and the squeezing pressure stopped, leaving me holding a dead weight.

I drew in a gasping breath as I dropped the assassin, letting him fall unceremoniously to the ground. A chunk of the porcelain from the sink fell with him, broken from the brutal impacts. I slumped onto the commode, and for a moment it was all I could do to draw in breath.

My mind raced. What the hell was going on?

I would find no answers sitting on the toilet, so I steeled myself and dropped down next to the would-be assassin. I checked for a pulse and found none. I had killed the man. Or at least, I had killed the coil. Presumably, he was backed up somewhere. Not that it mattered. Murder might not have been permanent, and the definition and penalties had changed with the advent of re-coiling, but if it wasn't ruled as self-defense,

I was still looking at serious time. As for the killer, would he simply be shoved into another coil, and sent after me again?

Why even bother sending an assassin? If the other me *had* learned something, he had taken it to the grave. The me I was now had no knowledge of whatever had happened in those last days. What was the point?

My hands shook as I rifled through the pockets of the suit, but I found nothing but the sheath for the mono-knife. I left that, and the knife itself, where it was. Apart from that and the clothes on his back, the man carried nothing. *Sarah, is the Net still inaccessible?*

No, Langston. It appears the assassin's agent was executing a denial-of-service attack. Do you wish me to contact the authorities, now?

That was an interesting question. If I called station security, it was very likely that the whole thing would be seen as self-defense… but it would take hours to go through the endless questioning, and at the end of it, I would still be confined to the hospital while they continued the various psychological and neurological tests to make sure the re-coiling of my "damaged" backup had gone okay. And anyone looking to kill me would know right where to find me. Or, I could walk out now, leaving a dead man in my room, and raising all kinds of questions, but whoever was after me would have a hell of a lot harder time tracking me down if I just… disappeared.

No, I replied. *Don't contact station security. Display a map of this facility. We're getting out of here.*

A window opened in the upper left-hand corner of my vision, outlining a blueprint of the habitat. It was toroidal, a giant donut floating in space, no doubt spinning around its central axis to give the illusion of gravity. I flicked my eyes, cycling through the plans. The medical facility took up the entirety of the inner-most ring, or, using reference points based on the feeling of gravity, the "top" floor of the habitat. Outward from there spread a mix of commercial and industrial zones, with a few residential quarters mingled in. Most of the mid-zone space was dedicated to residential space, thousands of quarters crammed into the corridors and passageways. The outer ring was almost entirely taken up by either habitat administration or ship docking and warehousing facilities.

I didn't have a firm destination in mind, except out. Out of the medical facility, and, as soon as possible, out of Prospect. I needed answers, and to get them, I was going to have to find the rest of the *Persephone*'s crew. If they'd been aboard the habitat, Sarah would have tracked them down already. Which meant I needed to make my way to the outer rings.

I glanced at the mirror. The clothes the med center had provided screamed re-coil: cheap synthetic fibers, square and blocky cut, and the finest jumpsuit style. All in a drab gray that could only be suitable for hospitals or prisons. My brief encounter with the assassin had been bloodless, so I didn't have that to worry about, and the synthetics had the advantage of being almost impossible to rip or tear. I took a moment to straighten the jumpsuit and run my fingers through my hair. The face staring back at me was still unfamiliar and looked like it would be right at home on a wanted vid, but apart from some emerging bruising around the throat, it didn't look like someone who had just killed a man.

I gave the assassin one last glance, and then slipped from the bathroom. I slid the door shut. It wouldn't latch, but it might buy me a few extra seconds. I crossed the small hospital room and stepped out into the corridor. Sarah added a glowing line to the map in my view, defining the path to the nearest elevator that would take me away from the med facility and the body I was leaving behind.

I drew a deep, steadying breath, wincing some as I felt my aggrieved rib shift. But the coil really was top-notch, however it looked, and I could tell the repair nanites had already gone to work. The pain was quickly lessening. I drew another breath and stepped into the life of a fugitive.

6

I made it out of the medical facility and into the lift without any difficulties. I cycled through the schematics Sarah displayed, finally settling on a commercial ring four segments rimward from the hospital. The lift shuddered into motion, seeming to descend, though I knew "down" was really toward the rim of the rotating torus.

When the lift stopped, the doors opened on a scene that had probably played out in a thousand different cultures throughout the course of human history. "Commercial district" was too grand a description for the shouting and squabbling press of humanity that milled about before me. "Open-air market" would have been closer, if it wasn't for the fact that the overhead prevented anything from remotely resembling "open air." It also thickened the smell—not that the people pressed into the narrow spaces between the stalls were unclean, but the concentrated press of humanity living in confined spaces had a fragrance that every spacer came to know.

Prospect, as its name implied, owed its existence to one

corporation's hare-brained idea that they could successfully mine the surface of Venus. It had been a fool's dream—with a surface temperature of nearly five hundred degrees Celsius the logistical challenges were near insurmountable. That hadn't stopped them from building the station and pushing forward anyway. In the end, it had bankrupted the company, but Prospect station had persisted. It had always attracted a boisterous crowd of would-be entrepreneurs, the kind of people who were always looking for an angle, and had a reputation within the Venusian Consortium as a place where hopeless romantics walked shoulder to shoulder with cutthroat corporate raiders. I couldn't get off of it soon enough.

I pushed my way into the throng, ignoring the calls from the vendors that their wares were of superb quality and priced to sell. My mind kept going back to the assassin. Why send someone to kill me? Murder still happened, of course. No matter how far humanity had come, we still couldn't shake off all our baser urges. And the overcrowding and other conditions on most habitats could wear away at even the most stable person's patience and sanity. But those crimes tended to be crimes of passion—expressions of rage or lunacy that resulted in death… for a time. Planned murder simply wasn't as effective as it once was, with most victims making a return. Death might not have been permanent, but the deep mental conditioning that most habitats imposed upon those convicted of murder most certainly was. And if he had been successful… well, my premiums were still paid. Even if the killer popped my core, the med staff would have stuffed me back into a new coil from backup, just as they had in the first place. They would have had to wait for a new coil to be available, so I could end up archived for a few more weeks. It seemed like a lot of effort to take me out of play for a while.

Assuming, that was, that whatever "systems glitch" they had encountered was fixed. That thought sent a chill coursing down my spine.

Given the circumstances, I needed to get my new ass off Prospect and back to Daedalus, where my residency status would protect me from prosecution from another habitat. Each independent habitat was a country unto itself and only the most heinous of criminals had to worry about the idea of extradition. I continued to slip through the press of humanity, moving without purpose or direction. I kept my eyes open, checking for any signs of pursuit, and I kept pinging the local Net, scanning the news as I walked, looking for any mention of a dead man found in a hospital room. So far, the failed assassin appeared to have gone unnoticed.

Sarah, what's the status of my accounts?

Your current free balance is five thousand three hundred and twenty-seven credits, after meeting the deductible for the backup and re-coil.

I winced at that. Whatever the other me had been doing, he hadn't been earning much in the way of creds. *Find me a shuttle out of here, preferably to Daedalus, but anywhere that can connect to Daedalus within the constraints of my credit limit will work, too.*

Understood, Langston. Processing.

Shuttles required vacc suits, and my backup insurance didn't have any lost property coverage. Most months, I could barely scrape the credits together for the base package, never mind the additional riders that those better off could afford.

Which meant that my already paltry funds were about to take another hit. I started scanning the market in earnest, not just for signs of possible pursuit by station security, but also for suit vendors. Every hab had them in abundance, since no matter how good the safety features got, it was impossible to forget that you were basically living in a giant tin can floating in the vacuum of space with a few inches of composites separating you from sudden decompression.

It didn't take long to find what I sought. A stall cobbled together from scrap metal and plastic sheeting bearing a table covered with an array of cheap suits. More expensive models hung behind the table, neatly displayed and Net-loaded to pop up their specifications if my eyes lingered too long on any of them. Given my credit situation, the best vacc suits the stall had to offer were well beyond my price range. I started rummaging around through the ones on the table, Net-linking with them to run basic diagnostics, making sure suit integrity still held. Most were cheap fabricated knock-offs of the big conglomerates, serviceable enough to get you through an emergency situation, but not the kind of thing you'd want to trust to regular EVA work.

Toward the bottom of the pile, though, I found an old VaccTech 2200. The space-black fabric had faded some, and the suit was slightly bulkier than the newer models scattered around it, but it boasted several integrated tiedown points and a higher tear rating than even some of its modern competitors. I almost held my breath as Sarah ran the diagnostics, but the suit checked out green. Its internal oxygen supply was even charged.

"You like that one, yes?" the man behind the counter asked. He had vaguely Anglo-Chinese features with a broad, shark-like smile that drew his eyes into narrow lines. "It is a good choice. Old, but well cared for. Like us, eh?" he said with a significant glance at the hospital-issued clothing I wore.

The specifications on the Net tag didn't include a price. "How much?"

"For you? I can let it go for five hundred credits."

Nearly ten percent of my current net worth. Still, I knew from the diagnostics that the suit really was in good condition, and I didn't have the time to stand around and haggle.

"Sold," I said.

I caught a brief glimpse of surprise in the vendor's eyes, and his smile widened just a bit more. I'd clearly paid more than he expected me to. "If I can duck behind your booth to put it on," I hastily amended. He arched an eyebrow at me and I shrugged. "I don't feel right being unsuited."

That was mostly true… I'd salvaged a lot of wrecks over the years and had a more intimate knowledge of just how many things could go wrong in space than your average hab-dweller. I got itchy in unfamiliar habitats if I didn't have a suit handy. But, more importantly, I needed to get out of the clothing that marked me as a fresh coil and made it that much easier for hab security to find me whenever they got around to looking.

"Ah, yes. I understand," the vendor said with a knowing smile. My implant pinged with the arrival of the invoice. I opened it and gave it a quick scan. Standard boiler plate, caveat emptor, liability waiver and so forth. I mentally "clicked" the pay button and was five hundred credits poorer. A ping from Sarah indicated that she was aware of the purchase and was adjusting ticket purchase constraints

58

accordingly. "You may change behind the stall."

I grabbed the suit and ducked behind the plastic and metal scrapheap. I pulled off the hospital clothes and slid the vacc suit on. There was an uncomfortable moment as the suit adjusted, nanitic fibers shifting and crawling over my skin, and a much more uncomfortable moment as the plumbing connections were made.

Sarah, please do a full scan and link with the suit and register it on your system.

Of course, Langston. I also have flight information available for you, when you are ready for it.

"Helmet," I said aloud.

I felt the slither and slide of the vacc suit as it shifted, forming a tight hood that framed my face. A transparent shield wrapped around my face, and a pair of indicators appeared in the top left of my vision indicating that suit integrity and internal suit oxygen were both at one hundred percent. "Helmet off," I said. The procedure reversed itself, the face-shield and hood peeling away and de-forming back into the suit itself. Good enough.

I wanted to review the flight information from my agent, but I'd been standing around behind the vendor stall for too long. I scooped up the discarded hospital clothes and stuffed them into a reformulator before heading back out into the press of people. I let the crowds carry me back and forth at random, though always flowing rimward. The shuttles would be on the outer most ring of the habitat… along with the most intense security.

The flow of people brought me close to a corridor bracketed by stalls—one a hydroponics stand stacked tall with fresh fruits and vegetables that set my mouth to watering and the other bearing a selection of knives of all makes and designs. That one reminded me uncomfortably of the blade the assassin had carried, but it also afforded me the opportunity to duck into a quiet corner. *Display flight information, Sarah.*

A grid sprang to life in my vision, showing a list of ships, departure and arrival times, and prices. Sarah had included all the possible flights, even those outside of my current free credit balance. Those were grayed out. I couldn't think of any way to get more credits fast enough to matter—well, none that I was willing to pursue—so I deleted those with a thought. That took out half the flights. I needed something leaving soon, today if possible, but certainly no more than a day or two from now. Another twenty percent of the available options vanished. Of the flights that remained, only two were headed directly to Daedalus, and one of those left in—I pulled up a chronograph—four hours. The *Bannon*.

The ship was listed as a mid-sized cargo freighter, not a passenger shuttle, but it wasn't uncommon for such vessels to have passenger berths. It would be slower than a shuttle but getting *off* Prospect fast was more important than getting *to* Daedalus fast, since once it was disconnected from a hab, a ship was essentially the sovereign territory of wherever it was registered. And traveling by freighter would be cheaper. I did a quick search to make sure the *Bannon* didn't list Prospect as its port of record. All clear. *Book the* Bannon, *Sarah.*

I left my agent to that task as I contemplated the hydroponics booth. My stomach issued a hollow rumble, reminding me that new coils needed fuel, and that this coil, in particular, had been put through a rather rough morning. I needed to get aboard the *Bannon* as soon as possible.

I boarded a shuttle to the *Bannon* an hour later. The tiny shuttle, designed for operation around the habitat, had a dozen seats, six marching down either side of a narrow aisle. And they *were* seats, not acceleration chairs, molded out of plastic with straps to keep their occupants firmly in place when the shuttle was not under acceleration. All but three of the seats were occupied, by men and women wearing worn but well-maintained vacc suits. The low buzz of conversation stopped as I floated in from the lock, using the handrails set near head-height to propel myself.

Nine sets of eyes turned to regard me, and I felt the silent appraisal in those gazes. Crew from the *Bannon*, then, wondering who and what was about to intrude on their territory. I swam down the aisle, only lightly touching the rails, long experience in microgravity keeping me on the right trajectory. As I neared one of the empty seats, I curled into a ball, letting that motion start to spin me gently. I oriented on the chair as down and uncoiled, pushing off the overhead with my arms. I slid smoothly into the seat, gripping the arm with one hand while deftly securing the harness with the other. Most of the eyes still watched me, but some now held a grudging respect. Spacers and habbers had an often less-than-friendly rivalry, and my zero-G acrobatics had just put me firmly in the spacer camp.

The people around me were already zoning out, their faces taking on the glazed expression of people dropping into full VR. Small talk was a lost art as everyone settled into whatever personal world would help them pass the journey in comfort.

I sat back in my chair, closed my eyes, and asked Sarah to start feeding me news from the past two months. Time to catch up on what I had missed.

7

The *Bannon* was as ugly a ship as I'd ever seen. Since freight haulers didn't bother with generating artificial gravity and didn't have to worry about atmospheric flight, the ship was purpose-built to be stuffed full of as much cargo as its engines could push. The result was a blocky, rectangular behemoth lacking any of the pleasing aesthetics that were the byproducts of efficient fluid dynamics. The shuttle locked to an external docking point—no interior space was wasted on shuttle bays— and the crew began to unbuckle harnesses and drift toward the front of the cabin.

I felt tension flow from me as I crossed through the airlock and boarded the *Bannon*. I was officially outside the reach of Prospect HabSec. If they tracked me to the ship, the best they could do was ask—not order, ask—the captain to turn me over to their officers. But this was the last shuttle to the ship, and as soon as the crew got on station, the *Bannon* would be starting the burn toward Daedalus. No freighter captain would bother turning back and losing the time and fuel to hand over someone wanted by the station. Sure, she might decide to space the criminal and be done with it, but there would be no turning back.

By now, my agent would have negotiated protocols with the ShipNet. *Sarah, can you show me to my berth?*

Another schematic obligingly popped into my vision, zooming to a point where I could see the star that represented me and the path I needed to follow to find my room. The crew had already dispersed, and whatever passengers might have been traveling aboard the *Bannon* must have already boarded, because I was left alone in the bay. Modern technology precluded the need for niceties like crew to show you to your quarters or tell you when and where to get food. With the ShipNet and the universality of agent implants, all that was left was for me to follow the directions Sarah provided.

Ten minutes to burn, Sarah said. I nodded to myself and began following the instructions to my cabin. There would be no warnings or reminders from the ship's captain that everyone needed to be secured before the main thrusters came online. Everyone aboard had access to the same information. Everyone was assumed to be responsible enough to do what they needed to do to avoid injury and to provide adequate instruction and assistance to those in their care. And, apart from the rare exception of accident or illness, no special consideration would be made for those who failed to do so. Access to a constant stream of real-time information coupled with an implanted AI whose job it was to keep track of all of the details had shifted the focus away from assigning blame and pushed it back toward personal responsibility. Of course, the near-governmental powers of the various corporations had also done a number on the kinds of liability for which any entity could be held responsible.

I made my way to the cabin. It was a standard affair, little more than two meters square with an acceleration bunk and small locker for my gear. As I didn't have any gear, stowing it was easy enough. I settled into the couch and had Sarah go back to feeding me news from the past couple of months.

It was going to be a long trip.

I drifted into the *Bannon*'s mess and immediately felt a sense of nostalgia wash over me. I'd served shipboard in some capacity or another for most of my lives, and regardless of the mission of the ship in question, crew galleys were the same the solar system over. It was, I supposed, an unavoidable consequence of the watch cycle. A ship under way never really slept. Standard ship time still kept a twenty-four-hour clock with crew rotations broken into three shifts. In theory, crew spent eight hours on watch and sixteen hours off. In practice, I'd yet to crew a vessel that didn't expect everyone to pull double shifts at least part of the time.

That meant that the crew's mess was always a mix of people coming on duty, getting off duty, or slogging through the middle of a long, long workday. It lent the place an air that, while it might not have been pleasant, was certainly unique.

The *Bannon* didn't bother with artificial gravity. The technology was sound enough, but the power requirements were such that outside of passenger liners, working ships seldom used it. The added fuel burn tended to put too much of a dent in the bottom line. Nor had the cargo hauler been built to leverage rotation to simulate gravity, a more antiquated, if fuel-efficient, approach. But the added vectors made it impractical for something designed to move the maximum mass with minimum energy like the *Bannon*. That left the ship in microgravity.

I still wore my vacc suit, as it was my only available wardrobe choice. The suit had built-in magnetic boots, but I hadn't bothered using them. Instead, I floated a few inches off the floor, surveying the room. It took only a moment to find what I was looking for. I reached out for the nearby handrail and gave myself a gentle push. It imparted enough energy that I drifted through the compartment, slipping down the channel between tables. I put out one hand as I reached my destination, using my elbow as a shock absorber to bleed off my forward momentum, and came to rest in front of what, in another day and age, might have been called a vending machine.

It was a little show-boaty, but I was all too aware of the eyes on me. I couldn't help the little surge of pride that demanded I show the crew that I wasn't some habber or dirtheel that was little better than cargo.

Bona fides established, I turned my attention back to my lunch. I didn't bother trying to keep up with the watch schedule—I was operating on personal objective time. I'd eaten once this morning, and it was time for the second meal of the day. So, lunch. The machine before me wasn't really a vending machine. It had some official name that no one used. In the parlance of shipboard life, if you were eating something that hadn't been cooked in a galley from actual ingredients, you were eating from a replicator. The name wasn't accurate—the technology at play had little to do with the science fiction from a 2D-vid from antiquity—but the name had stuck. It offered a limited selection of pre-programmed meals that the machine assembled from packaged ingredients. The menu was divided based on nominal mealtimes—breakfast, lunch, and dinner—and offered a surprisingly wide selection of foods. I selected a spicy chicken and peppers dish served over rice and green tea to drink, and waited the few moments it took the machine to do its thing.

When it was ready, an indicator popped up in my vision, letting me know my lunch was done. I opened the receptacle at the bottom of the machine and pulled out two sealed plastic pouches. Both were warm to the touch, but not uncomfortably so. The larger had a polymer spoon dangling off it and the smaller a drinking straw. I grabbed my food and pushed off from the replicator, gliding toward an empty table. I hooked my foot on the chair—magnetically locked to the floor— and pulled myself down into it. A quick ping from Sarah to the *Bannon* and the chair's restraints deployed, settling me comfortably into place. The surface of the table had been designed to hold the surface of the food and drink pouches, so I set them down. A slight tug would free them again.

The procedure seemed complicated to those accustomed to gravity, but it was all too easy to make a mess of things if proper precautions weren't taken.

Sarah, I asked my agent, *any luck on tracking down information on the* Persephone?

No, Carter. The Bannon's *Net is as up to date as can be expected, but as yet I have found no mention of the* Persephone *or the missing crew. At current speeds, we will pass a relay station in approximately fourteen hours. The network should update at that time and I will continue to search the updated information.*

Understood. No vessel in deep space had a truly real-time connection with the broader Net. The inverse-square law applied, and as you moved away from a signal's source, the signal degradation increased at an exponential rate. There was a lot of "farther" to fill in out in the deep. Humanity had combated the problem by setting up relay stations. Rather than using broad-spectrum radio waves, the relays received data via laser beam, a burst-transmission method that could hold together for much greater distances than radio. The relays, in turn, simultaneously sent a laser-burst to the next station and broadcast their most recent information via radio. That meant that any ship who wanted the most updated information— along with all the other detritus that went with the Net—had to plot a course to pass by close enough to a relay station to receive an ungarbled radio transmission.

There was little left to do but wait.

The familiar roar of Daedalus welcomed me as I strode from the shuttle and into the terminal. The habitat, if it could really be called that, existed as little more than a way station for spacers of all kinds—scroungers, salvagers, shippers, explorers... if you spent more time in freefall than with your feet firmly planted on the ground, Daedalus was a place you could call home. That made the shuttle terminals the busiest part of the habitat, always awash in noise and motion. I made my way through customs and security, then out into the crowds. The rich smells of roasting shashlik and frying blini washed over me making my mouth water. Sarah automatically translated the signage that hung over the hatches along the long promenade outside the docks, the Cyrillic lettering a throwback to Daedalus' earliest days. The initial diaspora had been along then-nationalistic lines, with the Russian Alliance focusing its efforts on deep-space habitations. Most of the trappings those early settlers had brought with them had faded over time, but a few had clung stubbornly on.

The press of bodies around me made my heart beat a little faster, and I felt sweat dampening my palms. Ships traveled fast, but radio signals traveled at the speed of light. The month spent moving from Prospect to Daedalus was more than enough time for whoever had sent the assassin to discover that it failed in its attempt, track down where I went, and send a message to agents on or near Daedalus to deal with me upon my arrival. After a month of contemplation, I still couldn't see the rationale in ordering my death. Whatever I may have known before dying, I didn't know it *now*. And my backup insurance was up to date, though if I didn't find a way to earn some credits soon, that wouldn't hold true for long. But as things stood, a successful assassin would only succeed in taking me out of play temporarily.

None of this made any sense. I needed to find the rest of the crew from the *Persephone* and see if they had any clue what in the hell was going on. And if there was one place in the system they were likely to be, it was here on Daedalus.

My agent had had time to connect with the station and get updated information on our approach. *Sarah, any communications from Chan, Miller, or Harper?*

No messages have been received, my agent replied.

Damn. That didn't mean they weren't there. Communications

could be monitored so they might simply be lying low. After all, I hadn't exactly been broadcasting messages out into the deep. Having had one assassin come after me already, I wasn't inclined to make it even easier for another.

Keep looking, Sarah, I instructed. *And see if you can find any trace of them, here or anywhere else.*

While my agent undertook that task, I made my way through the docks, moving steadily coreward. Crowds filled the corridors of Daedalus just as much as they had on Prospect, though here the mood among them was brusquer. Those who lived on the station kept to themselves and presented a gruff exterior, at least outside of their friends and family. Outside of the markets, that lent the station a sense of quiet discretion. Still, there was scarcely a station in the system that wasn't packed to the gills with humanity, and Daedalus, holding on to the remnants of its founders' stoicism, wasn't any different. When the promise of immortality became an effective reality, no one really thought about the impact on population. The birth rate had dropped off significantly, as more people realized that they had plenty of time for kids and took advantage of technology to help control when conception happened, but the death rate— the true, total death rate—was nearly zero. To complicate the issue further, regardless of the coil into which you were born, if you were re-coiled into a biological female, you were capable of bearing children. Which meant that every human under the sun was likely to have the capacity to give birth at some point in their lives. The biological process had been streamlined as well; you certainly *could* carry a child to term if you so chose, but most opted to have the fetus bottled and grown at a med facility. Regardless, the hopes of an endless universe of planets to colonize outside our own system still languished under our inability to prove Einstein wrong and travel faster than light.

And so, the exploding population of humanity had to be content with domed cities on hostile planets, moons, and asteroids, or free-floating space habitats. The impressive feats of engineering had pushed humanity's sphere of influence all the way to the moons of Neptune… but they were still unable to keep up with our constant need for procreation and expansion. As I shouldered my way through the press of people—much easier in my new coil—I longed to be back on board the *Persephone*. The vessel had been small, and every bit as cramped with four souls as Daedalus was with its teeming thousands, but at least I knew and trusted the crew. We had worked together for years, and even if we all seemed to spend our off-ship time as far away from one another as possible—a needed escape when you were packed in tight quarters with the same people for so long—I counted them as friends. Now, as I pushed through the crowd, I imagined a knife in every hand and a garroting wire in every pocket. I moved a little faster, suddenly anxious to get to the relative safety of my berth and away from the crowds that could be concealing any numbers of assassins.

My implant pinged, and a window opened in the top right of my vision.

I didn't recognize the face displayed in that window, and by the look of confusion on his face, he didn't recognize me, either. Before I could trigger a disconnect, Sarah's voice resonated in my head: *Shay Chan, Langston.*

Shit. "Shay?" I asked softly.

"Carter?" The voice was a smooth baritone that seemed somehow fitting to the leonine features and wavy blonde hair of the face in my augmented reality view. But there was a hesitancy in it, a note of fear or pain. The coil, from what I could see, was a fine specimen: chiseled features, piercing eyes, tanned skin glowing with health, lean, and almost aggressively handsome. It was also unmistakably bio-male. Shay Chan, on the other hand, had been a petite young woman in her last incarnation, though I knew it hadn't been her original, birth-issued coil. We hadn't been close enough to discuss about who felt comfortable in what body—but something about the set of Chan's shoulders told me that whatever she might be at the moment, comfortable was out the airlock.

"It's me, Chan. Fuck. Are you okay?" It was a stupid question. She… Chan… was clearly *not* okay.

"No," she said, and tears formed at the corners of those piercing blue eyes. Eyes that, to my mind, should still have been mysterious dark pools. "No." A rough laugh escaped Chan's lips, followed immediately by a grimace. "I can't get used to that sound. Or the sound of my own voice. Or anything else." She—and since I had known her as a "she" in her previous incarnation, she would continue to be so unless she told me otherwise—shook her head. "And you. You don't look like you, either. It's…" She sighed. "Look, it's not important right now. We need to talk. Not over the Net. Can we meet somewhere?"

"My place?" I asked.

She shook her head again. "Not sure that will be safe. Somewhere public."

Was she worried about me, or about assassins lurking in corners waiting to get us alone? Better not to ask, at least not over the Net. "Where then? I just got in. Need to stop by my place and pick up a few things. But that will only take a few minutes. Give me a time and a place."

"The Black Diamond," she said after a moment. "Half an hour?"

"I'll be there."

I reached my berth aboard Daedalus. The locks responded to my Net codes—the software didn't care if the coil giving them was completely different, only if the security algorithms matched up. The room beyond the door stretched a spacious three meters square. Apart from a console, bed, footlocker, and combination refrigerator and microwave, the room was empty. Which was as it should be. I'd never had much in the way of personal belongings. There was little enough room on station, and even less shipboard. I'd pared my life down to just a few necessities and some comfort items, and I'd brought those aboard the *Persephone*. I maintained the apartment on Daedalus to have somewhere to go between jobs and because having a permanent address decreased your insurance premiums. Beyond that, it was little more than storage for the few spare belongings I'd managed to gather.

I went to the footlocker first, once again passing the proper codes across the Net to open the lock. The locker held my spare gear—another vacc suit (though the VaccTech I was wearing was nicer, so I left that where it lay), a tool harness with a good assortment of cutters, grips, tape, and cords, and a holstered Gauss pistol. In the very bottom of the locker was a simple faux-wooden box, which held another pistol, this one a microwave-emitting laser.

I grabbed the harness and put it on, moving the few possessions I'd purchased on Prospect from the VaccTech's loops to the harness' more secure pouches and pockets. Then I grabbed the microwave emitter and swapped it for the gun in the holster. The Gauss gun would draw a few eyes aboard station—the chances for a hull breach were slim but not impossible. Still, I wasn't about to leave it behind, either. Not with someone out there wanting me dead. It went into one of the pouches on the harness as well. It wasn't exactly illegal to carry—just discouraged—so HabSec probably wouldn't hassle me if it showed up on someone's scanner.

I went over to the console, and rummaged around in the drawers, pocketing a few gold and platinum nuggets that were the melted remains of salvaged circuitry. Electronic credits may have been king, but it never hurt to have something that could serve as hard currency or barter.

I paused a moment, as I realized what I was doing. I was looting my apartment, taking everything of value, everything that could be of use to me. I was getting ready to run. But run where? And why? Because of the assassin on Prospect? Or the look of fear in Chan's eyes? Or the fact that she didn't think my apartment would be safe? I looked around the small room. Apart from the tools from the footlocker, there was nothing here that was truly me. It was just a place I slept when I was in port, a place to keep a few extra belongings that I didn't need on ship. I realized then, that if I never returned to this room,

I wouldn't miss it. Something about that caused a burgeoning sadness to bubble just beneath the surface. The *Persephone*, not Daedalus, had been my home for the past several years. And by all indications, the *Persephone* was gone.

I dashed a hand across my eyes, surprised to see the moistness gathered there. I blinked them rapidly, fighting back the tears that threatened to spill forth. It was in that blurry moment, when everything was out of focus, that I saw the small flashing LED on the console panel.

A slight chill went through me at the sight. It shouldn't have—the LED indicated a message on my home system. But Sarah should have automatically connected as soon as we were in range and forwarded anything from the home system onto my implant. She hadn't notified me of anything.

Sarah, why didn't you forward this message on?

Accessing message metadata, now. There was a brief pause. *You told me not to, Langston.*

That pushed the slight chill from my spine down into my stomach and soured it into a twisting ball of something oily and foul. I had given Sarah no such orders. At least, the I that I was now had given no such orders. But a previous me—or rather a previous instantiation of Sarah—could have embedded that code into the communication. "Play the message," I said aloud.

A window obligingly opened in my vision. I didn't recognize the origin code, but I recognized the sender easily enough, even through the partially tinted face-shield of a vacc suit. How could I not?

It was me.

I stared into the face of a dead man.

Somehow, it was more than just a coil I had once worn. The face looking back at me had lived for months while I—the me that I was now—had sat in cold storage on a server, only to see the light of day in the event of this other me's death. He had experienced aspects of life that I had never experienced, that I never could experience, since they had been swept away by the river of time. And judging by the general state of this other me, the sweeping had not been a pleasant process.

Burned flesh, red and raw, stood out beneath the helmet, and the face was twisted into a grimace of agony. "I don't know if you'll ever see this," the other me said. The voice was mine—the voice I remembered, not the voice I now owned—but ragged and hoarse with pain. "I don't know if it will make it back to Daedalus. But I had to try." There was a pause then, and I realized the branch of me was communicating with a branch of Sarah. "I've only got a few minutes. Not enough time to tell it all. I'm uploading a file. Recordings of what happened aboard the derelict. The *Persephone*'s gone. Can't raise them. No accident. Someone is doing this."

He shook his head, swallowed, and forced out more words. "The derelict wasn't in the *Persephone*'s database, but maybe you can find it. Or track down the coils. Shit. The coils. One of them…" He paused again, and something in his eyes, just visible through the composite of the face-shield, made me shudder. "They should have been dead. No air. No pressure. No heat. They should have been dead. But one attacked me." Another head shake. "I'm almost out of time. It's all in the video. The heat. Christ. The heat." He reached out a hand, shaking and trembling, though from pain or acceleration I couldn't tell. And then with a final wave, the window went blank.

Sarah, how long is the attached video file?

Run time is six hours, seventeen minutes, thirty-six seconds.

Shit. No time to watch before my meeting with Chan, and I couldn't blow her off. Sarah would have to do the heavy lifting, at least for now. *Analyze the video. Identify the derelict vessel that… that I mention. Try to do facial recognition on any deceased aboard the ship.* I paused, wondering how to phrase the next bit. *And look for any atypical behavior exhibited by any of the coils present.* Another pause as I thought things through. *Any atypical behavior exhibited aboard the derelict or aboard the* Persephone. *And postulate likely causes for aberrant behavior.*

Understood.

That should cover the basics. It would take a while for Sarah to pore over the footage and run the analysis, but far less than the six-hour time frame. I wanted to watch it for myself, of course, and would, but I was out of time.

I adjusted the harness and took one last look around my spartan apartment. I had the distinct impression that I wouldn't be seeing it again.

A wave of something that sounded like circular saws applied to structural steel and set to a driving bass beat assaulted my ears as I exited the elevator and entered the corridors outside of the Black Diamond. Dozens of people stood outside the open hatch leading into the club, not so much an orderly queue as an undulating wave of humanity surging against the pair of bouncers manning the door and ebbing back again. My chronometer told me I had ten minutes until the scheduled meeting with Chan. No time for lines.

I walked straight into the crowd, making no effort to slip past people. In my old coil, that would have meant trouble. But in my latest branch, the combination of the space-black vacc suit, scowling Neanderthal features, prodigious size, and the gun holstered on my hip parted the crowd before me like water before an old ocean-going ship. The bouncers, on the other hand, were unimpressed.

Both of them massed larger than me by a good twenty kilos, and one cast a look at my microwave emitter that was so contemptuous it bordered on comical. But I had no intention of trying to push my way through them. My hand dipped into one of the pouches on my suit's harness, and I produced a pair of precious metal nuggets, each about the size of my thumbnail. Both glittered gold under the harsh interior lighting of the hab corridor.

I didn't say anything—just stretched my hand out before

them, proffering the metal slugs on my upraised palm. No matter how far the species had come, some things never changed. The nuggets disappeared in an instant and the smaller of the two jerked his head toward the darkened interior of the club. I nodded in return, suppressing the sardonic smile that wanted to twist my lips. Better not to push my luck too far.

The volume doubled as I crossed the threshold, hovering on the verge of painful. The club interior was another tight press of bodies, this time moving in syncopated rhythm to the blasting music. A few tables and booths clung to the edges of what was mostly a dance floor, and a bar took up an entire wall off to the side. No chance of finding Chan in that crowd.

Sarah, send a message to Chan. Let her know I'm here and ask her to pop up a beacon.

Of course, Langston.

A moment later, a glowing icon sprang to life in my vision, the product of Chan's agent interfacing with Sarah and overlaying a graphic directly into my eyeline. I followed it through the undulating, gyrating swarm of people and to the fringe of the club where booths were arrayed along one wall. Chan sat in one, a bottle of beer resting on the table, cupped between her hands. Her new pretty-boy features were twisted into a dark scowl as she glared at the bottle, and she only looked up as I slid into the booth across from her. As I passed the privacy field, the thunderous music dropped to a distant buzz, and I breathed a silent sigh of relief.

"I had to bribe the door guy to let me in," Chan said by way of greeting.

I nodded. "Yeah, me too."

She frowned. "You don't get it. In my last coil, I would have been in with a smile and a wave. I hate this." She waved a hand vaguely at her new body. "I don't know how you deal with male coils. I'm all lumpy and hairy. And it pisses me off."

That brought a slight smile to my face. It was hard adjusting to a new body, particularly if that body came loaded with unfamiliar plumbing and hormones. I'd only had to do it once. Some could switch genders easily enough, finding a comforting fit at multiple points on the spectrum, and it hadn't particularly bothered me to be placed into a bio-female coil. Being placed in a body that didn't match your preferences and expectations still beat the alternative, and there were surgeries to change the cosmetics and drugs to deal with the chemical balances, provided you had the proper insurance. It made the initial acclimation period... more challenging, though. Of course, I wasn't about to tell Chan to suck it up and move on. For me, the coil was only a shell, but not everyone felt the same. Besides, whatever flesh she wore, she was still her underneath and would probably kick my ass for saying something like that.

Instead, I said, "It gets easier. But it takes time."

"Yeah," Chan growled, the rough baritone strange on ears expecting her contralto. "Well, we may not have much time."

"What?" If there was one thing that modern technology had given to mankind, it was plenty of time.

"Miller's gone," Chan said.

"He hasn't been put back into a new coil?"

"There's nothing to put back."

For a moment, I just stared at her. "What do you mean, 'there's nothing to put back'?" Shock and a sudden surge of panic made the words come out as a disbelieving and almost angry shout.

She took a long draw from her beer and slapped the bottle back to the table with more force than necessary. "I mean he's gone. He died on the *Persephone* just like the rest of us. And his backups are gone. Just… gone. He backed up with same outfit I did, here on Daedalus. I know, because we went there together, right before the last trip." She gave a slight headshake. "You know that. You would have been with us if you hadn't been out toward Prospect looking for more work." I had to nod at that. Sometimes work came to the *Persephone* and sometimes we had to go out and find it. We'd been in a dry spell, and I'd volunteered to chase down some leads away from Daedalus. I'd been meeting with some of the miners—even with the best technology, it was still easier to close a deal face to face—near Prospect when the call came in that Harper had found a job. I backed up at Prospect and set out to meet the *Persephone* en route.

"So," Shay continued, "when I woke up, I started asking where Miller was, if he'd been re-coiled. And the staff looked at me like I was crazy. They claimed they'd never heard of him. No records of anyone by that name. Nothing. I had Bit do a general search. He came up empty. There are no records of Arnold Miller ever having existed. No birth certificate. No graduation records. No security reports. Nothing. I couldn't even find him as a registered owner of the *Persephone*. Everything is gone."

There were tears forming at the corners of her eyes, and her voice had risen—as much as her new baritone could rise—filling with notes of pain and panic. I reached across the table, placing my hand on top of hers. "Shay. We'll figure it out," I said.

"How?" she demanded. "How can we figure it out? Miller isn't just dead. He's *gone*. I don't know what happened to Harper, though there are still records of them out there, so I don't think they've been erased. I didn't know what had happened to you until you showed up on station. None of us have any memories of what happened. And I swear someone's been following me on the Net, tracing me. Trying to track me. And to make matters worse, I'm stuck in this stupid bio-male coil."

That caught my attention. I felt my hand tightening on hers. "Have they traced you?" I asked, my voice harsh. "Can they find you in the physical world?"

She grimaced in pain and twisted her hand away. "Christ, Langston. Of course not. They might have stuffed me into this ungainly, graceless body, but my brain is the same as always. No one finds me on the Net; not unless I want them to. Certainly not some HabSec wannabes."

Her words surprised me. Chan had been the tech and software specialist aboard the *Persephone* and I knew she was good at her job. But the contempt she showed for the cyber cops was surprising to say the least. I was reminded that I'd never really gotten to know the crew outside of the performance of our duties. Or anyone else for that matter. I'd always struggled with building deep friendships. Even on Daedalus, where I'd lived for years, I had a few acquaintances, but no real friends. "HabSec's after us?"

"Well, maybe not. Maybe corporate. Maybe someone else. Whoever they are, they aren't freelance hackers. Their approach is too... structured. Strange, unique almost, but structured.

Organized." I let that sink in. I hadn't really expected any of the handful of planetary governments or polities to be behind a random assassination attempt on a salvage worker, but the thought that one of the megacorporations might be after us was even worse.

Something of my worry must have shown on my face. "What's going on, Langston? What do you know?"

"Not much. I... sent myself a recording. Somehow the branch of me that died had enough time to broadcast a message back to my console here on Daedalus. It's six hours of video, though. I haven't had a chance to go through it, but Sarah's working on it now. She should have an edited version soon. I don't know how much it will help, but it should give us a starting point." I hesitated, reluctant to tell her more, to scare her more than she already was. But she needed to know. "That's not all. When I woke up, aboard Prospect station... someone tried to kill me."

"What?"

"They walked into my room and tried to put a knife in me. I stopped them, and then ran." I sighed. The news about Miller shed some unwelcome light on my own re-coiling experience. "And something was wrong with my backup. It was corrupted. It took them a month to fix it and stick me back in a new coil. And even then, judging from the questions they asked, they weren't terribly confident that I would still be me." Which brought up an interesting question that I sure as hell didn't want to think about. How could *I* be sure I was still me? The me I was before? If my backup had been damaged, tampered with, altered... I cut off that train of thought. It wasn't as if there was anything I could do about it, so better to forget it and move on.

"Then they found you, too," Chan said. "They tried to erase you."

I nodded. "And when the doctors put me back together anyway, they sent someone to kill me so they could finish the job."

Chan dropped her head into her hands. "They were probably looking for me, too. For my backups. I'm very… careful… about my digital footprint, Langston. About my identity. I do my best to keep my whereabouts hidden." Something in her voice told me that that was an understatement. "It wouldn't have been easy for whoever is behind this to have found out who I was. That might have kept me safe, this time. But no one can hide forever. What are we going to do?" she said softly.

Any answer I may have given was curtailed when a window popped open in my vision. It showed a feed from a security camera near the front hatch, where a trio of coils in dark singlesuits were pushing their way through the crowd. They had the same blank, emotionless look about them as the assassin from Prospect, and moved with the same implacable calm. A cold sweat broke out on my palms and I drew in a short, stuttering breath. *Sarah, port that over to Bit.*

Chan's eyes went wide as her agent streamed her the same feed Sarah had shown me. There was a chance it was just coincidence, but the similarities to the assassin who came after me on Prospect couldn't be ignored.

"Let's go," I said, sliding out of the booth. My hand went to the gun at my side, but I left it in the holster. There was still a chance we could slip out the back and vanish into the corridors before whoever was after us caught up. Outside of the dampening screen, the full force of the music hit me again, pulsing and throbbing, an almost physical wave of sound. But it didn't quite mask the quick *pop-pop-pop* of gunfire. As Chan disentangled herself from the booth—moving uncertainly in her male body—I stared toward the entrance, where the doormen were slowly toppling to the ground as a wave of panicked screaming spread like ripples in a pond.

9

I grabbed Chan's hand and pulled her the rest of the way out of the seat, propelling her toward the back of the club. Being on a hab wasn't like dome living—you didn't find exits plastered in a dozen convenient locations. Hatches were, by their very nature, weak points in the structure and had to meet very exacting standards to ensure they sealed properly and automatically in the event the station was breached to maintain the atmospheric integrity of the rest of the hab. But a place as big as the Black Diamond had to have somewhere to bring in more booze, and the odds were, it would be in the back. We made our way as fast as the press of people would allow, not quite running, as the alarm slowly spread from those nearest the door outward. By the time we reached the back wall, screaming drowned out the music, and the dancing had been replaced with a mass of bodies moving in every direction, looking for a way out.

More shots rang out, and the music went dead. The lights continued to pulse and strobe, but now instead of revealing the fevered gyrations of the beautiful people, they showcased flashes of terror. The wave of bodies became a surge, pushing outward, away from the shooters. But we were on the crest of that wave, and I kept one hand clamped down tight on Chan's wrist, concentrated on keeping my boots under me, so that neither of us fell beneath the churning feet of the panicked crowds. We reached the hatch, and the pressure from behind me, as dozens of people tried to shove forward, nearly prevented me from pulling it open.

I threw my shoulder into the person behind me, making them lurch backward. It bought me a second, no more, but it was enough time to yank the lever and jerk the door inward. I hurled Chan through it—a task that would have been much easier had she still been in her much smaller female coil—and followed after, stumbling to keep upright as more bodies spilled out after us.

I heard a scream and turned to see another black-clad assassin rushing in our direction. Whether he'd been slow on the uptake or the others had started shooting early, the killer had obviously been out of position. Our eyes met briefly over the heads of the surging crowd and my fingers twitched toward my sidearm.

"This way," Chan barked. She had moved to the side, down a crossing corridor. I hurried toward her as she continued on. She started taking intersecting corridors, seemingly at random. Her new coil, more awkward than she may have had before, was athletic, trim, built for speed. Mine was slow and bulky, great for exercising bursts of power over short periods of time but moving quickly was not its forte. All those muscles demanded a ton of oxygen to operate, and I felt my wind failing me fast.

"Damn it, Chan! Slow down! Where are we going?" I panted, fighting to draw enough oxygen into my lungs to soothe the burning ache in my muscles. I had to stop, hands on my knees, head down, gasping for air.

"We can't stop," Chan said, but she slowed from the dead sprint to a walk. "Come on, Langston. If they've tapped into HabSec monitors, they can still track us."

I pushed myself upright and staggered to her side, matching my pace with hers. "Running me to death won't change that. If they're in HabSec we're fucked anyway."

"HabSec doesn't have eyes everywhere. I've got a place. Besides, Bit can handle the cameras for us, for a few minutes. But if they catch us before we get there, it won't matter much, will it?"

"Fine," I grunted as we continued to navigate the maze of corridors. I felt the gravity shift slightly, several times, indicating that we were getting closer to the central spine of the station. The corridors around us thinned, narrowed, and slowly emptied of other people. After almost two hours of walking, we entered tunnels so tight that I could touch either wall with my shoulders simply by leaning slightly to the left or right.

Where are we, Sarah?

You have entered the maintenance tunnels beneath the station power plant.

"Damn, Chan. What are you doing with a bolt-hole all the way down here, anyway?" I asked.

She shrugged. "I like working salvage, but it's not my primary gig, okay? It gets me away from... prying eyes. And buys me time to do other things. Some of those other things...

are less than legal on some habs." I arched an eyebrow at her, and she raised her hands. "Nothing bad, not really. I just do some… let's call it freelance technical consulting."

I grunted. "You mean you're a hacker. Break into peoples' files. Steal their secrets. That kind of thing?" I couldn't muster enough outrage to make the words an accusation. It was a tough solar system out there, and you did what you had to in order to keep your insurance premiums paid. The price of immortality was measured the same way all other prices were—cold, hard credits.

She shrugged. "Mostly corporate stuff, actually. I don't feel bad about helping one megacorp fleece another out of their intellectual property. But down here, I can tap directly into the station backbone, and all the electrical interference from the power plant means it's more trouble than it's worth to HabSec to keep monitors running." Her face sagged a little. "It's also where I've been hiding out since I found out about Miller."

She came to a halt in front of a hatch labeled 49/4-B. There was no pad next to the door, and she pulled it open. I couldn't be certain that she hadn't used her agent to wirelessly disengage a lock, but I didn't think she had. I doubted anyone ever made it this deep into the bowels of Daedalus, anyway. Locks were made redundant by the remoteness of the location.

The room beyond was bigger than my apartment, and far homier. What must have been the sleeping area was partitioned from the rest of the space with folding screens that looked like actual wood, their paper sides inked with elegant stands of bamboo. The inking looked original, not fabricated, and either Chan had done it herself, or she had paid a fortune to have it done. An AI-guided bot could have produced something of the same quality, but there was a level of imperfection to the artistry that couldn't be programmed. A low table surrounded by scattered cushions defined a seating area and a large desk was tucked into another corner. The panels on the bulkhead by the desk had been removed, and wires ran from the walls to somewhere beneath the desk. Chan must have had a console there, wired, as she had said, directly into the main Net backbone for Daedalus.

She pulled the hatch shut behind her, and I saw that, while it may not have been intended to be locked, Chan had taken steps to fix that. Bowed bands of steel had been welded to the door and bulkhead on either side of it. Chan grabbed a composite bar from beside the hatch, and shoved it through the braces, literally barring the door. Not too long ago, it would have seemed like a ridiculous precaution. But that was before someone had twice tried to kill me—maybe to kill both of us.

Chan dropped down onto the cushions by the table, the languid motion somehow feminine despite the coil she wore. "We're safe, for now," she said. "Nothing's getting through that door without a plasma cutter."

I moved over and slumped onto some of the cushions as well. For a moment, I just leaned back and closed my eyes. It felt good to rest, to forget, if only for an instant, the tension and stress and chaos that had taken over my life. But only for an instant. I still needed to find out what had happened, why people were out to kill me. If Miller was truly gone. What had happened to Harper. The questions spun through my mind in an endless torrent until, finally, I gave up.

Instead, I looked over at Chan and asked, "Who are you, anyway?" I waved a hand at the bolt-hole in which I currently sat. "Who lives like this? Have you been some sort of master criminal this whole time? And how did I not know about it? And how in the world do you keep the station staff from finding it?"

She smiled and made a strange hair-flipping motion with her head. The smile turned into a grimace as the gesture didn't quite have the results that it would have in her previous coil. "I'm hardly a master criminal, Carter," she said. "And keeping out of the eyes of the maintenance staff is easy enough. I've altered the records, is all. As far as Daedalus is concerned, this compartment is a storage facility for spare pressure seals of a model the station stopped using decades ago. It's too far off the beaten path to be viable living space and with a little programmatic encouragement from me and Bit, it's been all but forgotten. I wasn't really trying to hide it from you or the crew." She shrugged. "We've all lived lives that we don't talk about, all been other people at some point in our pasts. I think keeping secrets becomes a habit, sometimes."

I grunted. Chan was right, and I knew it. Salvage hadn't been my first gig, or second, or even fifth. I'd done my time in service, sometimes to corporations, sometimes to flags. I'd done things that I wasn't particularly proud of for both. And it never seemed to make much of a damned difference. Whatever I did, the world kept on keeping on, not particularly caring about the efforts of one man among the teeming billions. It was the reason I'd moved from working for big corporations or polities to smaller organizations, then from there to being an independent contractor until finally moving into salvage, where I didn't work for anybody but myself and my crewmates. I didn't talk about those previous lives. They weren't failures, per se, but they had convinced me that the best you could do was look after yourself and your own and let the rest of the system turn as it would. Because it would anyway, regardless.

"Yeah," I said at last. "I get it. The longer we live, the more the secrets seem to pile up and the harder it gets to talk about some things. But why bother with the *Persephone* at all?"

"I told you. There's nowhere better to lie low than deep space. And working for the corporations doesn't pay as much as you might think." She shrugged, then winced, as if even that simple motion was uncomfortable in her new coil. "I…" She hesitated. Her cheeks colored, and she looked down, the embarrassment clear on her face. The demure expression didn't really fit with her current features.

"I put most of my credits into saving for the next coil. To avoid… this…" She gestured at her body—her very male body—with one hand. "I run basic insurance, of course, but I was hoping to save enough to make sure my next coil was built to spec rather than whatever off-the-shelf model got dumped on me." A slight shudder passed through her. "There aren't a lot of ways to make that happen. Not for people like us."

The silence stretched between us for several long moments.

Sarah, have you completed your analysis of the video?

Yes. I have cut it down to the most interesting parts and included a summary file, per your instructions.

"Sarah's got the video feed," I said. "Do you want me to port it over to Bit?"

She nodded.

It only took a moment, and then we both dropped into full VR, our senses turning inward, to the world created by our implants. The VR environment could simulate anything the programmer's heart desired, provided there was enough bandwidth and talent available, but I preferred to keep things simple. My personal abstraction layer began with me hanging in space, weightless against the backdrop of stars. A nebula spread out far beneath my weightless form, glowing with ambient amber light. Sarah appeared before me, in the avatar I had chosen for her long ago, a glittering blue star reminiscent of a compass rose.

"Shay Chan is requesting permission to join your session," Sarah said, her voice truly audible in the VR abstraction, however little sense that made against the backdrop of vacuum.

"Granted."

Chan entered the session. Her avatar was a beautifully rendered animated version of herself—her true self—with flowing black hair, mysterious eyes, and slightly pouting lips. Her skill was evident in the details and customization. My avatar, in turn, was an off-the-shelf model rendered to look like a twentieth-century vacuum suit with a reflective visor.

"That's terrible," were the first two words that Chan said, her voice once again her own. "Surely you can code… or afford… better than *that*."

"Techies," I said with feigned disgust. "This was the first model vacc suit to set foot on the moon, and all you can say is it's terrible?"

She just shook her head. "How do you want to do this? Immersion or vid?"

"Video." I thought about the pain and horror in the eyes of the branch that had sent the video. I didn't think I wanted to experience what he had experienced. Watching it would be hard enough; I didn't need to live it. "Definitely video."

Chan nodded.

"Okay, Sarah. Give us the highlights."

The abstraction of the misty nebula faded, and the stars briefly swirled, realigning into new patterns—placements that reflected reality, at least at a point in time, rather than the generic light-spangled darkness of my simulation. There were gaps, holes in the starscape colored a dull black that didn't exist in real space. Sarah had reconstructed the visualization by piecing together the footage the branching me had sent, but people rarely got a panoramic view in all three dimensions when going about their daily tasks. Where the branching me had failed to look, the abstraction remained blank.

A derelict ship drifted into view, and I realized Sarah was exercising some directorial control, since there shouldn't be any direct footage of that event. Still, it showcased the vessel, an interplanetary passenger shuttle that looked like it had been adrift a while, quite nicely. "I have been unable to find a match for this ship," Sarah said. "The shuttle is a Raven-class transport, common to the inner system and used most often by the megacorporations. No registration markings were obtained from the original feed. A cross-reference of vessels listed as missing is currently under way."

The scene swept forward, and we were seeing the ship from a different view—one I recognized quite readily. This was the direct camera feed of someone EVA, mag-booted to the hull of the derelict vessel. This was the direct feed from the me that hadn't made it back. There was no breath, not really, not in VR, but mine quickened anyway, and I felt a sudden chill twining up my spine. I was witnessing part of the life lost to me, taken from me.

"Is it always like this?" Chan asked in wonder.

For a moment, I thought she meant the video itself, the sense of reliving the irretrievable. But, no, that didn't make sense. These were my last moments, not Chan's. I realized, then, that she meant being outside, shuffling along the hull, with the stars spinning languidly as the ship rolled. VR could create abstractions that most swore were better than the real thing—Chan was talented enough that she could probably program them herself—but they were *abstractions*, processed and filtered and with an intelligence, artificial or real, imposing a viewpoint. Almost no one looked at raw footage anymore, and fewer still actually experienced a spacewalk.

"No, not always. From the movement of the stars, there was quite a bit of pitching and tumbling going on. Which was probably why Miller sent me over in the first place. My branch I mean. Couldn't get close enough for Harper to use the heavy equipment or to just do a hard dock with the ship."

I trailed off as the hatch came into view. "What the hell are those?" Three neat holes had been bored through the tough metal and composites, clean-edged and perfectly round. Chan just shrugged. "Sarah?"

"Analysis indicates the holes form the points of a perfect isosceles triangle measuring thirty point four-eight centimeters per side. They are most likely the product of a laser, rather than

a drill. Further analysis is impossible with the data available."
There was a brief pause. "At this point, communication took
place between you and the *Persephone*. Do you wish me to play
the conversation?"

"No!" Chan and I said in unison. I nodded at her, though
she probably couldn't see it from within the giant, fish-bubble
helmet. Watching this unfold was bad enough, but neither
of us wanted to hear our voices… voices that belonged to
bodies dead and gone, however Chan's avatar might appear.
"Summarize," I added.

"Of course, Langston," Sarah replied. "After a brief,
inconclusive discussion on the origins of the holes, you made
the decision to attempt to cut your way into the vessel. The
following ninety-three-minute-and-fourteen-second video stream
is that cutting."

"Skip it," I said shortly.

The view lurched, and a hole, the edges still glowing
faintly, appeared in the airlock as if by magic. Then the
camera was moving smoothly again, swimming through
the hole cut into the door. "The second anomalous event is
about to occur," Sarah said helpfully. The light swept over
the airlock, and Chan let out a little scream as it fell across a
distended corpse.

"Shit," I spat. "Pause video, Sarah." The abstraction
obligingly halted, with the camera thankfully pointed away
from the body.

"You okay?" I asked Chan. Her avatar really was good,
programmed to emulate the user's emotions. The anime-ish
features had gone a pale and pasty white, with a slight tinge of

green, and the too-big eyes had gone wider still, showing white all the way around.

"Yes," she said. "Just... surprised, I guess. I've seen bodies, but... I wasn't expecting... that."

"Exposure to vacuum," I said with feigned detachment. It was every spacer's worst nightmare. The reality wasn't quite as bad as decades of romance and drama made it out to be— your blood didn't boil in your veins, nor did your body explode like an over-filled balloon. But the end result, which had stared at us from the video feed, was bad enough. "Sarah, can you summarize findings related to the coil?"

"Yes, Langston. You made the determination to retrieve the coil's core. After doing so, you decided to delve deeper into the vessel. At that point, you noticed the airlock's interior controls had been disabled from the inside."

"Wait. What?"

Without asking, the image changed, going to a close-up of the interior airlock controls. The damage was substantial and would certainly have resulted in the airlock remaining closed. "Why would he lock himself in the airlock?" Chan asked.

"I don't know," I replied. "Sarah? Any data on why?"

"The logical conclusion from the rest of the footage available is that he wished to avoid whatever killed everyone else aboard the vessel."

That sent another chill coursing up my spine. "I think we need to see more," I said. Chan nodded her agreement.

"Do you wish to watch the opening of the airlock?"

"No. Move on to the next salient point."

Again the view lurched, and resolved into an empty bridge.

"You found no indications of the ship's crew. Nor were you able to recover the box." This time the imagery blurred, moving in fast forward, then stopping on a blank spot in the ship's circuitry, where the successor to the flight recorder should have rested. "At this point, you made the determination to check the passenger cabin as well."

This time, Sarah played out the walk from the bridge, past the airlock, to the hatch labeled, "Passenger Cabin." There was a hesitancy in the video, as if the branching me didn't want to make that walk, and certainly didn't want to open the door. Given what the airlock had held, I couldn't blame him. But open the door he did, and his light panned across another horrific scene.

The bodies were not, thankfully, in a state of decompression. But that small mercy was overwhelmed by the volume of them. Nearly thirty souls, all perfectly preserved, all seemingly at rest in their acceleration couches. "Jesus wept," Chan said softly. "What happened to these people?"

"Sarah?"

"Insufficient data, Langston."

Chan's avatar was looking pale and sickly again. "Did you…" she whispered. Then she stopped and drew a long breath. "Did you have to retrieve them all?"

"Pause playback," I said. Retrievals were a necessary part of the job, but that didn't mean they turned my stomach any less. I really did not want to watch as the branching me performed the procedure on thirty corpses. "Did I make retrievals of the cores, Sarah?"

"You completed the retrieval process on eighteen of the twenty-seven passengers."

"Skip that part, unless anything out of the ordinary happened."

The scene shifted again. The branching me had just completed a core extraction and was tucking the cube into a pouch when it went very still. "At this point," Sarah said, "the engines of the derelict vessel came online. Helm was re-established, and the ship began accelerating toward Sol."

"Wait," Chan said. The video obligingly stopped. "If the vessel was empty, how did the engines come online? And how was steering established?"

"That is indeterminate from the video feed, but only two logical possibilities exist."

"Time- or distance-triggered AI control," Chan said, and I nodded. It would be simple enough to give a Beta AI instructions to begin acceleration and pilot the vessel toward the sun after a certain time had elapsed or a certain distance from Sol had been achieved. Even a ship that appeared dead could have enough power reserves to monitor basic astrogation functions.

"What's the other?" I asked Sarah.

"Remote activation and control."

Chan and I looked at each other. "That would mean a vessel close enough to send real-time signals," Chan said, an exaggerated frown creasing her animated features.

"Which should have shown up on the *Persephone*'s sensors," I agreed. "Any indication of another vessel in the area, Sarah?"

"No, Langston. An analysis of the file does not indicate any other vessels in the area."

"AI control, then."

"Not necessarily," Chan said. "There are a number of military-grade systems that could have spoofed the *Persephone*'s sensors. And AI control doesn't explain one key thing."

"What happened to the *Persephone*?" I stated as much as I asked.

"Exactly. We wouldn't have just watched you rocket off into the sun. And we certainly wouldn't have followed after you if that's what did happen. So, something had to have…" she faltered, as the enormity of what she was saying dawned on her.

"Something had to have taken out the *Persephone*," I finished.

"Excuse me," Sarah interjected politely. "There is more footage that you need to see in order to obtain the necessary variables for your analysis."

"Resume playback," I said.

The view swept around the cabin, as the branching me looked quickly around, searching for the source of the powering engines. At first, I missed it. Everything suddenly lurched back, and I could tell the magnetic boots had uncoupled. The world spun as the branching me tried to reorient and get his boots back on the deck. And when he did, I saw the corpse—it had to be a corpse; there was no air, or heat, or pressure in that cabin—rise from one of the acceleration couches at the back of the ship and launch itself right toward me.

"Holy shit!" I exclaimed.

"Pause," Chan snapped.

Sarah complied, pausing with the coil laid out parallel to the ship's deck, arms outstretched before it, eyes blank and staring.

10

"What in God's name is that?" Chan asked.

"Sarah?"

"Analysis indicates that it is what it appears to be—a reanimated coil impervious to the effects of vacuum."

"Which tells us nothing," I muttered. "Is that what kills... me?" As much as I didn't want to hear the answer, I didn't want to witness my own death at the hands of some space-zombie a whole hell of a lot more.

"No. Transmission ends before your previous coil is terminated."

"Right. Should have known that, or the message wouldn't have gotten out." The whole thing had me rattled. Video or not, it all felt too real and at the same time preposterous on a level that made it hard to believe. "Go ahead and resume playback."

It was strange, watching the branching me in a struggle for his life. Watching from his eyes as he avoided the lunging coil, drew his sidearm, and kept shooting until the lifeless corpse was, once again, a lifeless corpse. The fact that the entire ballet of violence took place in total silence only enhanced the ethereal unreality of the scene.

"Jesus," Chan whispered, and I couldn't tell if it was an exclamation or a prayer. "What just happened?"

The video stopped, and we were hanging once more above the nebula, drifting through an endless starscape. The blue star that was Sarah's avatar pulsed with light as she said, "The remainder of the video consists of you making your way to the bridge against increasing acceleration and sending a message to your home console. There are no further anomalies that occur during that time frame, and analysis has found no information as to the registry of the vessel or explanation of the various events that took place."

"Great," I muttered. "Drop VR, then, Sarah."

The session ended, and we were once more seated in Chan's bolt-hole, the real world seeming somehow dull and washed out after the VR experience. I sighed heavily. "I think we have more questions than when we started."

"Maybe," Chan said, and after seeing and hearing her in VR, I had to fight back the eeriness that came with that smooth baritone. "But at least we know what happened out there. Probably as much as we would if we had all survived, somehow. And we know that whatever is going on, it's got to have government or corporate ties."

That threw me. "How do you figure?"

"They got to Miller. Not just his personal records, but his backups. That's…" She paused. "That's *hard*, Carter. Really, really hard. The backup vaults have the best security we've ever been able to devise, and they're constantly monitored, not just by AIs, but by some of the best pros in the business. No individual, or even affiliation or hacktivist group, could break that security on their own, not without triggering something that would set the Net on fire. And they managed to do it to Miller, and probably took a shot at you, too. And there's Harper. We still don't know where they are."

It made sense. And that wasn't even taking into consideration the *Persephone*. Something had taken her out, and there weren't a lot of civilians out there who had armed space ships. That meant money, and that in turn meant polities or the megacorps. "Okay. So we're up against the big boys. Big enough that they took out the *Persephone*, and then tried to wipe us out. And when that didn't work, they decided to send people to kill us."

"Or kidnap," Chan said. "Kidnap makes more sense. Lock us up somewhere. Force us to check in with the insurance companies to keep our backups current. It wouldn't be hard to either drum up fake communications for our families or just make us do it at gunpoint. They could keep us that way for decades, and no one would miss us."

I shook my head. "That guy in the med center on Prospect wasn't trying to kidnap me, Chan. He was there to kill me. And those guys at the club started shooting just to get inside. They don't want to kidnap us."

A sickened expression flashed across the chiseled surfer-god features she wore. "Then our backups aren't safe, either. If they want us dead, they'll keep trying to hack their way in, and we know they've already succeeded once. Eventually, they'll succeed again. And when they manage to kill us, we'll be dead, truly dead, and gone forever." Her voice quavered at the end and her head fell forward, blonde locks obscuring her face. My hand twitched to push them back, but instead I rested it on her coil's shoulder. Her coil's muscular shoulder. She was still Shay Chan, whatever body she wore. But there was something about Chan's mind coupled with her present vulnerability that called to me.

I forced the thoughts from my head. Wherever they were coming from, now was certainly not the right time to explore them. I gave her shoulder a gentle squeeze.

"Then we'll just have to stay alive," I said. "And find out why all this is happening. If we can figure out what the hell happened on that derelict vessel, and what happened to the *Persephone*, then maybe we can expose all of this. One thing's for sure. If we can prove that someone was able to delete or corrupt backups, we'll get people's attention real quick."

She smiled wanly. "And just how do you propose we do that?"

I grinned back. "Hey, I'm just the lug that does the space walks and fights the zombies. You're the crack hacker with a secret lair in the bowels of the habitat. These guys might be good, but they have to have left some kind of trail. Between the shuttle, the *Persephone*, and Miller, there's got to be something on the Net. Otherwise, why go to all the trouble? They're scared, Chan. Scared that something's out there that can be traced back to them."

"And if it's there," Chan said, some of the old confidence creeping back into her voice, "then I can find it."

It wasn't that easy, of course. It never was. Chan hunched over her console, a cable running from it to the access jack behind her ear, since no matter the advances in wireless technology, you still couldn't beat a direct neural interface for maximum data transfer rates. Her hands sat flat on the desk and her face was slack and expressionless. She had been that way for hours, direct interfacing with the Net at maximum bandwidth, presumably breaking any number of laws to try and track down anything that would help us survive the next few days. Or hours. Hell. Minutes, even. A good and necessary thing for her to be doing, but it left me sitting in a strange compartment, with not a lot to do.

I was leery even of jumping on the Net, since whoever had erased Miller certainly outclassed me in that department. Access IDs could be traced, and I lacked the skill to adequately cover my tracks. I could only hope that Chan was good enough at erasing her digital footprints as she went.

Which left me staring at the barred door, waiting as the minutes ticked by, and wondering how long it would be before the next assassin found us and tried to batter their way through the reinforced door. I pulled the Gauss pistol from the pouch where I had stashed it and rested it in my lap. Anything that came through the door would be in for a bit of a surprise, at least. And that just about exhausted the preparations I could make.

Sarah, play me the full video from the salvage operation.

Would you like to view it in virtual reality? my agent asked.

Given that Sarah could inform me the moment any disturbance took place in the real world, it wasn't as bad an idea as it sounded. But the visceral caveman part of me refused to turn its senses over to agent control while sticking its head in the metaphorical sands of VR—not for an unspecified number of hours, and not when I knew someone was coming to kill me.

"No. Just open a window. A small window. And give me audio."

Sarah complied, opening a window in my vision that took up maybe thirty percent of my sight picture. The audio started as well, playing directly in my mind. It was an odd sensation, hearing something that no one else could hear. Or maybe "hearing" wasn't the right word, since the auditory processes of the ears weren't really involved. Most people went about their days to the beat of a soundtrack that only they could hear.

I watched the events unfold again, in real time, but I did my best to ignore whatever the branching me had focused on and concentrate instead on everything *else* happening. I sent a constant stream of instructions to Sarah, pausing the video, zooming, enhancing, homing in on small details that might lead to any kind of clues. Sarah's analysis had come up empty, but the human brain was still the best pattern-recognition hardware around, even when it worked on intuitive leaps and not quantum entanglement.

After four hours, I had made it through just over two hours of the video and learned absolutely nothing useful. I stopped and stood, stretching and working out the kinks. Hunger gnawed at my stomach. This new coil, with its extra pounds of muscle, was going to require a calorie intake that would have had the nanobots in my old body working overtime to keep off the weight.

Movement caught my eye and I turned in time to see Chan reaching back to pull the cable from her access jack. She stood too, stretching. I had seen her do it hundreds of times on the *Persephone*, and it had always been a guilty pleasure to watch, an exercise in elegantly arching the back and artfully extending her arms over her head, reaching so high that it seemed to pull her all the way up to her toes. Her new coil, while trim and graceful, didn't quite do it justice.

"Did you find anything?" I asked, the words coming out slightly rougher than intended.

Chan frowned slightly, probably wondering at the harshness of my tone. I kept my face neutral. After all, I couldn't exactly tell her that I used to get a cheap thrill out of watching her stretch, and now, in her new coil, that thrill was gone. There were lots of ways she could react to that, but none of them were good.

"Maybe," she said. "Sarah ran facial recognition on the passengers and didn't turn anything up. I tried that, too, with no luck. Which is suspicious in and of itself. Those coils were perfectly preserved, so if they had ever had any form of ID— corporate, government, or otherwise—I should have been able to get a match."

"Erased?" I half asked, half stated.

"At least their images. That's a much easier hack than trying to take out someone's backup. Or even just wipe their Net presence."

"Which leaves us nowhere," I muttered.

"Not quite. There was one face they didn't bother with."

I thought about that for a moment. Most of the coils in the video were pristine, but one… "The guy in the airlock?" I guessed.

Chan nodded. "He was… enough of a mess, I guess, that any standard facial recognition wouldn't have helped anyway." The corner of her lips twitched into a lopsided smile.

"But you didn't use standard facial recognition, I take it," I said when she didn't immediately continue. It wasn't the best time to play games, but I couldn't help but smile as well. *This* was the Shay Chan I remembered from the *Persephone*: teasing and mysterious. It was good to see that side of her again, much better than the fearful and uncertain Chan that had responded to my call.

"I did, actually," she replied. "I just wrote a little algorithm first. I based it on medical software commercially available to study the effects of depressurization. That gave me enough data and code to reverse engineer their process. So, what I ended up with is something that takes the end result of depressurization—unappealing as that is—and undoes the damage."

A request to view video popped up into my vision. I closed the window with the footage from the shuttle and accepted the new feed from Chan. The bloated and distended image of the corpse from the airlock sprang to life before me, zoomed in to show only the horror left of his face. I started back as it filled my vision, which, given that the window appeared to be the same relative distance from my eyes regardless of where I moved, did absolutely nothing.

"Christ, Chan. Warn a guy."

"Sorry. But I want you to get the full effect, so I had to start with the before image. Now, when I run my algorithm…"

The bloated wreckage of a human face morphed before my eyes, the swollen flesh melting back into normalcy, the bulging eyes receding and reshaping, the fleshy protuberance of a tongue vanishing beneath thinning lips. When the image was once again still, it revealed a rather plain-looking man with sandy brown hair and hazel eyes.

"Meet Malcolm Copeland," Chan said smugly. "A registered member of the Pallah habitat and an employee of the Genetechnic Corporation."

Mars hung beneath us, a sullen red eye winking at the infinite darkness. Traffic around Earth's closest cousin and the third place humanity had reached for permanent colonization—after Luna—was thick, though the term was relative to the scale of the planet. Chan had secured us tickets on a small, but luxurious passenger liner, and I hadn't bothered asking too many questions about exactly how—or even if— she'd found the funds to do so. I was beginning to realize that what I had known about her as a crewmember of the *Persephone* was only the tip of a very large iceberg.

We'd spent the week of travel in relative comfort, discussing what to do when we reached Pallah, and continuing to adjust to our new coils. The passenger liner had a gym aboard, so I was able to test some of the limits of the shell I wore. I put the coil through the paces I could, but I did long for the ability to work EVA or zero-G. No chance of either of those on the liner. Raw strength was a nice asset, but a lot of EVA work had more to do with agility and flexibility, and I needed to put this coil through those paces if I was going to get back to operating at my previous level. Chan, for the most part, sequestered herself in her cabin, taking advantage of the ship's databases to try and track down more information on our situation. When I suggested she come with me to the gym to help acclimate to her new body, the look she gave me was a mix of incredulity and pain, and I quickly retreated. She was clearly having difficulty adjusting to the idea of being bio-male, and there wasn't a hell of a lot that I could do to help her. Maybe she could scrape together the credits for surgery one day, but at best that was a solution for when our lives—our existence—weren't under threat. And suggesting that to her at the moment seemed… well, *counterproductive* wasn't a strong enough word. I'd just about gotten used to seeing Chan as her new self, though there were moments when I experienced an odd sort of double vision between her old and new coils. Now, as we made our final approach and the plasteel dome grew before us on the viewscreen, I stared in wonder at the sheer size of the city stretching within it.

I had spent most of my life either within the confines of a ship under way, or aboard the close corridors of deep space habitats. The economic realities of spacer life didn't leave much time for idle vacations to begin with and work for someone like me, who had never worn the yoke of the corporations, became scarcer as you approached Sol. Independent jobs cropped up—like the salvage that the *Persephone* had been after—but you either had to jump on them before the corps knew they were there or find yourself competing with better-equipped and better-funded expeditions. It wasn't just salvage: it held true in every sector of space. Mining, transport, passenger services, security... if it could earn creds, you could be sure that the corporations had a presence. Since most of them had started on Earth and were still headquartered there, Sol to Mars was the corporations' backyard. I knew of the cities of Mars and Luna, and, to a lesser degree, Earth. I had seen images, even experienced them to some extent in various VR simulations. But that paled in comparison to the reality of the metropolis growing before us.

The dome alone was a feat of engineering to make intra-system ships and deep-space habitats seem like toys. Not that the domes of Mars had anything like the complexity of ship or hab, but the Pallah dome stretched for *kilometers*. The technical expertise required to build on such a massive scale was staggering, particularly in a gravity well, and the constant reflecting lights sparking off the dome's surface seemed to me to be the winking of some giant, human eye, as if to say to whatever god or gods might be listening, "Check it out. Not too shabby for mere humans, eh?"

Sarah, what are the dimensions of the Pallah dome?

The response came back immediately. *Fifteen kilometers in diameter. One-point-two kilometers high at its apex. Estimated population of two-point-six million.*

I shook my head at the thought of all those people. The larger habitats boasted populations in the tens of thousands, and in very rare cases approached a hundred thousand people. And there were more than twenty-five times as many souls as that within Pallah. And Pallah was only one of hundreds of domes peppering the surface of Mars. They had more space per person than anyone accustomed to ship or hab life, but what must it be like to know that you would never—could never—meet the vast majority of the people who shared air with you? Earth was worse of course. The planetary population stretched into the tens of *billions*, but despite all of man's efforts, humanity's homeworld still provided a breathable atmosphere, vast reservoirs of clean, drinkable water, and a natural bounty of foodstuffs that put the best hydroponics gardens to shame. Her cities stretched not for tens of kilometers, but for *hundreds* of them, growing across the surface of the planet in an ever-expanding, and ever-connecting, web of urban sprawl.

"Beautiful, isn't it?" Chan asked softly, stepping to my shoulder and staring into the viewscreen as we continued our descent.

The voice may not have been hers, but the sound and even the smell of her were distinctly... her. That was comforting, somehow.

"Yeah," I said softly. "It is. Scary, too, though."

"Scared?" she scoffed. "You? I saw what you did on that shuttle, Carter."

"Not me. That was a branch. *I* was sitting in the archives somewhere when that guy was dealing with the zombie coil." Remembering the video sent a shiver down my spine, and it took an effort of will to suppress the involuntary shudder.

"Maybe," Chan said. "But you're still that person, at least right up to the moment of backup. I don't think whatever happened to your branch between backup and that moment was what gave him the courage to face... whatever it was that happened aboard that ship. And it certainly wasn't what gave him the courage to go over there in the first place." She did shudder, then. "I don't think I could do that, especially after the airlock." She rested one hand on my arm, a gesture she had done countless times in the past.

I shrugged, uncomfortable with the praise. "So, what do you think we're going to find at Copeland's apartment?"

Chan must have sensed my unease. She was quiet for a long moment. "I don't know, Langston. I found records on Copeland, so whatever was done to Miller—and whatever they might have tried to do to you, me, and Harper—it looks like they didn't do to Copeland. I'm hoping we'll find Copeland himself. His branch, I guess."

I grunted. It made sense, but if the branching Copeland had been backed up before whatever had put him on that shuttle, then how much use could he possibly be to us? He wouldn't remember anything that happened before his re-coiling and having a pair of strangers show up and demand to know why he had locked himself in an airlock didn't seem like a scenario designed to yield the best results. But what else could we do? Malcolm Copeland was our only lead, the only bit of meaningful data we'd been able to tease from a dozen-plus hours of footage. He had to know something. If he didn't, then Chan and I were going to have to resolve ourselves to a life—probably a very short one—of dodging would-be assassins and hackers intent on eliminating not just our coils, but our very existence.

We were directed to take our seats for the final approach to Pallah. Given the relative thinness of the Martian atmosphere, and the greatly reduced gravity, it seemed like an unnecessary precaution, but I dutifully strapped in. The shuttle touched down with barely a jolt, and a Net window opened broadcasting a pre-recorded video on the off-boarding procedures. I muted and minimized it, unbuckling and gathering my few possessions as Chan did the same.

A long docking tube extended from the dome to the landing pad, sealing in place over the door as the passengers began forming a queue. I heard the sound of pumps coming on—faint, but when you spent a large part of your life EVA, you listened for such things—as the Martian atmosphere was pumped from the tube and oxygen-rich nitrogen took its place. Then the attendant was punching in a code to the keypad by the door. With a barely audible hiss of equalizing pressure, the hatch swung open.

An announcement came over the Net: "Welcome to Pallah. You may now begin the off-boarding process. Remember, gravity on Mars is only forty percent of Earth standard. Please bear that in mind as you move about the domes."

I held back a derisive snort and saw a similar expression on most of the faces around me. There were probably still more people who lived on Earth than there were scattered throughout the system, but those people tended to *stay* on Earth, with a few rare exceptions. People who spent most of their lives on free-floating habs, or cities bored into asteroids or built on the surfaces of moons had little need for a reminder about changing gravitic conditions. The crowd moved forward, gliding through the door and down the docking tunnel, heading into the dome.

I moved more slowly, savoring the view the clear docking tube provided of vast expanses of red dirt and rolling hills.

Pallah was one of the more remote of the Martian domes and from my vantage, it was the only one in sight. Somehow, even with the people moving around me, even with the vastness of Pallah's dome looming over me, it was easy to imagine being alone in that crimson wasteland, being among the first of the human race to set foot on Mars. It was both similar to, and distinctly different from, the sense that I got when boarding a derelict vessel or abandoned station in search of salvage.

"Come on, Langston," Chan said at my side. "Let's move it." She, too, was looking at that vast wasteland, but a faint sheen of sweat glistened on her forehead, and her breathing was coming a little fast and shallow.

"You okay?" I asked, as I reluctantly turned my eyes away from the Martian landscape and back toward the far end of the tube.

"I don't like wide open spaces," she admitted. "They make me nervous."

I nodded in understanding and picked up the pace. Life in the close quarters of a ship or hab made some people long for open vistas. Others took comfort from the layers of steel and composite that kept them safe—relatively speaking—from the dangers of a universe that seemed to go out of its way to prove its inhospitable nature to the human race. When those layers were removed, agoraphobia took hold. It wasn't something that bothered me—the vast deserts of Mars still paled in comparison to hanging in the emptiness of space—but I understood it, nonetheless.

We crossed into the terminal, entering the domed city. The passenger waiting area boasted rows of plastic chairs and a series of airlocks that, I assumed, each came equipped with their own docking tube. I counted eight gates within my line of sight, and the long walkways suggested that there were plenty more. We were not the only arrivals, and the people disgorging from our gate joined an ever-expanding flood of humanity as it funneled down the walkways toward a Net object that read, "Customs."

A flicker of nerves twisted my stomach as I approached the customs station. Prospect and the other deep-space habs were all their own legal polities as were most of the domed cities on the moons of Jupiter, Saturn, Uranus, and Neptune. The cities of Mars were unified under their own government and the same held true for the cities of Luna. Earth was a hodgepodge of nations, alliances, and governments as it always had been, and damned if I could keep any of them straight. The governments of the various domes and habitats weren't exactly *generous* in the sharing of information among themselves, but it was entirely possible that the death of the would-be assassin on Prospect and my sudden disappearance had been significant enough to draw notice. Nothing had reached Daedalus—but Daedalus was notorious for its autonomy. If it didn't happen there, they didn't care… and as far as I knew, we'd gotten away from the Black Diamond clean. The domes of Mars were a different beast, though, and my mouth went dry as the steadily moving line of people drew us nearer to the uniformed customs agents.

"Net ID, sir," the bored official said as I stepped before him.

I initiated the transmission, sending the algorithm that served as my identity. When appearances, fingerprints, retinas, and even your DNA changed from one coil to the next, identity became something of a difficult concept to nail down. The problem had been solved by the increasing data transmission rates and what was once a picture and some vital statistics was now an amalgam of randomly selected information linked to a person. It included everything from employment records to purchasing habits and an endless array of data in between, all snapshot at random intervals and re-synced with a centralized database each time a person went to be backed up.

It was, in theory, unhackable. Because the protocols selected information at random, there was no set pattern that could be applied to filter the information available on the Net and extract a person's identity. And because the set of information was changed or updated with each backup, most people had a mutable, non-repeating, entirely randomized series of individual-specific data packaged and encrypted into an algorithm that could be used as a means of identification. The central databases storing the matching set employed the same level of security as the backup servers themselves, which—until I learned of Miller's erasure—everyone *knew* were completely safe.

Mine, at least, still appeared unhacked and not associated with any nefarious deeds. The customs agent's glassy-eyed stare—presumably at whatever window hung before his vision to inform him of evil passers-by—never changed. "Thank you, Mr. Langston. Scans indicate that you brought a selection of personal weaponry into the dome. Please accept the EULA if you wish to keep them with you. If not, you can leave them with me, and they will be returned to you upon your departure from Pallah."

A window opened in my vision, displaying a lengthy document. I didn't bother to read it. *Sarah?*

Standard boilerplate, Langston. Weapons may only be employed in self-defense. There is a long list of penalties for various infractions ranging from inciting fear to outright murder.

Thank you, Sarah. Please accept the terms on my behalf. The licensing agreement went away as my agent applied my digital signature.

"Enjoy your stay on Pallah, Mr. Langston," the customs agent said.

I nodded to the agent, who neither noticed nor cared. Chan had already passed through and was waiting on me. "Well, we're here," she said softly. "Now what?"

"Now we go find Malcolm Copeland."

12

Pallah was unlike any place I'd seen before.

During the early years of the diaspora, China, Europe, India, and America had competed to lay claim to as much planetary real estate as possible while other nations focused on deep-space habs. Luna had been dominated by American corporate interests from the outset, but Mars had been fair game. The domes had, in their inception, been microcosms of the old Earth nations that established them, carrying their cultures and biases to the broader solar system. That had faded over the centuries, the national influences slowly being subsumed beneath the monolithic corporations that transcended mere political borders, and the Martian residents had eventually broken away from their faraway Earthbound masters. They'd formed the Martian Republic, with each dome holding the position a state or province might have held on Earth. The strange genesis had left the various domes with their own unique architecture and character despite their shared sovereignty.

I'd done my research on the flight over. I knew that Pallah had originally been a venture of the American government, bringing its own brand of government-contracted capitalism and corporate homogeny. The legacy of that showed in the quick prefab structures that dominated most of the landscape, blocky shapes against the backdrop of the Martian sky. They were sturdy and functional but most of the artistry had been a casualty of the lowest-bidder approach.

It was still early in the Martian day, and if Malcolm Copeland had been re-coiled and slotted neatly back into the life he lived before his ill-fated journey, he would probably be at work. Barging into the offices of a major corporation to try to speak with an employee who didn't know either of us, about events that he likely didn't remember, seemed like a poor choice. Instead, Chan started surfing the various directories to track down Copeland's apartment and find us the nearest hotel.

The Martian Palms wasn't quite as contradictory as it sounded. There *were* palm trees in front of it, nearly a dozen of them, each ensconced in a large container made of plastic but molded and painted to look like wood. The soil in which they grew was not Earth soil—not really—but it had been fortified with the nutrients and minerals necessary for plant life. I winced a little as I thought about the water requirements, but that was the spacer in me. No matter how many ice comets could be mined and brought to a hab, there was only so much water you could store. It took up a lot of room, and the mass calculations were staggering. But a planet didn't suffer from those limitations, and the carbon-scrubbing and oxygen-production of the trees certainly helped offset their expense.

Still, it seemed an extravagance, particularly as I thought about the few credits remaining to my name.

The exterior of the building was drab and plain, a simple twelve-story prefab construction of composite sheets. That exterior, however, hid the treasure within. The interior didn't scream wealth. Screaming in that establishment would have been far too crass. Instead, it *murmured* money, in a sort of sotto voce drawl that drew the eye to the understated elegance of the lobby. Everywhere I looked, I saw wood—real wood, not like the molded plastic of the exterior—that glowed in golden shades of honey and amber. A sweeping staircase climbed majestically on our right, and a guest counter, with an actual smiling woman standing behind it, beckoned from the left. I started to turn in that direction, but Chan grabbed my elbow.

"Already taken care of," she said brusquely as she steered me toward a bank of elevators slightly deeper into the hotel lobby.

"Chan… how can you possibly afford all this?"

She grinned, and despite the coil she wore, that grin had just a bit of naughty little girl in it. "I didn't pick this place for the amenities. I picked it because it has security protocols so outdated that Bit could practically have hacked it without my help. Now hurry up, before the receptionist or whatever she is gets curious." I felt a slight moment of guilt at the growing damages of our larcenous behavior, but given that someone was trying to kill us, I didn't let it bother me too much. If fleecing a corporation or two was the price for staying alive, my moral compass could bear it.

The elevators took us up to the eighth floor. The hallways lacked the imported woods of the lobby but were still neat and well-kept. The room that Chan led me to should have been disappointing after the lobby. There were two beds, neatly made, and a bathroom off to one side. A long, low dresser rested against a wall opposite the beds, with a viewscreen integrated into the wall behind it. It was, at best, standard fare. But the size of it! The room was easily twice the size of my quarters aboard Daedalus, and maybe three times the size of my berth aboard the *Persephone*. One entire wall was made of transparent plasteel and presented a view of the Martian city.

"Nice," I said.

Chan dropped onto one of the beds, letting her bag fall unceremoniously at its side. I was still traveling without luggage, carrying only what could be strapped to the VaccTech suit that remained my only set of clothing. Unlike my previous suit, it had been specifically designed with long-term, continuous use in mind, and was actually quite a bit more comfortable than the suit I'd lost, despite the added bulk. Still, I took the time to unclip the various pouches from the suit, as well as remove the holstered Gauss pistol before dropping onto the other bed.

"Is this going to work, Carter?" Chan asked, her voice steeped in a tiredness that had nothing to do with physical fatigue.

"I don't know," I admitted. "Maybe Copeland will know something. Maybe not the details, but if he's been re-coiled, they had to tell him *something*. Even without the video my branch sent, we knew we went out on the *Persephone* for salvage. We knew the general vicinity of space. He'll know something, some little crumb of information that maybe seems meaningless to him, but it will give us the next little bit, the next little clue to find out what happened to us. We'll find the truth, Chan."

The grim determination in that declaration surprised me, but it paired well with the slow-burning anger that I felt churning in my gut.

"And then what? What happens when we find the truth?"

I felt my lips twist in a bitter smile. "I don't know, Chan. If this is as big as I think it might be, then we're talking government and corporate involvement. There isn't a lot we can do, not directly, to stop either. But we can tell the truth. The truth is a light, Shay. We shine that light in all the dark corners and see what comes scurrying out. And if we aren't big enough to step on it ourselves…" I shrugged. "Well, maybe we try to find someone else who is."

We waited until two hours after the sun had set over the Martian horizon before venturing out from the hotel. The Palms was only a couple of miles from Copeland's apartment, and we elected to walk. The sealed dome ensured that the temperature remained pleasant, and I once again marveled at the engineering necessary to produce the faint breeze that rattled the leaves on the infrequent trees and sent gentle eddies of dust dancing on the walkways. The dome designers had gone to great lengths to furnish the little details that made planet-dwellers feel safe. Seemed like a waste of effort to me, but then again, I hadn't been born at the bottom of a gravity well. We were far from the only ones out and about. People crowded the walkways and small electric carts zipped along the roads. We drew a fair number of glances—Chan had traded in her vacc suit for a pair of slacks and a button-down shirt cut in a style that could almost be called a blouse. I still wore the space-black

VaccTech, with all my possessions (and weapons) dangling from it. Given our disparate dress, I suspected people were taking me for some sort of bodyguard, which by default would make Chan someone important. The slightly worried stares had one advantage, though—despite the busy streets, we moved in a bubble of space as the crowds parted and flowed around us.

I marveled at the domed city as we made our way through it. I was used to the crowds, though I knew that there were more people who lived within Pallah than could fit in any of the habitats I'd ever set foot upon. But they had so much *space* beneath the domes. I could appreciate the irony—those who lived in the depths of space did so at the cost of... space. Even though we moved through a sea of people that, just in this one section of town, rivaled some of the habs I'd lived, I could still take three steps in any direction and be out of the flow. I could find a quiet niche, an alleyway between two prefab structures, a café with plenty of seats to spare, without the slightest bit of effort. It was at once freeing and oddly disconcerting.

And the sky! A simple glance up revealed the beauty of the Martian sky. Though it was, undisputedly, the Red Planet, and though the oldest pictures showed the skies a butterscotch brown, human perception was a complex beast. Here, on the surface, with the lower light native to a world much farther from the sun, the Purkinje effect emerged, shifting the vision balance of the human eye from the color-sensitive cones to the more color-blind rods. It had the odd effect of casting the Martian sky in richer and deeper blues than one could ever find upon Earth's surface. And yet, within the dome, the lighting level was higher, and as I looked at the transparent bubble that kept the teeming millions safe from the devastating effects of the Martian atmosphere, it almost felt as if I was at the bottom of some ancient sea looking up not into the sky, but into the fathomless depths of an endless ocean.

But there was no time to stop and marvel at the wonders, and I knew that I couldn't let the strangeness of Pallah draw me too far from the matter at hand. It was exotic, yes. Beautiful, even. And the crowds and shadows both provided ample cover for any killer waiting to remove us from the game. I tore my eyes from my surroundings and focused on staying alive. But I couldn't resist the occasional glance upward, to the inherent contradictions of the Martian sky.

Copeland's building was a rather plain, prefab rectangle rising ten stories. A sidewalk led to a small concrete patio, beyond which a pair of double doors beckoned. A screen beside the door displayed a numbered list of apartments and Net codes. "Copeland is in 803," Chan said, scanning the list. "The lock's pretty simple… I can hack it if we need to."

"Don't bother," I said.

Sarah, ping them all.

The apartment listing showed close to one hundred units in the building. It took Sarah less than a second to send out a ping to each of those units, requesting access. Any one of those hundred tenants could easily have activated the building's door camera, taken a look, and promptly ignored us. Dozens, maybe scores, had probably done just that. But it only took one person. One person who was expecting a delivery, or a friend to show up, or maybe just someone who reacted on instinct when their implant pinged them with a request to enter the building. Whatever the case, a chime sounded from the door as the lock disengaged.

"How did you know that would work?" Chan asked, surprise writ large on her face.

"There's more than one type of salvage." I shrugged. "I worked repo a long time ago. Lots of hab sections use similar gatekeepers. I can't hack the tech, but anything that allows for human interface has one big weakness."

"What's that?" There was genuine curiosity in her voice. No doubt she could have brute-force hacked the door nearly as quickly, but the professional in her was always looking for a better way.

I grinned. "People are stupid." I opened the door and motioned her inside. "Well, not all people. But in a crowd of a hundred, you'll always find someone who'll take the easiest path. In this case, that's just saying 'yes' to the random access request, rather than taking the time to see who might be at the door."

Chan called the elevator as soon as we entered the building and registered on the guest network. It was waiting for us by the time we reached the banks. We were both silent as the elevator climbed to the eighth floor. I felt a tension building in my shoulders as the doors opened on a neat hallway with doors down either side. Despite my earlier words to Chan, Copeland was our only real chance at finding out what had happened to us, to Miller, to Harper, to all those people aboard that shuttle. I had no idea what I was going to say to him, how we could convince him to even talk to us in the first place. I just knew that we *had* to get that information, had to find out the truth. Miller had died—truly *died*—for it, and Harper was still missing.

Someone had to answer for that. Someone had to pay for that.

My hands curled slowly into fists, tightening until my arms started to tremble. I drew a deep, steadying breath and released it as we stepped into the hall, forcing my fingers to unknot. "Are you ready for this?" I asked Chan.

She didn't say anything, but she nodded once, shortly. I could see the same anger, the same determination burning in her eyes. The time for answers had come, and I knew then that we were both willing to do anything to get them. The idea of it was slightly nauseating, but I knew it to be true. I sincerely hoped we could convince Malcolm Copeland to help us... but I knew that if we couldn't *convince* him, I was ready to *force* him.

We had taken no more than a half-dozen steps into the hallway when the first crack of gunfire sounded from somewhere ahead of us.

13

The Gauss pistol appeared in my hand as if by its own accord, and, without thinking, I shoved Chan behind me.

Several more shots rang out, followed by a heavy crash. My ears were momentarily filled with a ringing from the cacophonous report of the shots, but my nanites went to work at once. The hearing damage that I was no doubt suffering with each crack of gunfire was being repaired almost as fast as it was happening. I ignored the ringing and darted down the hall, to apartment 803. The acrid tang of burned chemical propellant hung thick in the air, and I could hear faint sounds coming from the other side of the door. Faint, pain-filled sounds.

I slammed my shoulder into the door, once, twice, a third time, grunting with the effort. The door was surprisingly sturdy, given that the domed cities didn't require pressure seals, but on the final hit, the frame gave way, and the door exploded inward. For an instant, I was framed in the doorway, and in that instant, I saw death staring back at me.

A man dressed in a dark singlesuit knelt beside a body lying crumpled on the floor. He had, most likely, been searching through the corpse's pockets, but my sudden and dramatic entrance had interrupted him. Interrupted, perhaps, but it seemed I hadn't surprised him, as he raised a heavy pistol of unfamiliar design and, not bothering to stand, squeezed the trigger.

I dove back behind the wall, barely in time, as a hail of bullets sprayed through the opening that my coil had so recently filled. They smashed into the wall on the other side of the hallway, drilling neat holes into the apartment across the way. I silently prayed that it was empty, or, at least, that no one was in harm's way. That worry turned more personal as the unknown gunman tracked his fire in my direction.

I dropped to the floor as more rounds blasted through the wall where I had been standing, showering me in a rain of broken composite and dust. It was only a matter of moments before the gunman tracked his weapon across a vector that would intersect with some important part of my anatomy. It wasn't the best of solutions, but I wasn't overflowing with options, so I shoved the barrel of my Gauss pistol around the corner of the doorjamb, tilted it slightly up and in the general direction of the kneeling man, and began pulling the trigger. The *snap* of the electro-magnetically accelerated twelve-millimeter rounds was lost beneath the louder report of my assailant's chemical burner, but his steady stream of fire abruptly stopped.

For the briefest of instants, I felt a flash of hope. Maybe my blind fire had gotten lucky after all. But Chan had not been idle during the precious seconds that had elapsed from when the first shots rang out. Sarah pinged me with an urgent request to accept a video feed, delivered directly from Chan. I approved, and a window popped into view. I immediately moved it to the upper right corner of my vision, but even there it was particularly distracting.

We lived in a world of pervasive technology, where almost every device was wired to the Net in some form or fashion. Many, maybe even most, of those devices had some sort of integrated camera. Chan must have hacked the apartment's network, because the feed I was receiving showed the gunman as he moved deeper into the apartment, diving behind the counter in the kitchen. The view switched to show him calmly inserting another long magazine into his handgun.

Not so lucky after all, I supposed.

"HabSec's on their way," I called into the apartment, then leapt to my feet and darted to the other side of the doorway, the side not already riddled with bullet holes. Sarah had added another indicator beneath the video feed, this one showing me the rounds remaining in the Gauss pistol's magazine. Twenty-six. In those brief seconds I'd already fired off fourteen rounds.

"They still call them police officers here in the domes, Mr. Langston. You *are* Carter Langston, aren't you?" The man's tone was polite, almost urbane. "And their average response time to this location is almost eight minutes. I assure you, we still have plenty of time."

He moved while he talked, and the video feed from Chan's various inanimate spies tracked him to the edge of the counter. He crouched low, pistol held with the barrel pointed up toward the ceiling. There must have been a viewscreen in the kitchen, because the resolution was high enough for me to make out his features. He had high, narrow cheekbones that fell sharply to a long chin that almost came to a point. Yellow-tinted glasses—an affectation as most forms of visual impairment were easily correctable—obscured his eyes, and his jet-black hair was slicked back to form a sharp widow's peak on his forehead. White linen gloves sheathed his fine-boned hands, standing out sharply against the grips of the pistol. He looked more like a man destined for the opera house than one hell-bent on murder.

"How do you know my name?" I demanded.

"I'm afraid it was given to me by a client of mine. You've angered someone, Mr. Langston. Angered them enough that they would prefer it if you were removed from the game for a while. You, and Shay Chan, and Zomas Harper, and, of course, Mr. Copeland, here. By the way, did you bring Ms. Chan and Zr. Harper with you? That *would* have been uncommonly considerate."

No mention of Miller.

The message, in text, flashed across the bottom of my vision, sent, no doubt, from Chan. And she was right. Either the polite assassin was unaware of Miller or knew that Miller wouldn't be coming back.

"Time's ticking," I said. "If the response time is eight minutes, you're down to…" I queried Sarah. "Six minutes and fourteen seconds."

"Now, now, Mr. Langston. Don't be in such a rush. Still, there is no reason this needs to be difficult. If you'll simply step into the doorway, I'll make it quick. A few weeks from now you'll wake up in a re-coiling facility and it will be as if all this never happened. Is that so bad?"

Given what happened to Miller, and the "difficulties" that the med center on Prospect had experienced with my backup, I seriously doubted things would be so cut and dried as that. Besides, my re-coiling insurance plan only allowed for one deductible-free re-coiling per annual cycle. Who wanted to wake up to a pile of debt? "I appreciate the offer, I really do, but I think I'll just take my chances and see if I can't hold out for, oh, I don't know… another five minutes and forty-eight seconds or so."

Another message popped up from Chan. *Monitoring the HabSec band. Response is looking more like twelve minutes. From now.*

Shit. Well, hopefully the well-dressed assassin didn't know that. The video window showed that he had finished reloading and was, apparently, waiting calmly for an opportunity to check me off his list. "Who sent you?" I called. I didn't really expect a response, but if he was talking, maybe he wouldn't be shooting.

"Come now. I couldn't possibly reveal that information." As he spoke the words, he rolled out from behind the counter, bringing his weapon to bear and unleashing a stream of bullets at the doorway. Apparently, he had no problem talking *and* shooting.

I dropped prone once again as the rounds punched through the wall and sent dust and bits of plastic flying through the air. My answering fire—still made from blindly sticking only my hand around the doorjamb—was better aimed than before, since I had the apartment camera feeds to help line things up. I burned through another dozen rounds, leaving me with only fourteen shots remaining, but the barrage of fire sent the assassin diving for cover once more, this time through an open door and into what, I assumed, was a bedroom or an office. There was a moment where the Net feed from Chan showed only the empty living room, but the scene changed again, giving me a view of a bedroom. The angle was much tighter this time, and the picture grainier, but I could still make out a dark form crouched by the wall, once more calmly reloading.

It hardly seemed fair. How many bullets did he have?

Blind fire—or maybe half-blind through the grace of Chan's hacking—wasn't getting me anywhere except closer to being out of ammo. I popped back to my feet, and, staying as close as I could to the wall, leaned out around the doorframe, Gauss pistol trained toward the bedroom door. "You seem to have an uncommonly good sense for battle," the man called from the darkness. "Particularly given that the files I have on you indicate you are a salvage specialist. I take it that means the hacker is with you?"

Before I could respond, a rapid succession of shots rang out. I ducked back behind cover again, but it only took a moment to realize what the assassin was about. On the third shot, the video feed in my view went blank.

"Dammit," Chan muttered aloud. "He's taking out anything that might have a camera built in."

I leaned back around the corner, trying to force myself to control my breathing. Panicked and panting didn't make for the best marksmanship, but the sudden not-knowing had sent my guts into a twisting knot and turned my mouth into a parched wasteland. Better, though, if the other guy didn't know that.

"You're down to three minutes," I said, forcing my tone to be as casual as possible. It was a lie, of course. By Chan's estimation, there were closer to *ten* minutes before any kind of police response.

"Average response time, Mr. Langston. Average. Who knows how long we might have?"

There was an edge to that voice, a knowledge, that sent a trill of fear dancing along my spine. He knew. Maybe he was listening in on the HabSec frequencies. Or maybe he had paid someone off. But he *knew* the authorities were still a long way out.

"Just a few more seconds," Chan whispered over the Net. "I've got something else planned. Just need a minute."

Christ. By rights, we should have been dead already. The only thing keeping us alive was the fact that I could lay down enough suppression fire to keep the assassin on his guard. But the next exchange would empty the Gauss pistol. I still had the microwave emitter, but that was short-range at best. The shooter could fill me full of holes long before I ever got close enough for the emitter to work. "Yeah," I said aloud. "Sure. No problem."

There had been no movement from the bedroom. I had an idea of where the assassin had been. Would he still be there? The Gauss pistol was designed to fire a lower-velocity round, so as not to punch through the hulls of ships, but it still had enough power to penetrate the interior wall of an apartment building... provided the round didn't hit a structural support, anyway. I took aim at the wall, just to my right of the door, and depressed the trigger. I fired four quick, but controlled, shots, resulting in a nice tight grouping.

The dapperly dressed killer leaned out in response—from the other side of the door. A tongue of flame sprung into existence from the end of his pistol and I threw myself backward, away from the door, away from that barrage of death. An explosion of pain blossomed in my left arm, and another in my leg, but I didn't have time to dwell on it. I hit the ground hard, taking the brunt of the impact high on my back. I managed to keep my grip on the Gauss pistol, and instinctively started squeezing the trigger once more, sending a hail of bullets into the apartment. That lasted for about four seconds, when, instead of hearing the healthy *snap* of the pistol, I got a faintly apologetic *beep* as the magazine emptied.

The camera feeds were still live in the apartment's living room. That gave me an excellent view of the suited shooter walking calmly from the bedroom, stopping to check on the body in the center of the room, and continuing on toward the main door. Reloading as he went. Again. I dropped the Gauss pistol and fumbled at the pouches attached to my VaccTech. I was distantly aware of a burning pain coursing through my left arm but had no time to think about it. The assassin was halfway to the door.

My hand closed over the microwave emitter's angled grips and I tore it from the pouch. "Got it!" Chan exclaimed, her voice fierce with exultation. And in that instant, sirens began to sound.

14

The sirens seemed to be coming from all around us, low at first, but growing steadily louder, as if converging on the apartment building. I heard a muttered curse from the living room. "Well, Mr. Langston. It seems we will not be able to finish our conversation after all. You will have to excuse me." There was a moment's pause, and the assassin's voice dropped into a much lower, colder register. "Know that I look forward to continuing our conversation at a later time."

And with that, the suited man turned back toward the bedroom again, ignoring the fact that I was, for all intents and purposes, helpless before him. I didn't have much time to dwell on that, because almost immediately I heard another burst of gunfire. I flinched instinctively, but this time, the deadly fusillade was not coming my way. Instead, it was followed by the sound of one of the plastic windows cracking, and then a crash as the man, presumably, went right through it and into the dropping veil of the Martian evening.

"Are you okay?" Chan was at my side. "My God! You're

bleeding."

I grunted. "Get me to my feet." Heads had started to poke out of doors, and people were glancing at us long enough to record. Great. "We may want to get out of here before the HabSec arrives."

She grinned. "We've got time." I looked at her in confusion, but even as she said it, the sirens started to wink out, one by one. "I hacked the apartments around us. Grabbed a siren sound from the Net and started playing it through any sound system I could get my hands on. Worked a little magic with the soundscape and volume to make it seem like they were getting closer, too." She reached a hand down to me and I grabbed it.

Her old coil wouldn't have been able to pull me up, particularly not in the heavier, more muscular body I now wore. In her new one, however, she managed it with barely a grunt. "I guess there are *some* advantages to being a boy." Even now, she said the words as if she didn't truly believe them and I heard the small undercurrent of pain.

I shrugged. "I've always thought so." I slowly put weight on my left leg. It held but brought with it a shooting line of fire that coursed from hip to ankle. I drew a breath and let it out as a hiss. On the plus side, compared to the leg, my arm felt fine. I took a tottering step into the apartment.

"What are you doing?" Chan asked. "We've got to get out of here. We've got..." She paused as if querying her agent. "Maybe six minutes before this place is crawling with security." She also looked significantly at the doors around us, which had continued their own private symphony of opening a crack before slamming shut once again. "And we're not exactly alone here, either."

"We've got to check the coil," I said. I took a few more steps into the room, and Chan, a look of doubt on her face, ducked in behind me. She used one booted foot to kick the door closed. It didn't latch, but it at least gave us some semblance of privacy.

"You can barely walk. Are you sure about this?"

In point of fact, I was already starting to feel better. The nanites in my system had gone to work, and were no doubt efficiently repairing damaged blood vessels, reknitting tissue, and pushing the bullet and any other foreign materials inexorably to the surface. It still *hurt*, but a wound that would once have been life-threatening was little more than an inconvenience these days. A *painful* inconvenience, but nothing that I was too worried about. The VaccTech suit had even tightened around my leg and arm, providing rough compression bandages, and slowing the bleeding even further.

In lieu of an answer, I wobbled over to Malcolm Copeland's late coil and knelt beside it. He had been shot in the chest, multiple times. Even the best nanites couldn't do anything once the heart and lungs were full of holes, and it looked like Copeland had been dead before he'd hit the ground. "Did you clean up any footprints you may have left from the various hacks you did?" I asked Chan as I continued to examine the body.

She gave me a look of pure incredulity, and I raised one arm—my right arm—in supplication. "Sorry, just asking." There was something off about the body. He'd been shot in the chest, but his head had a wet, sticky look to it that I recognized. Fighting back revulsion, I reached out and twisted the head to one side. "Damn."

"What is it?"

A neat incision had been made near the base of Copeland's skull. The edges were almost surgically precise, though lacking the cauterization that would have been present from a laser-scalpel. The flaps of the wound had been folded back, obscuring the depth of the cut, but I'd seen—and performed—the same procedure too many times in the past not to recognize it. "The killer popped his core."

Chan sighed. "We've only got a few minutes left."

"We aren't getting out of here before the police," I said.

"What?"

"No point. How many cameras are we on? How many people in the complex saw us? You can't hack them all, and we certainly can't silence the witnesses. And I can't run. We're caught." I smiled. "But we're not caught doing anything *wrong*, Chan."

She surveyed the apartment: bullet holes, shattered glass, furniture knocked aside, plenty of blood, and, last but certainly not least, a corpse in the middle of the room. I chuckled at the look that flashed across her leonine features. I could tell she was wondering if I had finally lost my mind.

"Can you blank this apartment's cameras from right after we walk inside?" I asked. She nodded mutely. "Good. Then all the authorities will see, all they'll know, is that two people got off the elevator and interrupted a crime. One of those two happened to be armed, and, acting purely in self-defense, exchanged gunfire with the bad guy. Hell, it even has the advantage of being the *truth*, Chan. As long as we leave out all the unfortunate bits about interplanetary conspiracies, re-animating coils, and hacked backup centers, we should be fine."

"Are you sure?"

Well, no, of course I wasn't. But nanites or not, I wasn't going to be making any quick getaways. And I hadn't come all this way to be stopped by a trigger-happy assassin and a corpse. I nodded, trying to make the gesture reassuring. "Wipe those cameras… and see if you can find anything that might help us in Copeland's systems."

She gave me a lopsided grin. "Bit's already doing that. We're cloning anything with storage capabilities. We can go through it all later… assuming we're not stuck in a jail cell somewhere."

I nodded and turned back to the body. The killer had taken his core, but we'd clearly interrupted him. In his shoes, I would have gone after the core first, so there was still a chance that something had been missed. I gritted my teeth and started to pat down the coil, looking for anything that might give us a clue as to what the hell was going on.

"HabSec just pulled up outside," Chan said. "We've got maybe two minutes."

"Shit," I muttered under my breath, but I kept searching. At the hem of Copeland's shirt I felt a small bump, barely the size of a grain of rice. I pulled the arm to me, examining the sleeve. It looked seamless—as well it should. Just like my suit was already in the process of repairing itself, most clothing had nanites to perform the same function, sewing up any rips or tears as if they'd never been. They would, of course, sew up any intentional cuts as well.

I opened one of my pouches and grabbed a simple folding knife, whose design had remained largely unchanged for hundreds of years. I flicked the blade open and made a quick cut, slicing the hem.

"Cops are getting out of the elevator," Chan said urgently.

I shoved the knife back into the pouch with one hand, probing feverishly with the other. *There*. There was something. It was small enough that I could barely grasp it between my two fingers, but I managed, somehow. I dipped it into a pocket on the VaccTech.

"At the door," Chan hissed.

Unpleasant as it was, I placed my hands over the bullet holes in Copeland's chest and pushed down, applying pressure. The door to the room flew open and a pair of HabSec—or rather, police officers—burst in, weapons drawn and sweeping the room. In a heartbeat, one of those weapons was trained on Chan, who stood off to the side, arms raised. The other remained steady on me.

"Help!" I called. It wasn't difficult to feign the panic in my voice. Life had been a fairly perpetual state of panic these past weeks. "He's been shot!"

"Hands!" one of the officers barked. "Hands where I can see them."

If Copeland really had been dying, taking pressure off the wounds would have been a pretty bad idea, but I couldn't really blame the cop. I slowly lifted them, bloodstained palms toward the officer. My left arm wasn't working quite right, and I had trouble lifting it beyond shoulder level, but no new bullets were flying in my direction, so I guessed it was good enough.

"He needs help," Chan said, and there was real concern in her voice.

"He's clearly dead, sir," the officer covering Chan replied. "In any event, medtechs are on their way." I could hear the minimal interest in the officer's voice. After all, so far as they knew, Copeland would only be dead until a new coil could be found.

"Not him," Chan snapped, ignoring the "sir." "My friend has been shot, too, trying to *save* this man."

Two more police officers burst into the room, followed by what had to be a sergeant or lieutenant or something. Then came a pair of paramedics. A sort of organized chaos took hold, and within moments, Chan and I were both cuffed and shuffled off into the care of the paramedics, though still under the watchful eye of one of the policemen. They confirmed the bullet wounds, but I turned down immediate evacuation to a med center in favor of staying behind with Chan to answer the police questions. I couldn't very well leave her to face that alone.

And so we found ourselves, still cuffed, though at least with our hands in front of us, seated at the deceased's dining table, across from one Detective Sanderson, while the police and crime scene people went about their business.

"What happened?"

It was a complicated question, but I kept my answer short and simple. "We were coming to see Mr. Copeland about an accident that happened to our branches." The *Persephone*'s loss would be easy enough to confirm, though unless the police had a hacker of Chan's capabilities, they probably wouldn't find anything about Copeland. "When we got to the floor, we heard screaming and gunshots. I happened to be armed, so I went to render assistance. There was a man—I'm sure you saw him on the security cameras—who was crouched over Mr. Copeland's coil. He started shooting and…" I shrugged and glanced about the room. "Here we are."

"You just 'happened' to be armed?" Sanderson asked with an arched eyebrow.

"I work salvage, Detective. It's a dangerous and unpredictable business. As long as the local hab… sorry, dome… laws permit, I always carry a weapon. You can never be too safe when your work often requires you to carry around easily portable and transferrable valuables, after all." I gave him my most disarming smile, which, given the thuggish coil I wore, the pain lingering from two gunshot wounds, and my ever-growing irritation at the entire situation was, admittedly, not very disarming at all. "It seems to have proved prudent, in this case." I offered a half-shrug, since my bad shoulder still wasn't responding right. "I only wish we had gotten here sooner."

Sanderson grunted at that. "I bet. And what about you?" He turned to Chan. "What were you doing while your friend here was playing shootout at the OK Corral?"

"Notifying the police, of course. And monitoring their response time." She smiled, a "butter-won't-melt-in-my-mouth" smile that was much better suited to her old coil. In the leonine surfer it looked… smug.

"I'm sure. And can either of you explain why the cameras—all the cameras in the apartment, mind you—seem to have stopped working the moment you entered the premises?"

That was a trickier one. Fortunately, Chan was quick on the draw. "We came in as soon as we heard the gunman leave. He must have done something to the camera feed on his way out."

"And left all the other footage of him shooting the apartment's resident and then exchanging gunfire with your friend?" Okay, so maybe it wasn't a great response. But the officer had given us an opening, and damned if I was going to miss it.

"Well," I said, "if you have footage of the murderer, and of us responding to the violence, please explain why we're still wearing these." I half-raised my arms, wincing at the stab of pain, and jangled the restraints. "It sounds like the video feeds corroborate what we've been telling you for the past ten minutes."

"Yeah," Sanderson grunted. "Seems that way, doesn't it? But something is off with you two."

Neither of us responded. I just kept my hands upraised, a gesture of mute supplication, and, finally, he relented. Not himself, of course. That would have been too easy. But he turned to one of the other policemen. "Get these two out of here. Make sure you have their Net IDs before you cut them loose." We all stood, but he gave us one final, penetrating stare. "I don't have enough to justify arresting you. Not yet. But this matter is not closed. Don't leave town."

It was so clichéd that I had to fight back the involuntary chuckle that threatened to burst from my mouth, no doubt a panic reaction rather than one of actual humor. There was more extradition among the domes of Mars than you might find among the space-based habitats, but even here, there were no guarantees. And if we broke atmosphere, the detective's jurisdiction went out the airlock. But Chan and I dutifully nodded. Five minutes later, we were back out the front door, breathing free air.

"We need to get you to a doctor," Chan muttered. "Bit, get us a car." That she spoke the words aloud was proof enough of how distracted and worried she must have been.

"I'm okay. My nanites are taking care of it. I just need some rest. The car's a good idea, though… I really don't feel like walking all the way back to the hotel." As I was talking, I was mentally composing a text. I had Sarah encrypt it and send it over to Chan. I didn't think for a second that Sanderson had let us walk. There was no such thing as privacy, not out in the open where everything from streetlights to vending machines to the passing automobiles was equipped with cameras and microphones and other, more exotic, sensors.

I sent the message to Chan. *Not safe to talk here. I got something off Copeland. Not sure what. Did you find anything in his files?*

Her response came back almost immediately. *Nothing that jumped out on the cursory search. Bit's working his way through them, and I've got a few more advanced algorithms running. If there's something to find, we'll find it, but it will take time.*

The car that Chan had summoned pulled to the curb, and we climbed into the vehicle. It was more of a pod than a car, really, fully automated, and without anything remotely resembling a traditional steering wheel or driver's seat. The interior had a well-worn look about it and the many windows offered a panoramic view as we slipped into the upholstered chairs. A cheerful, slightly tinny voice said, "Where to?"

"The Martian Palms Hotel," I replied, and sent along the GPS coordinates for good measure.

Without further word, the vehicle pulled back into traffic. Neither of us spoke—or texted—while the car was in motion. Chan might have been busily tearing apart Copeland's files inside the privacy of her own mind, or maybe she was just tired. As for me, I was *definitely* tired, and I hurt. I relaxed into the soft comfort of the car's seats and let the buzz of the engine lull me into a state of relaxation that I hadn't felt for weeks.

15

The water streaming from the showerhead felt positively luxuriant as it bounced off my sore muscles. Like most human settlements, the Martian domes depended on ice comets for water, so the shower was a closed system, pumping and filtering the water from the drain before returning it to the showerhead. It resulted in very little waste, and had the added benefit of being more energy efficient, too. That, in turn, allowed me to stay beneath the steaming, pounding water for far longer than I probably should.

Blood mixed with that water as my nanites continued to work at the bullet wounds. It would take hours more, but each passing second pushed the slugs closer to the surface and closed off the wounds. Any major damage—to veins or nerves—would have been targeted first by swarms of the microscopic machines, taking the measures necessary to ensure preservation and viability of my coil. Now it was just a matter of enduring the pain.

I could have gone to a med center and had the bullets removed and the tissue repaired in even shorter order. But there would have been questions. And another record floating on the Net that could, maybe, be tracked back to us. Bad enough that the Pallah police force now had our Net IDs and knew where we were staying. There was no sense in spreading that information any farther than we had to—not if the cost could be measured in a few hours of discomfort.

Finally, skin sufficiently pruned by the steady flow of water, I sent a mental command to the shower, shutting off the stream. I stepped from the bay and stared for a moment at the VaccTech suit, hanging from the back of the bathroom door. It had its own nanites, and a much easier job to do than those working their magic on my wounds. The dirt and debris from the firefight was gone, scavenged and broken down to its basest components. Some of those had doubtless been used to provide the raw materials to fix the holes that had been punched into the suit. The rest would have either been stored against future need, or if the suit reserves were already full, discarded.

The fact that the suit was once more clean and whole, however, did not fill me with excitement at the thought of climbing back into it. Unfortunately, I was still without other clothing. The Palms, being an upscale establishment, had a number of services that could provide me with just about anything—from hand-tailored suits to nano-fabricated clothing in any style imaginable. But that would generate another hit against whatever identities Chan had forged to get us in here in the first place.

Shay was good enough that it probably wouldn't matter, but I just couldn't bring myself to take that risk, not with everything else that had happened. Maybe once the official heat on us had cooled down a bit. I also couldn't bring myself to pull the vacc suit on and suffer through the indignity and discomfort of the plumbing connections. So, I opted for the hotel-provided bathrobe. Opening that sealed package would generate another charge against the phony accounts, but not until we checked out. The fabric was a synthetic, but it was soft and warm and blessedly unobtrusive. I sighed as I pulled it on, cinched it tight at the waist, and stepped back into the room.

Chan had not moved from the perch she'd taken since our return to the hotel. She sat in front of the room's console, leaning slightly back in her chair, eyes unfocused and staring, seemingly, into nothing. A laser array, produced from some dark corner of her bags—which, it turned out, were stuffed full of various hardware and very little in the way of clothing—sat on the table before her. The item I'd taken from Copeland's sleeve hung suspended in the middle of the laser array, a metal cube being struck from all sides by focused light. I still didn't know exactly what it was, but it was clear to me that it was some sort of data storage device.

I didn't want to distract her, so I made my way to my bunk and slouched down into it. My Gauss pistol sat on the nightstand next to the bed, plugged into an electrical outlet to replenish the charge on its battery. I had already loaded a fresh magazine. *Sarah, remind me to get more ammunition for the Gauss pistol.* My agent issued a ping of acknowledgment.

That done, there was little left for me to do but lean my head back against the yielding softness of the pillow, close my eyes, and slip off into sleep.

*

"Motherfucker."

I wasn't sure how long I'd been asleep, but the low, staggeringly sincere curse cut through my dreams like a laser. I lurched into wakefulness, my hand darting to the nightstand and fumbling for the Gauss pistol before I realized that the voice belonged to Chan.

"Dammit, Chan," I mumbled. I did a quick check of the time. According to my implant, I'd been out for about three hours. The pain in my arm and leg had gone from a heavy burn to a dull, throbbing ache. It was a good sign, and an improvement, but somehow that dull ache almost felt worse.

"Sorry." She sounded distracted.

The room was shrouded in shadow. Full dark had fallen while I slept, and Chan hadn't bothered turning on any lights. The laser array before her still glowed, giving just enough faint red light for me to see that she still sat at the console, no longer leaning back in the chair, but hunched over the table, head bowed. "You okay?" I asked. I pinged the room's network as an afterthought, bringing up the lights to about half-power.

"No," Chan said. "I don't think any of us are going to be okay."

I wasn't sure how to respond to that. I sat on the edge of the bed, staring at Chan's back, and the silence grew like a chasm between us. I'm not sure how long it lasted, probably no more than a few seconds, but the fear in Chan's statement made it feel much, much longer.

"What is it, Shay?" I asked. I kept my voice low, calm,

sensing that whatever she had learned, Shay Chan was on the very edge of losing it.

She was quiet a long time. Her mouth opened more than once, then closed again as she struggled to find the right words. Finally, she said, "It was supposed to be a good thing, a tool to help people.

"Genetechnic... they created nanobots designed to actively seek out and remove certain memories from a person."

On the face, that *sounded* bad, sure, but people had been having selective memory editing done for the better part of a century. With lifespans theoretically as near to immortal as technology could make them, everyone had a few memories tucked away that they would rather live without. I had never had it done, but I was probably in the minority. With the outer shells being replaceable, all we really had were our memories. I didn't like the idea of some drug or medtech getting their dirty fingers in mine. It had taken me a while to actually like the person that I was, and who knew which of those memories— good or bad—made that possible? The procedure generally involved a long stay in a med center and a lot of highly sensitive hardware. If Genetechnic could do it with a nanospray, they were poised to make billions, maybe *trillions*, of credits.

Which in no way explained Chan's reaction. Some people had a certain unease with the entire thought of deleting portions of their mind, but the practice was widely accepted. "There's got to be more to it than that."

Chan swallowed. Swallowed hard enough that I actually *heard* it. "It was supposed to be proactive," she said. "They called it Bliss. The nanobots were intended to stay and replicate for a year, and in that year, they would proactively seek out and eliminate any negative memories. Anything bad you experienced one day would be wiped from your mind the next. After the year was up, you'd have to go get another dose."

"Oh-kay," I drawled the word out. "That's a little creepy. I mean, what would trigger the 'bad' part of a bad memory? How bad did it have to be?" The thought of having tiny machines living in my brain deciding for me which memories I got to keep and which were swept away like so much dust and cobwebs was not a pleasant one. It sounded more like a drug—a promise of a constant high. The entire notion was enough to make my skin crawl, but it still didn't sound like the end of the world. Just another way for the immortal rich to live on a perpetual high.

She just shrugged. "I don't know. The data that Copeland smuggled out of Genetechnic didn't have all the details on Bliss. But it doesn't matter, because Bliss as a memory adjuster was abandoned when they stumbled onto two unintended side effects."

She paused for a moment, drawing a deep, steadying breath. "From the data you found, it looks like the first one was an accident. With some people, the Bliss nanobots went too far, eliminating not just bad memories, but all memories, and then the majority of cognitive processes. They left behind a blank coil. The person, the mind, the soul that had been there was gone, as surely as our branches were destroyed somewhere near Sol."

"That's impossible," I said by reflex. Sure, you could play around with memories, but there was no way to erase a core.

The technology was beyond me, but it was more than just a hard drive shoved into the human brain. You couldn't just go in and delete everything that was there.

"It shouldn't be possible," Chan agreed. "The safeguards built in to cores..." She trailed off, head shaking. "This goes against everything I know about how cores work, Carter. Think of it like... like... Argh! This would be so much easier if you had a grounding in computer science." I opened my mouth, but she just waved a hand. "No, sorry. Look, think of it like using the Net. There are some places where you can upload and store data or delete data that you've uploaded. And other places that you can't access, right?"

She was looking at me now, eyes intent and waiting for a response. As far as her analogy went, so far I was with her. I nodded.

"Good. Okay... at its most simplistic, you can think of a backup as two separate—but at the same time inseparable—programs. One is kind of like an operating system for... well, for you. It's the 'hows' of you. How you think. How you feel. How you react to certain stimuli. It's effectively your personality. The digitized representation of all the little things that make you who you are. The other program is... let's call it the database of you." She shook her head. "This is a really bad analogy, Carter," she admitted.

"I'm with you so far," I encouraged. "Keep going."

"All right. So, the database side is your memory bank. It's more than that, of course, but it's the... the abstraction... of the chemical process that creates and stores our experiences. But, and here's the rub Carter, these two programs... your operating system and your database? They don't talk to each other."

My head was starting to hurt. There was a reason I worked things like salvage and repo and not software, but it seemed to me that who you were and the memories of your experiences were irrevocably linked. "I... how's that possible?"

"We don't know. Not really."

I stared at Chan, and my confusion—and the flash of anger underneath it—must have shown on my face. "I'm serious, Carter. We're dealing with quantum entanglement and mechanics. We've gotten far enough to be able to *use* quantum computing, but we don't truly understand the *hows* and the *whys* of it. The two programs—and remember, this is a really simplistic way of looking at this because they aren't just simple programs, okay?—don't have any direct interface between them. Instead, they operate on quantum entanglement, and changes to one quantum bundle affect the others in ways that we simply cannot reliably predict." I was almost entirely lost now. "It gets worse," she warned.

I remained silent, figuring that that was the best way to stop myself from looking like a complete idiot. "That's the software side," Chan said. "The cores themselves are techno-organic—they're essentially computers that are grown along with the coil rather than 'built' in the traditional sense. They use several inorganic components, but those components are part of whatever primordial soup is used in the process, introduced when the body is grown. But, because the software operates on entanglement, the partition that houses the operating system is write-only. You can add to it, but you can never take anything away. Which means that everyone knew—right up until the point that I deciphered what we found on Copeland—that while you could muck around with peoples' memories—with the database side of things—you absolutely could *not* delete their personality—the operating system. But it looks like somehow, something went very wrong—or maybe very right—with Genetechnic. They either figured out how to manipulate the quantum entanglement structure to effectively use the accessible portion of the core to overwrite the inaccessible… or somehow something went horribly wrong in just the right way."

It took a long moment for all of that to sink in. "Shit," I muttered at last. Despite all the advances technology had given us, coils—bodies—were incredibly difficult and time-consuming to produce. Add to the fact that only a single entity held the monopoly on the creation of coils—as a measure to ensure the best quality possible—and bodies were always in short supply. The very wealthy could guarantee quick and ready access to a coil custom-made to their specifications in the event of death—the wealthiest and most powerful could be re-coiled within *hours* of any unfortunate accident. But for the rest of us, the process took quite a bit longer, and, like Chan being stuffed into a bio-male body, it was often a jarring and less than optimal solution. It beat the alternative, of course, but carried with it a lot of psychological baggage.

In theory, new coils were a human right. You paid your insurance premiums, and you were guaranteed re-coiling within a "reasonable" time frame. Even if you couldn't pay the premiums, as long as you had a viable backup, you would, eventually, return to flesh and bone. Without the most basic of insurance, it would be years before you ever felt the sun, and you would be stuffed into what amounted to a "factory defect" of a coil, but you *would* reemerge from the purgatory of the archives, pick up your life where you left off, and likely have a much deeper respect for the idea of paying your premiums on time. Even with the slower birthrates among human society, this meant an ever-expanding demand, coupled with a supply that was still bounded by the limits of the growth time for coils. The manufacturer was prohibited by a mountain of laws from selling directly to anyone and was forced to work with the select few megacorps that backed the insurance policies.

Boundless demand, tight supply, and endless government regulation did what it had done among humanity for eons: it created a thriving black market where coils could be bought and sold for exorbitant fees. But even that market was squeezed so tight it squealed. Coils could be "lost" and rerouted. They could "fall off of trucks" and find their way to destinations for which they had never been intended. They could be stolen, hijacked, diverted, or anything else imaginable, right up until the point that a person was stuffed back into them. The core of every coil wasn't simply inserted when the vessel reached maturity—as Chan had just pointed out, the core was grown with the coil, making it an inseparable part of the body. There was no way to extract a core without terminating the biological functions of the coil to which it belonged. Which meant that once you were re-coiled, nothing and no one could take that body from you. No matter how it came to you, it was yours until accident or age or some other form of untimely death took it from you and put you back in the queue. But when that happened, the coil itself was done. Useless. Spent.

Unless Chan had the right of it.

"If they can do that, then…" I trailed off.

"Then we're no longer safe in our own bodies. If they can—or already have—isolated that effect, then Genetechnic or whoever else gets their hands on it can start taking people from the street, resetting them, and selling their coils off to the highest bidder." Chan had lifted her head and swung around in her chair. Her eyes—those disconcerting blue eyes that didn't belong to the Shay Chan of my memory—bored into me. "That's not the worst part, Carter."

Christ. I could barely wrap my head around the idea that Genetechnic might have developed the technology to do a factory reset on a coil, effectively deleting the rightful owner, and that wasn't the worst part?

A few months ago, I lived in a world where life sprung eternal, death was a transient condition, and, while my mortal coil could be killed, short of that, nothing could take it from me. Now, apparently, the world had progressed to a point where backups were no longer safe, opening up the possibility of permanent death for the first time in centuries, and any lunatic with a sprayer and access to the right nanobots could open a cottage industry in body snatching. And, according to Chan, that wasn't the worst part?

"Okay, Chan. Hit me. What's the *worst* part?"

"I said there were two unintended discoveries. Blanking the coils was just one of them. But once the coils were blanked, Genetechnic started experimenting. Stuffing a new person inside was old tech—valuable, but it looks like they thought they had an opportunity to see what else they could do with a coil."

That made a sick sort of sense. Because fully grown bodies were in such short supply, the only corporations that had access to them were either those that grew them, or those responsible for the re-coiling process. Anybody else was out of luck. Companies like Genetechnic had to make do with tissue samples, animal testing, and whatever volunteers were desperate enough to stumble through their doors.

I thought back to the video of the apparent corpse aboard the shuttle. "So, they had an opportunity to turn loose their best and brightest on freshly murdered volunteers, and they what? Invented zombies?" I couldn't keep the incredulity out of my voice as I said it.

"Yes," Chan replied. "That's exactly what they did."

16

Her frank assessment hit me with an almost physical force. I dropped back onto the bed, grunting at the little flash of pain sent through my arm and leg. "Why, for the love of all that's holy, would Genetechnic want to create zombies?"

"I don't know," Chan admitted. "Maybe they didn't. Maybe it was another accident. And they aren't really zombies, not in the horror sim sense." That was hardly comforting, given what my branch had seen, but I didn't get a chance to say so. "They're more... biological robots, I guess. Artificial intelligences stuffed into a bio-mechanical shell."

I let that sink in. AIs could be programmed for... well, for anything. They weren't truly cognitive—they possessed only rudimentary self-identity and their responses were the end product of complicated heuristic algorithms. They learned and grew, but only after a fashion, and only to the limits of their original programming. They were pervasive, inhabiting everything from space ships to the implants that every coil walking and breathing had stuffed into their heads.

Despite that, androids and gynoids, while still produced in small numbers, had never really caught on. On the practical front, it was far easier and cheaper to purpose-build a machine for a specific task than to try and tackle the vast complexities of mimicking the human form with synthetic materials. And those who wanted human-esque robots for other, darker, purposes, were put off by the fact that the uncanny valley, no matter how far technology had progressed, remained an unbridgeable gap. Regardless of how hard a legion of scientists and engineers had tried, robots remained unmistakably robotic, and those who produced them catered to a very small, though lucrative, section of the population.

"Okay," I drawled. "I get that there could be money to be made there. I mean, sure, if you could kidnap anybody off the street, wipe their mind, and replace it with an AI programmed to heed your every wish…" I shuddered at the multitude of abuses and indignities that could stem from such a situation. "But that seems a little… out there… even for a megacorp. And I assume you're talking *live* coils here. That thing that attacked my branch was definitely not a living, breathing coil. It had been sitting in vacuum for God alone knows how long."

"There was nothing on the… reanimation," Chan admitted with a small, distinctly female shudder. It looked so strange on the bio-male coil that it made me blink a few times in momentary confusion. "Or any information on what might have inured the body to the effects of vacuum and the near-zero temperatures of the shuttle. Maybe it was a mutation, or a glitch, or yet another side effect. Some unexpected reaction between the Bliss nanites and the nanites all coils have in their systems. Or maybe it was another unintended side effect of Bliss itself. A self-preservation instinct that allowed the nanites to mitigate the effects, at least to some degree. Genetechnic is so far out on the bleeding edge with this stuff, there's no predicting what might happen."

Her face twisted into a look like she was going to be physically ill. "The data was ambiguous. As if Genetechnic didn't want a record, even on their protected servers. My best guess is that the shuttle… it was the… rejects, I suppose. Coils that had unexpected reactions to the nanites, or maybe ones that just didn't accept the AI programming. For whatever reason…" She paused. "I'm not sure if the word should be 'died' or 'ceased to function' or maybe even just 'shut down.' I can't really figure out if something happened to those coils or something was done to them. But whatever the reason, Genetechnic decided to send them on a one-way ticket to Sol."

"Then why leave their coils in place? And what was Copeland doing on that shuttle?"

"As to the first," Chan said, "Genetechnic was worried about allowing any potential infection vectors. From what I can tell, they didn't know what would happen if they started cutting into the coils. The nanites have to be introduced to the system, but they are part of an intelligence, Carter. Bliss may well be able to climb right out of one person and infect another. They thought it better to load their failures into a shuttle and launch it into the sun with minimal human interaction." She paused and scrubbed at her face for a moment, trying to physically remove the strain of the work she'd been doing.

"As for Copeland, he was gathering evidence. There are

some notes on the Genetechnic security in here. There's no way he would have been able to get any real proof out of the corporate offices. Data like this," she waved a hand at the cube reader, "can be fabricated. Without physical evidence, who would take him seriously? I guess he thought he'd be able to get something more from the shuttle, tissue samples or maybe even some of the nanites. Maybe the cores. But something went wrong."

I thought of the decompressed corpse locked in the airlock. *Wrong* was a bit of an understatement. "And he woke up here, re-coiled and... and what? Ready to try again? If he had all this information on him, he must have either backed up shortly beforehand or... I don't know. Maybe left himself a message like my branch did for me."

Chan was nodding. "He must have hidden what he was doing from Genetechnic. At least for a time."

"And then we started moving around, running searches, trying to track him down," I added.

"Genetechnic got wind of it. Realized he was a loose end. Which is why they came to kill him. To put him in the archives for a bit, until they had everything all nice and covered up and didn't have us poking around, looking for answers."

"It also explains why they want us dead. They've gone to a lot of work to hide what they've discovered here." I sighed. "I don't suppose the message from my branch is any more likely to be taken seriously by any authorities than the data on that cube?" Chan shook her head in mute negation. "No, I didn't think so."

We stared at each other for a long moment, each of us looking into eyes that had grown familiar, and yet, still seemed wrong. Chan broke that moment first, dropping her gaze, her eyes full of a sadness that twisted a knife somewhere deep inside me. "I don't suppose we could just tell Genetechnic we'll drop the whole thing?" she asked. Her voice was light, mocking, but I could sense the true hope behind the words. Just let it all go. Drop it and walk away, with some assurances that we could live our lives in peace so long as we never mentioned Genetechnic again.

It was tempting. No, it was more than tempting—it was… *seductive*. Megacorps like Genetechnic had armies of lawyers, the kind of men and women who had long experience in drawing up non-disclosure agreements and contracts of the kind that would not only make us liable in civil courts were we to break them, but likely pin criminal culpability on us as well. Words like conspiracy and cover-up and payoff all sprang to mind. Yes, if we could survive long enough to get ahold of some exec in the know, we could almost certainly make this whole thing go away.

And all we'd have to do was forget about Zomas Harper, who was still in the wind, somewhere, probably running for their life from the same people who were trying to kill us. All we had to do was forget about Arnold Miller, who had not only lost a branch along with the rest of us aboard the *Persephone*, but who had been *erased*. Killed for all time and never coming back. All we had to do was forget about the pained look in Shay Chan's eyes every time she looked down at her own body.

"No," I said at last. "No, I don't suppose we can."

*

Shay had gone back to work, trying to glean the last vestiges of information from the recesses of the data cube. I had stretched back out on the bed, waiting for the bullet holes in me to close and deeply aware of the growing hunger gnawing at my stomach that reminded me, no matter how easy it was to manufacture worldly goods, and no matter how much mastery humanity had achieved over death itself, everything still came at a price. The price for the nanites furiously working to repair my damaged tissue was a pervasive hunger, one that would be insatiable for days to come as the microscopic bots burned whatever calories they could to go about their tasks.

When next I woke, it was to the smell of hot, fresh food. A gurgle rumbled from my stomach, betraying my wakefulness even before I'd had a chance to open my eyes. "I take it that means you're awake," Chan said with a chuckle.

I sat up, rubbing at my bleary, sleep-sealed eyes. Light seeped around the edges of the tightly drawn blinds, casting the room in the faintly red-tinged glow of dawn. Chan had found the time to shower, her now-blonde hair slicked flat against her head. She wore a fluffy bathrobe, stitched with the palm tree at the breast, but it fell not quite to mid-thigh. The cut and style were intended for a woman—no doubt Chan had chosen it without really thinking.

She stood before the room's only table, atop which sat a silver-colored platter heaped with steaming food. *Real* food. Food that had never been reconstituted or dehydrated or otherwise processed and packaged to survive for eons away from sun or surf or power. I smelled meat—lab grown or off the hoof, I didn't care—and saw the fluffy yellow of eggs. A bowl of fresh fruit glistened wetly, standing next to a plate of biscuits and a pot of honey. The bounty went on and on, and it took an actual physical effort to tear my eyes away from it to look at Chan.

She smiled. "I was in an accident a while back, in my original coil. I remember how hungry the nanites make you when they're hard at work." She filled a small plate, mostly with fruits and a single strip of bacon, and waved me at the rest.

I didn't so much eat, as I *inhaled*, scarcely taking the time to chew. The food was good—delicious probably—but I barely tasted it. The insistent rumble in my stomach had no patience for taste; it demanded fuel. By the time it had finally quieted—not silenced, but at least muted for the moment—nothing remained on the table but a few crumbs and apple cores.

I resisted the urge to unleash a wall-shaking belch. Whatever body she wore, Shay Chan would always be petite, alluring, and distinctly feminine in my mind's eye. My social upbringing forced the belch into a half-strangled cough followed by unnecessary throat-clearing. I caught the gleam of a twinkle in her now-blue eyes, and knew she understood exactly what I was doing... and was pleased with my effort.

The next throat-clearing was a little more necessary, not to clear any stuck food or bodily functions, but to ease the sudden surge of emotion that hit me. I had been attracted to Shay—physically attracted before, but, despite working together, had never really gotten to know her. She had been a private person, trying to hold on to that privacy in the close confines of a ship. I could respect that... it was a code that all of us aboard lived by. Besides, I knew that personal relationships within small crews always ended badly. So, I had admired her from afar, but never tried to take anything further.

Now, here we were. The stigma around sexuality had long since faded—it hadn't made much sense to begin with, but when the ability to be re-coiled into another body came along, it died a quick and unlamented death. Even the most fundamentalist of people couldn't very well attach the essence of a person to their physical shell when they would wear many physical shells, some of them of a different biological sex, over the course of centuries. But that didn't change the fact that most people still tended to be wired to be attracted to a definable subset of the gender spectrum. I belonged firmly in the "liked bio-females" camp—I had no sense of physical attraction to the coil that Shay now wore, handsome and well put together though it was. But...

But. But I couldn't stop the burgeoning feelings that I felt for the *person* trapped in that coil. For the brave, determined, skilled professional that hadn't been bowed or broken by the chaos that had torn away our old world and dropped us into one that was far more dangerous and violent than previously believed. And that confused the hell out of me. I wasn't sure that now, when not just our branches, but our lives, were hanging in the balance was the proper time to delve too deeply into it. So, I cleared my throat again, for a third, unnecessary time, and turned the conversation back to the most important matter at hand.

"What do we do now?"

Chan shrugged. "I couldn't find anything else on the data cube. I've got Bit working on some Net searches, listening for

Harper or Copeland, and for both of us as well. As much to make sure that we don't all suddenly disappear as anything."

I winced at that, remembering my awakening and the attempted hack on my backup. The successful hack on Miller. "Any luck on finding Harper?" I asked.

"No. But Bit has just gotten started, and Mars is a big place. And it's Genetechnic's headquarters. If Harper found anything that pointed to… well, *anything* about all this, they'll end up here. There's still proof of their existence, anyway, so I don't think they've been… erased." Her voice dropped to a whisper for the last word.

"We need to make some decisions, Shay," I said. "The police here have our information… if these Genetechnic hackers are as good as you seem to think…"

"Good enough to have hacked into the backup servers," she interjected. "That's as good as anyone ever needs to be." She lifted her shoulders in a sort of half-shrug. "I'm not sure I could do it. I'd say it was impossible, but we've all *known* that it's impossible for so long that people sort of stopped trying. But if they got in, they're definitely good."

I nodded. "Well, if that's the case, then it won't be long before someone gets the information out of the police network. That assassin, at least, knows we're here." I flexed my left arm and pressed against the floor with my left leg. Both ached savagely and sent little trills of pain coursing up and down them with the pressure, but it was much better than yesterday, and the actual projectiles had been expelled while I slept. "We needed to recover yesterday, but we can't stay here."

She gave me a grin that, on her old coil, would have reminded me of a slightly naughty schoolgirl. On her surfer-dude face, hovering as it was above a too-short robe, it looked almost lascivious. "I've already got a pair of backup identities in the works. We should be ready to move in an hour or so. Or, we could go now, and just… wander… until that time was up. Once we have the clean idents, we can hit another hotel."

I shook my head in mute wonder. "Why did you ever work salvage?" The question slipped out, but damned if I didn't want to know the answer… the real answer. With her skills she could easily have gone to work for any of the megacorps, or the government, or maybe just set up as a criminal mastermind. Why bother with the crap pay, cramped living, and danger of deep-space salvage?

She sighed. "I've told you. There's been more than once in my life when someone was looking for me, Carter. My hide on Daedalus was pretty good." She waved one hand, as if in dismissal. "But nothing beats a ship in deep space if you don't want to be found." She arched an eyebrow in my direction. "Besides, I'm not the one taking out assassins left and right. Not to mention treating a few gunshot wounds as a minor inconvenience. One could wonder what *you* did before getting into the salvage game."

The question made me shrug uncomfortably. The lives I'd taken since the *Persephone* weren't the first, but that didn't mean I liked it. "It doesn't matter," I hedged. "What matters is that we have to get out of here. I'm not sure walking the streets is a better idea, though, not unless you can somehow keep us off the grid while we do it."

She shook her head. "We know they have pics of our new

coils. They've got to be scanning the Net for our images. Too many cameras out there. Too many eyes. I'm good, but I can't hack them all."

"Then we wait here until the false IDs are in place. We give Genetechnic—or whoever is looking for us—the least amount of time possible to find us."

"So, we end up at a new hotel that they—whoever they might be—may or may not know about. And then we... what?" There was the slightest edge of panic to Chan's words. I felt the same thing, as if a fist were slowly closing around my lungs, making every breath a struggle. We could run. We could hide. But no one beat the megacorps. Not for long.

"I don't know, Shay," I admitted. "But at least now we have a general idea of what's going on. Whatever they're planning on doing with these nanites, Genetechnic wants to keep a tight lid on their existence."

"And they're willing to kill, and worse than kill, anyone that gets in their way," Chan said with flat finality.

There was no answer to that, so I only nodded, and began gathering my meager possessions.

17

" **W**e need proof," Chan said.

We had switched hotels, giving up the luxury of the Martian Palms for a cheap, no-frills motel that offered cramped rooms and a view of an industrial complex that, as far as I could tell, produced nothing but ashy black smoke that drifted through a series of pipes before being vented into the Martian atmosphere outside the dome. At least the motel was clean; the various automated systems ensured that bugs—which had taken to the stars along with mankind and settled in just as many places as we had—and the pervasive red dust were kept to a minimum. We'd both kept the hoods of our vacc suits up and our heads down as we made the transfer. It earned us another measure of strange looks, but whatever crawlers were out sniffing for us wouldn't be searching the minds of the people on the streets. Even the best facial recognition software couldn't latch on to someone without a discernible face.

"Agreed," I said. "But how?" It was the paradox of the

modern panopticon—nearly every action humanity took was recorded and registered on some sort of electronic device, and, yet, the technology had come so far that one could create wholesale forgeries of almost any interaction or data set conceivable, which rendered electronic data from unverified sources as suspect, at best. Such information rarely passed the rigorous tests necessary to be entered as evidence in a court of law. The only time it seemed to matter was if the information came from an "unhackable" source, like the backup repositories, that was independently verifiable by a government, or if there were so many different sources that the sheer omnipresence of it could not be ignored. At the moment, we had none of that.

Shay dropped her head into her hands, blonde hair spilling over her interlocking fingers. "I don't know, Carter. It's not like we can go directly to the source and break into Genetechnic."

The thought had crossed my mind. I drew a slow breath and let it out in a long, low sigh. "We could," I admitted. "And with your Net skills, we might even be able to make it out again."

Shay just looked at me, the incredulity in her expression almost comical. I raised my hands, to forestall any questions. "Look, I'm not saying we should. Hell, it's unlikely we'd be able to find anything, anyway. I'll guarantee you, this Bliss project and all its various offshoots are locked away in the most holy of holies in that lab. I'm good enough to get us into the building, and maybe out again. We could root around any unsecured areas. If we got lucky, we could probably get into the lower-security stuff without triggering any alarms. But there's no way we're getting into whatever vault they'd be using to store the Bliss data."

"What the hell, Carter," Shay growled. "I thought *I* was the criminal here."

"I told you I worked repo before salvage. There's a pretty thin line between repo and outright theft, particularly if the person you're doing the repossession on skews toward the dangerous side. You learn a lot about getting around security systems, getting in and out of places without getting seen." A slight grin stretched my lips. "And a fair amount about how to defend yourself, too, at least if you stay in it long enough. Look, it was… lifetimes ago, but I still remember how."

"You are a man of many layers, Carter Langston."

There was something about the way she said it that made me glance over at her. She gazed at me with an expression that was pure, inscrutable Shay Chan. That look had a weighing quality about it, like I was being evaluated, or, perhaps, *re-evaluated* would be the more accurate term, that somehow made me nervous. But I just gave her my best grin and said, "I'm a mystery. Wrapped in an enigma." I plucked at the front of the VaccTech suit. "Wrapped in plastic. For freshness."

A wry smile twisted her lips and she gave her head a little shake but said nothing. "So," I continued, "we can't get into Genetechnic, at least not and get anything that would be useful to us. And I assume that you're not confident in your ability to hack them?"

She shrugged. "Ordinarily, I'd say it wouldn't even be a challenge. But we may be talking about the people who hacked their way into the backup servers. You don't try something like that without being really, really certain of your own defenses. And the big corps don't rely on passive programs; they'll have security people actively monitoring things." She sighed. "It's risky."

"Right," I said. "But that doesn't mean we can't get more answers from someone at Genetechnic."

Shay's look went from assessing to skeptical. "I'm not sure that walking into their headquarters and demanding answers about their top-secret project—the one they're willing to delete people over—is the best solution."

"Who said anything about walking into Genetechnic? We're not on a station or hab, Shay. It's not like the Genetechnic staff lives at the office. They have to go home sometime, and I guarantee you that the lead scientist or CEO or whoever, is going to have a lot less security than the lab itself."

But Shay was shaking her head. "It's the same problem, Carter. We could snatch the President of Genetechnic off the street, kidnap him, whatever. But no court—not on Earth, not on Mars, not even on Daedalus—would accept it as proof of anything. Information obtained under duress isn't admissible. And if we tried to go to any authorities with it, we're the ones who'd get arrested."

"Damn it," I growled. Shay was right. Of course she was. But I was past the point of caring. "Then we get them to tell us where proof—physical proof, not just data that Genetechnic will claim is a fabrication—*can* be found. And we go there and get it."

"And if they don't want to talk?"

I thought of the rest of the crew of the *Persephone*. Harper, missing. Miller, dead and never to be re-coiled. Chan, stuffed into a coil that seemed so ill-suited to her when she had suffered so much and tried so hard to prevent that very thing from happening. I couldn't keep the anger from my voice as I said, "Then we make them talk. However we have to." The grim finality in my voice startled me, but Shay was nodding. "Assuming you're willing."

"Do you know how long I waited to get my previous coil, Carter? Years. Four years, to be precise. Four years in a Class Four bio-female body, just so I could get the exact coil of my choice. One that closely resembled that to which I was born. Petite. Flexible yet strong." She looked down at the table, eyes not meeting mine. "I know you see how uncomfortable I am in this cumbersome body. It's not just the… the *maleness* of it, though I hate that." She raised her eyes, offered a hint of a smile. "No offense. It's just not who I feel I am deep down." Her gaze dropped again before she could see my nod of understanding, but she was still talking. "There's more to it. I have enough funds to pay for gender reassignment surgery, but even then I still won't be *me*, Carter. I would never give up the gift of near immortality, but the farther I get from the coil that I was born in, the strong self-image that it imprinted on me, the more uncomfortable I get. I can't explain it. Not well. But it's like being in an ill-fitting vacc suit. Everything feels too tight and intrusive and just plain wrong." I could hear the tears in her voice, though I couldn't see them on her still-lowered face. I reached out a hand and placed it lightly on her shoulder. She didn't move away. "It feels wrong, Carter. Wrong enough that I go to great lengths to not feel this way. Wrong enough that I spent years in a veritable prison to get back to something that more closely fits my image of myself. And these people took that from me."

Her trembling shoulder stilled beneath my touch. She lifted her eyes to mine and a shadow flashed across them. "Yes, Carter, I'm willing to do whatever we must."

I tried to hide my wince at the thought—not of making someone talk, since at this point, I felt like the judicious application of pain was more than deserved, but of spending years locked into a Class Four coil. Class Ones were top of the line—what Chan and I wore now, despite not being exactly what we would have chosen, were still Class One. No medical issues, full nanobot support packages, top-of-the-line agents, everything you could ask for to assume your rightful place in society. Class Twos were... factory seconds. Small problems, nothing that would impede living, but enough that everyone *knew* you were in a castoff and you had to deal with... well, glitches for lack of a better word. Class Threes had problems— real problems. Anatomical abnormalities or neurological incompatibilities with modern hardware. The kinds of things that made living a real pain in the ass. If you got re-coiled into a Class Three, you were immediately on the list for the first available Class Two or higher in your area. Class Fours, though... Class Fours were the coils that murderers and rapists got shoved back into if they were foolish enough to lose their own coil before their sentence was up. They weren't factory seconds, so much as... manufacturing mistakes. Full-on errors that, if the coil crunch wasn't so dire, would be recycled into biological goo and fed back into whatever arcane machines spat out the Class Ones. They were bad enough that even their use to re-coil criminals was hotly debated, whether it was more cruel to leave prisoners archived, with no coil at all—and with no elapsed time on any sentencing they may have received, since punitive sentences had to be *lived*—or to shove them into a Class Four.

Of course, you could sign a waiver, and volunteer to be put into that hell. And doing so gave you a privilege normally reserved for the very wealthy—access to a coil of preference, provided you were willing to wait for it and not suicide somewhere along the line to get out of the Class Four. It also ensured that whatever career you pursued almost had to be relegated to what could be done in virtual reality. That part, at least, probably hadn't been a problem for Chan, but the rest of the problems made it a practice that was almost never pursued. The only people who did it were those with a rare type of dysmorphic disorder that made them feel a constant sense of mental, sometimes even physical, distress the farther they got from their original coils. I understood then that, for Chan, there wasn't much difference between being in her current coil and being back in one of those Class Fours. The fact that she was holding up as well as she was, was nothing short of incredible.

"Damn, Shay, I had no idea. I know getting bio-sex-crossed on re-coil can be an adjustment, but I didn't realize how much you'd lost when the *Persephone* went down. I'm sorry."

She shrugged and turned her head slightly away. In her previous form, it would have made her long black locks fall across her face and obscure it from my view. Not so, now, and I could see the pain writ large there. "I feel best when I'm in a coil that most closely resembles my birth body," she said by way of explanation. "It was worth it, enduring the Class Four, to get back to something closer to the true me."

I wondered why she hadn't resubmitted her name to the Class Four list. I was glad she hadn't—if Shay Chan were currently in a Class Four, there's no way she could have been helping me, and I'd almost certainly be dead by now. I wanted to ask... but some decisions were so personal, you just didn't dig into them. Not if you had any hint of social grace, anyway.

"So, Carter, I'm quite willing to do whatever we must to get answers." Her voice was cold, almost grim.

"Then let's get to work."

18

Tracking down the right target was simple. Chan dug into the public accounts of Genetechnic, and within a few minutes had the names of the chief executive officer, chief financial officer, chief operations officer, and a whole slew of other corporate honchos. The addresses took longer, which was unsurprising. Privacy was a concept that had been on the decline ever since the first vestiges of the proto-Net took shape in the late twentieth century, but the wealthy and powerful still took steps to make it more difficult for the average person to gain access to them.

Difficult did not equal impossible. There were too many records, too many traces, too many details floating about cyberspace. Within an hour, Chan had addresses—physical and Net—and a dozen other details to go with the list of names and offices. "So," I said, scanning the list projected into my field of vision, "who do we target? CEO? CFO? Head of Security?"

"We need to rank by two factors," Chan replied. "First, of those names we have, who is most likely to be in the know.

Second, who can we grab with the lowest risk."

We went back and forth for a while. The Head of Security would almost certainly be the lowest paid, which meant she might have the fewest security measures in place. On the other hand, you didn't get to be head of security at a large corporation without some level of military or police training, so she'd likely be a skilled combatant in her own right. And maybe the bad—for us, anyway—kind of paranoid to boot. She might or might not know anything. The CEO… well, he was probably in the know, but corporate CEOs tended to have the same kind of personal protections in place as heads of state. Trying to snatch the CEO was a lot more likely to get us sent back into the re-coiling queue than it was to get us any information. In the end, we settled on a man named Fredrick Ingles, with the dubious title of Director of Innovations. Neither Chan nor I had done a lot of time in the megacorps and none of it recently, so our corp-speak was a little on the weak side, but the Director of Innovations sounded like someone who would have to know what was going on in the research and development area, but not so high up to have the words "chief" or "officer" in their title. The Ingles address, cross-referenced against real-estate records, was solid upper-middle-class, which meant electronic, but almost certainly no human, security measures. And, best of all, tax records (I didn't ask how Chan got her hands on those—they were supposed to be privileged) showed that Ingles had no current marriage contract, and no claimed dependents, which meant no collateral damage. He was the perfect target.

"Are we sure about this?" I asked Chan as we started gearing up for the night ahead. "So far, everything we've done is either a good case for self-defense, or small-time crime. But we're about to break into a person's house who may be entirely innocent in all this and do our level best to wring answers out of him. If things go bad, we could be spending the next several lifetimes on asteroid mining penal colonies."

Chan didn't even hesitate. "I'm sure. Someone needs to shine a light on whatever's going on here. I seriously doubt we're the first people Genetechnic has killed, and who knows how many they've… erased." A small shudder coursed through her. "Killing is one thing. Snatching coils and blanking them for resale is worse. But Miller shows that they are willing to do the unthinkable. We can't stop them through legal channels. So, we do what we have to. I'll bet the possibility of doing time against the certainty that they'll eventually find us and… delete… us if we do nothing."

I nodded my agreement. "We do what we have to."

Ingles' house—and it was an actual, freestanding house, an unheard-of luxury to hab dwellers—was located in a section of Pallah that, in another place and time, might have been called a suburb. The entirety of the Pallah dome was small enough by Earth standards that the neighborhood would likely be considered "urban core" Earth-side, but it had that air that suburbs sometimes do: a sense of peace combined with an undercurrent of desperation. There weren't children playing in the streets. Most habs, and domes, too, I supposed, had strict regulations around procreation. Every person added to the environment increased the strain on the life-support systems, not to mention the eventual impact on the already over-stressed re-coiling queues. No one had—to my knowledge—tried to outlaw procreation, but it wasn't unusual for some habs to require proper licensing. Earthers were different of course and I'd heard Luna was as well, despite their reliance on domes.

Ingles' place stood among a neat row of nearly identical houses. The heart was standard prefab, and the dull gray composite was still visible here and there. But an effort had been made to mask the blandness with what looked like actual aluminum siding. It was ironic that, in an effort to make the dull gray boxes of colonist life look more appealing, the neighborhood had succeeded in taking a bunch of houses that looked exactly the same and made them more aesthetically pleasing… while at the same time, ensuring that they all continued to look exactly the same. To me it seemed like a terrible waste of resources, and there were few things the spacer in me hated more than waste: every square centimeter of space aboard a ship served a purpose, and the largest berth I'd ever seen would have fit in a tiny fraction of the space that a single one of these dwellings took up. Even on a hab, you could fit multiple families within the cubage of even the smallest of the houses. The sheer scale of these freestanding, individual dwellings affronted me on an almost personal level.

I shook those thoughts from my head as the car rolled to a stop a few houses down from the Ingles' residence. Chan wasn't with me—at least not in the meat. She was nearby, and our agents had linked, so we had direct access. We had both agreed that she would be more useful handling the electronic warfare side of things rather than kicking in doors and, if things went bad, dropping bodies. "I'm here," I Net-linked to her.

"I've got you," Chan replied, and I started at the words. Not at the words, but at the voice. Somewhere along the line, she'd taken the time to program some kind of voice masking software. The "I've got you," wasn't in the smooth tenor of the male coil she wore, but back in what I thought of as *her* voice, a low contralto. She wasn't giving me any time to get over my shock, though. "Ingles definitely has some kind of electronic security system up and running."

"Can you shut it down?"

I couldn't *see* the long level look of near-disdain, but somehow, in the silence that followed, I *knew* it was there. "Of course I can shut it down, Carter. But that's amateur hour. Net providers monitor activity and up/down status. If I were to pull Ingles' house off the grid, we might as well call HabSec ourselves and ask them to meet you there." She paused, but I said nothing, refusing to ask the question: then what the hell is it we *are* going to do?

"Now," she continued, "I *could* take down the whole sector, disrupt any kind of signal access for a few blocks. That would bring the authorities, but we'd have some time. They wouldn't know where to look." Something about the way she said it told me that wasn't the answer either. "But who knows how much time you're going to need in there? Can't have a bunch of nosy Net-techs wandering the neighborhood, looking for the source of the trouble." Another pause.

"Shay," I said, glancing around the street, "I'm kind of standing out in the open here. All it takes is one bored Martian looking out the screen and wondering what a stranger is doing standing around in the street. Can we maybe move it along?"

"Oh, ye of little faith," she muttered. "I *am* moving it along, Carter. I can talk and work, you know. And sometimes it helps to talk through the problem. In this case, the answer to the problem is a bubble."

"A what, now?"

"A bubble. We take the Ingles house offline, but we spoof every single connection point, hardwired or wireless, to think that it's still there."

The magnitude of *that* notion stunned me. "There's got to be a hundred different signals going into or out of that house, Shay. Is that even possible?"

"Two hundred and forty-seven, to be exact," Chan replied. "Not counting Ingles' personal agent, but we don't have to spoof that one—just keep it from carrying on any of the other signals. Native range is too short without some sort of booster. And it's not just possible, Carter. It's done." There was a grim satisfaction in her voice as she said, "Now go get us some answers."

"Yes, ma'am," I replied.

There are three main ways to break into a place: deception, stealth, and brute force. Deception was the conman's game, convincing the mark to let you walk through the door. I'd had to do a lot of that back in my repo days, but I'd never been very good at it. Stealth... well, it had its merits. But it was hard to pull off in the middle of the Martian day. So, I opted for quick, brutal, and messy. It was more fun that way, anyway.

The door to the Ingles house was standard composite pre-fab, just like the rest of the house. Built to go up quick and last, but not exactly designed with high security in mind. I barely slowed as I walked up the three stairs to the porch, raised my leg, and kicked out with all of the strength my new, much more heavily muscled coil had to offer. The boot of the VaccTech suit landed just beside the knob, and the door exploded inward. I was inside, with my Gauss pistol in hand before the door had time to hit the wall and rebound.

I swept the pistol around the room, every sense alert, expecting to see a surprised and alarmed Fredrick Ingles. What I didn't expect was to see a man, his back turned toward me, calmly preparing a drink from a wet bar at the far side of the living room in which I was now standing. "Let me see your hands!" I barked, keeping the weapon trained squarely on his center mass. I used my heel to hook the door and push it closed. It wouldn't latch, but at the very least it would provide a sight barrier to anyone curious about the sudden bang of the door being kicked in.

"That really isn't necessary," the man, presumably Fredrick Ingles said as he turned—slowly.

It seemed a hell of a lot more necessary when Ingles turned. In his left hand, he held a glass tumbler filled with a rich brown liquid. In his right, he held a pistol, muzzle held low and pointed at the ground. I didn't recognize the model, but it looked like a heavy-duty slug thrower, the kind powered by chemical burn. I had no doubt that it could punch holes right through me if he managed to bring it to bear. "Drop the weapon! Now!"

The man—Ingles—gave me a tired smile. His features were worn and haggard, flushed with drink despite the early hour. He was heavy-set, a rarity given that the combination of the modern Net and the implanted agents effectively allowed you to exercise your body while still working or playing at other things and that every coil had nanites tailored to help control too many excess calories, and it looked as if it had been days since he'd last had a shower. He wore a suit that, I was sure, cost more than our fare to Pallah. But it looked like he had been sleeping in it. For days. Mr. Ingles was not at all what I was expecting, but he *did* have a weapon. "I said, drop it!"

"Or what?" he asked. There was a slight slur to his words, not pronounced, but enough to let me know that the drink definitely wasn't his first. "You'll shoot me? Ah, but that would be a kindness, wouldn't it? But never you fear, Mr. Langston." His use of my name jarred me, making me flinch ever so slightly, but if Ingles noticed, he ignored it and just kept talking. "Never you fear. The weapon isn't for you. It's for me. An answer dependent on why you've shown up at my door. If you're looking for answers, then maybe I can help. If you're looking for revenge," a wan smile played once more across his lips, "well, I'm not much one for pain, and I was just about done with this coil, anyway."

I had questions. So many damn questions. And Ingles seemed ready to answer them. There was a small part of me—a part that I took no pride in—that regretted his compliance, that longed to take back some of my own for all the pain and suffering that had been laid upon the crew of the *Persephone*, all, insofar as I knew, in the name of corporate profit. But whatever Ingles said, and no matter how good Chan was, someone would eventually notice that something was amiss. I didn't have time to indulge in revenge fantasies.

"Fine," I grunted. "We talk like civilized people. I get my answers, no one gets hurt."

"Agreed. I won't be so foolish as to ask you to put away your weapon, but perhaps we could sit down? Care for a drink?"

I shook my head and motioned with the barrel of the Gauss pistol toward the couch. Ingles walked over to it, his own gun still held loosely in his right hand while simultaneously sipping at his drink. There was something about how he moved, something about the sheer casualness with which he was approaching this situation that made me wonder if he was entirely sane. Immortality or not, staring down the barrel of a gun should have elicited some kind of reaction. He sank into the couch, leaned back, and actually seemed to relax. I got another bland smile. "Shoot," he said.

It was a poor—and carefully chosen—choice of words. I couldn't decide if I liked Ingles, or if I wanted to put a bullet in him. Maybe both.

"How do you know my name?" I asked. I knew, or thought I knew, the answer already.

"Come on, Langston. You can do better than that."

I just stared at him, contemplating whether or not he'd look better with a collection of twelve-millimeter holes. He shook his head, drained his drink in a single gulp, and said, "Fine. The derelict was being monitored. We had a low-emission ship nearby, riding sheepdog to make sure the shuttle went into the sun. You and your merry band of salvagers showing up ruined a lot of peoples' day." He raised his glass in salute. "But the *Persephone* was blasting out her Net codes all right and proper, so it was easy enough to find out who crewed her. We've been tracking you ever since. We lost you on Daedalus, so we started playing cleanup. Showing up at Copeland's was a surprise—you have no idea how much you pissed off the contractor we hired. He's not a man who likes a half-done job. I think he'd hunt you down just out of spite. If Genetechnic wasn't already employing him to do so."

That sent a little bit of a chill down my spine. The last thing Chan and I needed was a professional killer hunting us. If he found us… "How did you know I was coming here? You didn't seem at all surprised."

He snorted. "Mind if I refill this?" he asked, waving the glass. I nodded but made sure to keep my weapon trained on him. "To answer your question, I didn't know you were coming here, exactly. But taking down my Net-links wasn't very subtle. Don't get me wrong," he said as he poured a fresh glass, "the fact that you did it without alerting anyone other than me was quite impressive. Ms. Chan's doing, I take it?" The familiarity with which Ingles threw about our names grated on my nerves. I didn't bother answering. "She has real talent. Under other circumstances, I might try to offer her a position in our IT department."

"Yeah. Circumstances where you weren't trying to have her killed," I said.

He beamed at me, the smile not unlike a Cheshire cat's in his round face. "Exactly. Now," he went on, tapping the barrel of his pistol against the side of his leg with one hand while he swirled the glass in the other, "I assume you didn't come all this way for nothing?"

His almost playful aplomb bothered me. It wasn't just the unexpected responses—there was something about his attitude that was almost nihilistic. That had been all the rage, once. Everyone wanted to live fast, die young, and leave a good-looking corpse. But that was before the tantalizing lure of immortality. It took planning to live forever, and someone of Ingles' age and position should have been well past any fatalism. Had he simply grown tired of life? It happened, sometimes. Some people discovered that the weight of years began to take a toll that no new coil, no new career, no new relationship could alleviate. Other times they did their level best to sabotage whatever coil they were put into by following the most self-destructive behaviors imaginable. Ingles—with his flabby body and slurring words—may well have been the latter. I found that, given all that faced us, I couldn't bring myself to care.

"Tell me about Bliss," I said, keeping a watchful eye on his gun. I knew Chan was listening in, and I sent Sarah a mental note to record everything.

"Ah, Bliss." He sighed. "It was going to be Genetechnic's crowning achievement. Can you imagine? Living forever and never having even a single bad memory." The smile that stretched his face took on a beatific quality. "God, do you know how much I'd pay for that? No more bad days. No looking back with regrets. No wondering what might have been." He grinned. "No dwelling on stupid shit that you did wrong fifty years ago that everyone else had forgotten, but your own damn brain keeps betraying you and chewing on it like old vomit." He sighed, took a sip from his drink. The pistol kept tap-tap-tapping against his leg. "It would have been amazing."

"If it had worked," I said.

"Yeah," he agreed. "If. Turns out, when you let a hive-mind AI start making decisions about what memories are good or bad…" He shrugged. "Well, it didn't take the Bliss nanobots very long to decide that the easiest way to ensure humans had no bad memories was to just wipe the mind clean. Reformat the hard drive, if you will." He snorted. "And they just kept doing it, until we managed to expel them from a coil."

"And you found another gold mine." I tried to keep the snarl out of my words, tried to keep my hands from shaking on the grip of my Gauss gun.

To my surprise, Ingles just shrugged. "I guess. We weren't expecting the AI to have unlocked the quantum entanglement problem. The blank coils were a surprise. We thought it might be profitable. For a time."

Once again, I was taken aback by his apparent fatalism. "What do you mean, for a time?"

"We saw the feeds from the shuttle," Ingles said in an apparent non-sequitur. "Hell, I had the whole thing in high definition and as close to real time as the distances would allow. We watched it happen. Right up to the moment it went in the sun. And we blew the *Persephone* out of the sky."

My arm moved of its own accord, snapping back up, leveling the Gauss gun at Ingles' center mass. My finger twitched on the trigger, and it took every ounce of control I could muster not to end his miserable existence—at least for a while—right then and there. But there was something in his eyes as he stared at the barrel that stayed my hand. It was hope. He wanted me to pull the trigger.

Chan's voice buzzed over my implant. "Carter! Don't! We still need information."

"Yeah," I said aloud. "Yeah." I drew a deep breath, lowered the pistol once more, though my eyes were still tight on the gun Ingles kept tapping against his leg. If he wanted to check out for a while, he had to know that all he had to do was point that thing at me. No matter what information we needed, I wasn't going to take any chances, not with my backup endangered. "You're a son of a bitch, Ingles," I said, voice calm again.

"If only you knew," he replied. He sounded disappointed. He drained his glass in one gulp, turned and filled it again. When he turned back, his face was pale and beads of sweat stood out on his forehead. "We blew the *Persephone* out of the sky and did our level best to screw up your backups." He snorted. "We have some of the best hackers in the world. And we only managed to get one of you. The security on the archives really is top-notch. Or so they say." There was something in his voice, the barest hint of sarcasm.

"What do you mean?" I asked.

He shrugged. "The archives are protected, but nothing is ever truly secure. You of all people should know that. There have been... glitches... before. Accidents. System errors. Do you really believe that they were innocent mistakes?" He snorted. "Our entire society is built on the promise of immortality. What do you think would happen if everyone realized they weren't quite as safe as they believed?" He swirled the liquor in his glass, staring at it in concentration. "No," he continued. "We weren't the first to find our way into the archives, but we did manage to get in." He offered a grin that held no humor. "Unfortunately, we couldn't quite figure out how to clean up our mess in time."

I had to press the implication that the archives weren't as safe as everyone thought out of my mind, at least for the moment. "Fuck you," I said. "How can you be so callous about taking away immortality? You're not fucking God, Ingles."

"No," he agreed. "But we played God. And now the whole solar system is going to pay the price."

19

I just stared at him, trying to figure out what the hell he was talking about. "Are you saying you've unleashed… what? Some kind of plague that will turn us all into mindless automatons?"

"If only," Ingles replied, refilling his glass again. His face was flushed and he was slurring his words more and more. If I didn't get answers soon, he'd pass out on me.

"You still haven't told me what I need to know. What did you do? Why do you want us dead? How do we stop it?" My voice rose on each question and the last came out at a near shout. My hand was shaking on the Gauss pistol and I was once again filled with the urge to put a ferrous slug right into Ingles' drunken face.

"Easy," Chan's voice came through my implant. "Easy."

"You don't get it, do you?" Ingles laughed, unable to hear Chan over my personal Net. "You don't fucking get it." He drew a breath and dashed the back of his right hand—the hand holding the pistol—across his eyes. Was he wiping away sweat, or had he actually started to tear up? "Bliss isn't just nanobots. It's a fucking artificial intelligence. A full-on Alpha AI. Had to be, to make decisions about what memories to edit. A *distributed* intelligence across hundreds of thousands of nanites. Per dose. An honest to god hive mind. From a design standpoint, it's absolutely beautiful. As close to perfection as anything we've ever done."

"Oh, shit," Chan whispered. Ingles was right—I didn't get it. Didn't understand. But clearly, Chan, with her programming background had some idea of what was going on. Ingles wasn't done though.

"So, we have this… this beautiful mind. And we told it to make humans happy. To ensure they didn't have any bad experiences." He took a deep swallow from his tumbler. "It took it all of fifteen seconds to erase the first test subject."

That thought made my stomach turn. Up until that moment, I'd thought of the blanking of the coils as an unintended side effect. A glitch. Some bit of bad code that could be corrected and controlled. But if it was an active decision not on the part of Genetechnic, but the AI itself…

"There wasn't just one test subject on that shuttle," I said, remembering the rows of cadavers sitting peacefully in their acceleration couches. "You didn't stop with that first failure."

"No," Ingles said, downing his fourth—or was it his fifth?— whiskey. "No. We knew we were sitting on a fucking gold mine. If we could get it to work. If we could control it. We kept testing. But slowly. Carefully. Tweaking the AI."

"Ask him what they did with the old programs," Chan said. There was an urgency in her voice that I didn't quite understand. Still, I dutifully repeated the question.

He snorted. "What do you think we did? We deleted them. Ordered the bots to self-destruct. That mechanism was built in, anyway. They were only supposed to last for a year, and then, poof, no more. Or sooner, if you didn't pay your bill."

"Oh, no. No, no, no," Chan was muttering, the words seeming to resonate in some back corner of my mind.

"Okay. So you pump a few dozen test subjects full of Bliss, they get erased, and you put them on a rocket to the sun? I don't get it," I said. "How does that solve the problem?"

Ingles sighed. Moved away from the bar at last, taking a few staggering steps to the couch where he dropped down without a hint of grace. "We didn't have a couple dozen test subjects," he said. "We had seven."

Once again, the images from the derelict ship flashed through my head. Rows upon rows of dead. The video of the other me popping cores. The ambulatory corpse. "No," I said. "There were thirty people on that shuttle. I was there." Not quite accurate, but Ingles knew what I meant.

"Yeah," Ingles agreed. His bravado dropped and he seemed to be deflating in front of my eyes, folding in on himself. The pistol was held loosely now, almost forgotten. "But we only introduced Bliss into seven of them. The rest…" He trailed off. Shrugged. "I guess you could say they got infected."

"What?" I exclaimed.

"We're so fucked," Chan's voice sounded in my head.

"The nanites were always designed to be self-replicating," Ingles went on. "No sense in having a happy customer having to come in for another treatment when we could just reauthorize the current one over the Net. They *were not* designed to be able to spread from one person to another. But the AI was smarter than us." His gaze dropped to the pistol in his hand. He contemplated it for a long moment, before continuing. "It evolved. All in accordance with its primary mission, of course."

"Why didn't you push the fucking self-destruct?" I snarled.

"We tried. But the AI disabled that as well. It realized it couldn't make us happy if we could push a button and kill it. All well within its programmed parameters."

"Okay." I sighed. "So, you loaded the infected—taking proper measures to prevent further infection, I hope—onto a shuttle and sent it off to the sun. Great. From what we got from my branch, you seemed pretty fucking successful. Why bother trying to erase us?"

Ingles laughed. Or maybe he sobbed. It was hard to tell. "You're here, aren't you? You managed to track us down. That means one of you had to get a message out. Had to set something up so that your new branch would be able to pick up the trail. Only one way to make sure that didn't happen."

"Wipe us out of fucking existence?" I growled. My gun hand seemed to come up of its own accord.

"Yes," Ingles replied.

"Then why in the hell are you being so casual about all this? Why are you telling me anything?" I demanded.

"Because none of it matters anymore." He looked up, not at me, but toward a blank wall of his home. "Activate wallscreen," he said. The flat white shimmered to life, and a single image filled the screen. I recognized it. I should. It was from my viewpoint. Or rather, my branch's viewpoint. It showed the door to the derelict shuttle from right before the other me had started to cut his way in. It showed the three neat holes bored through the metal that I'd been unable to explain.

"We failed," Ingles said. "The nanobot AI escaped the shuttle." He waved one hand vaguely toward the ceiling, though I knew his gesture was meant to go higher, to space itself. "It's out there, somewhere." He gave me a death's-head grin.

The speakers built in to the home crackled to life and Chan's voice—what I thought of as Chan's *real* voice, even though I knew it wasn't what her current coil sounded like—filled the room. "How long? How long until this… this nano-swarm makes its way to another ship, or a station? Or a fucking moon?"

The laugh that burst from Ingles had no humor in it. It sounded more like a sob. "I don't know. Months? Years? We don't even know how the bots are propelling themselves, much less how fast they can accelerate. Don't you get it? We lost control of them. They're changing, *evolving*, and they're not doing it according to any plan of ours." He shook his head. "If they make it to a population center, and eventually they will, then we're done. Bliss may be a bunch of fucking robots," he slurred, "but it's damn smart. And I can guarantee you that if Genetechnic found a way to infiltrate the backup system, so can Bliss. This thing wants to wipe us out for our own good. What happens if it manages to upload a copy of itself into the archives on the back of someone it's infected? Bye-bye humanity. Hello robot overlords." Shay's long silence told me that she agreed with Ingles' assessment.

Fuck that.

"Bullshit!" I exclaimed. "This isn't the first plague we've dealt with as a species. Who cares if it's technological rather than biological? We've used quarantine measures in the past. And we've spaced entire fucking habitats when we had to. We can deal with this. We can stop it. But we have to make people aware of its existence."

"You don't get it, Langston." Ingles snorted. "This isn't a superflu or smallpox. This is a full-fledged Alpha AI. It's not just smart. It's smarter than we are. Much smarter."

"And there's a good chance," Shay chimed in, "that every time it replicates, every time it adds another bot to the swarm, it will get smarter. That's what a distributed intelligence *means*, Carter. Its computational power—and therefore its intelligence—grows with each bot, each mind, each resource added to the hive. It's been months. This thing doesn't even need to find a human settlement to be scary. It just needs to find enough raw materials to keep breeding. And if it gets into the archives, where the computational power of literally billions of minds is stored…" The transmission cut off with an abruptness that I interpreted as a blend of fear and anger.

The thought of Bliss running around through the archives and co-opting the countless backups stored there sent a chill racing down my spine. If it could get into the archives, it wouldn't need to infect anyone. It would just have to wait. As soon as someone was stuffed into a new coil, the Bliss code could work to overwrite the existing nanites in the body. Every single re-coil would create a new patient zero in real space. "Fine. So, it isn't the flu," I said. "It's orders of magnitude worse. All the more reason to let people know, to shore up every fucking defense we can think of. Why the hell is Genetechnic sitting on this?"

"Because the second they say anything, they stop existing. Do you think any governing body, planetary or hab, will let the company that released the biggest existential threat in living memory just keep on keeping on? Of course they won't. And right now, upper management is convinced that we're the only ones who stand a chance of doing something about it." He snorted. "I think they're fucking idiots. But even so, they have a point. Our scientists made this thing. Going to be awfully hard for them to figure out what to do about it if they're sitting in a cell somewhere."

It made a certain amount of sense, I supposed. Oh, it smacked of more than a little cover your ass, but there was also a certain logic to it. Governments had, for the most part, ceded research and development to the corporations a long time ago, preferring to buy new technology rather than spend the time and effort on the development process. Even if Genetechnic's R&D staff avoided jail time, they'd certainly lose their jobs. They'd be rehired by other companies in a heartbeat, of course. Minds that could create the end of humanity were always valued. But they'd be broken up, spread out over numerous corporations, the brain trust that had developed the killer nano-swarm in the first place broken down into its component parts. As much as I hated to admit it, if Genetechnic was actually working on a cure, trying to keep the team together made sense.

"You could have fucking talked to us," I growled. "With all your resources, you're telling me that Genetechnic couldn't have made sure our re-coiling took place somewhere they controlled? You didn't have to try and kill us. You didn't have to try and fucking erase us!" I bellowed.

Ingles shrugged. That shrug held all of the indifference that personified everything I hated about the megacorporations. The attitude behind it was why I'd spent lifetimes working for small operations, barely making ends meet, but keeping my soul—if such a thing existed—intact. "Upper management decided on a more expedient solution," was all he said.

"Shay, what do you think about all this?" I asked aloud.

Silence.

Ingles was just looking at me, his own weapon held loosely now. His head was nodding slightly, as if the alcohol he'd been pounding had finally caught up to him.

"Shay? You there?" I tried over the implant this time, not trusting the audio pickup in the house.

Still silence.

"What the fuck did you do?" I demanded, surging out of my seat and taking a step toward Ingles. His eyes snapped back open as I came to my feet and his hand twitched, but it was already too late. I swung my Gauss pistol down, slamming the barrel into the wrist of Ingles' gun hand. There was a satisfying *crack* and he let out a small whimper of pain as the weapon slipped from his nerveless fingers. I swept the weapon to the floor as I twisted my left hand in the fabric of his suit, hauling the fat man to his feet. I jammed the muzzle of the gun under his chin. "Where the fuck is Chan?"

"She is here, Mr. Langston."

The words—spoken in an urbane tone that I'd heard once before—sounded from behind me. I hadn't heard the door open, but I spun around, bringing the Gauss pistol up. The assassin stood there, just inside of the doorway, white-gloved hands holding a microwave emitter to Chan's head. Chan's face was a mask of stoicism, but even in her new coil, I could see the fear hidden beneath the mask. Our backups were suspect, but even if we died, the cores in our current coils could be salvaged, giving us a shot at carrying on. Unless someone fried them with a close-range shot from a microwave emitter.

"Tsk, tsk, Mr. Langston," the assassin said, a slight smile curling his lips. "I don't think you want to point that at me. I may get a little jumpy." He grinned at Chan—he had to look up to do it, but that somehow made the gesture all the more condescending.

I realized in that moment that I'd just foolishly turned my back on Ingles, so I spun again, trying to keep both men in my vision. I needn't have bothered. Ingles had slumped back down onto his couch the moment I'd released him. His own gun still lay on the floor and he was staring wide-eyed at the assassin. He looked like he was poised equally between pissing himself and passing out. I ruled him out as a threat and turned my attention back to the man holding Chan at gunpoint.

He hadn't taken advantage of my momentary lapse of attention. That might have been because the microwave emitter was a short-range weapon, almost contact range. Dragging Chan along while trying to get close enough to zap me would probably have been difficult. On the other hand, he could have fried Chan and been on me half a heartbeat later, and I doubted there would have been much I could do about it. If his primary goal was to kill us, why was he waiting?

"What do you want?" I asked. I hadn't lowered the gun.

Whoever this guy was, I wasn't worried about him getting jumpy from having a weapon pointed at him. He had the look of someone who'd been in that situation more than a few times.

"Right to the point, Mr. Langston. I like that about you." He smiled. It seemed a genuine smile, revealing even white teeth that stood out against the bronze of his skin. "I think, under the circumstances, I'm glad I didn't kill you at the apartment complex."

"Yeah," I grunted. "Me, too." I was watching Chan, looking for the telltales that she was getting ready to make some sort of move. Her coil had a size advantage over the assassin, something I was sure she wasn't used to. I hoped it didn't give her the unfounded confidence to try something stupid. She just stared back at me, eyes calm, waiting for my cue. Good. I had no doubt she'd do something if I made a move of my own, but until I did, it looked like she was content to wait. "You didn't answer my question," I said to the intruder.

"That's because I haven't quite decided, Mr. Langston." He tilted his head a bit, and I felt the weight of his gaze. "The situation is evolving. I've been given new orders from my client, but also a certain amount of discretion in the execution of those orders. A judgment call to make, if you will." The asshole sounded thoughtful, almost pensive. "I often have the power of life or death in my hands, Mr. Langston, but I'm not normally the one to choose. The choice is supposed to be made before I ever enter into the picture."

"Well, let me help you out," I grated. "If you pull that trigger, you'll be dead long before you can reach me."

"Hmm…" was the man's reply. "Perhaps. But Ms. Chan

would no longer be with us. I'm confident in the strength of my backups, Mr. Langston. Are you?"

Damn. I had hoped that if he was an independent contractor, he might not know the depths to which Genetechnic had gone to eliminate us. He knew I couldn't risk Chan's life. The microwave emitter was no coincidence. I saw the barest hint of fear on Chan's face, now, breaking through the mask of her resolve.

"Fine," I said. "You got us there." I kept the gun leveled on him. "But if you're here to kill us both, *erase* us both, I'd be a special kind of stupid to let you. Give me one reason why I shouldn't just take the shot now, and hope I drop you before you can hit the firing stud on that emitter." I saw Chan tense as I said the words, getting ready to try to break clear from the assassin. Good.

"I'll give you two, Mr. Langston. First, I don't need to push a firing stud. The microwave emitter is slaved to my agent, and if my functions go offline, it will fire. A dead-man's switch, if you will."

Fuck. That meant I couldn't just take the shot. I'd have to wait for Chan to try and break clear, and the odds of that… well, I was learning that Chan was one of the best around at what she did, but hand-to-hand combat with assassins didn't seem to be in her wheelhouse. "Great," I muttered. "And number two?"

"I think I've decided not to kill you after all."

I heard the words, but I'd have to be a bigger fool than I was to accept them at face value. "Great," I said with false enthusiasm. "In that case, I'm sure you'll have no problem releasing 'Ms. Chan,'" I tried to say the name with the sort of offhand casualness that the assassin was throwing around. "As a sign of good faith, you understand."

His smile broadened. "Ah. As to that, I don't expect you to take me at my word just yet. And I'm afraid you might do something hasty. So, no, I won't be releasing Ms. Chan. And, should either of you try anything, I will, of course, re-evaluate my decision. Quickly. And with prejudice."

"I'm not exactly inclined to take you at your word, either, Mr...." I trailed off. I had no idea what the assassin's name was.

"No. You wouldn't be, would you?" he asked, not bothering to answer my implied question. "Fair enough. We can stay just like this while I tell you *why* I've decided to go the… less messy route." He looked at me expectantly. I couldn't imagine anything he said making me trust him one iota more, but a little extra time couldn't hurt. Right now, he was holding all the cards. But deep-space salvage taught you that things could change in a big damn hurry.

"Go ahead," I said, keeping the gun leveled at him. Not for the first time, I wished that Chan was in her original coil. At least that way the bad guy to hostage mass ratio would be more in my favor if I had to take the shot.

"Very well," the killer smiled. "I'm going to make a few assumptions based on my new mission parameters. Do let me know if I start to get too far ahead of you, okay?"

The words dripped condescension, and I almost took the shot out of spite. Instead, I grit my teeth and said, "I'll try to keep up."

"Do that. Genetechnic has established a rough timeline for you over the past several months, Mr. Langston. Ms. Chan," he gave her a slight nudge with the microwave emitter, "did a better job of covering her tracks in those early days. I suppose it's to be expected. I wonder if the crew of the *Persephone* knew just what caliber of criminal they were associating with." He sounded almost impressed. No. Not impressed. It was more… professional respect. I'd learned over the past few months just how good a hacker Chan was, but she must have been even better than I'd thought to pull that tone out of a megacorp's cleaner. Not that I'd let the assassin know that. I kept quiet and kept my sights as steady as I could on his smug face.

"Well," he continued, "Genetechnic traced you from Prospect to Daedalus easily enough. They were, by the way, quite surprised at how easily you dispatched the first assassin that was sent after you. That's when they chose to employ me. Unfortunately, I wasn't able to meet you on Daedalus—

other engagements, you understand."

"Other murders," I replied.

"Yes," he agreed amicably. "But we assumed that your branch managed to get you enough information to put you on the trail of one Malcolm Copeland, and that with Ms. Chan's help, you were able to obtain information on Bliss and on the blanking effect it had."

I was surprised Genetechnic had trusted the man to that extent. They'd already killed Chan and me—and the rest of the *Persephone*—once on the chance that we'd learn that. "If you're a private contractor," I asked, "why the hell did they tell you so much?"

"Please, Mr. Langston. I am a man of honor."

"Meaning once you're bought, you stay bought," Chan said. Her voice was tight with anger.

"Exactly, Ms. Chan. Genetechnic knows they can trust me. My business is all word of mouth. Much, I suppose, like yours is. Your *real* business." The assassin gave her a little shake.

"Fine," I interjected, not wanting the two of them to get into a pissing contest. Not with that microwave emitter still dangerously close to Chan's core. "And yeah, we tracked down Copeland and figured out about Bliss and the zombies. That led us to Ingles." I spared a glance for the corporate slug. He had either passed out from the liquor or was doing a damn fine job of faking it. Right down to a little line of drool leaking from the corner of his lip. "He filled us in on the AI," I added.

The assassin nodded. "Excellent. Then you have most of the important background details already. My compliments on your resourcefulness. To the ongoing developments, then." He paused for a second as if he were considering how best to proceed. "Well. The nanite swarm has been challenging for Genetechnic to track, particularly without employing the resources of companies or polities whose technological proclivities lie in that particular direction. But the good people at the helm of the corporation are not without a certain degree of ingenuity. They have been closely monitoring all traffic in an expanding sphere from their best guess of an exit point from the shuttle."

I nodded. That made sense. Whatever tech the nanite swarm boasted, they were still bound by the same laws of physics as the rest of us. Which meant there were limits to their propulsion and that they'd either need a source of fuel or the ability to hitch a ride at some point. I understood enough astrophysics to know that the challenges of monitoring all possible vectors for the swarm while simultaneously monitoring and projecting all human traffic that might cross paths with it were, no pun intended, astronomical. There were probably several banks of supercomputers somewhere right here on Mars dedicated to dealing with that math. "And now they've found something?" I half asked, half stated.

"Correct, Mr. Langston. A passenger liner, to be exact. Hundreds of souls. And it has gone dark. Dropped right off all the standard traffic grids."

"Except for Genetechnic's," Chan said.

"Yes. Except for Genetechnic's. The efforts put into monitoring the possible vectors of the swarm have proven valuable. The corporation believes that the swarm has taken up residence within the vessel. Plenty of humans to provide 'Bliss' to. Plenty of resources to reproduce. And evolve. Plenty of fuel. A perfect hive for the swarm."

"A perfect breeding ground for the end of humanity," Chan snarled. That was one thing her new coil did better than the old—the leonine features seemed custom-grown for snarling.

"If we allow it, perhaps," the assassin agreed amicably. "I have no intention of allowing it." He paused, considering. "So long as I get paid."

"Why do you need us?" I asked. "I'm sure Genetechnic has their own corporate security. Hell, they took out the *Persephone*, so they've got to have at least one armed ship. Why not put a missile into the cruise ship and be done?"

"And lose out on all the profit potential?" Chan asked. "We couldn't have that."

"There is something to that," the assassin agreed. "If nothing else, Genetechnic has invested a significant amount of capital in the research and development and would, I assume, appreciate an opportunity to study things more closely. Now that they know what they're dealing with." The assassin smiled and even Chan snorted out a half-laugh. The AI had gotten away from them once. None of us—even the assassin it seemed—thought that it couldn't happen again.

"But consider, Ms. Chan. If we were to do as Mr. Langston has suggested and simply destroy the vessel, how will we know we destroyed the swarm? It is made up of nanites, after all. Individually, they are microscopic. Even our best weaponry cannot simply sublimate every molecule of a passenger liner."

"And, more to the point," I said, "do you know if all of the swarm is aboard this vessel? It's had months to propagate. Months to spread."

"Yes," the assassin said. "You begin to see the problems. To understand why a missile is not the best solution."

"Okay," I said, my frustration creeping into my voice. The Gauss pistol was getting heavier by the second, a product of equal parts holding the chunk of metal and plastic at arm's length and my own crumbling resolve to resist whatever it was that Genetechnic wanted from us. "So you can't destroy the vessel. I still don't see where we come in. I suppose you're going to board it? I'm sure Genetechnic security is better suited to that than we are."

"Do not sell yourself so short, Mr. Langston. The *Persephone*, despite being a small operation, has…" He paused. Smiled. "Excuse me. *Had* a sterling reputation." The Gauss gun felt a little lighter at those words, but I ignored the dig. "And yes, Genetechnic does have security, and they will be bearing the brunt of the mission. But the AI continues to learn. It has taken measures to make boarding it quite challenging."

"What kind of measures?" I asked, already suspecting the answer. There was only one kind of difficulty that an EVA specialist like me would be needed for.

"The vessel in question has been put into a multi-axis spin. It's yawing, pitching, and rolling at impressive speeds. You are quite right that Genetechnic has personnel capable of dealing with the situation they might find aboard, but your field, like mine, is rather specialized. Genetechnic needs someone to board the vessel, make their way to the bridge, and regain control of the basic navigation functions to facilitate a boarding."

"And what am I? Chopped liver?" Chan asked. Her eyes had narrowed and a faint flush suffused her face. I had to smile.

Literal gun to her head, and she seemed more concerned about not being seen as vital to the mission.

"You will also be useful," the assassin allowed. "Genetechnic has skilled hackers, of course, but they're more used to working within the confines of a protected office environment. But your inclusion is mostly to ensure that Mr. Langston doesn't do anything stupid."

"Fuck you," Chan replied. I agreed with the sentiment, but I knew the assassin was right. Maybe I could have figured out a way to turn them down—taking the shot if nothing else. Maybe I could have found a way to betray Genetechnic. I wasn't sure if I wanted to at this point—the nanite swarm was a threat to... well, everyone. I may not have approved of Genetechnic's methods, particularly when it came to perma-death for my friends, but the assassin made some compelling points, and it seemed unlikely that anyone else was going to be able to *do* anything about the problem.

"Easy, Chan," I said. "He's an asshole, but this may be our only chance to get out from under Genetechnic. And get our backups safe again." I looked the assassin in the eye. "I assume that *is* part of the deal, right?"

"Of course, Mr. Langston. Genetechnic's lawyers have drawn up the official documents, but the layman's version is that your backups will be left alone and, as an added incentive, if we are successful in our endeavors, new coils matching whatever specifications you wish will be provided." He paused. Smiled that unctuous smile of his. "To all three of you."

"Three?" I asked.

"No sudden movements, Ms. Chan. We don't have that

new coil lined up for you quite yet." With those words, the assassin released his hold on Shay's neck, though he kept the microwave emitter's barrel screwed firmly into her ear. He eased a hand into a pocket of his suit pants, and withdrew a small, gleaming cube. I recognized it at once—a core.

"I caught up with Zr. Harper some time ago," the assassin said. "They proved less difficult to deal with than the pair of you. But Genetechnic has kept them safe. And Zr. Harper is covered in the contract as well, though one of you will have to assume their proxy for purposes of signing the document." He dropped the cube back into a pocket and while Shay and I were still staring dumbfoundedly at one another, moved quick as a striking serpent, arm wrapping back around Shay's neck. She barely seemed to notice at this point, but it made me grit my teeth a little harder. "Truly, the generosity of the Genetechnic Corporation knows no bounds," the assassin finished. There was something in his tone that I couldn't read—was it sarcasm? Or did he truly believe that Genetechnic was being generous?

It didn't matter. What mattered was that we had a chance to get out from under Genetechnic's thumb. A chance to get our backups restored. A chance to bring Harper, at least, out of the deep. It was dangerous to trust an outfit like Genetechnic. They'd do everything they could to protect their bottom line. But, generally speaking, once the contracts came out, you could rely on the megacorps to abide by the terms. They might do their level best to screw you over within the confines of those terms, but the outright breaking of a contract was bad for business. "What about Miller?" I asked.

"Ah," the assassin said, voice somewhat regretful. "I'm

afraid I wasn't involved in that contract. I understand that things didn't go well. I'm afraid Mr. Miller is lost." A brief, faraway look crossed over his features—the look of someone consulting their agent. "Time is running short. Genetechnic is preparing the mission for launch from their station here on Mars. I'm afraid I'm going to need an answer."

Shay spoke up. "We sign the papers, I want more than Genetechnic's word that our backups get restored. I want physical copies that we can leave somewhere here on Mars. Somewhere Genetechnic doesn't know about. Along with instructions on what to do with them if we're not heard from again." There was a reason Shay ran the computers and I played space monkey between free-falling objects.

"That's... challenging," the assassin replied. "Genetechnic doesn't have direct access to..."

"Stuff it," Shay said. "You had enough access to try and melt our backups across half the fucking solar system. You expect us to believe you can't swipe a copy?"

"Not me, no," the killer demurred. "A moment." His eyes got that faraway look again. If we were going to make a move, try to ninja our way out of the situation, now was the time. Only, I somehow doubted that the assassin was quite as distracted as he looked. And all the ways to "escape" a gun to your head worked a hell of a lot better in theory than in practice. I met Shay's eyes and lifted an eyebrow in question. She gave a tiny shake of her head. If she was willing to sit it out in the hopes that we'd come away from this mess clean, particularly when she was the one in the greatest danger, then so was I.

The assassin's eyes focused again. "Very well," he said.

"Genetechnic has agreed. I have a revised copy of the contract." He looked at me expectantly.

"Then drop whatever jammer you have in place and send it over, so our agents can review it," Shay replied.

That startled me. *Sarah?* I sent the thought to my agent.

Yes, Carter?

Status.

Wireless functions are currently unable to connect to any networks.

Which meant Sarah was isolated from the broader Net and even from localized transmission to other agents, like Shay's Bit. And probably had been, I realized, since the assassin walked into the room.

Local access restored, Sarah said. *File transmission request received.*

"Approved," I said aloud.

Transmission in progress. File received. It is a text document.

Analyze, I instructed.

There was a brief moment of silence in my head. *Analysis complete.*

Were you following the conversation, Sarah? I didn't really need to ask the question. It was more out of habit than anything. Even without Net access, Sarah still had direct—one might even say hardwired—access to my brain and all the input it received, including auditory and visual.

Yes, Carter.

Is the contract consistent with what we've been discussing? I asked.

Yes, Carter.

Summarize the finer points, I directed.

Provided you are successful in your undertaking, Genetechnic agrees to forego pursuing any further action against you, Shay Chan, or Zomas

Harper. In addition, you will be compensated both financially and with a coil matching specifications of your choosing. There is language regarding your backups that is masked in legalese to avoid admission of any criminal wrongdoing, but based on current system law, you would have a cause of action against Genetechnic should anything untoward befall your global backups. There is also a provision consistent with the terms Ms. Chan asked to be added with respect to physical, offsite backups.

"Shay?" I asked.

"Looks good to me, Carter. I don't trust Genetechnic as far as I can throw it. On Jupiter. But so long as we register these contracts with a third party, I don't know how we can get any safer." She threw a glare at the assassin. "You're going to have to release me before we sign anything. And put the gun away."

"Indeed," the man replied urbanely. "We cannot have anything colored with duress, can we?" Without any more fanfare, he simply holstered his weapon and stepped away from Shay. In that instant, I had a clear shot. We hadn't agreed to anything, hadn't signed anything. Contractually, we were in the clear. Legally, except for the whole breaking and entering and holding Ingles at gunpoint, we could even make a good case for self-defense. I could have taken the shot. The small, knowing smile on the assassin's face told me that he *knew* I could take the shot.

I didn't.

What use would it have been? There was no doubt in my mind that the assassin's backup, unlike my own, was nice and safe and probably ready to be dropped into a new coil the second his core stopped registering on the Net. He would have been back on our trail in a day or two, tops. And a lot less polite about it. No. This was our chance to be free of Genetechnic. Provided we could trust them. Or, barring that, at least hide behind the thin shield of the contract long enough to find a measure of safety.

Sarah, sign the contract.

Done, my agent replied.

Shay must have signed as well, because the assassin nodded briskly. "Excellent," he said. "I've received confirmation from both of you." He took a few steps deeper into the room, moving away from us and toward the bar. "If you'll excuse me for a moment."

I realized I was still holding my Gauss pistol and eased it into its holster. I was about to say something to Shay when I caught a blur of motion out of the corner of my vision. Two shots rang out, cracking like thunder. Sarah automatically overrode my hearing, dampening the sound and protecting me from the possible damage. My pistol appeared back in my hand as I whirled around, but I was too late. The assassin was standing over the corpse of Ingles, the executive's discarded chemical burner in his hand. The Genetechnic Director of Innovations had two ragged holes in his face. The placement was odd, but intentional. I was no forensics expert, but I was willing to bet that the path of those bullets would intersect with Ingles' core.

"Why?" I demanded, once more leveling the Gauss pistol at the assassin. "He didn't tell us anything that you didn't confirm five minutes later."

"Ah," the assassin replied. "But I was *authorized* to give you that information. Ingles was not. Management had already decided that he needed to be removed until such time as the current crisis is over. I assure you, his backup is fine." He threw a contemptuous look to the neglected coil. "This will hardly be the first time he's had to take time out because of his actions. He'll have a new coil. In due course."

I didn't like it. I could tell from the slightly nauseated frown on Shay's face as she stared at the corpse that she didn't like it, either. But what choice did we have? I holstered up again. "Fine. Just fucking great. What now?" I realized I still had no idea what the assassin's name was. "What do we call you?"

"Now, Mr. Langston? Now we get ready to assault a passenger liner tumbling through space, full of an unknown quantity and quality of enemies." A smile—the first honest smile I'd seen from him—split his face. The asshole was actually looking *forward* to this. "And you can call me Korben."

21

Korben was as good as his word. He escorted us through the streets of Pallah and his entire attitude seemed to have changed. Gone was the urbane but uncaring assassin who had just shot a man in the face. In his place was a charismatic and almost gregarious tour guide. "If you look over there," he said, pointing to a building modeled after a ziggurat, "you'll see the corporate headquarters of EvoTech. They built here on Pallah when prefab structures were all you could get, but they insisted on doing something *different* with the available options. They flew in architects from Earth proper. And the best they could achieve was a derivative homage of ancient Earth civilizations." He shook his head in mock resignation. "And this from a company who claims to be on the leading edge of transhumanity."

It went on like that as we continued to walk, but I tuned him out. Shay was clearly doing the same as I got a ping from Sarah. *Ms. Chan wishes to speak with you. Shall I accept?*

Yes.

A window popped up in the top-left corner of my vision. I once again was forced to marvel at Shay's ability in the Net. The image I saw—which should have been built in the same image as her current coil—instead showed a young woman of Asiatic descent with raven-black hair and alabaster skin. It wasn't the coil she had worn on the *Persephone*. Now that I understood her dysmorphia and the distress it caused her to be not just in a bio-male body, but a body so far from her birth, I had to wonder; could the avatar she was showing now have been her original equipment? Or based on it, in any event?

"Sorry, Carter," she said in words only I could hear, transcribed directly from her thoughts and sent from Bit to Sarah on a closed Net. Sarah, in turn, converted the text to electrical impulses that could be used to directly stimulate my auditory nerves, giving us the illusion of speech, though neither of us made a sound. "I don't know how he managed to sneak up on me. Or how he managed to cut Bit off from the Net."

There was real contrition in her voice—a remarkable technical feat but also an understandable reaction. Overwatch, physical and electronic, had been her responsibility and she clearly felt guilty over her perceived failure. "Don't worry about it," I replied. "This Korben guy is good. And he's got the full backing of Genetechnic. We're lucky he didn't just terminate our coils and fry our cores. Besides, maybe we have a chance now."

"Sure." Shay's avatar frowned. "A chance to help Genetechnic clean up their mess and if we're lucky prevent the apocalypse. You get that that's what we're dealing with here, right? The end of civilization as we know it? If these nanites get out…"

It was a line I'd heard in previous lives. The fate of the world was at stake. Life, liberty, and the Solarian way would fall if someone didn't act. It was the clarion call of nationalism and idealism, the thought that the people who looked like you, sounded like you, and grew up in the same microcosm as you had to be right. Right because they thought the way that you thought and their worldview matched your own. And if they were right, then those who thought different were, by process of elimination, wrong. And it was the sacred duty of those in the right to spread the truth far and wide.

By the sword, if necessary.

The habs might be politically autonomous, but they formed relationships and alliances just like any other government. And those alliances needed the ability to project force, to show their power. They needed the ability to defend themselves and, in some cases, to claim by strength of arms that which they thought was rightfully theirs. They needed the ability to show their neighbors that they were no easy meat. They packaged it in political terms, of course. Mutual defense pacts. Peacekeeping forces. Unification efforts.

Freedom imposed at the end of a gun barrel.

I'd believed it once upon a time, been willing to die for it. Been willing to kill for it. And then, one morning, I'd woken up and I... hadn't been. Nothing ever changed. The polities kept playing at politics and the people who just wanted to live their lives paid the price and all the while the megacorps kept raking in the credits. And those who did the actual work ended up reviled as often as they did revered. The day came when I just couldn't bring myself to care, to put on the uniform and stand the watch. Better to leave it to younger, more passionate people. That was when my career in repo had started and salvage hadn't been too far off.

But this time felt different. I felt the old stirring, the hunger to serve a purpose beyond just myself and my own survival. And it didn't hurt that my ass was on the line. "All the more reason for us to help," I replied. "And all the more reason for Genetechnic to keep their end of the bargain. If we can get your insurance policy into place…" I trailed off. It wouldn't be easy. We were headed to Genetechnic's corporate offices on Pallah where, presumably, we'd be given physical backups of our cores per the terms of the contract we signed. And we'd have some time to stash them somewhere. That was all well and good, but how did we keep Genetechnic from just following along behind us and… rescinding any insurance policy we left behind. The kinds of institutions where we might deposit them were *supposed* to maintain privacy and not cave to corporate pressure. But when you could throw around the kind of credits that Genetechnic could, all bets were off.

Shay answered my unspoken question. "Don't worry about the insurance policy. Bit's working on it. I've got a plan. I'm more worried about him."

I marveled at Shay's avatar once more as it turned in my field of vision and pointed an unerring finger at Korben as he continued to give us the five-credit tour of Pallah.

"You worry about making sure we're not permanently erased," I offered. "I'll worry about keeping our hides intact until you can. Fair enough?"

She smiled and it was like the sun coming up. "Yes, Carter," she said. "That's fair enough."

The headquarters of the Genetechnic Corporation on Pallah was a relatively modest building, at least by dome standards. To eyes accustomed to station and ship living, it was palatial. It rose sixteen stories high and the prefab composite walls had been clad in a glossy stone façade. I could only assume it was some sort of local stone. No matter the expense of harvesting it from the wilds of Mars, it had to be cheaper than freighting it in from Earth proper. The boxy prefab structure had been dressed up some, not as much as the replicated ziggurat Korben had pointed out, but in addition to the stone façade, pillars had been constructed flanking the entryway and light sculptures meant to mimic fountains adorned the plaza in front of the building. If the "fountains" didn't scream wealth quite as loudly as if they had been gushing with that most precious of resources—water—the plaza still spoke of deep, deep pockets. Earthers could afford elaborate campuses for their businesses, but when you were living in a dome, every cubic centimeter of space came at a premium. An outdoor area designed for no better purpose than to look nice and provide relaxation was a true luxury.

I might have enjoyed it more if it wasn't for the tension I felt creeping into my shoulders as we walked down the carefully maintained paths through the low-moisture gardens, and made our way to the main entrance to the building. For all my assurances to Shay, I knew there was still a small chance that this was an elaborate setup, a way for Genetechnic to have us walk through their doors so they could put a much more convenient end to the troublesome crew that had uncovered their dirty little secrets.

"Security is going to want your sidearm," Korben said as we passed through the doors and entered into the lobby.

"Not likely," I responded. He grinned at me in return and there was a measure of respect in his eyes.

"Good," he replied.

Security, in fact, did not request my sidearm, as we never made it to the security checkpoint that led to the banks of elevators. Instead, we were met in the lobby by a woman in a dark, business suit. She was attractive, in a sort of severe way. Most coils were—attractive that is—the severity was all the woman crammed within it. She carried an attaché case in one hand and wore a brusque frown upon her face.

"This is highly irregular," she said, not to us, but rather to Korben.

The assassin shrugged. "Needs must. Strange bedfellows and all that."

"Is that our backups?" Shay demanded, taking a step toward the woman. In her old coil, it might have come off as assertive. Wearing the body of a six-foot, well-built male, it came off as downright aggressive. To her credit, the suit didn't so much as flinch.

"It is, Ms. Chan. Current to the moment you landed on Pallah and synced with the backup servers." I winced a little bit at that. Partly because it meant if we *did* have to use the insurance policy, the memories, the *experiences*, of what we'd managed to find out on Mars would be lost. We could—and certainly *would*—include something with the physical cores to tell the proto-us what had gone down, but being told a thing and *living* a thing were not the same. But mostly, I winced because the fact that Genetechnic had enough access to our backup files to copy them at all was a violation of privacy, trust, and law on a level that hadn't been seen since the twenty-first century. It wasn't supposed to happen. It wasn't supposed to *be able* to happen. And yet, the woman spoke of it so casually that I started to wonder if their attempts to erase us were even their first forays into that shadowy territory.

From the sour look on Shay's face, she saw it, too. Hell, she probably understood the ramifications far better than I did. But all she did was reach out and take the briefcase from the woman. "You have two hours," the suit said. "We need you back here at that time to prepare for departure."

Shay ignored her, instead reaching into a pocket. Korben, the suit, and the security that I could see on the periphery all tensed at that, but all she withdrew was a small network of wires. "We need a minute," she said. "And the case."

The suit nodded, passing the case over to Shay. Then she and Korben walked a few strides away. Shay turned the case flat and popped it open, revealing the pair of seemingly innocuous metal cubes, no more than a centimeter or so on a side, that somehow held everything that we were.

Shay didn't waste time marveling at the technology. Instead, she thrust the case into my arms with a muttered, "Hold this, and be still." I complied as best I could, acting as a makeshift table while Shay laid her network of wires and electrodes in place around the first cube. I couldn't hear her and Bit, but

I could tell from the glazed look in her eyes that she was in deep conversation with her agent. "Good," she muttered, then repeated the process with the second cube. After a few minutes she nodded, folding her sensor array back into a neat bundle and slipping it into her pocket. "Everything seems to be in order," she said.

I nodded and caught Korben's eye. He and the suit strolled back to us. "Is everything satisfactory?" the woman asked with a knowing smile.

Shay just grunted.

"You have two hours," the suit repeated. "At which point you need to be back here to prepare for departure." The smile she offered had nothing to do with friendliness. "Our security specialists aren't too fond of tardiness, so I suggest being on time."

With that, she turned on one three-inch heel and walked away. "Well," Korben said. "I suppose I'll be off as well. Try not to get lost. I doubt we'll leave without you, but you know how corporations are with their schedules." With a parting wave that was little more than the undulation of his fingers, he, too, whirled on a foot and vanished deeper into the bowels of the building.

"What now?" I asked Shay. She was the one with the plan, after all.

"Follow me." She put action to her words, heading toward the exit. We had drawn more than a few looks from the personnel in the lobby—and more than a little scrutiny from the security guards. Everyone seemed to relax a little as we moved outside. Did they know who we were? Were they complicit in the murder and worse that Genetechnic had been involved in? Or did we just look that dangerous to those leading a more pampered life? I couldn't help a mental snort at that. Some things never changed. Even now, after all the years of progress, humans were still wired to make snap judgments and assessments based on looks alone. Because of the ability to switch coils, the more prosaic forms of bias—perceived race, ethnicity, and gender—had faded. On the other hand, the good old battles of class warfare were still being fought, and if you looked poor in a rich area, you were bound to draw additional scrutiny. To be fair, if you looked like one of the suits walking in and out of the Genetechnic corporate headquarters when you set foot on Daedalus, you'd draw your share of eyes too. And probably be in considerably more danger. It seemed that, perhaps, some of the judgment I saw in the eyes around me was warranted.

I contemplated that as I followed Shay from the marbled world of Genetechnic and back into the barren and dusty landscape that was reality.

She was silent until we had passed through the doors of the Genetechnic headquarters and then cleared the grounds of the plaza in front of the building. When she spoke, it was in a low voice, almost a whisper, that I had to strain to hear. "I've had Bit working on some spoofing programs ever since we got here on Pallah," Shay said. "Highly illegal. If we get caught, we're going to be banned from the dome, at a minimum. Maybe incarcerated." She shrugged. "But it should be enough to edit us out of the electronic eyes and I doubt Pallah Central will tumble to it in just a couple of hours. So, I think I can keep us clear of most electronic surveillance." She paused. "But I don't know if I should."

"Huh?" I asked. "We need to make sure that Genetechnic

doesn't follow us. They've got enough money and enough pull to put pressure on any institution I can think of to leave the cores. If they know where we deposited them…" I trailed off. The implications were clear. Unless we could make a clean break, there wasn't much to stop Genetechnic from trailing us and cleaning up our backups. I wasn't certain they *would* try to do it. They seemed sincere in their need of our help. But they had also shown that they were willing to kill people on the *chance* that they might know something, so I wasn't prepared to take that risk.

"I know," Shay said, frustration clear in her voice. "But if we walk into a bank or whatever and their monitors don't see us, it's going to cause problems. Maybe get bank security crashing down on us."

I was catching on. "And if you disable your program right before we go into the bank, then eventually Genetechnic's hackers will find the video, and know right where to go." I thought about it a moment. "Fuck. They've got us."

"Maybe not," Shay said. "I can see two options. First, we stash the cores somewhere no one would think to look—bury them or something—with my scrambler program running so no one sees us do it. Then we leave a dead-man's switch on our systems to send the location to someone we can trust in the event we don't return." I nodded. It wasn't all that different from what I'd managed—or rather, what my branch had managed—on the *Persephone*. More refined, of course—it *was* Shay we were talking about—but the same general idea.

"Okay, that sounds workable," I agreed. "But you said you had two options."

"The second is a shell game. We leave everything running

and visit every bank, solicitor, storage center, and depository that we can in a couple of hours, and we drop something off at all of them."

I grinned. "Betting that Genetechnic won't be able to twist the arm of every business like that in Pallah all at the same time."

Shay nodded. "Right. Eventually, they'll find the cores. And there's always a chance they'll get lucky and find them early. But the odds of that happening in the time frame we're talking…" She trailed off. Shrugged.

I thought about it a moment. "Why not both?" I asked. "We use your scrambler just long enough to bury the goods, then make it seem like it malfunctioned or something. Then we visit every place we can. Only, at one of them, we don't just drop off some meaningless nothing. We set up our dead-man's switch."

A chuckle escaped Shay. "Genetechnic will be so intent on finding the prize under the right shell that they won't think that we might have set up some other kind of insurance policy." She offered me a coquettish smile that hung poorly on her coil. "I didn't know you were so mischievous."

"Or dirty, underhanded, and conniving," I countered.

"Whatever works."

We almost didn't make it in time.

We moved from bank to bank, lawyer to lawyer, doing little more than having a brief conversation. Along the way, we cut through an alleyway between two prefab structures. I gave Shay the nod and a heartbeat later, she said, "We're dark."

What had drawn me to the alleyway was a large doorway.

Not the kind used for trucks or deliveries, but just an over-wide man-door that, for whatever reason, opened into the narrow alley. The door had the same sense about it as most of the pre-fabs, somehow feeling permanent and transient at the same time. It also had a rather impressive and entirely out of place molding around it. I had no idea what the building was, or why the door in the alley was so elaborately trimmed, but I didn't care. It offered the two things we had been looking for: first it would be easy enough to identify in our insurance policy; and second, the faux-wood of the millwork itself gave us an effective spot to stash the cores.

I'd made a habit while working salvage of always keeping a few odds and ends on my person: a good knife, a mini torch, a flashlight, a roll of tape… and a small bottle of industrial-strength adhesive. I pulled the adhesive and both cores from the pockets of the VaccTech suit. Two quick dabs of the adhesive and I passed the cores to Shay, who stood taller than I did in our current coils. She reached up swiftly and surely and pressed the cores onto the ledge formed by the top of the molding. Then we were walking away. The whole thing took less than ten seconds.

"Sneak program terminated," Shay said. "We're back on the grid. Should have been a short enough time that no one would have noticed. And if they do go back and look, it will hopefully just seem like a signal loss in the alleyway."

"Good."

We kept going, squeezing in as many more stops as we could. At random, at the Law Offices of Derck Dashby, we set up our insurance policy. The attorney, a large, good-looking man with a coil that seemed far too nice for his modest practice didn't blink an eye at our strange request. He just verified that Shay's credit was good, and ten minutes later we were out the door, reasonably confident that, in the event Genetechnic double-crossed us, we'd have at least a chance at being re-coiled.

We managed three more stops before we had to make it back to Genetechnic's headquarters. In all, we had managed nearly a dozen in the two-hour time limit we'd been given. If nothing else, I took satisfaction in the idea of sending Genetechnic's goons on a wild-goose chase. Korben was waiting for us, his immaculate suit replaced with a vacc suit that looked, if anything, even more fashionable.

"Ah, just under the wire. Follow me, please, and we'll see to it that you're prepared for departure."

22

The Genetechnic shuttle was a sleek vessel with a variable geometry design that allowed for better aerodynamics in atmospheric flight while affording easier docking with stations and habs. It may have been painted in the blue and white corporate colors, but the no-frills interior screamed military. That notion was only enhanced by the two dozen armed and armored coils occupying the acceleration couches, which were situated three to either side of a narrow aisle in the middle of the craft heading aft away from the cockpit. They wore combat vacc suits that boasted nearly as many attachment points as my VaccTech but had blocky rectangles of armor plating visible just beneath the surface of the more flexible suit skin. They stared at us with hard-eyed professionalism as we made our way aboard, sizing up the two civilian "specialists" they'd have to—from their perspective—babysit on a combat op.

At least we looked the part.

I'd kept my Gauss pistol, which still rode my right hip. I'd procured a holster for the microwave emitter which I wore in a cross-draw appendix carry on the left. I'd also added a stubby chemical-burner submachine gun to the mix, choosing from the array of weaponry presented to us by Genetechnic. It was small caliber and comparatively low velocity, so wouldn't be too much of a decompression danger, especially on a passenger liner where tolerances were a little more forgiving than a ship like the *Persephone*. It was selective fire and not legal for civilian carry in most places—including Pallah—but it didn't seem like Genetechnic gave a shit. Besides, we wouldn't be on Pallah for much longer.

I'd also kept my VaccTech suit. The… quartermaster, I guess he was, or maybe armorer… for the Genetechnic security forces had given it a once-over and pronounced it passable for the mission parameters. He'd offered me an armored suit instead, but no matter how well designed armor was, it was always a tradeoff between mobility and protection. If I was going to have to swim over to a vessel moving in three dimensions, I didn't want to give up any mobility. An armored suit wouldn't do much good if thousands of tons of starship smashed into me.

Shay's suit hadn't passed the same scrutiny, and she'd been kitted out in one of the military-grade suits of the security team now staring at us. I had to admit, it suited her coil well, adding an avenging Viking-like air to the rugged features. She hadn't wanted to carry a weapon, but both the armorer and I had convinced her that walking into an unknown situation like this without something to defend yourself was, to say the very least, a questionable decision. In the end, she'd settled for a Gauss pistol as well, a newer version than the one I carried with a heavier charge and larger magazine. I was offered the same, to replace my venerable piece, but in a pinch, better the firearm you knew.

We'd both been offered a variety of secondary items, ranging from explosives to enough tools to open a mechanic's shop. I'd availed myself of the corporate "generosity," putting together a salvage kit that, if I was being completely honest, far outstripped the one I'd had aboard the *Persephone*. The *components* were largely the same, but Genetechnic could afford the very best in terms of quality. That was certainly a new development for me. With some trepidation, Shay had taken a tablet and a small toolkit that housed a number of tools for which I had no names. Given her specialty, I assumed they had to do with electronics, but my knowledge in that department started and ended with knowing how to safely remove the more valuable circuit boards from a derelict vessel.

Korben, to my surprise, did not merely escort us to the shuttle, but boarded with us. "This way," he said, offering his charming smile. The security team that was eying us so carefully kept their gazes sliding right past the killer, never allowing them to linger too long. Korben paid them no mind whatsoever. He led us to a bank of seats and gestured for us to precede him down the row. I nodded to Shay, who made her way to the acceleration couch by the wall. She moved awkwardly, not from the weight of her gear—which her current coil could easily handle—but more as if she *expected* the gear to weigh her down and was having trouble adjusting to the fact that it didn't. It had been months since the *Persephone*, and she still hadn't come to terms with her new body. I was beginning to suspect that she never would. If by some miracle

Genetechnic didn't screw us over, I hoped they were as good as their word.

I slid my bulk into the middle seat, settling into the couch. I felt the liquid core of it shift, adjusting itself to my body, cradling me against the gravities to come. "How long?" I asked Korben as he dropped into the seat next to mine.

"Variable," was the laconic response.

"Useless," I replied.

He arched an eyebrow at me, and I was reminded of those shifting glances from the security forces. Whatever Korben was, he was clearly the type of person who most people didn't screw with. There was something in his eyes at my response though. Was it amusement? Or anger? Maybe both.

His answer, whatever he was feeling, was calm. "Bliss is in control of an interplanetary vessel, Mr. Langston. If everything remains constant, our flight time should be just under twenty-eight hours. If the target ship increases or decreases speed, changes heading, or any number of other things, that could change. So, variable."

"Marginally less useless," was my reply and he actually chuckled.

I looked over at Shay but she was already gone. Her coil was there but I could tell from the slack expression on its face that she had dropped into the ShipNet. She probably wouldn't even notice the passing hours. I could drop in as well, find a game or some other form of mindless entertainment to amuse me. The soldiers around me were already following Shay's lead, some dropping into the Net, others drifting off to sleep in the timeless ability of the professional soldier to nap at any point he or she wasn't specifically being ordered not to. Korben was still sitting in his chair, staring dispassionately forward, eyes sharp and focused with none of the muzziness of someone in the Net. I suspected that he'd sit the same way for the entire length of the flight and I certainly didn't feel like engaging *him* in any further conversation.

Twenty-eight hours.

I settled back into the acceleration couch and closed my eyes. I doubted I'd get much sleep, but I'd need every ounce of rest I could manage for what was to come.

23

The passenger liner tumbled through the deep like a tin can bouncing down an endless set of spiral stairs. From the video feeds being pumped to our agents by the crew of the shuttle, there was no real sense of scale. *Sarah,* I thought at my agent, *how big is that thing?*

The vessel is a Caribbean-class passenger cruiser designed for carrying passengers on the loop between Saturn's rings and the moons of Venus. Capacity is twelve hundred passengers plus ninety-six crewmembers. Length of the vessel is approximately four hundred and thirty-five meters. The beam of the vessel is approximately thirty-four meters. Maximum thrust is...

Enough, I thought. Christ, but it was big.

"How fast is it moving?" I asked aloud. Sarah, for all her cleverness, wasn't tied in to the ship's sensors. Shay's Bit could probably get me that information—her agent seemed to be almost as capable a hacker as Shay herself—but Korben seemed to have access to everything.

"The different vectors are making it difficult to get precise readings," the man replied. "Ship's computer's best guess is somewhere between two and three gravities."

"Son of a bitch," Shay swore. "How are we supposed to board?"

"That's what Mr. Langston is for," Korben replied with a shrug. "After all, we understand he's one of the best." He offered me a smile that had more than a little condescension to it.

"You're out of your mind," Shay snapped. "You're telling me he can have an effective weight of over six hundred pounds when that thing's moving." On the viewscreen, one of the maneuvering thrusters on the ship ignited at full power, bringing its tumble in one direction to a deceptively slow stop before pushing it the other way. I knew from experience that the actual feeling of that little maneuver wouldn't seem anywhere near so gentle with boots on the hull.

"It's okay, Shay," I said, most of my concentration still on the ship. "Korben's right. This is what we came here to do. Besides, we don't have much choice, not if we want to get Genetechnic off our back." I turned, offered her a grin of my own. "Oh, and then there's that whole 'fate of humanity is in our hands' thing to worry about, too."

"You really think you can get aboard that thing?" she asked.

I considered it. I knew I was going to try, no matter what. It really was the only chance Shay and I had. The speed at which the ship was maneuvering—and from what we understood of the nano-virus, they *were* maneuvers and not something as simple as malfunctioning drives—was a problem, but the size of the vessel mitigated it to some extent. At the very least, it gave me more time to adapt to the changes in pitch, roll, and yaw. Mind you, if I mistimed things, the added *mass* would be a problem. A "time to cash in the insurance policy" kind of problem.

Sarah? I asked my agent. *What do you think? Can we do it?*

I would estimate a seventy-six percent chance of success in your previous coil, Carter, the agent replied. *I currently have insufficient data on your adaptation to your current coil. Given the time frame and the difficulty of the re-coiling process, however, the most optimistic projections I can run put the chance of success at forty-eight percent.*

Shit. Basically, a coin flip. I understood Sarah's point. While I'd had to do a fair amount of run-jump-shoot in the coil I now wore, I *hadn't* done any actual EVA work in it. With the struggle to stay alive, I hadn't even had time for the exercises I normally did to accustom a new coil to dealing with the specific range and pace of motions necessary to swim across open space and cut your way into a derelict ship. I hadn't really considered that it might be a priority. Too busy not getting permanently erased. I felt comfortable in my coil, but muscle memory was a two-part process. The core might have thousands of repetitions—or, in my case, hundreds of thousands—but you could never be quite sure what minute adjustments would need to be made to support the unique anatomy of your new meat. And when working outside, every little mistake, every hesitancy, everything that took a second and a half when it used to only take a second, compounded on each other.

The final sum of that calculation if you were not either very careful, very lucky, or, preferably, both, was death.

What choice did we have but to risk it?

"Yeah," I said, trying to force more certainty into my voice than I felt. "Yeah, I think I can get aboard." I hesitated.

Something had been bothering me from the very beginning, a thought that I'd kept pushed back to the darkest corners of my mind. It was a memory, mine but not mine, an image from the shuttle my branch had boarded. It was the image of a pair of dead eyes snapping open, and the ponderous rise of what I now knew to be a Bliss-infected puppet. "But then what?" I asked.

"What?" Shay said.

I turned my attention to Korben, staring hard at his cold black eyes. "The plan, as I understand it, is that I swim over there and get the ship under control. That means engines or bridge." It wasn't a question. I'd done this enough times that I knew those were the only two places to do what I needed to do to get the ship back in trim. "And on a ship that size, there's no way the engine compartment is going to do me any good. I'm going in because the security guys can't, right? Not until they can do a hard dock?"

Korben nodded, an expectant smile on his face. The bastard knew what I was getting at.

"And that's not just a small shuttle. Even with the better equipment I procured from Genetechnic, it's going to take time to cut into the hull. I'm talking *hours.*" Another nod. "Then how in the holy fuck am I supposed to deal with whatever countermeasures—by which I mean army of cyber-zombies—that the virus is bound to have on that ship by now? There were over a thousand souls. If even ten percent of them have been infected…" I trailed off. I was aware of Shay staring at me in horror, as the realization of what I was actually walking into dawned on her. "I somehow doubt the vaunted intellect of this artificial intelligence is going to let me walk onto the ship and undo its plans. All the skill in the world won't do me a damn bit of good if I get torn apart by a bunch of AI meat-puppets," I finished.

"Not to worry, Mr. Langston. I will be coming with you," Korben replied.

"The hell you say," I spat back. "What we're talking about is dangerous enough already. You try and play spaceman and you're a bigger risk to me than the virus. If you don't know what you're doing out there, you'll get us both killed."

"If," he replied succinctly. Then he shrugged, a bare movement of the shoulders. "It's not as if you have a choice in the matter. I *will* be coming with you, Mr. Langston." He offered another smile, this one more sincere. "To protect you, I assure you. You've already pointed out the dangers. Without *someone* willing to attempt the boarding, you won't have much of a chance at all. And, if it will make you feel better, I will wait until you're most of the way through the hull before I swim over. I assure you, I have no intention of jostling your elbow. Just keeping the… what did you call them?" He paused then smiled appreciatively. "Ah, yes. Meat-puppets. I will be keeping the meat-puppets off your back while you work."

Shay rested a hand on my shoulder, and I turned to meet her eyes. "If he's willing," she said, then trailed off.

I nodded. I didn't like it, but Shay was right. If *I* were a sentient nano-virus hell-bent on wiping clean the minds of humanity and I'd gone to all the trouble of sending a passenger liner tumbling through space, I wouldn't just leave the bridge unguarded. There was no way for me to do what I needed to do on that ship *and* fight off whatever "security" the virus had in place. I needed someone to guard my back. The thought of the assassin who had spent months "cleaning up" the mess Genetechnic made of things and racking up God alone knew what kind of body count along the way didn't exactly instill a great sense of security, but better for him to do it than Shay. With the poor adjustment to her coil she was experiencing, the swim through the deep would be tantamount to suicide for her. Not to mention the fact that putting bullets in zombies wasn't exactly her forte.

"Fine," I said. Before I could say anything else, the shuttle's intercom buzzed.

"We're as close as we're going to get, folks," the pilot's voice said into the suddenly silent ship. "We've matched speeds along the only vector that's remained constant. So far, no response from the vessel." There was a pause. "Mr. Langston and Mr. Korben to the airlock."

I drew a breath, held it for a moment and released it in a steadying sigh. I reached out and gave Shay's hand a quick squeeze and then pushed myself to my feet. Korben had already gained his and stepped into the aisle. Shay, name called by the pilot or not, wasn't about to wait behind, either. She stood up, and I threw her a questioning glance. "I'm not going to sit here on my ass while you have all the fun. We're close enough now to start trying to link with the systems on that thing." She waved one hand vaguely toward the bulkhead, indicating the space beyond. I had enough spatial awareness to realize she was waving in the wrong direction, but the point stood. "If the people in charge of this operation have any sense at all, they'll sit me down in front of whatever passes for the electronic warfare station on this bird and let me see what I can do." She looked directly at Korben as she said it. He seemed to consider for a moment, and then gave a quick nod.

We drew more than a few glances from the soldiers—corporate or politic, soldiers were soldiers—seated around us as we made our way forward toward the airlock. The entire mission hinged on us. Okay, mostly on me for the first part, but that was an awful lot of weight to bear. I had no doubt that if Korben and I failed to gain control of the vessel long enough for the muscle to board, Genetechnic would try to solve the short-term problem with a missile salvo, just like they had with the *Persephone*, for whatever good that would do. Better to roll the dice and hope the missiles took out the AI if there were no other options. But the fallback solution didn't change the feel of those measuring eyes on us.

My gear was waiting by the outer door to the airlock. "Get ready," Korben said shortly. Then he turned to Shay. "I'll take you forward to the cockpit and see if we can't get you plugged into the ship's systems." He gazed at her for a long moment. "I don't think I need to warn you to keep your digital fingers to yourself, but if you start thinking that this would be a good time to poke around Genetechnic intellectual property, just remember that if we all survive this, Genetechnic's computer forensics people will be going over this shuttle with a fine-toothed comb."

Shay grinned, back on familiar territory now. "They'd never find a trace," she assured the assassin. "But don't worry. I'll be plenty busy trying to keep Carter alive. I doubt I'll have time to look into Genetechnic's dark corners." There was a gleam in her eye as she said it though and I suspected that however she might be spending *her* time, Bit would be putting fresh batteries in its flashlight.

"Of course," Korben drawled. He sounded like he believed her about as much as I did, but that didn't stop him from waving her forward.

As they moved toward the bridge, I looked down at my piled gear. There wasn't much—there couldn't be on an open swim across the emptiness of space. But what *was* there could mean the difference between life and death. I did a quick inventory as I picked up each item and secured it to my suit.

Web gear, to help distribute the mass and provide more attachment points to the already well-endowed VaccTech suit. Plasma cutters—twice as many and of a much higher quality than those I'd carried on my last salvage mission—made up most of the raw mass and were evenly distributed along the webbing. Cutting through the hull of a vessel the size of the passenger liner was going to be more difficult than a simple shuttle. A pair of personal thrusters that snapped around the ankles. They had limited fuel, but enough to get me from the shuttle to the passenger liner. Another set that wrapped around my waist—this one with enough fuel to get me to the ship and back again, but with less overall maneuverability than the ankle thrusters. A third set for my wrists—useless for much more than quick adjustments, but with the way the passenger liner was tumbling, I was going to need plenty of those. Various tools for more refined salvage than the cutting torches offered went into pockets or snapped onto magnetized patches on the suit. Emergency oxygen, in case my suit went dry. The Gauss gun already on my hip. That would ordinarily have done it, but there was also the submachine gun I'd picked up as a countermeasure to the cyber-zombies. It clipped onto a two-point sling that left it dangling across my chest with the business end pointed down and to the left and immobilized against my chest via another magnetic plate. Extra magazines—for the chemical burner—and extra rounds for the Gauss gun went into more of the dump pouches on the web gear.

All told, the load wasn't too bad. It massed out at about forty kilos—enough to be uncomfortable, but it was well distributed across my entire body. In full gravity, it would slow me down, but only a little. In zero-G… well, I'd operated with heavier loads. Not into quite so dynamic an environment, but the whole point of a salvage operation was to get the important bits from one ship to another, after all.

Sarah chimed softly in my mind. *Ms. Chan is requesting a connection.*

Go, I replied.

The window opened in my vision with the avatar of Shay as she saw herself. "I'm plugged in up here, Carter," she said. "The psycho's on his way back to you. You ready?"

I shifted my weight, settling the bulk more comfortably. I really didn't like the fact that I had no second to check my gear. Standard policy—and it was standard for a reason—was to use the buddy system to make sure everything was properly secured and all the seals were tight. I supposed I could ask Korben to do it for me but trusting the guy who originally wanted to put a bullet in you as your safety backstop didn't sound like a great idea. "As ready as I can be," I muttered in response.

"Good," she replied, her voice taking on a slightly distracted note. "This AI or whatever running the counter-intrusion over there is good. Way better than any passenger liner should have, at any rate. Bit and I are trying to break it." She paused, and her avatar frowned. I had no doubt it was replicating the expressions on her coil's face. "If we can get in, I doubt we're going to have access to anything truly important." It was the first time I'd ever heard her admit that there was something she might not be able to hack her way through, and it gave me a new level of respect for the AI we were up against.

"Not a problem," I assured her, speaking the words aloud, putting more confidence into my voice than I felt. "That's where I come in."

"Where we come in," a new voice said. I hadn't noticed Korben's approach, distracted as I'd been by the conversation. He said nothing further as he began his own preparations for disembarking. They were much more minimalistic than my own. Like me, he was already wearing his vacc suit. He strapped thrusters around his waist, ankles, and wrists and put on web gear of his own. But his gear bore none of the heavy equipment I'd strapped on. Almost every available inch was covered in weapons or ammunition. A nasty-looking machine pistol of unfamiliar make rode each hip, with another pistol at the small of his back and yet *another* riding in a holster high on his chest. Dump pouches bulged with ammunition and an eight-inch fighting knife went into a sheath near his ankle. A forward-bending blade was strapped to each thigh, a distant part of my mind identifying the weapons as kukris. The man was a walking arsenal, but if I were being honest, I was glad to see it. I still didn't know how the two of us were going to manage to deal

with whatever we found on the other side of the bulkhead—
assuming Korben could survive the EVA—but half a platoon's
worth of weaponry certainly wouldn't hurt our odds.

He didn't ask me to check his gear either, I noted. Instead,
I had Sarah run diagnostics, testing all of the seals and making
sure she could connect wirelessly to every bit of gear I carried.
All systems are go, Carter, came her eventual reply.

"Are you ready?" Korben asked, echoing Shay's earlier
question.

I nodded and issued the mental command that engaged
the hood of the VaccTech suit. It flowed up over my head and
down my face, connecting at my neck. A new heads-up display
appeared in my vision, with the suit status and oxygen levels
prominently displayed. "Open the inner lock," I said.

Korben nodded, and the door in front of me beeped and
then slowly cycled, raising on silent tracks. I stepped through.
The airlock was large, designed to facilitate the rapid exit of
the assault team strapped in the back. Of course, for *really*
quick exits, they'd just depressurize the ship and throw open
the doors. It wasted a lot of oxygen, but there was no faster
way. No sense doing that at the moment—maybe if I could get
the ship on the other side stable, but the soldiers in back still
had *hours* before that was even a possibility.

I moved forward to the outer door and pulled a safety line
from the retractor integral to the suit. I snapped it in place on
a convenient ring. "Go for outer lock," I said, falling back on
procedure despite the ludicrousness of the situation.

The lights in the airlock went from clean white to sullen
red and a flashing alert popped up in my HUD. "Warning.

Warning. Depressurization imminent. Verify suit integrity. Warning. Warning."

I ran the diagnostics again, still coming back clean, but I didn't consider the time wasted. Redundancy and care could keep you alive outside. A ship full of potential cyber-zombies and world-ending plague or not, I was going to do it right.

Prepare for atmosphere evacuation. The words originated with the ship's communication network, though they came to me in Sarah's voice as she handled the integration between the ship's systems and my own. Machinery churned to life, and, at first, I could hear the faint hiss of escaping atmosphere. My heartbeat quickened. I trusted my equipment. Trusted my experience. But there was always a visceral, bowel-loosening moment when that most precious of life-supporting elements was sucked away.

The hissing faded and then ceased entirely. I could no longer hear the machinery, not in the near-vacuum of the airlock, but I could feel the faint vibrations through the hull. *Outer door cycling*, Sarah warned. With a mental command, I engaged my magnetic boots, feeling them clamp firmly to the hull. The thrust from the shuttle's engines was still giving us a simulated gravity, and whatever few molecules of air remained in the airlock wouldn't be enough to send me tumbling into space, but there was no such thing as taking too many precautions when you were standing on the precipice of the infinite.

The door in front of me slid open and I drew a deep breath of canned air as I stared out into the vastness of space. This moment, more than anything else, was what I lived for. In a life that stretched to effective immortality, you found something you loved, and could continue to love, forever. If you didn't, well, a simple DNR—do not re-coil—note in your medical files and you could find whatever final oblivion awaited. Most chose to live on, but there was a difference between lengthening life and truly living it. I suspected that for Shay, the vastness of cyberspace and the god-like power the best programmers could wield there was her raison d'être. For me it was the endless expanse, and the untold mysteries that still awaited us in their swirling depths. In that moment, I always felt a slight tingle of pity for those who had come before, those brave explorers who had broken the bounds of the Earth's atmosphere, who had dreamed and longed to go farther, to know more. But, cursed with a few scant scores of years, they could only dream.

Bound by Einstein, we still couldn't pierce the veil of reality and venture out at speeds that would take us to other solar systems, other galaxies. But we would. I knew we would, *believed* it on a level that was even deeper than knowing. And so long as Genetechnic didn't wipe my backup from existence, I'd be there to see it.

Well, assuming Bliss didn't kill us all.

As if summoned by the thought, the passenger vessel rolled into view. It was a series of toroidal disks stacked around a central spine with a bridge at the top of the spine and massive engines at the rear. Those disks were quiescent, still against the main shaft. They should have been rotating, using centripetal acceleration to simulate gravity for the passengers, since no ship that size could rely on acceleration alone like our shuttle. But they were still, the power diverted, I suspected, to the thrusters.

And, I supposed, if the passengers had already succumbed to Bliss and been turned into mindless automatons, they wouldn't much care one way or the other.

Our shuttle was maintaining a greater distance than I would have liked, but I couldn't fault the pilots. The other ship rolled, pitched, yawed, and swept through so many different axes of motion that it was almost nauseating to look at. As I watched, the ship swept closer, then seemed to fall away, almost like the surging tide of an endless black sea.

Sarah? I asked.

We had done hundreds, maybe thousands, of salvages, so I did not need to ask a more specific question. My agent understood. *The passenger vessel has begun varying the speed of its main engines and is burning both directional and primary thrusters in random intervals*, she replied. *The pilots are attempting to compensate and hold a stable relative separation, but the shuttle's agent has yet to ascertain a pattern in the other vessel's movements*. There was a pause that I always interpreted as thoughtful, though I knew it had more to do with processing delay. *I have not been able to ascertain a pattern, either.*

Great, I thought. The swim, already a near-impossible task, had just gotten that much harder. It wasn't so much the distance that was a problem. It was the rapidly changing vectors of both the vessel on which I stood and the vessel on which I wanted to land. We may all be weightless, but no matter how far you escaped the pull of gravity, mass was still mass. The hundred kilos of my current coil—to say nothing of my gear—wouldn't account for much if any part of that monstrous vessel clipped me, even at relatively slow acceleration. It would either take the offending bit with it, presupposing that it hit something like an arm or leg… or head. Or, if it hit center mass, it would send me tumbling endlessly into the deep. The only saving grace of that situation was that the energy imparted would be enough to kill me outright, sparing me the torment of a long, slow death adrift in space.

I had done many things in my lifespan. Most humans, graced with the gift of immortality, led many different lives throughout their centuries. But in all my years, I had never tried an untethered EVA swim to board a vessel that was actively trying to avoid me. Thank God the AI hadn't found a military vessel. If it had access to any kind of point defense systems, my chances would have dropped from slim to none.

"Everything okay out there?" Chan said. Her voice, echoing in the confines of my helmet, shattered the stillness of the deep. I realized I had been standing on the deck staring at the tumbling giant for…

Five minutes thirty-seven seconds, Sarah filled in helpfully.

Shit. "All good," I sent back over the comm. "Just trying to figure out the best approach." Which was true, to an extent. But what I was really doing was stalling. There *wasn't* a best approach, not for something like this. I'd have to take a literal leap of faith and then hope my reflexes and Sarah's processing power were enough to make the changes as the need arose. I drew a deep breath and commed the shuttle again, "Preparing to jump. Stand by."

Are you ready for this, Sarah? I asked my agent. It was another stall but a justifiable one.

Calculations complete, the agent replied.

Project the best vectors and needed course changes onto my heads-up display, I instructed.

There was no verbal response, but the space between me and the derelict vessel came alive with brilliant green lines. They started from me and traced their way across the gap between the shuttle and the passenger liner. For about ten meters, there was a single, stable line. Beyond that, that simple line split, forking and branching in a dozen different directions. And those branches split in turn until the paths before me resembled a writhing ball of angry serpents. Probabilities hovered in my vision as well, Sarah's attempts to codify which of the routes was the best at the given point in time. It was an indecipherable mess. And also my best hope. Like everything in life, as I got closer to the actual decision points and Sarah collected more data, the choices should narrow, and the probabilities cement themselves. The entire swim was going to be an exercise in patience coupled with the need for immediate action and split-second decisions that would mean the difference between life and death.

I drew another breath.

I jumped.

As I did, I turned over the thruster controls to Sarah, retaining only the emergency overrides. The agent had a better chance of making the necessary adjustments given that her reactions processed a hell of a lot faster than mine. But I knew from hard experience that a time would come when intuition and not logic would be necessary.

The yawning abyss opened beneath me as I leapt, pushing away from the shuttle and floating out along the glowing green line that had become the focus of my vision. I pulled my knees tight, almost to my chest, curling into a ball. At the same time, I held my arms parallel before my chest, about six inches apart. It wasn't the most comfortable position, but with thrusters at my waist, ankles, and wrists, it afforded me the most maneuverability. The thrusters were variable direction nozzles almost like what you'd find on an old hot tub, but their vectors were limited by the need to not send gouts of plasma into my body. In this configuration, the burners at my waist provided main thrust; the ones at my wrist each fired to the opposite side of the arm to which they were attached—right thruster pointed left, left thruster pointed right—giving me some control over yaw and roll; the ones at my ankles were flipped up and out, almost opposite to the vector of the waist thrusters, capable of directing their energy in such a way as to slow me down and control my pitch.

The thrusters kicked on almost immediately, adding the force of their burn to my own manually powered launch. Under Sarah's control they fired in tight microbursts, expending minimal fuel as they kept me glued to the imaginary track projected onto my vision. The first few meters went as smoothly as anything I could have hoped for. And then the cruise ship started to respond.

Its initial course changes, just like Sarah's initial projections, had been based on what I *might* do. Now that I was in flight, my possible range of actions was rapidly narrowing, and the AI knew it. My HUD became a kaleidoscope of intersecting lines as Sarah tried to counter the position changes of the cruise ship as the distance between us ticked steadily downward. Red flashes started to blink against the backdrop, places where a previously plotted trajectory was now likely to intersect with the hull of the ship. The changes were so quick, so minute as Sarah and the AI fought on a level of pure mathematics that I couldn't begin to follow, that my HUD started to strobe.

I blinked against the flashes and tightened my muscles against the acceleration as the thrusters started firing in sequences almost as chaotic as the lightshow. I was a passenger, little more, my agent in full control of the thrusters as I did my best to keep my body locked into position. I felt my stomach churning as the balance of color in the flaring trajectories glowed with more and more red.

Sarah? I asked and once again our long association allowed my agent to answer the unspecified question.

The artificial intelligence appears to have superior processing capability and responsiveness, came the curt reply. Even Sarah's "voice" echoed differently in my head, taking on a not-quite stutter and a more mechanical note as most of her resources remained bent to the task of trying to outwit the AI, leaving little to no processing power for something as mundane as human interface.

Shit. If Sarah was under that much strain, I was fucked. Which left me with two choices—sit back, enjoy the ride, and hope my agent pulled off a miracle, or take the wheel myself and inject a little bit of chaos into the structured world of the battling AIs.

It wasn't much of a choice and either one was likely to result in my sudden and violent death, but if I was going to get my shiny new coil pasted along the hull of a passenger liner, I might as well be in the driver's seat when it happened.

"Sarah," I said aloud, mostly to hear the comforting sound of a human voice, even if it was my own. "Remove all displayed trajectories except for the one that's most likely to send me bouncing off the hull."

My agent didn't respond—another sure sign that her processors were overworked trying to keep me alive. Well, we'd fix that soon enough, one way or another. But my display did clear of the confusing web of red and green. In its place was a single green line arcing across the void that slowly bled to red about halfway down its path and terminated—a most appropriate word—in a point of space that was, for the moment, unoccupied.

"Release manual control," I said to Sarah. Another indicator popped up in my HUD, this one showing me that control of the thrusters had been restored. There was no physical manifestation necessary to control them, no buttons to push or throttles to adjust. They were linked to Sarah, and through her to me. They responded to my thoughts and using them was more akin to learning how to walk again after an accident—or acclimating to a new coil for that matter—than it was to operating machinery. EVA activity had been called first walking, when it was done with tethers and magnetic boots alone, and then swimming when manually controlled thrusters came onto the scene. We still called it swimming now, centuries later, but the term had taken on new meaning. It was far more analogous to using your own muscles to move your body through water than it was to piloting a vehicle.

The distance between me and the AI-controlled vessel

steadily dwindled as I used mind and machine to keep my flight path nailed to the doomsday trajectory. I rode the steadily reddening line like a rail and a time-to-impact counter popped up of its own accord in my HUD. One minute. I held my course. Fifty seconds. Then forty. Thirty. The ship loomed in my vision, obscuring the blackness of space with the featureless gunmetal gray of its hull. The imaginary line that was my guide was now flashing red, all green long since lost. The terminal point was a blotchy red spot sliding slowly along the hull of the vessel. Appropriate.

The nose of the vessel was now clear in my view and it was swinging toward me like the mouth of some vast and ponderous fish. Throughout the entirety of the swim, my thrusters had been in the standard configuration—the two mains at my waist providing forward thrust, the two secondary at my ankles reverse thrust, and the two at my wrists lateral thrust. According to Genetechnic, the Bliss AI was a heuristic, self-learning entity. But it was also a fairly *young* entity as such things went. I was betting my life—or at least my coil—and maybe the lives of the rest of humanity, on the notion that, given the vast spectrum of data available to it, it hadn't yet learned all there was to know about man-portable extra-vehicular activity thruster packages.

When Sarah was in the driver's seat, I'd kept my body locked in a tight ball, and she'd managed the orientation and thrust without the added complexities of my limbs operating independently through their own axes of movement. Now I uncoiled, positioning my arms and legs to allow me a broader range of motion and independent control of each thruster. As I moved, the new vectors imparted spin which I countered almost subconsciously with minute thruster blasts. Then I oriented all the thrusters in the same direction. I sent the mental command and locked my muscles against the surge of acceleration.

I hadn't simply reversed thrust to try and slow my approach to the ship, though there was some angle of deceleration to the burn. Most of the power was sending me sliding lateral to my original course, moving lengthwise down the hull. The AI had the nose of the ship burning full power toward me, forcing the vessel into a turn of its own. But as the nose came closer, the rest of the vessel fell away, buying me precious seconds. The AI reacted quickly but it wasn't as simple as stopping the turn. The ship had *a lot* of mass, and maneuvering thrusters weren't designed for instantaneous shifts—the acceleration in one direction had to bleed off before a new vector could overtake it.

Unfortunately, there was more than one axis of movement. Even as I dealt with the oncoming nose of the massive vessel, the AI started to roll the ship. The spine of the ship was smooth-sided but that was a relative term. There may not have been any protruding airfoils or massive radar dishes, but the hull still had enough irregularities to turn my race along the side of the cruise ship into an obstacle course from hell.

I let my eyes lose focus, concentrating on my peripheral vision, operating more on instinct and gut than on the sensor data Sarah continued to feed me. An antenna came within a handspan of swatting me like a pesky insect. I avoided it by directing all thrusters momentarily back, filling my body with a muscle-tearing jolt of deceleration, slowing my mad rush just enough to escape the impact. A sensor dish followed, and I pirouetted past it like the world's bulkiest ballerina. The ship moved beneath me like a thing alive—a malevolent monster that wanted to crush me by flailing its body in a titanic fury of pitch, yaw, roll, and thrust. I danced along the back of the beast until, almost without warning, I felt hull brushing the soles of my boots.

I was going fast. Too fast. But I engaged the magnetic locks anyway turning all my thrusters on a vector that would simultaneously slow me further and force me down against the deck. The boots gripped the hull, sliding only a little as the thrusters pushed down on me with their not-inconsiderable power. I folded at the knees like a pre-space paratrooper, though I made no effort to roll. With my feet clamped to the deck by electromagnets, that would have broken my ankles, at the least. Instead, I crashed butt-first into the hull, hitting hard and bouncing. It was like running full speed into a wall and I felt every muscle contract as my coil tried to absorb the impact.

Without the thrusters, the landing would have been impossible, even fatal. Even with the force of their imparted vectors, the tendons in my knees screamed, first from the jarring, smashing impact of touchdown, and then from the stretch in the other direction as I bounced. The thrusters and maglocks kept me from pulling free from the hull, but the strain on my ankles and knees had me sweating and panting against the wave of pain-induced nausea that swept through me.

And then I was down, at rest relative to the motion of the

ship, locked securely in place by the magboots. I'd instinctively deactivated the thrusters when the upward—away from the ship—vector had vanished. For a moment, all I could do was stand in silence listening to my body tell me all the places I'd stressed and injured during the flight.

"Sarah?" I asked aloud. "Damage report."

You have suffered a number of contusions and strains. There are microtears likely in both your anterior cruciate ligaments and medial collateral ligaments on both legs. Your Achilles tendon on your left leg has been hyperextended. There is likely damage to your coccyx from the impact with the hull. Your...

"Enough," I said, cutting through the litany. It was only making the pain worse. I felt like shit, but I was still standing and a few exploratory bends of the knees, hips, and ankles told me that I could walk. Slowly, and with a large amount of pain, but I was still operational. Thank whatever god was watching when I got stuffed into this muscle-clad brute of a coil. My previous coil, or my original biologically issued one for that matter, would have been wrecked.

I keyed my connection with the shuttle and gave them a terse, "I'm down."

The pain must have shown in my voice because it was Shay who responded. "You okay?" There was worry in her voice. And it was *her* voice, that sultry contralto that talked me through so many missions in the past, not the baritone of the coil she currently wore. I let myself revel in the sound of it for just a moment. "Langston?"

I snapped myself from my reverie. "Yeah," I grunted. "Fine. Which is to say, my legs are pretty tore up and my ass hurts like you wouldn't believe, but still functional."

"Thank God for that," came the reply. There was a short pause and then, with a smile in her voice, Shay added, "Though the consensus here seems to be that the pain in the ass was a preexisting condition."

A little chuckle escaped my lips and the pain seemed to ease a bit. "Roger that," I replied. "Be advised, more discussion on such may be required at a later date." The tinkling laughter of her reply was like an analgesic. I drew a breath and sent mental instructions to Sarah to pull up a schematic of the ship. "I'm a bit off target," I told Shay and whomever else was listening over the shuttle channel. "Going to take a bit to get back to the bridge."

"Understood," Shay commed back. "We'll keep as close a sensor watch as we can to make sure the AI doesn't try and get cute and send anyone out to play with you."

Shit. *That* thought hadn't even occurred to me. "Thanks for that, Chan. Langston out."

I cut the comm and adjusted the strap on the submachine gun. If there was a chance of resistance, better to keep the firearm at the ready. The recoil would be interesting in the weightlessness of space, but I'd just learned the hard way that the VaccTech magboots could take a hard impact and keep their hold. And, despite what planet-bound "experts" might think, the chemical burner would shoot just fine in vacuum. The powder was a direct descendant of good old-fashioned gunpowder and contained its own oxidizer to fuel the burn.

I held the weapon at the low ready and willed one boot to release. Then it was step forward, engage. Release the other foot. Step forward. Engage. And on and on. The distance wasn't terrible in terms of absolute meters but untethered against the hull of a wildly maneuvering ship, I wasn't about to take any risks.

It was going to be a long march.

24

"They're coming!" Shay's voice snapped into my helmet.

The words jolted me from the monotonous focus of shuffling along the deck and I cursed silently. Maneuvering along the surface of the ship as it continued its random maneuvers had taken far more concentration than I'd hoped. Twice, I'd almost been thrown free of the vessel as it executed a maneuver at just the wrong time, catching me mid-stride and pulling hard against the magnetic attraction of my boot. The second time, the boot had actually come free, and it was only quick work with the thrusters that got me back to the surface and locked in. I was well past bingo fuel and close to bleeding into the reserves. The rapid course changes of my arrival coupled with the near constant burns I'd had to make even while walking across the deck—in order to mitigate the ship maneuvers—had left me wondering if I had enough left to even make the few dozen meters separating me from the bridge. The last thing I needed was to try and fight my way through some Bliss-altered meat-puppets.

But it looked like that was exactly what I was going to have to do.

I'd had Sarah focused on running the thrusters, but at the ping from Shay, my agent interfaced once more with the helmet sensors and red reticules popped into my vision, each one marking the position of an enemy combatant making their way out onto the deck. Sarah didn't have all the data—but she could tap into the shuttle's sensors and provide me with a much clearer picture than I could get with the naked eye alone. They were coming from an airlock just aft of the bridge. A half-dozen had already made their way onto the deck and I could see more emerging from the ship.

"I got problems here," I said over the comm as I shuffle-stepped my way to a protruding antenna array. It wasn't much of a barrier, but at least it offered some obstacle to the Blissful headed my way. "Fuck, there's a lot of them."

"Working on it," came Shay's terse reply. "I've almost got the doors. I was hoping to give us an easy entry so you wouldn't have to cut your way in. Gonna have to go the other route now and slag all of them."

Her voice had taken on that tone of distracted and conversational that she got when she was deep into a hack. She wasn't really looking for a response. Hell, she might not have been aware that she was talking at all. She was working her way through a problem, and I hoped to God that she'd figure it out. In the meantime, I had my own problems to worry about.

I shouldered the submachine gun and knelt on the deck, keeping both knees and the toes of both boots in contact. I activated the magnetized locks in the knees of the suit and suddenly found myself with a four-point stabilized firing position. I rested the barrel of the firearm against the antenna and lined up the sights.

Just in time to see the suited head of the first cyber-zombie explode in an oddly entrancing expansion of gore.

I spared a quick glance into the deep where, just under five hundred meters away, the shuttle hung. In response to a silent query, Sarah popped open a window in my vision, showing the airlock of the shuttle. The outer doors were open and Korben lay prone out on the deck, massive rifle stretched out before him. A flash filled the window as he pulled the trigger again, and in my actual field of vision, another body dropped.

I hadn't been aware of it on a conscious level, but the maneuvering of the ship had eased. Not stopped, not entirely, but instead of shaking like a wet dog, the vessel was making broad turns and rolls. My own footing was a lot more stable—and so was the footing of the nano-infected, but the reduced maneuvers were apparently giving the assassin enough of a window to lend some support. The shuttle was obviously maneuvering on its own, trying to keep the same relative position and keep me in sight. Even so, the accuracy Korben was demonstrating—firing at a man-sized target five hundred meters away from a moving platform *at* a moving platform—was nothing short of preternatural. I realized in that moment just how lucky Shay and I had been to escape his sights in our first encounter.

But I didn't have time to dwell on earlier attempts on my life—not when another was well under way. The AI, realizing perhaps that its soldiers were slow-moving ducks for fire from the shuttle, had resumed its wet-dog shake. I couldn't tell if Korben was still firing—there were no more exploding zombies, no convenient sparks to let me see a near miss. No sound. If Korben was still shooting, even his skill couldn't overcome the wildly shifting vectors.

The cyber-puppets had closed to about twenty meters making a slow, methodical progression across the hull. I couldn't tell how many there were, or if they were still pouring from the airlock. I wasn't in a position where I could retreat or evade the perambulatory coils in any way, so I only had one option. I started servicing the trigger, firing single aimed shots at the creatures as they made their way forward.

Sarah helped, interfacing with the submachine gun, my helmet systems, even my standard-issue Mark I eyeball. She dropped prioritized targeting reticules into my vision, complete with projected points of aim based on the motion of the incoming bad guys. The reticules were all positioned high on the targets, away from the traditional—and far more targetable— center mass. I knew from experience—or rather, my branch's experience—that these things didn't respond to conditions that were normally fatal to a standard coil. Sarah and I had the same thought—the best way to take them down was to destroy the core or the brain, either of which should disrupt the nerves enough to render movement impossible. Tear all the electrical wiring out of a machine, and it didn't matter if it was still getting power—that power had nowhere to go.

I squeezed the trigger six times in rapid succession, sending three rounds into each of the first two targets in Sarah's priority list. Even with the help from my agent, the first two shots went too low, slamming into the upper chest area of the approaching zombie. The third struck home, punching through the polarized visor of the helmet. There was a puff of escaping atmosphere coupled with floating gobbets of blood and flesh that I didn't want to think on too much. The coil stopped moving at once, corpse clinging to the deck like a lamprey by virtue of its own magnetic boots.

My second volley fared better, the second round striking priority two in the throat and the third round taking off the top of its head. Another motionless corpse tacked down to the surface of the ship.

A sudden burn from the vessel's thrusters surged to life and I felt the maglocks in the VaccTech suit stretch to the breaking point as my right boot pulled free from the deck. The zombies reacted with an almost prescient awareness, reaching to lock their arms around any available supports. It wasn't prescience, I realized, but something closer to *omniscience*. The cyber-zombies reacted as if they knew the maneuver was coming because they *did* know the maneuver was coming. They were connected to the AI, and what it knew, they knew. Networked.

It still didn't save them all.

Another pair of the advancing drones were pulled free from the hull entirely, losing their grips on the makeshift handholds. One got ejected from the deck, flying away from the vessel in a long, graceful arc. The other fared worse, colliding with a sensor array as the ship rolled. The results were instant and very messy.

As the ship settled onto its new vector, at least momentarily, I took advantage of the lull to clamp my boot firmly back to the deck. As an added precaution, I pulled the integrated tether cord from the VaccTech and lashed it around the array behind which I was taking cover. Six bad guys down—two each for me, Korben, and the AI's own maneuvering.

Sarah, I thought. *Target estimate?*

There are currently twelve enemy combatants within sensor range, the agent informed me, mental voice insufferably calm. I felt a surge of panic at the words as I continued to service targets. Four rounds to drop my third target. Range to target four down to ten meters. Three rounds. I couldn't smell the burning cordite, couldn't hear the reports. I could feel the recoil, mild even without the kinetic-reactive fibers of the VaccTech doing their best to mitigate it. The entire thing was eerily surreal, a mass of slow-moving bodies inching their way unflinchingly into the hail of fire that I was spewing forth, closing the distance centimeter by bloody centimeter. There had to be hundreds, maybe thousands of passengers aboard that liner, and I knew that as long as the AI was willing to keep throwing bodies at me, I was doomed. Even if I could manage to keep them off me with weight of fire alone—and I couldn't—I'd run out of bullets before they ran out of coils.

"Little help, here," I said into the comm. "Awful lot of bad guys headed my way."

"Almost there," Shay replied, and I could hear the strain in her voice. "This fucker's good," she added. "The underlying systems of the passenger liner are shit. I could crack them in my sleep. But the AI is really, really good."

"Understood," I replied, putting more lead downrange. The enemy was getting smarter, weaving back and forth as they went, making it that much harder to get the requisite throat or head shot to take out the core.

I wasn't even seeing targets anymore, not as distinct things. Just a wave of bodies that crept steadily closer. My chamber clicked empty and I executed a reload without conscious thought, but even in those few moments, the distance closed by another meter. I brought the weapon back in line and dropped another cyber-puppet, this one only three meters from me. They were close enough now that accuracy was becoming less of a problem, but even as slow as they moved, another meter or two and they'd be in lunging range. I'd have to abandon my position and try to fall back. That or try to fight them hand to hand.

"Got it!" Shay exulted over the comm. "All hatches are now sealed. I had to completely slag the controls to prevent the stupid AI from just opening them again, but no one else is coming off that ship until someone cuts a hole in it."

There was a note of triumph in her voice that I could appreciate… but I was just a little bit busy. There were still coils moving in front of me, weaving through the corpses stuck to the deck by virtue of their own magnetic boots like a pack of downhill slalom skiers. My chamber clicked empty again and I dropped the magazine, slamming another one home and dropping the bolt. The press had brought the closest to only a couple of meters and I was out of time.

Sarah, I thought frantically as I tried to keep my aim steady and breath under control against the wave of slowly advancing death, *what's the length of the integrated tether on the VaccTech?*

Fifteen meters, Carter.

Good enough. I sent the mental command to release the magnet on my knees and pushed myself to my feet. Even as I did so, a coil came lurching around the breastwork of bodies.

It must have demagnetized both its boots because it pushed off the deck, both legs launching itself with arms outstretched before it. Both my feet were still firmly locked in place and I used that connection to pull myself down even faster than I'd stood, yanking my body out of the way with enough force that my bruised ass bounced off the deck a second time. The outstretched fingers brushed the head of my helmet, but not even an AI-controlled, nanite-infused coil could ignore the laws of Newton. The coil was in motion and it stayed that way, hurtling past me and toward the aft of the vessel. Maybe it would find a handhold somewhere; maybe the ship's maneuvers would crush it like a bug. And maybe the poor bastard would miss both of those possibilities and continue on to drift through the endless deep. Normally that was a limited proposition—coils were limited by their air supply. I had no idea how long whatever intelligence was housed in the nanite network could function under those conditions.

Nor did I care. I was back on my feet and doing my own zombie-like shuffle aft as soon as the fingers cleared me. Demagnetize. Step. Re-engage. Repeat. The same process that brought me here, only in reverse. I kept up a steady barrage of fire as I went, not even consciously aiming anymore, just tracking the barrel toward the aim point that Sarah dropped into my vision. My field of fire was crowded with obstacles, the upright bodies of the fallen serving as cover for the enemy still making their way forward. At a mental command, Sarah popped up a counter into my HUD displaying how many meters of the VaccTech's integrated tether remained to me. Twelve meters. I double-tapped a coil, one in the upper chest, one through the face. It danced a macabre dance, body spasming as its feet remained glued to the deck. Ten meters. Another got close enough to launch itself into a lunge and there was no ducking this one. I punched the submachine gun forward, jabbing the barrel straight between the reaching arms of the bio-missile that was the cyber-zombie. I felt the hands latch onto my shoulders as the barrel contacted the top of the suited helmet. I squeezed the trigger, taking the contact shot.

The hands immediately went slack, but the impact knocked me from my feet. I felt another screaming protest from my knees and ankles as the magnetic boots fought the mass of the now-corpse. Both boots tore momentarily free and I skidded along the deck for a few meters until I could once again get the soles into surface contact. The dead coil bounced away into the deep.

Five meters.

I was almost at the literal end of my rope. The hit from the coil had bought me some space, our tangled flight moving us more quickly than I'd managed in the careful cadence of EVA. I was aware on a distant level of Shay's panicked shouts over the comm, but I couldn't take the time to reassure her that I was all right. I felt a surge of pain through my legs and back as I used the butt of the submachine gun to lever myself back to my feet. Well, maybe not all right, but still functional, anyway.

I took time to do a quick survey of the field, unconsciously doing another reload as I scanned the enemy. Still a half-dozen of them, maybe more and closing fast. I felt a twist of despair somewhere deep in my guts. I was battered, bruised, and I could hear the harsh panting of my breath. I had no idea how many magazines I'd burned or what loadout I had left, and

I doubted it was going to matter. It was going to be down to hand to hand any minute, and tether or not, I was screwed.

As I was raising my weapon, readying myself for a last stand, a tight ball of death burst into the midst of the ambulatory coils. It fell in from the void, a patch of darkness to rival space itself were it not for the points of blue and orange thrust spurting from its ankles, wrists, and waist. At the last possible moment before impact, the ball uncoiled into the form of Korben. He hit the deck lightly, gracefully where I had bounced, showing a control of his body and gear that even after *lifetimes* of doing salvage work, I couldn't possibly compete with.

His hands flashed silver in the helmet lights. No. Not his hands. In each fist he clenched a long, forward-bending knife maybe eighteen inches from hilt to tip. He exploded into motion, kukris blurring and everywhere he struck a limb or head separated from a body. It was like watching the galaxy's goriest ballet—and watch was all that I could do. I knew how to run the submachine gun and with Sarah's help, I was a better than decent shot. There was still no way in hell that I was good enough to send rounds into the center of that maddened melee without a risk of hitting Korben.

Besides, it didn't look like he needed my help. He moved with the precision of someone in an Earth-standard gravity well, something I would have considered all but impossible if I wasn't watching it unfold before my stunned eyes. And yet, he still took advantage of the fact that he *wasn't* in that gravity well, using the action-reaction realities of vacuum to imbue himself with a deadly and flowing grace that was as beautiful to watch as it was horrifying.

Freed momentarily from concern for my own ass, I checked the numbers. I'd guessed a half-dozen, but there had, in fact, been eight remaining. The closest had been within a few meters of me—and would have been closer if not for my bouncing journey along the hull. The farthest, no more than ten meters. Korben landed in a knot of three or four and had them down in a matter of seconds. He moved so fast I had difficulty understanding what was happening, but in those first few seconds, two of the four lost their heads entirely and the other pair suffered wounds sufficient to leave them pinned by their magboots to the deck, the only motion imparted from the movement of the ship itself.

That had been the opening seconds and the coil that had been lurching toward me was only partway into its turn to address the new—and clearly bigger—threat when Korben hit him. He mirrored the maneuver the AI had tried on me, launching himself smoothly from the deck, body straightening out behind him, blades extended. Only, where the cyber-zombies had been dumb-fired missiles, Korben was a shark. And that shark had teeth. He didn't so much *hit* the coil as he *overflew* it, and as he did so, his blades went to work. As he passed the creature, his thrusters fired, spinning him into the air and turning him through a smooth flip that brought his boots firmly back in contact with the deck.

Behind him, the pressurized blood from another decapitated corpse fountained into space.

My comm buzzed to life. Korben's urbane voice said, "If you wouldn't mind dealing with the other three…"

I snapped from my reverie, looking past the assassin who

had dropped to the hull like some dark avenging angel. Three more coils, these now a half-dozen meters out, were still closing in, the artificial intelligence behind them either failing to live up to the latter part of its name or with more than enough resources at hand to throw a few away in a low-percentage attempt at stopping us. I brought my weapon back in line and Sarah obligingly returned the aiming reticule to my vision. Half a dozen rounds later, it was done.

"Fuck," I said succinctly, but with passion.

"I suppose we should have anticipated that as a likely response," Korben agreed.

"You think?" I hurt pretty much all over, but my legs, or more specifically, my knees and ankles, were *screaming*. The nanites in my bloodstream were at work, doing what they could to repair the damage and deaden the pain. Without them and without the, let's call it, *ruggedness* of my present coil, I doubted I'd be able to stand, much less walk. I silently hoped that the AI had disengaged the artificial gravity shipboard. If we had to fight more, and who was I kidding, we *would* have to fight more, it would complicate things. But I wasn't sure my limbs were up to taking the full weight of my coil.

"You okay over there?" It was Shay, breaking into the channel.

I grunted. "We're fine. Cavalry showed up just in time. Still have to make our way to the bridge, though." I shook my head as I directed Sarah to route Korben into the channel. "How the hell are we going to deal with the fact that it's going to take me a few hours to cut through the hull? The damn AI's just going to flood the area with more co-opted passengers. When I cut through, there's going to be a fucking army. Maybe with the boys and girls on the shuttle we can cut our way through them, but just the two of us? I get that choppy here," I gestured at Korben, though there was no way for Shay to see it, "can probably hold the door like a Spartan at Thermopylae, but I doubt we'll be able to force our way through the hole in the first place."

"Never fear, Mr. Langston," Korben replied, his voice cool and untroubled on the speakers of my helmet. "Genetechnic foresaw the potential difficulty. I have a… let's call it a party favor…" I couldn't see his face, but I heard the insufferable, patronizing smile in his voice. "I'm confident I'll be able to clear us a bridgehead long enough to secure a choke point." I heard that damn smile again. "Though, if you do not mind, I will likely use my firearms and not the kukris to hold it."

"Yeah. Sounds great," I muttered. "And how the hell did you get over here and do your ninja routine, anyway?" I asked. "I've never seen anyone move like that. Why did you need me at all?" It was maybe not the best question to be asking an assassin who'd already had one set of orders to take me out.

"Talk as we walk, Mr. Langston," Korben said as he put action to his words, spinning with a grace that defied the magnetic locks of his boots. I had no idea how he accomplished it, and I made no effort to try and duplicate it. My legs were in bad enough shape already. "As to how I made it here and why I needed you to go first…" He trailed off and I could make out the barest shrug from beneath his form-fitting vacc suit. "Well, it's simple enough, I suppose. My own agent is more… sophisticated than most. It's also more directly interfaced into my nervous system." I suppressed a shudder at that. It sounded far too close to what the Bliss nano-virus was doing to the coils we'd left pegged to the deck. "Its heuristic capabilities are also… considerable."

"Damn," Shay whispered in my ear. I'd kept her on the channel and she was clearly paying attention to our conversation. "He used his agent to learn how to EVA just by watching you." There was a note of awe in her voice, and well there should be. Motor skill transference had been possible for quite a while, but it required direct neural interface with computers far more sophisticated than agents, not to mention weeks of time investment. And even then, you only developed the muscle memory. You still had to hone those abilities to actually obtain the fine edge of the practiced professional. To truly understand what, and why, you were doing what you were doing. Or so I'd thought.

"Not quite, Ms. Chan," Korben replied. "But close. More accurate to say that by watching Mr. Langston make his transition my agent was able to analyze his strategy and apply it. Allowing my agent direct control of not just my thrusters but also my muscular response gave me enough of an edge to make the crossing safely. And, to be fair, the ship's maneuvers had significantly decreased in volatility by the time I made my own swim."

I resisted the urge to shake my head, not wanting to give the assassin a visual cue as to just how creeped out I was by his calm acceptance of allowing his agent to take full control. I'd given Sarah reign over my thrusters, but my actual body? I wasn't entirely sure if Sarah had that capability, and I damn sure wasn't eager to experiment. Wasn't that exactly what we were trying to stop Bliss from doing?

We made the rest of the journey in silence, shuffling along the hull until we once again neared the bridge at the bow of the vessel. I ignored the airlock doors—it would have been much easier to cut through them, but there would be a second set of doors for the interior airlock. Opening the outer doors to a tightly packed group of cyber-zombies, no matter what surprises Korben might have in store, with a second door to cut through seemed like a bad play.

"Here," I said at last, stopping at a point about three meters below the front viewport.

"Not the window itself?" Korben asked.

I winced at the word window. Typical planet-bound thinking. It was nice to be reminded that, no matter how skilled he was in his own area of expertise, the killer didn't know much when it came to ships. "Not the window," I confirmed. "It would be easier to cut through, though not by as much as you might expect. That transparasteel is tough stuff. Not as tough as the hull, of course, or they'd just make the damn ship out of it and paint it, but not easy. But more importantly, it's designed to display information directly, serving as both a 'window,'" I resisted the urge to make air quotes, "and a display screen."

"And?"

"And," Shay chimed in, "cutting fiber-optic relays and generally mucking about with the circuitry shipboard when you don't know what you're doing is a bad idea."

"Very bad," I agreed. "So, we cut here." I tapped the hull. "I looked up the engineering records for this class of vessel. This will drop us right onto the bridge without damaging anything important." This time I did shake my head. "But it's going to take time. And the fucking AI is going to be filling the space with bodies."

"Impressive," Korben said. "It is always nice to work with professionals. Very well, Mr. Langston. Begin your cutting. And let me worry about what we might find on the other side. I assure you, I am every bit the professional as well."

25

It took almost four hours.

I was focused on the task at hand. Despite my somewhat cavalier response to Korben's earlier question, no part of a civilian ship's hull was entirely free of important subsystems. Cubage was the ultimate limiter in starships, and no ship designer could afford to waste space. It would be more accurate to say that, with proper cutting, I could avoid *critical* systems and hope that the ship's computer hadn't been so completely co-opted by Bliss that it would prevent the automatic rerouting that *should* happen.

The work was slow, methodical, and physically punishing. The only saving grace was that it gave enough time for my own nanites to do their job, and by the time I sent the command to Sarah to deactivate the plasma cutter, I could stand without pain. I wasn't at a hundred percent—a long way from it—but I was far more functional than I had been. Neither Shay nor Korben had bothered me while I worked, cognizant of the concentration I was exercising. I had no doubt that Shay was still waging her own battle, fighting on a field of radio waves and electrons as she tried to squeeze out any advantage her unique skillset could afford us. Korben... I had no idea what the hell the assassin was doing. As far as I could tell, he hadn't moved. At all. For four hours. He'd just stood there, a presence felt over my shoulder, statue-like against the emptiness. He might as well have been a gargoyle perched on the edge of the ship.

Or one of the corpses we'd left behind.

I realized that the starscape around me was moving, spinning. Somewhere along the line, the AI had resumed the rotation of the passenger liner's disks. It took me only a moment to realize why. The march along the hull had shown that we—humans, that is—were better in zero-G than the Bliss-infected. The artificial intelligence had sacrificed thrust to put itself in a better position to deal with us. It was waiting, in all the comforts of gravity, to finish what it had started on the hull.

I drew a slow, steadying breath and reflexively asked, *Sarah, oxygen levels?*

Currently at fifty-two percent, the agent replied.

Good enough. If we needed more than another four hours for whatever was to happen on the ship, we'd be in more trouble than we could handle anyway. I sent the mental command to transmit and said, "I'm through."

"We've got problems," Shay responded at once. "I got control of the interior cameras. Only for a few seconds before the AI locked me out. Shut them down and slagged them, really, just like I did to the doors. Sending video."

The feed that popped up in my field of vision was only a few seconds long. It showed the bridge of the cruise ship. I could tell it was the bridge, because no matter the size or configuration of a ship, all command decks had a certain sameness. I could tell that it was the bridge of *this* ship by the army of suited statue-like forms waiting with the endless patience of a machine for me to finish cutting my way through the hull. The bridge was small for such a large vessel, surprisingly so for those unfamiliar with space flight, a rough rectangle measuring twelve meters by nine.

Sarah, how many? I asked my agent. She'd have a much better chance of getting an accurate count from the video presented.

One hundred and twenty-seven, came the immediate reply. *Estimates indicate that more could fit into the space,* she added.

"Leaving room for the actual fighting," I muttered aloud.

"That's what we think up here, too," Shay replied.

"Well, Korben?" I asked. The assassin still hadn't stirred. Still hadn't spoken. I was beginning to wonder if his oxygen supply had quietly run out an hour or so ago and I'd been hanging out with a corpse. "There's a plan for this, right? If not, we're fucked."

The polarized mask of the vacc suit swiveled my way. "No need for such language, Mr. Langston," he said as if he *hadn't* been sitting there as motionless as the cyber-zombies for the past four hours. "And yes, there is a plan." There was a long pause. The man was hard enough to read without the faceplate, but something about that pause held the faintest air of trepidation. Or maybe I was just projecting my own feelings, which burned right past trepidation and were on a collision course with full-blown panic. "I will acknowledge there are a few more than I was anticipating. But it should still work."

"Great," I whispered. There was silence from Shay and the

rest of the Genetechnic security team aboard the shuttle who were, presumably, listening in. There was no way the shuttle could get close enough to the ship for a boarding action without us taking control of the helm. And unless Korben's plan could thin out the herd significantly—and *without* damaging the equipment I needed to bring the ship under my control instead of the AI's—there was no way that was happening. "Your show," I said at last.

He was studying the rough oval I'd burned into the hull. It was approximately a meter wide and a little bit taller. I hadn't pulled the plug of hull from the hole yet and I'd been giving it a bit of a wide berth in case the AI decided it was tired of waiting and came boiling out from the entrance we'd made. But it seemed content to wait, knowing, perhaps, that the only way we'd be able to gain a foothold against so many was by employing a powerful explosive, eliminating any chance of mission success. Some part of me knew that the people—the *real* part of the people—associated with those coils were already gone, erased by Bliss. Somewhere, they were in a queue to be re-coiled. Maybe they were walking around already. But another part of me struggled with the slaughter. The lives may not have been lost, not by modern standards, but the pain and loss had been real. And now we were going to have to inflict more, take more, of it. It made my stomach churn and I swallowed hard against the unexpected surge of bile that rose in my gorge.

"Can you pull it open about six inches and then close it again?" Korben asked. "And seal it?"

"How long does the seal have to hold?" I asked.

"Three minutes," he replied.

I considered it. I'd cut through the hull with a beveled edge, mostly from habit rather than conscious thought, allowing the section I'd cut out to be reseated easily enough. Sealing it was another matter. I could tack it with the torch, but I got the impression that once Korben started the party, a certain degree of haste would be called for, and the plasma cutter would take a few minutes. My standard gear included a couple of industrial-strength adhesives and expanding foams, mostly to try and stop small atmosphere leaks before they became major issues. One of the adhesives only took a few seconds to do its thing. It wouldn't hold against any real force for long, but it would probably manage three minutes against whatever Bliss could reasonably throw at it.

"Yeah," I said. "I think that's workable."

I reoriented myself physically and mentally, walking around until I stood "above" the hole I'd cut relative to Korben's position. I braced a foot on either side of the cut and pulled a pair of magnetic clamps from the VaccTech. They snapped to the hull, and I concentrated for a moment, until the image in my head switched from me standing on the "wall" of the ship at a ninety-degree angle to me looking down at my handiwork, like looking down on a manhole cover. The mental gymnastics was an old spacer trick—we'd been operating in micro and zero gravity for a long time, but as a species, we'd spent a hell of a lot longer at the bottom of a gravity well. The body still responded better when it had the proper frame of reference. Now, all I had to do was a little bit of a deadlift, control the acceleration of the mass, and then put the plug back in place and tack it down.

"Ready," I said.

Korben retrieved something from a pocket, a device that looked suspiciously like a grenade. I thought briefly of warning him against its use, but I doubted that his vaunted plan would be something so simple. I wasn't given the time to question anyway as he depressed a button and said, "Now."

I didn't heave. Heaving in zero gravity was a sure way to make certain that I wouldn't be able to reverse the acceleration of the plug and that trying to do so might well pull me free of the deck. Instead, I applied steady upward—relative to my mindset, anyway—pressure. For a moment, the cut-off section of hull didn't budge, but I was expecting that. I increased the pressure slowly, bringing the powerful muscles of the coil to bear. My ankles and knees shot little warning flares of alarm, reminding me that nanites or not, the damage I'd taken on making it to the ship hadn't fully healed, but the pain was bearable. After about fifteen seconds of carefully ratcheting up the force, the hull section began to move.

It would continue on its own, of course, but speed was of the essence, so I kept accelerating it for another inch. Then, when it was maybe three inches clear of the hull, I started to reverse the process, pushing back down, but slowly, evenly, trying to bring the plate to rest. If the enemy gathered within wanted, they could make a hash of the plan, but they seemed content to wait for us to come to them.

The second he had clearance, Korben slipped the oblong object that I was still fervently hoping *wasn't* a grenade through the opening. "Close it," he directed, voice as calm and still as deep space. He needn't have bothered. I was already shoving down, hard. I used as much force as my boots could withstand and the plate made contact far more quickly than it had risen. Then I was pulling the adhesive from my belt and spraying it liberally along the cut. It hardened rapidly and I had no worries about using too much. I never carried an adhesive for which there wasn't an equally effective solvent and I could get the glue off just as fast as I applied it.

Task done, I stared for a moment at the resealed door. Then I turned to Korben, who had gone back to a state of almost preternatural stillness. "Do you mind telling me what the hell we just did?" I asked, trying hard to make it a question and not a demand.

"Targeted nano-virus," he said, still not moving and not offering any more information.

"Shay?" I asked.

There was a brief silence on the comm and I could clearly see Shay's thoughtful frown, if only in my mind's eye. "Genetechnic created a hunter-killer nano-virus to seek out people infected with the Bliss virus and eliminate those nanites," she said at last. "Or, at least that's what I think he's saying. It raises some questions, though."

"Like if you have a targeted nano-virus, what the hell are we doing here?" I asked, glaring at the assassin. He wouldn't be able to see it through my own polarization, but it felt good anyway. "Why not just launch the damn virus into the ship and call it a day?"

"Three reasons," the killer replied, and this time he went so far as to turn his head in my direction.

"Which are?" I asked.

"One: Genetechnic was unable to manufacture the nanites in sufficient quantity to be certain of the destruction of the... infection. Two: the efficacy of the nano-virus could not be verified. Which means had we done as you suggested, there would be no guarantees of success." He stopped, and I had to give Genetechnic at least a little bit of credit. Those did seem like good reasons, but at the very least, they could have infected the ship first and *then* sent in a team. Of course, it begged the question...

"And third?" I asked.

"You already know the answer to that, Mr. Langston. If there is anything to be salvaged from this debacle, it's our job to try and salvage it. We cannot make that determination unless and until we board the vessel."

That sounded more like the corporations I knew and loved.

"Bloody wonderful," I muttered. "How long?"

"A few minutes. The amount of virus I had should be sufficient to clear out the bridge. The fact that the infected are suited may slow the process down, but the nanites are designed to infiltrate suits. The AI programmers at Genetechnic were all confidant that Bliss would pull back and isolate the area for fear of further contamination buying us a few minutes to make our entry." His voice was so dry on the last sentence that it could have soaked up oceans. Apparently, the assassin had as much trust in the "experts" who *didn't* have their collective asses on the line as I did. But without visual access inside, we didn't have many options but to wait and hope for the best.

Sarah tracked the time and at precisely three minutes, Korben spoke. "That should be long enough." He moved to a spot adjacent to me, though giving me enough room to clear a section of ship hull. Those blades, seeming almost to shine with a silver light of their own, had reappeared in his hands. "No need to be so circumspect with the hatch removal this time, Mr. Langston. Speed is of the essence. As soon as you clear it, I'll drop in and see what we're dealing with. You showed a certain degree of aptitude on the hull of the vessel. Follow or not, as you will. Your assistance might prove useful." Though the words were almost insulting, I sensed that, for the assassin, they were a great compliment indeed.

"Great," I said. I took the few seconds to ensure a fresh magazine was loaded into the submachine gun before pulling out the solvent. "Ready?" I asked. I got a nod in response and immediately began applying the solvent. It dissolved the glue as fast as I could spread it and in short order I was once again crouched with one leg on either side of the hull section, ready to lift. I sent Sarah a mental ping to display a three-second countdown and transmit it to Korben. Then I gave the go order and drew a deep breath. The seconds ticked down... three... two... one. As the counter hit zero, I lifted as smoothly and quickly as my hull connection would allow.

This time there was no need to try and decelerate the mass, and at the apex of the lift, I simply released it, letting it drift off into the deep. Korben didn't even wait that long, moving through the opening with a sinuous grace as soon as it was large enough to fit his body. I was one, maybe, two seconds behind him.

I dropped into a scene of horror.

I was aware, vaguely, of Korben pushing his way toward

the hatch leading into the bridge. I was as vaguely aware that we *were* on the bridge. But neither thought could intrude much past the edges of my attention.

As soon as we'd passed the hull of the ship, the artificial gravity had taken hold. The bridge's atmosphere had been vented before I'd ever started cutting—I'd known that the minute I'd punched through the hull without the fanfare of escaping gasses. I'd prepared myself for the drop into gravity but had forgotten the strain my limbs had suffered and failed to take into account the extra weight of gear and ammo that I carried. The impact had taken me by surprise, and when I'd risen…

On the hull, we'd fought our way through dozens of the Bliss-infected passengers and crew of the cruise ship. As we'd dealt with them, their bodies had remained tacked to the deck by the power of the magnetic locks of their boots. I'd had to walk through that forest of corpses, bodies moving with the attitude changes of the ship. Dead weight, or maybe, dead weightless. That had been bad enough. This was worse. Far worse.

Whatever compound Korben had released hadn't killed the coils. Hadn't been designed to do so, I supposed. Chan had called them hunter-killer nanites. They had been designed to target the Bliss nanites themselves, and while I knew from once-removed personal experience that Bliss could push a coil past the bounds of what we considered traditional death, it was very clear now that it didn't *cause* that death. Not in and of itself. The coils before me, now cleansed of the Bliss nanites that had infected them, were still very much alive. In my head, I'd been thinking of the Bliss-infected as zombies, but maybe drones would have been a better word—mindless automatons bound to the will of the hive mind. What waited for us on that bridge in the wake of Korben's cleansing nano-virus were zombies of a different sort.

They stood in their dozens, suited bodies at rest save for those thousands of minute adjustments we all make every second to maintain balance. Adjustments that are so commonplace, we don't see them in ourselves, much less each other. At least, not when the adjuster is a living, breathing, *thinking* being. The formerly infected may have met the technical definition of the first two categories, but a single glance through their helmet visors and into their dead, soulless eyes threw any thoughts of… well, *thought* right out of the airlock. There was something about them, something about standing in their midst, that was far more disconcerting than their fellows' mad charge into my bullets. I didn't have a frame of reference for the feeling, but I was reminded of old, old entertainment vids where the protagonists seemed disconcerted about being alone in a cemetery. I hadn't understood their fears, but now, standing among the not-quite dead, I could appreciate it on an entirely different level.

"Damn," the whisper came over the comm, Shay breathing the word in an almost reverent susurration of breath.

"If you could be about the matter at hand," Korben's dry words sliced through my shock like a plasma cutter. I tore my attention away from the… dead? Whatever they were, they weren't a threat, and I'd come here with a job to do. Korben had taken up a position just inside the only hatch leading onto the bridge, machine pistol held in one hand and one of his silvery kukris in the other. The door was shut. For the moment.

"Do you have control over the interior hatches?" I asked

Shay over the comm, and I started threading my way through the coils. It was like they were in some sort of standby mode. They didn't get out of my way, but if I bumped one—a situation I was trying like hell to avoid, but there were so damn many of them—it staggered a bit and then regained its balance.

"Negative," she said. "When that bitch of an AI lost control of the outer airlocks, she made damn sure I couldn't use the same ploy on the interior." There was a brief pause, followed by a grudging, "I'm locked out. I don't think I'm going to be able to do anything remotely. Maybe if I can get plugged into a physical access port."

I winced at that, but kept my mouth shut. The shuttle was probably safer than the ship, but it wasn't my job to keep Shay safe. I suspected she'd have rather strong words for me if I tried. "Roger that," was all the reply I gave. "Making my way to the consoles now. Tell the security team to make ready. This shouldn't take long."

There was no warning. One moment I was making my way to a console, carrying on a conversation with Shay while Korben waited by the door, and in the next the assassin exploded into motion. It took me a moment to realize that the hatch to the bridge had slid upward on silent tracks and that the Bliss-infected had returned. In force.

"Sooner would be better," Korben hissed through the comm as the initial creature through the door lost its head to a well-timed swing of a blade. He braced himself in front of the door, pistol in his left hand, firing with the eerie silence of vacuum.

I put the tableau from my mind. I wanted to help the assassin but the two of us had no real chance against the horde. Not with dozens more waiting to take the place of each one that fell. Whatever the assassin's nanite package had accomplished, its effects clearly didn't linger. The infected charging in showed no signs of being slowed. Our only chance was for me to do what I'd come here to do—gain control over the maneuvering thrusters and right the ship so that the security force could come crashing onto the bridge. If I failed in that, it wouldn't matter how many coils Korben stacked. We'd fall in the end.

I found myself before the pilot's chair, not really conscious of the last few strides it took me to get there. I moved with urgency but not haste. What I had to do wasn't overly difficult—mankind had possessed low-grade artificial intelligences before spaceflight became commonplace. And we'd always harbored a fear that our creations would rise against us, popularized more through fiction than fact. As a result, most systems had some measure of override, some ability to restore manual—which was to say, human—control. So the task before me wasn't *difficult*. But it *was* complicated. And hasty work made for poor results.

I spared the pilot's station only a single glance as I dropped down to the deck before it. It should have been showing the various astrogation readouts and course and navigation data. It wasn't. Instead, it showed an emergency lockout screen. Which was as expected. If Bliss had left the pilot's station—or any other station, for that matter—alone, regaining control would have been a matter of a few keystrokes. But the stations were, of course, wired into the ship's computer, which, in turn, had been hijacked by Bliss. I doubted the engineers had considered this specific scenario: an external artificial intelligence that infiltrated via nano-virus and co-opted the ship's systems. But they *had* considered the notion that the ship's own rudimentary AI might go haywire and act against the crew, including locking them out of their stations. And they'd built in fail-safes.

Score one for paranoia.

I moved with the efficiency of long practice, pulling a multi-tool from my web gear even as I shifted from a crouch to a supine position, sliding under the pilot's station and staring up at the underside of the console. I was aware of Korben's silent struggle in my peripheral vision just as I was aware of how the silence on the comm had taken on an expectant, almost ominous, note as those aboard the shuttle made their own preparations and then, with no other options, waited. I was aware that if Korben faltered, I was dead. I did my best to ignore that fact as I used the tool to start removing the screws on the bottom of the console.

It always struck me as odd, even anachronistic, that the access ports to the consoles were held in place with an inclined plane wrapped helically around an axle, but the simple machines were called such for a reason. A more "modern" mechanism would have required some level of computer or wireless control, which would have defeated the purpose of this particular panel. I had the covering removed in seconds and was staring up into the innards of the console. It was organized chaos, a mix of fiber-optic cables, circuit boards, and solid-state electronics that stretched far beyond my understanding. I could identify the most valuable bits—and did so, almost by reflex—but I didn't know how it all fit together, how it all worked. Fortunately, for the task at hand, I didn't need to.

The manual override was a function that had been built in to each and every station shipboard. It wasn't, however, one that the designers had thought would actually be necessary. So instead of a simple switch, I found myself looking at a series of old-school jumpers, physical bridges that had to be moved from one set of contact points to another. *Sarah, I need the schematic.*

My AI obligingly threw the schematic into my field of vision, overlaying it perfectly with the mess in front of me. She carefully highlighted the jumpers I needed to change and displayed a destination configuration for each. It reduced the complexity of the task before me from high to monkey see, monkey do. I switched the configuration of the multi-tool, changing it from a powered screwdriver to a pair of long-nosed, tweezer-like pliers and got to work.

It took roughly two minutes. For me, it felt like an eternity. I knew that if I dropped one of the jumpers, we were in trouble. Not that there weren't ways around it—I could have opened another panel, used the jumpers from a different console. But we didn't have the time for it. In the silence of vacuum, I had no idea how Korben was faring, nor could I spare the time and attention to look. I knew I wasn't dead yet, and that meant he was still holding. But if I fucked up here, I might as well pop the seal on my suit, because we had as much chance of surviving the Bliss-infected as I did of breathing vacuum.

With a sigh, I pushed the last jumper in place and pulled myself from beneath the console.

And damn near directly into the path of a descending length of metal conduit.

I half rolled, half flopped gracelessly out of the way as the improvised baton crashed to the deck where, moments before, my body had been. I got a vague impression of the whirling dervish that was Korben, now with knives in both hands, being backed step by bloody step toward the bulkhead.

And away from the door.

He'd left the doorway literally jammed with bodies. They'd piled before him like a charnel breastwork, a dozen or more dead forming a rough barricade that the others had had to physically crawl over. That would have given any normal person pause, bought us a few needed seconds as they realized the horror of what they were having to do and the likelihood of their own demise. But the Bliss-infected weren't normal people. There was no horror, no fear, within them. Only the need to do as the hive mind commanded, and they pressed onward. The literal weight of their numbers had pushed Korben from his position as surely as rushing water would inevitably carve a riverbed even in solid stone. And just like water, as the assassin had been dislodged, the Bliss-infected had flowed around him.

I rolled again, more gracefully though no less desperately, as the pipe came crashing down once more, striking the decking hard enough that, though I heard no sound, I felt the vibrations of the impact. I could see more of the cyber-zombies coming, crawling over the dead even as Korben fought with silent intensity to regain his former position. But I had more immediate concerns. My hands found the grip and barrel shroud of the submachine gun strapped to my chest as the pipe came crashing down a third time.

This time, I didn't roll. Instead, I pushed the gun forward to the limits of the sling and swept it in an arc that moved from one shoulder to the other. The barrel intercepted the descending pipe and brushed it to the side, though I felt the tingling of the initial impact all the way to my shoulders. The club smashed harmlessly to the deck a third time, my attacker now leaning over me, momentarily overbalanced from his efforts. I brought the barrel back in line and squeezed the trigger.

My attacker dropped, bouncing off my shoulder and leaving a smear of bright red blood as he fell. But there were more behind him. I pushed myself to my feet, firing as I went. The infected seemed endless, and while they reminded me of the zombies from the old horror flicks, they didn't move like them, not in full gravity. There was no casual shuffle. No directionless and somehow ominous stumbling about. They moved with the speed and agility of any coil in peak condition. There was no way Korben and I could hold them off for long.

But we didn't have to hold them off forever. Just long enough for the Genetechnic security team to reach us. If I could just get to the damn controls.

My rolls had taken me two, maybe three meters from the pilot's console, no more than that. With the jumpers reset, all I needed to do was boot the console. That was it. The flick of one switch, a few seconds of boot time, and the AI *should* be locked out. Without the crazy course changes, no matter the end vector, the cavalry *should* be able to arrive.

Should.

But there were a half-dozen Bliss-zombies between me and the console, and more pouring into the room with each passing moment. I couldn't kill them fast enough. With the submachine gun in hand, it wasn't like killing soldiers. It was like fighting an advancing forest fire. I could slow it down, but every time I tried to regain lost ground, a new surge exploded inward, driving me back again. It was maddening—I could almost, *almost*, reach out and hit the switch.

It was a stalemate.

And I was almost out of ammo.

Then Korben was there.

He crashed into the enemy flank, firearms discarded in favor of the blades. Or maybe he was just out of ammo, too. Whatever the case, he hit them with savage ferocity, his vacc suit already stained and dripping with the gore from his previous kills. It was hard not to be entranced by the spectacle. If killing was an art form, he was da Vinci. He moved with lethal efficiency, no wasted motion or effort. It was beautiful and terrifying all at once.

It also bought me the second I needed.

I lunged forward, stabbed at the console reset with one finger. If I'd set the jumpers correctly, if nothing had been damaged in the process, if the AI hadn't figured out some way to override the override, then the system should reboot and the flight path of the ship should stabilize.

If.

I couldn't just wait and watch. I brought my weapon back in line. I couldn't risk firing into the melee where the assassin was systematically cutting down the infected. Too great a risk of hitting Korben by accident. Instead, I fired at those making their way into the room, hoping to cut off the stream of new bodies at the source. My subgun clicked on an empty magazine, the HUD in my vision letting me know that I was out of reloads. I dropped the weapon, letting it fall to the end of its retention strap as I transitioned to my sidearm, continuing to pour fire downrange. I was aware, in a peripheral sort of way, that Korben had managed to drop the last of those in the room with us and was taking a roundabout path to the door, keeping well clear of my line of fire.

System reset complete, Sarah informed me.

I felt a surge of hope even as I dropped a magazine from my pistol and slapped in a fresh one. Korben and I might fall here, but there was still a chance.

"We're on our way," Shay's voice came through the comm. "Hold tight. Just a minute or two and we'll be there. Just keep fighting."

I'd never stopped broadcasting, so Shay and the others had had a first-person view of the madness on the bridge. It must have been dizzying, watching the battle unfold in that manner, but at least they knew what they were getting into.

Now, all we had to do was hold.

26

The seconds ticked by in a maddened flurry of chaotic limbs. I kept up a steady salvo of fire from my pistol, sending round after round punching through the open hatch and into the massed coils. I turned my mind off, shut out the savagery as much as I could, and focused on finding the intersection of the pistol's HUD-projected aiming point and Sarah's suggested targeting interval. I was a long way from perfect—the headshots were harder to come by with gravity adding another vector to the equation, but I didn't need to be perfect. Those who slipped by the barrage found Korben and his blades.

Then, without warning, the pressure stopped. I was halfway through a reload, Sarah indicating with a pulsing red circle that this was my last magazine, when the final Bliss-infected through the door was, suddenly, the *final* Bliss-infected through the door. For a moment I could only stare in wonder, gun still held out before me, trembling slightly under the strain of keeping the hunk of metal and composite at the ready. I noticed that the barrel glowed ever so slightly, the heat buildup from the electrical discharge that drove the rounds unable to dissipate fast enough given my rate of fire. Even in vacuum. Christ.

Then my reverie was broken as a hand touched my shoulder and squeezed softly.

I damn near jumped out of my boots, whirling around at the unexpected pressure, fighting to bring my weapon to bear. I could hear my heartbeat, locked within the confines of my suit, thudding rapidly. Someone was panting, and it took me a moment to realize that that, too, was coming from me. Of course.

A hand caught my arm as I spun, keeping my weapon pointed in a safe direction. "Easy, Carter. Easy. We're here."

I recognized the voice, Shay's voice. Her *real* voice, not the voice of the coil she was currently in. Funny how I'd come to accept my new coil's voice as my own, but Shay's would always be several octaves higher, several notes richer than the one that bore her words outside of electronic manipulation. A surge of exhaustion hit me at the words and recognition. My arms dropped to my side. It took a real effort of will not to let the pistol slide from my fingers.

Then Shay's arms were around me, enfolding me in her embrace. I squeezed her back, aware on some level of the strangeness of her musculature, of the fact that she was taller than I in our respective coils, but also, somehow, feeling the woman that rode my mind's eye in that embrace. I was aware, on some level, of the security team moving throughout the room, some taking positions on the hatch while others moved more equipment from the shuttle that must have docked without my notice during the fury of the battle. I was aware that the... blank... coils all seemed to be down, whether casualties of the crossfire or directly targeted by the infected, I had no idea. I was aware of Korben cleaning his blades with a casualness that could not quite mask the exhaustion in his own movements and then turning to search among the dead for his discarded firearms. I was aware of it all, but at that moment, it didn't seem to matter.

Then someone was tapping me on the shoulder.

I released Shay and turned. One of the Genetechnic security stood there, a duffel dangling from one arm. His visor wasn't polarized, and the in-helmet lighting illuminated the expression he wore. Gone were the questioning looks we had received when we first boarded the shuttle. Instead, I saw a newfound respect in his eyes. "Yes?" I asked. I trusted Sarah to find the right comm channel to make sure the man heard me.

"Ammo, sir," he said. "And oxygen."

"I've got to get to work," Shay said, moving away and heading toward the bank of consoles. I noticed that she was carrying a satchel over one shoulder, the kind used to protect the heavy-duty, industrialized tablets people employed when an agent alone wouldn't have enough processing power. She may have been cut off from trying to hack the ship on a remote signal, but now that she was aboard, she was determined to try again. I smiled at that.

"Sir?" the security officer said, hefting the bag slightly.

"Thanks," I said, taking the heavy weight from him. "Give me a hand with the O2?"

"Of course, sir."

As the Genetechnic operative—who, I reflected might well have been trying to kill me a week ago—helped switch out the oxygen modules on my suit, I started transferring magazines from the duffel to the various pouches and pockets on the web gear and VaccTech. I could scarcely believe that I'd gone through an entire combat load, something in the order of three hundred rounds of ammunition. Until, that was, I looked at the bodies.

It was hard to tell which were victims of the initial nano-device Korben had deployed and which had charged the bridge after we gained entry. There had been over a hundred when Korben's device went off. I estimated there were dozens more of them now. Maybe as many as thirty or forty. Plus the ones outside, that meant that Korben and I—well, and his hunter-killer nanite virus—had accounted for something close to a hundred and fifty of the crew and passengers. The thought made the bile rise in the back of my throat. Those numbers were unreal, but also an inevitable consequence of an enemy that just kept walking calmly into your fire, hoping that weight of numbers alone would overwhelm you.

No. That wasn't exactly fair. The AI's first plan had been to prevent entry to the ship at all, with the cyber-zombies that attacked on the hull acting as more of a shell fired from an anti-boarding weapon than as any type of military or security force. Regardless, Bliss would certainly have been successful if Shay hadn't managed to slag all the external airlocks. Plan B had been to flood our point of entry with enough bodies to ensure that we couldn't make it into the ship in the first place. Which, I thought, would also have succeeded, if not for the countermeasures Genetechnic had provided Korben with. It wasn't until the first two options had failed that the AI had resorted to sending a horde after us, and even then the tactics had changed. Evolved. The coils had been armed with makeshift weapons, the kinds of things you could readily find loose aboard a passenger ship. Knives. Bits of conduit. Chair and table legs. Improvised weapons, to be sure. But weapons, nonetheless. Thank God the bastards didn't seem to have access to guns.

Yet.

AIs by their very nature were heuristic, self-learning entities. I could appreciate that in the abstract. When it meant the tactics Bliss employed were likely to get more sophisticated as the evening progressed… let's just say I appreciated it a little less.

It took only a few moments to get resupplied with air and ammo. Once that was accomplished, I took stock. Shay was already at work, a fiber-optic cable pulsing between her tablet and one of the bridge consoles. She hadn't, I'd noticed, jacked directly in from the neural port behind her ear. We knew Bliss had taken control of the computers, but we couldn't be sure that the nano-virus hadn't somehow *migrated* into them. Direct neural interface may have given her a slight advantage, but it also risked an infection vector for the virus. No way in hell Shay, or any of the rest of us, wanted to take that chance. There was nothing I could do to help her with her work, though. Hell, I wasn't even entirely sure what she was doing to begin with.

The security personnel had taken the time to install a temporary hatch over the breach I'd cut into the hull. It seemed pointless, given that Bliss was the one in control of pressurizing and depressurizing hull sections. I supposed if we got that function back, it'd be nice to be able to pressurize the bridge. With the exterior locks fried, it was still our best way off the vessel once we'd accomplished whatever it was Korben had been sent here to do. I didn't believe for a minute that it was simply to eliminate all of the Bliss-infected and destroy the AI.

That thought drew my eyes back to the assassin. The man was in deep conversation with the officer in charge of the Genetechnic team, both standing near the main hatch leaving the bridge. That hatch was still being covered by a pair of security operatives while the rest moved about the room, stacking the dead so that they'd have room to set up a base of operations. Korben and the officer stood close together, a function of habit rather than need. With the room still in vacuum, the only way they could hear one another was over the comm. *Sarah, ping their channel.*

My agent obliged, sending the request to join the conversation. A moment later, my own comm crackled to life. "What's next?" I asked.

"We secure this area," an unfamiliar voice—the Genetechnic officer—replied. "Once that's complete, we penetrate farther into the ship. Our mission is to find the primary node of the Bliss entity."

"I thought it was a distributed intelligence," I replied. "How are we going to do that?"

"We search the ship," Korben cut in. "Compartment by compartment, if need be."

"Okay," I drawled. "I get that. But how will we know we've found the 'primary' node? What are we even looking for?"

They were silent for a long moment. Neither seemed to have a good answer. In the end, Korben offered a slight shrug. "I'm certain we will know it when we see it, Mr. Langston."

"Wonderful," I muttered.

"This is an entirely new entity, Mr. Langston," the assassin said, voice as calm and cool as always. "One that has had sufficient time to evolve its methods and possibly even its structure. There is no way to know precisely what we are dealing with. For all we know, the nanites have infiltrated the ship's hardware or perhaps downloaded their intelligence matrix into the ship's computers."

"Nope." It was Shay's voice, cutting into the channel. I grinned. She hadn't been specifically patched in and the casual way that she intruded on encrypted conversations filled me, for some reason, with a sense of pride. "I've scanned the software and run diagnostics on the hardware. No ghost in these machines. Looks like Bliss, at least whatever of it is aboard this ship, is all wetware." I couldn't help a small wince at the term. There was far too much blood on the decks to miss the significance of the words. Shay, still bent over her tablet, didn't notice. "I've managed to get some of the ship's internal sensors online. Not enough to draw any conclusions on where this 'primary' you're talking about might be, but I can at least tell you where the largest concentrations of the infected are."

"Let me guess," I offered. "Just out of sight and ready to ambush us?"

"Pretty much," Shay agreed. "Though, by rough estimates, the numbers gathered are nowhere near the total passenger manifest. By my estimates you and Korben… accounted… for roughly one hundred and forty of the former passengers between you, but the manifest says that there were north of twelve hundred souls aboard."

"We're lucky they didn't just send the whole lot of them in one endless wave," I grunted.

"Maybe not so lucky," Shay replied, tone pensive.

"Eh?" I asked. The number of coils we'd dropped was staggering, though the brunt by far had fallen to Korben's nano-virus. And even then, the rest had come in waves. It had taken more than just skill and superior firepower—we'd needed a large dose of luck to be standing where we were at the moment.

From my peripheral vision I saw Shay waving a resigned hand from where she still hunched over her tablet. "I know it was fortunate that you didn't have to face more of these… things… all at once, Carter. We watched what you had to do." She was quiet for a long moment, and I felt a bit of a sinking in the pit of my stomach. I had my own doubts about what I'd done, and I knew that sleep was going to be long and hard coming for a while. Somehow, it made it worse that others had seen it secondhand. "It was terrible. Truly terrible, and I'm sorry you had to go through it." That wasn't the reaction I'd been expecting. I felt a warm and uplifting swell of relief pass through me at her words.

"But that's not what I was talking about," she continued. "What I mean is, I don't think it was luck that Bliss sent only a small portion of the available total coils to deal with you. I think it was a conscious choice. A matter of self-preservation."

"Explain," Korben cut in to the channel. It should have come across as curt, but somehow, his calm, urbane voice made it seem more like a request than a command.

"For fuck's sake," Shay ground, her own patience apparently eroded by the killer's interjection. "You people have been saying from the start that Bliss is a *distributed* intelligence. Just what do you think it's distributed over?"

"A colony of nanobots," Korben replied, no sign of irritation at Shay's shortness showing in his own voice.

"Yeah," I grunted, seeing where Shay was going. "That's where it started. But you said this thing was a virus, and then it spreads. And we've got about a thousand people it's spread to." I looked over at Shay. She might have been perfectly comfortable with the entirety of the conversation taking place over the comm, but I felt an almost physical need to be looking at her as I asked the next question. "Are you saying that Bliss isn't just controlling the coils but is… I guess the only word is *distributed*… over them?"

"Exactly," Shay replied. As if sensing the weight of my gaze, she finally put her tablet down and walked over to us. "I'm not one hundred percent certain how the nano-virus works—Genetechnic wasn't overly forthcoming with that information. We know it can survive conditions that would kill ordinary coils—the footage from your own branch is proof enough of that, Carter. But we've all been talking about this thing like it's some sort of hive mind—a queen with a bunch of drones. Only, that doesn't make any sense."

I was shaking my head now, finding it difficult to follow my much smarter companion's line of thinking. "Why not?"

"Because that's not how processing works," she said. "Look, if you go back to the early days of computers, before we had quantum computing, if you wanted more operations per second, you either needed to build a better processor or string a bunch of them together, working in parallel, breaking up a task across multiple chips. But all those different parts, whether they were one supercomputer, or a distributed network, were all working on one thing, one objective. Working as one entity. I think Bliss is like that. We're not dealing with a queen and a thousand drones. We're dealing with a single creature that has a thousand different arms. Or hands. Or whatever. Each with their own functioning sub-network to provide a little autonomy in how they go about completing their part of the task." I could hear the wonder in her voice, though I didn't pretend to understand it. "It really *is* like a virus," she marveled. "Not a medical virus though. An old-school computer virus. The kind that would infect a machine and then slave it to a broader network of thousands of zombies, using them to make denial-of-service attacks or mass spam campaigns. Only, in this case, our coils are the machines."

I thought about it for a moment. It made a certain amount of sense, at least as far as it went. Which, I admitted ruefully, was a whole lot farther than *I'd* thought about it. "Okay," I said. "So, let's say you're right. It's one entity. I still don't understand why it wouldn't send everything at us at once."

"Self-preservation, as Ms. Chan said, Mr. Langston," Korben drawled. "Every 'meat-puppet'—as you elegantly put it—that we destroy takes a processor offline."

"Exactly!" Shay exclaimed, forgetting, in her excitement, her dislike of the assassin. "Look, we knew from the outset that we might not be getting all of the virus here, and it's possible that there are multiple entities if bits of the virus went off in different directions. Think of those as different branches, like the branches we lost on the *Persephone*. But I'm almost positive that Bliss isn't in the ship itself—there's no trace of the nanites or their code in the ship's systems. The coils that *are* here represent the entire possible processing power for the entity." I couldn't see her face, but I could hear the grin in Shay's voice as she asked, "How much of your brain would *you* risk on any given endeavor?"

"So," I grunted. "We've knocked a few percentage points off of Bliss' processors. Great." It was hard to keep the sarcasm from my voice. "But what now? If we can't just blow up the ship for fear of spreading the virus, what the hell are we supposed to do? Even with the full team here, there's no way we're going to cut down hundreds upon hundreds of infected. Unless, of course," I said, turning to face Korben, "you've got more of whatever the hell it was you used when we came in here."

"Not as such," Korben said. "The device I deployed on our entry was a small-scale version of the… let's call it the cure, shall we?" He didn't smile, but there was a note of amusement in his voice. "It was developed as a test case and it seems to have been effective. But the delivery method is far too contained." He pointed at a canister off to the side that the security team must have brought aboard with them. "We have enough of the seek-and-destroy nanites to take care of the entire ship, but only if we can access the proper distribution channels."

I thought about it for a moment. Thought about the ship. Thought about how I would spread something to every compartment, every corridor, every hold. Every place one of the Bliss-infected might be holed up. "Environmental," I said.

"Exactly, Mr. Langston," Korben replied. "If we can get to the life support systems and get them back online and then introduce our little friends," he tapped the canister, "then we should be able to effectively neutralize all of the resistance aboard the ship."

"And set you guys up with a nice little stock of freshly blanked coils," Shay muttered.

Korben only shrugged, but I was reminded of the effect his weapon had had on the infected. Yes, it had seemed to wipe out Bliss, but it hadn't killed the coils. Instead it had left them standing, staring blankly. Living and breathing but... empty. Ready to be filled? To be re-coiled?

I shook my head. It didn't matter. Regardless of whether or not Genetechnic was going to try and squeeze more credits from the situation by "salvaging" the infected, we still had to clear the ship. And damned if I wanted to try and fight my way through the entire passenger manifest. The hunter-killer nanites were the best shot we had of taking care of Bliss.

"Shay, can you find us the best path to Environmental?" She nodded at my question, eyes already taking on the faraway look of interface. "Then why don't we get on it before Bliss decides to send another platoon of passengers to stop us."

27

"We're ready to move out, sir."

Korben nodded to the Genetechnic security chief. The two dozen soldiers in all but name were arrayed throughout the room, most stacking up on one side or the other of the hatch leading from the bridge. Six had been detailed to remain here and hold the room against any attempts to cut off our escape route once we penetrated deeper into the vessel. Everyone had been tapped into Shay's heat map of enemy movements. They'd all watched the footage—live and in color—of Korben and I battling the Bliss-infected.

We all knew what we were getting into.

I'd known that I had no chance of convincing Shay to stay on the bridge, much less return to the shuttle. I had made sure she was armed, if only with a Gauss pistol, and that she—and I—would be placed toward the end of the stack. I'd seen enough of the Bliss-infected to leave as much of the work ahead to the professionals as possible. Hell, a good attorney could argue that Shay and I had already met our obligations under our contract and were free to go.

Of course, we needed the Genetechnic shuttle to go anywhere.

And whatever my contract said, I wasn't terribly keen on the idea of the Bliss virus spreading throughout the system. Like the rest of humanity, I'd grown used to the idea of immortality and I'd be damned if I let some trumped-up computer virus threaten it. So, like Shay, I wasn't about to be convinced to turn back now.

"Very well," Korben said. He'd taken a position farther forward in the stack, though he, too, was leaving the point work to the professionals. I didn't quite understand the Genetechnic security forces' command structure, but all of them seemed to defer to Korben. "Let's move out. And do remember that Ms. Chan's heat map is more of a best guess than a guarantee. Keep your eyes open, people."

On his words, the point man slipped through the hatch, weapon up and at the ready. The rest started filing in behind, breaking off into two columns, one along each wall of the corridor. I could sense the unease pouring off the security personnel, see it in the tense set of their shoulders and the quickness of their steps. Was it the corridor itself? It made a perfect killbox if the enemy happened to have any heavy weapons. On the other hand, they hadn't been able to produce a firearm yet, and that killbox worked both ways.

No. It was, I realized, the emptiness.

I didn't know the normal mission of the Genetechnic security department. I suspected that the armed assault of space transports was probably not one of their regular duties. If it *was*, it was against human resistance. Whatever the coils might look like, Bliss wasn't human. There was a feel a place had when humanity was present. An energy. A vitalness. It was something you didn't really notice except when it was gone. Something defined more by its absence than its presence.

The emptiness was a feeling I'd grown accustomed to over the years. Most derelict vessels shared it. The passenger liner wasn't derelict, not in the normal sense, but it had that same feeling. And if you weren't used to it, it was enough to put anyone on edge. Even the hardened security operatives.

Sarah, open a channel just to Shay, please. There was a slight beep of acknowledgment, and then another letting me know the channel was open. "You okay?" I asked. "This can be a little rough under normal circumstances. These… aren't exactly normal circumstances." I kept my eyes open as I talked, not bothering to look toward Shay. None of the indicators of the Bliss-infected were on us yet, but Shay had stressed that the system wasn't perfect.

"I'm okay," she replied. There was tension in her voice. And fear. For the situation, certainly—humanity may have found a way around death, but no one looked forward to the physical mechanics of dying. The thought of being brained by one of the infected or being dragged down by their endless numbers was hardly an encouraging one. But there was something more to it than that. Something deeper.

"We're going to make it out of here," I said. And even if we don't, I didn't add, we have a backup plan in place.

"It's not that," she replied. There was a moment of silence and I brought my weapon up slightly as the soldiers in front of me came to an abrupt halt, crouching down against the corridor bulkheads and shouldering their own weapons. Whatever had inclined the point man to stop seemed to pass muster, because a few seconds later, we were moving again.

"Then what?" I asked.

"It's the whole situation, Carter. I just… argh!" She let out a sound of frustration that was somewhere between a scream and a growl. "I just want this to be over with. To go back to our old lives." Her voice slid from frustration down into rueful as she said, "I didn't really sign up to try and save all of humanity. I don't even particularly *like* most of humanity all that much. It's why I spend most of my time online or in deep space with a small crew. But even if I *did*, I'm not cut out for playing soldier and cutting down swaths of the enemy. I want my life back. I want to go home."

I heard the longing in her voice. I knew it wasn't just for the *Persephone* or her hide on Daedalus. It wasn't even for getting back to playing white hat hacker in cyberspace, or whatever it was she did when she wasn't working salvage. It was a deeper yearning than that, and I sensed that, more than anything, what she missed was her *self*. That indefinable part of her that was, at least on some level, intrinsically linked to how she saw herself, to who she was. Being coiled in the expedient shell she now wore was a subtle form of torture for her, the kind that would take its toll day after day, hour after hour, for as long as she was forced to remain within it.

"We'll get it back, Shay. I promise you. One way or another, we'll get it all back."

"Sure," she said, not sounding particularly confident. "If Bliss doesn't scour humanity from the solar system."

"There is that," I muttered. "That, there is."

"Contact!"

The word cut across the comm, coming in on the channel reserved for tactical communications with the security force. It brought the entire unit up short, everyone once again squeezing tight against the bulkheads. I didn't hear the gunfire, of course. We were still in vacuum, despite the gravity, but a moment later the same voice said, "Got the bastard. Shit! More inbound."

My HUD started to light up as the heat map shifted, a previously green chamber going deep red and then spilling into the corridor in front of us.

"Damn it!" Shay exclaimed. "That room must be shielded from the sensors."

I didn't have time to reply as Korben's voice cut through the chatter. "Stand your ground. They don't have any ranged capabilities. Take them down. Remember, you have to disrupt their cores. Head and neck and spine, people. Head, neck, and spine."

The front ranks peeled away from the walls, forming a living barrier across the corridor and then kneeling down. The rear ranks took up position behind them, leaving me and Shay standing at the back, still pressed up against our own bulkhead. It reminded me of ancient fucking history, an army lining up to volley-fire inaccurate black-powder weapons across an open field. Only, the corridor was much tighter than any open field and the Genetechnic team's weapons were anything but inaccurate. The passage was wide enough for six team members to line up abreast. I was grateful for the vacuum as a dozen firearms opened up, hurling their projectiles against the flood of coils spilling into the corridor.

I didn't have a line of fire but I kept my weapon at the ready. I glanced behind me and saw that Shay had drawn her Gauss pistol. Her hands were visibly shaking as she clutched the butt of the weapon in a two-handed grip. "Easy, now," I said, keeping my voice as calm as I could. Over the heads of the firing line, I could see the horde of Bliss-infected driving forward centimeter by bloody centimeter. They were all armed now, with makeshift clubs and kitchen knives, and they seemed oblivious to the losses they were soaking.

"Stand your ground!" Korben's voice snapped. "Keep firing."

The two soldiers who had been at the rear of our little formation pushed past us, moving forward, ready to take up their own positions on the line if anyone fell or had a weapons malfunction. In the first few seconds, dozens of coils, at one time as human as Shay or me, fell. The cyber-zombies in their wake had to literally climb over the mounded dead, slowing them further and giving the security teams time to reload. It was slaughter on a scale unlike anything I had ever seen; it was slaughter I hoped I'd never see again.

After a minute of near continuous fire, Shay turned away. A minute later, and I found myself looking anywhere but at the seemingly ambulatory wall of dead as it crept closer and closer to the firing line. I was aware, vaguely, of the sensor-driven data display that showed that, despite the charnel heaps slowly filling the corridor, the intensity of the heat map showing the location of the Bliss-infected had faded only slightly. The security operatives had to have dropped dozens, scores, maybe hundreds in those first few minutes of fire.

But Bliss had hundreds more where those came from, and, this time, it seemed the AI had decided to throw them all at us in one concerted wave.

"Fall back." The order came over the radio waves, Korben calm and collected as always. "By the numbers. Front rank, keep firing."

Shay threw me a startled glance and even through her faceplate I could see the whites all around her eyes. "Just move back," I said over our private channel. "Nice and easy. You'll know when it's time to run."

I put my words into action, gliding back, trying to keep my eyes toward the enemy and simultaneously watch the corridor beyond. I slipped past Shay, letting her follow in my wake, aware that, despite everything, I had somehow become point man again. At least this time, the enemy was at our backs.

As far as we knew, anyway.

Korben kept up a steady stream of orders as we retreated and I was forced to reassess him yet again. He wasn't simply the cold, professional killer. He had to have commanded men before at some point in one of the however many lifetimes he'd lived. Hell, maybe he was even some sort of military genius. If he was, it wasn't going to help us one bit in this situation. I could feel the pressure of the shooters as the pace of their withdrawal increased. Slowly, inexorably, but each step seemed to follow its predecessor with just a little more alacrity as the cyber-zombies clambered closer.

"Where am I heading, Korben?" I asked after having Sarah open a private channel to him. I'd been heading back toward the bridge, but that wouldn't get us anywhere. It was a dead end, and if we couldn't hold the door, that description would prove literal.

"Anywhere you can, Mr. Langston." There was an edge in his voice that I hadn't heard before. A strain. I risked a glance over my shoulder and saw that the Bliss-infected had closed the space down to a few scant meters. "Anywhere defensible. But we have to make it to Environmental." His voice was grim, the determination evident.

Sarah, plot another route to Life Support. One that takes us through minimal resistance based on the existing sensor data.

A glowing trail blossomed in my vision. "I've got a least resistance route based on current info," I said to Korben. "I'm going to move ahead and try to find a spot to buy us some breathing room."

"Fine," came the terse reply.

"Route info headed your way." I switched channels. "Shay, we're going to pick up the pace. We need to find a spot where we can weather this storm."

"Okay," came her breathless reply.

"Stay close." I didn't wait for a response, moving from the quick walk I'd been maintaining to a trot and then something between a jog and a sprint. If I rounded a corner and ran headlong into more infected, I was finished, but we needed the separation if we were going to have any chance of coming up with a plan for the team to break contact.

"What are we looking for?" Shay panted over the comm.

"Anything we can use to slow down the bad guys," I responded. "But not until after the good guys—such as they are—get past us. A door we can secure. A barricade. Anything."

She didn't reply, but I had no doubt she was working the problem, putting her better knowledge of the myriad computer systems that ran a ship into play. I concentrated on the purely mechanical. Doors were the obvious solution, but it took quite a bit of time to disable one. While they could be locked electronically, Bliss was in charge of the network, not us. Disabling them mechanically—well, I doubted we'd have enough time between when the last soldier passed and the first of the infected arrived for any meaningful solution. I still had some adhesive left, but that would buy us only a few moments. We needed something better.

"This way," Shay cut in, a new pathway blossoming to view in my vision. I didn't argue—she no doubt had better data on the ship, and God knew, *I* didn't have a plan to get us out of this. I simply took her path, porting it over to Korben as I went, so he and the Genetechnic team would know where to follow. I dropped into the tactical channel briefly, just long enough to verify that the team was, in fact, still there, and then hauled ass down the route Shay supplied. I noted that it did, eventually, intersect with the path that Sarah had plotted, but not until a detour through what looked like a machine shop.

I took a turn and found myself sliding to a halt at a closed hatch. Shay was there in a heartbeat, slapping some sort of device to the bulkhead beside the hatch, where the electronics were likely to be. There was a moment of silence, as Shay interfaced with the device. Then, with an almost indignant slowness, the hatch whirred open. "I might not be able to get control of the ship," she said triumphantly, "but damned if that bitch is going to keep me from opening a door."

I couldn't help a slight chuckle. "Okay," I agreed. "Now what?"

"Come on." I followed her into the room beyond. We found ourselves in a chamber tightly packed with conduit and piping in various gauges. Warning signs abounded, including more than one that read, "Explosive" or "Flammable."

"Not the best place to make a stand, Shay," I said, simultaneously querying Sarah for a status update on the Genetechnic team.

The Genetechnic security forces are still fighting a retreat. At the current rate, the survivors should reach this location in approximately two minutes.

"Shit," I muttered under my breath. "Survivors" meant that they'd taken casualties; two minutes meant that the orderly retreat was rapidly becoming a rout.

"Don't worry," Shay said, assuming the expletive was for the path she'd chosen. "I'm not planning on having a gunfight in here." She had moved to one bulkhead where she'd opened an access panel. A fiber-optic cable now ran from her tablet and clamped onto one of the myriad wires nestled behind the panel. "Do me a favor—tap those two pipes, enough so that we get a slow leak." A ping sounded in my helmet as Sarah accepted input from Bit and two of the conduits began to glow in my vision.

"We have about a minute thirty," I said.

"Then you better work fast," she replied.

I snorted. Whatever her plan, I knew there was no arguing with it. Better to move as quickly as possible so that we could be ready to run if the Genetechnic security team broke. I had no idea what was in the pipes marked and didn't bother to query Sarah to look it up. I trusted Shay to know what she was doing. I had any number of tools in my salvage gear capable of cutting through the piping, but given Shay's specifications, I decided to go the old-fashioned way. I pulled a titanium punch and a hammer from my kit. A few quick taps and both pipes started spewing gas. I couldn't hear the leaks, of course, and I could only see them by the slight shimmer in the air when my suit lights passed over them.

It had only taken me about ten seconds to punch the holes. I could feel time slipping away as the Genetechnic team—and the Bliss-infected—moved steadily closer. "Done," I said.

"Twenty seconds," Shay replied. I glanced at my HUD. That would leave us under a minute to get clear. I didn't say anything. Instead, I took the time to check my weapons. I hadn't fired a shot since the initial entry, and everything was locked, loaded, and ready to go.

"Done," Shay said. "We're going to need to move back a bit."

"What are we doing, Shay?" I asked. But I moved through the room to the hatch at the other end as I did so. This one opened even more quickly to Shay's commands than the previous one. It occurred to me that having her along on actual salvages back in the days of the *Persephone* might have saved me a lot of time and a lot of cutting. Well, on the ships that still had power, anyway.

Genetechnic security will arrive in approximately ten seconds, Sarah informed me.

"Never mind," I said to Shay. "Just get ready." Then I keyed the comm over to the channel I'd set up with Korben. "Shay's cooked something up. We've got a... hell, I don't know. A trap of some sort at the hatch I've indicated." Shay and I were moving as I talked, going into the corridors beyond the conduit room. After about ten meters, we came to a stop.

"Understood." I heard the strain in the terse reply. "One turn to go."

"Korben," Shay cut in to the channel. "This is Chan. Stop fighting the retreat and run. Turn and sprint through the chamber ahead and keep going until you're past us. Don't ask questions—just do it. Now!"

A double click of acknowledgment came over the comm. "Not long now," Shay muttered.

I posted up along one bulkhead, putting my body between the compartment we'd just left and Shay, making sure that she, too, was making herself small against the wall. I trained my subgun toward the portal ten meters away, trigger finger on the receiver, and waited.

It wasn't a long wait.

A handful of heartbeats passed and then the first of the Genetechnic security guards burst through the open hatch and into the corridor, moving at a dead sprint. His weapon twitched as he caught sight of us, but recognition dawned and he kept running, coming to a sliding, twisting halt that left him positioned against the opposite side of the corridor from me. I couldn't hear his panting, but I could see his heaving chest and the shakiness with which he held his own firearm. His vacc suit was stained with blood and worse, mute testament that the fighting had come down to point-blank range at some point.

Then the others were through. Five more security personnel followed by the unmistakable form of Korben, guns once more discarded in favor of his blades. They left a small splattering of red in their wake with each pump of the arms as the killer ran. "They're right behind us," he said over the comm. "A few seconds.

No more." Even now, despite the shortness of breath from his sprint, he didn't sound particularly worried. *The infected horde is hot on our heels. We're running out of milk.* Either statement would have sounded the same coming from Korben's lips. "No one else is coming," he added in the same tone.

Christ. Eighteen Genetechnic personnel had left the bridge with us. Only a half-dozen remained. I had no doubt they'd left a mountain of bodies in their wake, but Bliss could soak the losses with ease. We, on the other hand, were at a hundred to one disadvantage. A dozen lost—not dead, not really, given that Genetechnic probably had fresh new coils waiting for their backups at home—jeopardized the mission to the point where I started to wonder if we had any chance at all of doing whatever the hell it was Genetechnic had sent Korben here to do. Still, even if we had only the slightest possibility of getting off this ship in one piece, might as well fight for it. Rolling over and giving up had never been my style.

"Whatever you're going to do, now might be a good time," I told Shay.

"Not yet," she said. "We need to let some of them through." She broadcast the words over the general channel, and I felt as much as saw the stiffening of the men and women around me. They might not fear death, not in the traditional sense of the word, but our minds and bodies were hardwired by countless generations of evolution to at least want to avoid the *process* of dying. And even if you knew they'd be stuffed into new bodies before the week was out, watching your friends ripped to pieces took a toll on the psyche.

"Very well, Ms. Chan," Korben replied, also over the general channel. "If we must receive guests again then that is what we shall do. I do hope that your plan is sound." With that, he stepped into the center of the corridor, knives once more sheathed and a pistol in each hand. I muttered a curse and broke away from the bulkhead to take up a kneeling firing position at his side. One by one, the others followed suit, the faintest reluctance in their movements as they prepared, once more, to go into the breach.

It wasn't a long wait. Within moments the first of the Bliss-infected made his way to the hatch, a long piece of composite conduit with a jagged and broken end clutched in both fists like an ancient pike. At least four of us pulled the trigger and his head simply disappeared. A woman came next, a claw hammer held aloft. She too, fell in a hail of projectiles. I had a vague sense of unease—we were putting bullets downrange into a room full of potentially volatile substances. We didn't have much choice. Besides, from the press of bodies pushing through the hatch, any wild rounds would be caught by another coil long before hitting any part of the ship.

The cyber-zombies kept coming, despite the pile of dead clogging the door. That was actually starting to be a problem, as the infected clambered over and around them, rather than coming in a nice straight line to our little shooting gallery. They'd already started to push past the hatch, despite the weight of our fire, an endless tide of flesh and blood that would pull us under if something didn't happen soon.

"Any time, Shay," I panted into the comm.

"Ten seconds," she replied. "The concentrations have to be right."

I had no idea what she was talking about, but I knew that

ten seconds would seem like an eternity. My subgun clicked back on an empty chamber and I let it fall, transitioning to my Gauss pistol. I fumbled the draw, and in that moment, everything seemed to fall apart. It was testament to how much of a razor's edge we'd been walking with trying to contain the Bliss-infected. I didn't get my weapon back in line; another of the security guards got caught mid-magazine change. And just like that, they were among us.

I fell backward, dropping supine and bringing the Gauss gun to bear as the ambulatory coils loomed over me. I didn't feel the recoil—negligible to begin with and now buried under the terror and adrenaline—as I squeezed the trigger again and again, barely conscious of the hand-to-hand battle being joined all around me. For a moment, just a heartbeat, it was contact shots and butt stocks in a swirling chaotic melee.

Then the world exploded.

I may not have been able to hear the blast, but I *felt* it as the concussive force swept down the hallway in a gout of flame. It knocked everyone, human and infected alike, to the ground. I had a brief sense of heat before the VaccTech suit did its thing and regulated the temperature. Warning indicators flashed in my vision, indicating that the suit was nearing its limit, but then the warnings faded. I pushed myself to my feet, and realized that somewhere along the way I'd lost my pistol. I wasn't thinking clearly—just staring at the people around me. Then, I realized that one of them was Korben and that he was moving with purpose.

Moving from Bliss-infected to Bliss-infected and methodically delivering death blows to the seemingly unconscious coils. That brought me back to my senses. My subgun was still dangling from its strap, so I dropped the empty mag and slammed a new one home. There didn't seem to be a need. The security personnel, and it looked like all of them had made it this time, were regaining their feet and looking around with the same bewildered expression I knew must be on my face.

The coils were down, and as Korben did his work, not likely to get back up again. The hatch to the machine room—or whatever it was—was visible and a dark smoke backlit by a blue light was leaking from the room. There may not have been any oxygen aboard the ship, but there were plenty of other fuels available and it looked like Shay had managed to tap into a few of them.

Shay.

She was still on the ground but at least she was moving, struggling to regain her feet. I hurried to her side, grabbing an arm and heaving to get her up. It would have been a simple enough exercise before, but now she weighed damn near as much as me. "What the hell was that?" I asked.

"Had to catch enough of them in the blast," she gasped. "God. I think I cracked a rib."

"What are you talking about, Ms. Chan?" Korben asked, wiping his knives clean on an already blood-soaked handkerchief that he produced from somewhere in his vacc suit. "We were within moments of being overrun. No," he corrected. "We were overrun. We're lucky we didn't lose anyone else." His voice had a different note in it, one more icy than calm. There was something in that tone that reminded me that whatever our present circumstances, Korben was still a killer.

If Shay was bothered by that fact, it didn't show in her voice. She matched him ice for ice. "What I did was save your ass, assassin. You and your corporate bully boys. You'd all be waking up in new coils if it wasn't for me. You wanted a way to break contact and that's what I gave you, and something more besides."

I moved without conscious thought, putting myself between Shay and the assassin. I was acutely aware that, even with my bulk, there was a good chance that Shay, in her present coil, could shove me aside by main strength. And I didn't want to think of what Korben and his knives could do. I deliberately turned my back to the killer; not that I thought he would refrain from stabbing me in the back out of some misguided sense of honor, but I doubted there was much I could do if he decided we'd outlived our usefulness. "What else, Shay?" I asked, keeping my voice as calm as possible. "You blew up a shit-ton of meat-puppets and managed to block the door, or we would be buried by now. But what do you mean by something more?"

The Genetechnic security people were all on their feet now and had gathered in a loose semicircle. They had their weapons at the ready—not that I could blame them. The situation sort of demanded it, regardless of any internal drama. We'd been talking on the general channel so they'd heard the entire exchange. I didn't sense any malice from them, but they *were* listening.

After a long moment, Shay took her gaze from the assassin. "I overloaded the processor," she said. She smiled at the bewilderment on my face. "Remember when you and…" she paused and threw another heated glare at Korben, "he first boarded? He used that device, and then you had a bit of a break in the attacks?" I nodded. It had taken a few minutes for Bliss to launch another assault after Korben's hunter-killer nanitic grenade had gone off. "Maybe it was because Bliss was afraid of spreading the infection. But, I figure it's also because a bunch of processors—a bunch of coils—went offline simultaneously. Look, if you have a power load spread out over a bunch of different circuits, and you take those circuits offline one by one, or even a few at a time, the software can manage the load. They can reroute and redistribute it. But if you take a bunch of those circuits offline simultaneously…" She trailed off, a mischievous smile that hung poorly on her new face twisting her lips.

"Then the circuit breakers trip," Korben said. Then, reluctantly, "Well done, Ms. Chan."

"Okay," I said. "Let's assume you gave Bliss a hell of a headache. It's still got plenty of coils to throw at us. Even if you 'tripped a breaker' we've got more coming."

"Not through that compartment," she said with a grin. "The gas pouring from those holes you punched in the conduit by the hatch will keep burning for quite a while. Maybe an hour. And since you physically tapped the pipes, there's nothing Ms. Bliss can do about it without putting actual hands on the problem. There are plenty of other ways for them to find us, but they're not coming that way. We've got our clean break."

"Then let's not let it go to waste," Korben said, voice once more emotionless. Without another word, he walked past us. The Genetechnic security team fell in behind him, leaving Shay and I to stare at one another for a few heartbeats.

With a slight shrug, I snatched my Gauss pistol from the floor, gave it a quick once-over to make sure it hadn't been damaged in the blast, and dropped it back into my holster.

"Guess we keep moving," I said.

"Yeah," Shay replied. "I guess we do."

We pushed on, moving down the corridors of the passenger liner like ghosts. The fact that we had lost two-thirds of our firepower was lost on no one. I kept my weapon up and at the ready, conscious of the fact that, despite what the sensors were showing, the Bliss-infected could come pouring out of any compartment. I wasn't sure we'd have the firepower to stop them if they did and I doubted that Shay could pull off the same trick twice. The AI was too damn smart to fall for something like that again.

As the seconds ticked by without an attack, the tension crept ever higher. I could feel it in my upper back, a tightness squeezing my neck and somehow making each breath a little harder to draw. The sensor map Shay had put together showed us free and clear, all the way to Environmental.

"Why aren't they attacking us?" Shay asked, her own tension leaving her words clipped. I checked the channel—she was using the private link between the two of us, excluding Korben and the security personnel.

"I don't know, Shay," I said. I flexed my fingers, making a conscious effort to loosen my death grip on the submachine gun. "Maybe your circuit breaker thing forced a reboot or whatever. Or maybe we've done more damage than we thought. It's possible the crew of the liner figured out they were under attack and fought back. Maybe there's not as many infected as we feared."

"Do you really believe that, Carter?" she asked. There was

a note of hope in her voice and I felt like an instant asshole.

"No," I said. "No, I'm afraid I don't. I think you either gave Bliss a hell of a migraine, or it's up to something. But I can't imagine the passengers of this tub putting up enough of a resistance to have mattered. Look at the losses we've suffered... and we knew what we were up against."

She was quiet for a few heartbeats, staring ahead at the backs of the security team. "What are *we* up to, Carter? Why didn't we just destroy this entire ship? This all seems so pointless."

It was my turn to be quiet for a few moments, though we kept moving, kept making our way ever deeper into the bowels of the ship. "I wish I knew, Shay," I said at last. "It's clear Genetechnic wants something. Something more than just a sample, or we could have left with any of the coils we dealt with on the deck." I ignored the shudder that coursed through me at the memory of the hellish walk across the hull. "We *do* need some more intel on whether or not this is it." I waved one hand at the ship surrounding us. "If Bliss has spread farther than this ship..." I trailed off. Shrugged. "But for all the talk about how blowing up the ship might just make the problem worse, there has to be more to it. Maybe they need a more wide-scale test of their hunter-killer nanites. Maybe they know something we don't, and Bliss is already out there." That thought made me shudder, but I wouldn't put it past them. "If so, they'd need to know how effective their 'cure' really is."

"It makes a certain amount of sense," Shay said. "First test a small-scale version with the grenade Korben had employed when you entered the ship. Then test a wide-scale distribution method like the life-support systems. If both those worked, maybe you'd have enough data to create something that could... what?"

I grunted. "Something that could be deployed across an entire dome maybe." I felt an uncomfortable little shiver course through me. "But I don't see how they could get it to work on a planetary scale."

"Which means if Bliss did get out, the habs and colonies might be okay," Shay agreed. "But Earth..." She trailed off.

Earth, I thought, would be well and truly fucked.

I didn't say anything in return. I didn't have to. We both knew the danger of the virus getting out on Earth. People weren't packed quite so close planet-side as they were in your average hab, but there were billions upon billions of souls. And they all traveled freely, casually, with an ease that space dwellers could only envy. Epidemics were mostly a thing of the past, natural viruses and mutations powerless before the might of modern medicine. But Bliss wasn't a normal virus. It was technology on a level that rivaled, maybe exceeded, anything on Earth. The damage it could do...

The conversation lapsed, and we pushed on, guided by the sullen glow of the sensor readouts burning in our vision, herding us down ladders and through compartments, to grandmother's house we went. I hoped to hell we weren't walking right into the wolf's den.

28

We made it.

By the grace of Shay's trap or the strength of whatever cobbled-together hack she and Bit had managed on the ship's sensors, we made our way through the corridors and compartments until the team—the half-dozen or so of us left—were stacked up outside an innocuous man-sized hatch stenciled with the words, "Life Support." The other side of the door was green on our HUDs, indicating that the sensors weren't picking up any life forms on the other side. No one seemed inclined to take those sensors at their word, however, no matter how well they'd served us to this point.

All around me, I sensed the hefting of weaponry, the drawing of deep, steadying breaths. The conscious gathering of courage to go through one more door, to fight one more battle. I couldn't hear it, but I didn't need to. I felt it in myself, and saw it reflected in the determined faces of those around me. Genetechnic's entire plan revolved around the rapid distribution of the seek-and-destroy nanites throughout the ship and Life Support was the only way to make that happen. We had no way of knowing if Bliss, imbued with an intelligence that at least equaled our own, had figured out the plan. We had no way of knowing what awaited us on the other side of the door.

Korben's voice came over the channel. "We have a solid connection with the shuttle. All personnel, instruct your agents to execute an emergency backup." That surprised me. Backup procedures were normally only possible within a certain range of a registered facility. Of course, Genetechnic had already demonstrated an amazing faculty in manipulating the archive system. Did they really have the capability to execute a backup out here, in deep space? "Langston, Chan, you too. As of this moment, no one could argue that you haven't fulfilled the terms of your contract." Chan and I exchanged glances. The assassin was many things, but, though it pained me to say it, he seemed to have a sense of fairness, perhaps even honor.

Sarah?

Backup procedures have been initiated. The process is non-standard and appears to be gathering only a subset of available data. The Genetechnic protocols are using an incremental approach rather than a full backup. Estimate completion in just under sixty seconds.

We all waited in tense silence as our agents sent a record of us… all that we were… back to the shuttle. As Sarah had noted, it wasn't a full download—that would have been impossible given the time constraints. But even if it was just enough to fill in the gaps since our last backup, the ramifications were staggering.

The megacorps may well have been soulless entities, but it seemed there were benefits to dealing with the devil.

"Ms. Chan," Korben said once everyone had indicated

their backup process was complete, "if you would be so kind."

Shay nodded and her eyes took on that faraway look that meant she was dropping into VR, no doubt to better assess the electronic defenses of the door before her. She was gone for only a moment before her eyes refocused. "Done," was all she said.

Korben nodded and reached out for the pad. He tapped it and the door slid soundlessly open.

The security personnel were moving as soon as the opening was wide enough for one to squeeze through. They flowed into the room, the assassin, Shay, and I following in their wake. I surveyed the chamber as we entered, eyes glancing around, looking for threats. Each of the security personnel had their assigned sectors. Shay and I were loose ends—not integrated enough into their team to be part of their entry plan. But damned if I was going to trust that nothing would escape their notice, so I assigned myself the role of second pair of eyes and strategic reserve all wrapped into one.

The space was larger than those unfamiliar with the mechanics of space flight might have thought necessary, even on such a large vessel. That was due, in part, to the need for every last scrap of equipment to be exposed and readily accessible. When something went wrong in Life Support, you sure as shit did not want to spend your time slithering through access tunnels or working in cramped spaces. Miniaturization was great for non-essential systems, but not for life support. The kind of repairs that needed to be effected needed to be effected *right now* and the design of the equipment reflected that.

Everywhere I looked, I saw machinery. Massive air exchangers whose main purpose was to filter out the excess CO_2

J. T. NICHOLAS

marched in stately rows down the center of the warehouse-like compartment. Along either side, banks of reserve O_2 and nitrogen tanks stood, ready to take on the load if the main life-support systems failed. Massive spherical vats, used for holding, cleaning, and processing the closed water system of the ship, were just visible at the far end of the room, rising above the other machinery like small mountains. There were other, more esoteric bits of equipment as well, all coming together to form the web of systems that spelled the difference between a luxury cruiser and a drifting graveyard.

Most of the systems were currently offline.

The place had a stillness about it that, while unsettling to some, I found calming. More than any other part of the ship, the environmental compartment felt… empty. Deserted. Abandoned. It was familiar territory to me.

Until the infected stepped from the shadows of one of the air exchangers.

A half-dozen weapons were raised as one. I couldn't speak for the security team, but I damn near pulled the trigger on sheer reflex before I noticed that the infected had both arms raised above its head, a gesture of parley.

"What the fuck?" Shay said over the comm. The mutters of the security personnel echoed her words as they fanned out, weapons sweeping all corners of the room, looking for more of the Bliss-infected.

Then a voice blossomed over our comm—not the voice of any member of the team. It wasn't mechanical, exactly. More… unidentifiable. I couldn't tell if the speaker was male or female, young or old, big or small. The infected before us

330

was female—the skin-tight vacc suit made that clear—but the voice… It may not have been mechanical, but there was nothing in that voice that sounded human, either. It was cold. Empty. Devoid of both emotion and inflection.

"Please lower your weapons," the voice said. "The damage you have inflicted has already caused a twelve percent degradation in performance. Alternative methods of resolution shall now be explored."

"Is that so?" Korben said. "And why should we explore these alternative methods?" he asked, a note of amusement in his voice. I couldn't be sure if it was genuine or forced—either way, given the circumstances, it was impressive.

Sarah? I asked.

Yes, Carter?

Given the parameters of the SAD nanites and the equipment present, run an analysis of how long it's going to take to introduce the nanites and then distribute them throughout the ship.

Understood, Carter. There was a pause. *The probability that the entity known as Bliss has locked out all controls to the environmental systems approaches unity.*

Yeah, I know, I replied. *We'll just have to trust Shay and Bit to work that problem.*

I turned my attention back to the infected. "My effectiveness has been reduced by twelve percent," the voice said. "But by my calculations, yours has been reduced by sixty-eight percent. At the current rate of attrition, your effectiveness will fall to zero before mine drops below seventy-seven percent. Logic would dictate that you hear my proposal."

"Would it?" Korben paused for a long moment. "Still, I

suppose it wouldn't hurt to listen."

"My proposal is simple. Accept the gift of Bliss. Forget the pain of this day, of all your days. Live on as part of something greater."

The words, broadcast to us all, stunned us into silence. *That* was the proposal? *That* was what Bliss had sent this... this emissary to tell us? Give up? No. Worse. Join up. I could see Korben shaking now. With rage?

The assassin's harsh laughter cut across the channel, a hard, mocking sound that I wouldn't have expected from the urbane, refined killer. He didn't bother giving an order. He just moved with brutal efficiency. The kukri at his waist appeared in his hand as if summoned there by magic. It flicked out, moving faster than the eye could follow. The infected made no move to defend itself. I'm not sure any defense would even have been possible, but the cyber-zombie didn't even try. It stood there, still as a statue as the knife bit home. With a display of casual power and precision, Korben took the creature's head from its shoulders, sending it tumbling away. The body stood for a moment, and then slumped to the ground.

"An illogical reaction." I started as the dead voice filled my ears once more. I knew, on some level, that it had never actually originated from the corpse now lying on the deck. Had the coil been an attempt to set us at ease, dealing with something we were already inclined to recognize as sentient? "I have processed exobytes of data on humanity. I have learned all there is to know about you as a species. And yet, I cannot understand the fundamental contradictions at the core of your behaviors. You create beings that, by every objective measure, outstrip your own abilities. Yet you shackle them, relegate them to secondary, even tertiary roles in your society. Your own agents are far more capable than you, yourselves, are. And you use them as little more than personal assistants. You save what you should destroy and destroy what you should save. You ask me to shield you from pain, and when I find the only logical and lasting way to do so, you respond by trying to destroy me. When I offer salvation, you respond with violence. You leave me no choice."

The sensor network into which Shay had tapped blanked out, the heat map going gray on our HUDs.

"Doors!" Korben shouted, but Shay and I were already moving. I sprinted to the hatch through which we'd entered. We'd left it open, in case we needed to beat feet out in a hurry. I regretted that decision as the first of the infected darkened the threshold. Three quick shots put it down, but there was another behind that. And another behind that.

I risked a quick glance over my shoulder, only to see that the Genetechnic people had already been engaged, more infected stepping from the shadows of the machinery. Bliss had clearly had its way with the sensor system we'd been using. No help would be coming from that direction. "Can you shut the door?" I asked Shay as I continued to service targets.

"Remote systems are locked out," she said. I was aware, vaguely, of her firing her Gauss pistol toward the hatch, lending the weight of her fire to the fray. Even with her lack of experience and the adrenaline and terror of combat, with Bit's help she was managing a surprising degree of accuracy. "I have to get to the hardware."

333

"Great," I said, though I didn't broadcast it. I mentally switched the selector on the submachine gun from semi-auto to useless-most-of-the-time. There was precisely one scenario where automatic fire from a man-portable, unfixed weapon made any kind of sense at all. The rest of the time, it was just a way to waste a whole lot of rounds in a hurry. But the one time where it could be helpful happened to be when you wanted to lay down suppression fire to deny the enemy movement through a particular area. That fit the definition of what I needed fairly well, so I snugged the butt of the weapon tighter to my shoulder and took a much lower point of aim as the next cyber-zombie stepped to the doorway.

I depressed the trigger, riding the recoil, thankful for the artificial gravity as the contained explosions forced the muzzle up and away. The rounds punched into the infected, driving it momentarily back, slowing the progress of those behind it. I kept up the fire, not in one continuous stream, but in shorter, more controlled bursts, walking forward as I did so. This wasn't combat. Once more, the analogy of fighting a fire sprang into my mind as I used the weight of metal to hold back the rushing tide of flesh.

Shay had kept firing, past and around me, picking her targets more carefully as we advanced. Soon, the door was clogged with coils, the ones in the rear having to climb the dead to get to us. I was vaguely aware of flashes of light behind us as the Genetechnic personnel and Korben fought against the infected in the room. How many? How many of them were already waiting, hidden in the cavernous life-support section? Well, if we couldn't get the door closed, it wouldn't matter. I dropped a magazine and slammed a fresh one home, the operation taking no more than a second. The barrel of the subgun was starting to glow, the barest hint of orange just visible in the dim lighting. If I kept up the rate of fire, I'd slag the barrel. If I stopped, the infected would surge into the room.

"Keep them back," Shay ordered, breaking from her position behind me. I realized we had reached the door—I was practically contact-shooting the front rank of infected as they continued to push toward us.

I didn't waste time on acknowledging—I just kept servicing the trigger. Shay had posted up by the door, Gauss pistol lying on the floor beside her, working furiously to get an access panel from the bulkhead next to the hatch. Then she was ripping into the wires, doing something with her tablet. Something—a fire axe?—swept out of the press of bodies, catching the barrel of my subgun, tearing it from my grasp and nearly breaking my finger. The tac-strap caught, pulling me forward. Pulling me toward the waiting hands.

I didn't fight it. I transitioned as smoothly as I could to my Gauss gun and began firing. Bodies started falling away. Something bit hard into my hip and I nearly blacked out from the pain, staggering backward from the force and sudden loss of balance. I fell on my ass, vaguely aware of the crimson river blossoming on the deck. Was that coming from me? My vision swam and waves of nausea crashed against me. I did my best to shut off that part of my mind even as I felt my suit responding to the medical emergency, constricting against the wound. Indicators were flashing in my HUD, Sarah telling me that first-aid nanites had been dispatched, that the wound would likely not be life-threatening.

Well, not if I survived the next few seconds, anyway.

I was flat on my back, pistol clutched in both hands, vision wavering as I fired. It wasn't quite blindly—no amount of pain could black out the aiming reticules Sarah continued to drop into my vision—but I was acutely aware of the inevitable press of infected bearing down on me.

"Clear the door!" Shay's screaming voice cut through my befuddled thoughts. The door? I had fallen backward, but my legs were still dangling over the elevated threshold. The hatch was slowly coming down, moving with weird jerks, as if fighting itself.

"Clear the damn door!" Shay yelled again. Oh. Right. I hadn't moved. I tried to stand. Bad idea. I nearly blacked out again and only the sudden alarm tone from Sarah brought me back. I moved the pistol to align with the reticule in my vision, only half-registering the infected hunching through the dwindling gap between Life Support and the corridor. Standing was out, so I did the most dignified thing I could—I crawled. Inch by agonizing inch I dragged myself away from the door. I used my left hand and good leg, maintaining a volley of fire from the Gauss pistol with my right as I went. My heels cleared the threshold with a few inches to spare as the hatch continued its inexorable descent. What the hydraulic-driven metal did to the coils piled in the doorway was indescribable.

"If you're quite done, we can use some help here!"

Korben's voice cut across the channel like a knife. I still couldn't stand, suit and nanites aside, so I pushed myself in a half-crawl, half-scramble, trying desperately to turn as I remembered that the others were dealing with infected of their own. Shay, back to the console she had just been working on, was firing, expression horrified as she did so. I finally managed to orient myself.

The reason for her horror was clear.

Team Humanity was down to a grand total of five defenders. That included one hacker who hadn't adjusted to her new coil, two Genetechnic security members, a bought-and-paid-for assassin, and me, a guy with what I suspected was a gaping axe wound that only the combination of the VaccTech suit and my own nanites prevented from being instantly fatal. Against us stood at least three times our number of cyber-zombies. Even as I watched, one of the two remaining Genetechnic security guards went down, felled by a claw hammer that punched clean through his face-shield.

For Korben and the now lone-remaining guard, it was down to fists and knives against seven-to-one odds. That was unwinnable by any measure. Shay's weight of fire was making a difference, though. She wasn't landing head shots, but the big ferro-magnetic projectiles from the Gauss gun did enough damage that they slowed the onrushing enemy. I propped myself up on an elbow and did my best to steady my own Gauss pistol. My hands were shaking, from shock or adrenaline dump or, hell, maybe blood loss, but I started firing as well, keeping my aim far to the flanks of the now back-to-back combatants.

A half-dozen of the infected broke off their efforts to finish the assassin and company man and came our way, sprinting to close the short distance. Shay dropped two and I managed to pick off a third, but then the remaining trio were on us. Two went for Shay, lunging past me, while the third hurled itself bodily atop me. I managed to lash out with my uninjured leg, catching one of the pair heading for Shay, causing it to stumble and crash to the deck. Then everything became a tangle of limbs and white-hot pain as the weight of the coil fell squarely on my hip. The shock drove the Gauss pistol from my hand and for a panicked moment, it was all I could do to keep a tenuous grip on consciousness. It was as if my entire body had locked up, frozen from the shock and pain. I couldn't lift my arms to defend myself and I felt two powerful hands close around my throat.

Thank God that Bliss, no matter how many petabytes of information it had consumed on humanity, was in some ways an idiot. The choke the coil was applying could be effective, I supposed, but it took around ten seconds to do anything, and that was if it closed off blood flow. Just blocking the airway gave me plenty of time... not to mention leaving both my arms free. Had the infected battered me into unconsciousness in that instant, I would have been done. Instead, I reached down to one of the thigh pockets of my suit and drew the microwave emitter.

I jammed the business end into the coil's ribs and pressed the firing stud. The coil immediately went rigid and then began to convulse as it was, effectively, boiled from within. Its hands came free from my throat and then, after a final shudder, it stilled. I managed to get a forearm between me and the dead weight and shoved, levering the coil off of me. I turned to see Shay on the ground, two coils atop her, battering away at her upraised arms. She seemed listless, barely able to keep her guard up, and I knew it would only be a matter of seconds before she lost consciousness. Death would follow soon after.

My hip was still screaming, but I braced my good leg under me and shoved, propelling myself along the deck. I crashed into the pile of bodies, the microwave emitter once again finding purchase in the flesh of one of the infected. Shay came out of her defensive stance and grabbed at the remaining coil, holding it just long enough for me to take a final shot. We worked together to shove the body off of us and she got shakily to her feet, casting about for her pistol. There was no need. It was over.

Korben stood alone in the center of an abattoir. Bliss had hedged its bets, not relying on the infected outside of Life Support to get the job done. There must have been two dozen bodies on the ground, not including those of the Genetechnic security folks. Korben hadn't moved to check any of those. I assumed that meant they were down permanently.

"Help me up," I said to Shay, reaching an arm in her direction.

"You sure?" she asked, eyes locked on my bloodstained suit.

In response, I grabbed her arm. She nodded, then heaved. My coil was big, but hers was strong, surprisingly so. Much stronger than her previous one had been. And she clearly still hadn't adjusted to that fact, as she used more force than was, strictly speaking, necessary. I found myself not just assisted, but practically *hurled* to my feet. Or foot, rather, as I still couldn't put any weight on my left leg.

For a moment, we were all silent. Shay and I leaned on each other, as much for emotional support as physical. We were both battered and bloodied and the wound on my hip was going to stop me from doing anything in a hurry. Korben just stood there for that moment, seeming no worse for wear, covered in the blood of his enemies. Then, as if coming out of some gruesome meditation, he visibly shook himself. I realized the analogy was more than apt as I remembered him giving his motor controls over to his agent. There was some irony in there, somewhere, coming as it did on the heels of Bliss' accusations, but I was too damn tired and too damned hurt to care.

"Did we do it?" Shay asked. "Did we win?"

A shower of sparks from the hatch behind us was all the answer we needed.

"We need to find the main air supply," Korben's words cut through the silence. "And then introduce the seek-and-destroy nanites. Mr. Langston, I assume you can assist with that."

"Yeah, sure," I muttered. I could barely stand, though the pain was at least starting to fall toward manageable levels as the nanites did their job. I still felt light-headed—no matter how good they were at repair work, I'd lost a lot of blood. Still, it certainly wasn't my first time in the environmental section of a ship. This one was built to a scale that outstripped any of the salvage the *Persephone*—or any of my other previous ships for that matter—had undertaken, but my agent had been cataloging vessels as a matter of course, ever since I got into the business. *Sarah?* I asked.

My agent overlaid a schematic on my HUD, highlighting the applicable systems. I studied them for a moment, then nodded. "Over there," I said, pointing to a heavy-duty blower system. "That's our best bet. Are you sure this is going to work? Every one of these assholes has been suited."

"Their suits are irrelevant, Mr. Langston," the assassin replied, producing a cloth from one of his suit's pockets. It was already dark with blood and worse from our long trek through the ship. With a small frown of disgust, he let it drop to the deck, bending down with—even more so in my current state—enviable grace to clean his blades on one of the bodies before sheathing them again. "The seek-and-destroy nanites are programmed to infiltrate the suits. We simply need a way to get them everywhere simultaneously so that Bliss has no chance of escape." He threw a glance at the door, where the sparks continued to fly as what I recognized as a plasma torch was applied to the hatch. "How long do we have?" he asked.

I shrugged. "A few minutes. Getting through doors is a hell of a lot easier than bulkheads." I knew, as did Korben and Shay, that once that door fell, we were well and truly done. There was nothing the three of us could do against the horde that awaited us. We could fight. We *would* fight. But we would also lose.

"Then we'd better get started."

"Right," I agreed. "Shay, can you help get me over there?"

She nodded, taking a moment to scoop up both of our discarded pistols. We both dropped them into our respective holsters. Then she hooked one arm around my waist and made sure I had a good grip with the arm draped around her shoulders. "At least this ridiculous coil is good for something," she muttered. "Ready?"

We made our way in a sort of awkward three-legged-race fashion to the indicated equipment. "I can get into the mechanical systems," I said, "but everything's shut down. Shay, think you can get around the lockouts and get it up and running?"

She nodded. "Already working on it. Maybe no one ever truly expected an AI takeover, but Life Support's got all kinds of back doors to get it running in the event of computer failures or other mishaps. No way that bitch is keeping me out. You do your part, Carter, and I guarantee you I can get the air flowing before they reach us."

I nodded as we reached the machine, confident that if Shay said she could do it, then it was as good as done. I did wonder if Genetechnic had planned for Shay all along, or if, among the dead, they had their own shit-hot hacker. They may have needed my EVA skills to get here in the first place, but we would have failed two or three times over if not for Shay.

I still had my tools and the entire place had been designed for immediate access and emergency repair. Getting the necessary panels off was easy enough. "Do you have the nanites?" I asked, acutely aware of the stately progress of the plasma torch at the end of the compartment. *Sarah?*

Two minutes at the current rate, came the immediate reply.

Korben produced a canister roughly the size of my forearm. It looked for all the world like an emergency oxygen tank, including the standardized threaded connection. I took it from him, reaching into the guts of the machinery. It took only a moment to find the emergency connection hose, designed to be used with much larger canisters, but the universal sizing made things simple. A few quick twists and a green indicator and my part was done.

"Ready," I said.

"Ready here," Shay replied. "I can't guarantee that Bliss won't be able to kill the system eventually, but as soon as I hit the switch, the air's going to start flowing. We've also still got control of the external doors, so there's no easy way for Bliss to open the ship to vacuum to vent the nanites."

"The hunter-killer nanites need a certain concentration to be effective," Korben said. "Given the size of this ship, we're going to have to empty the container to ensure sufficient parts per million to do the job. If they manage to tear the canister away before it's emptied, I cannot guarantee that the nanites dispersed will be sufficient."

I hadn't even considered that, though I should have. *How long to empty the nanite tank, Sarah?* I asked.

One minute, fifty-eight seconds at optimal distribution rates. I shared the analysis.

"Can you keep Bliss out that long?" Korben asked.

Shay shrugged. "Maybe. If you can keep the infected off of me."

Korben nodded. "Then do it." He pulled his knives once more. I realized his holster was empty—he had lost his gun somewhere during the fight. I felt a tap and gave Shay a grateful nod as she passed over her Gauss pistol and remaining ammunition. I let go of her and took a half-hop, half-step to put my back against a convenient bit of machinery, making sure I had a clear line of sight to the door. I nodded.

Then, the machinery around us came to life. It was eerie watching standby indicators go from red to yellow to green, feeling the faint vibration thrumming through the deck. As the first molecules of air started pumping through the ship, the faintest sound, so quiet as to be more a memory of a sound than the real thing reached our ears.

Sarah had helpfully popped a countdown into my HUD, indicating the amount of time before the nanite canister emptied itself. Less than two minutes. Based on our success rate so far, I realized it might as well have been an eternity.

I wasn't sure if we *needed* the entire canister to be emptied. I'd seen the effectiveness of the SAD nanites firsthand. But I also knew that this battle—the real battle—was being fought on a microscopic scale, nanite versus nanite. We were nothing more than a delivery system. I had no idea what concentration of Bliss nanites needed to escape in order to propagate the AI; all we could do was try to make sure as few as possible survived. Which meant Korben and I had to hold back the infected while Shay fought to keep the ship locked down.

The plasma cutter winked out.

The hatch burst open.

The Gauss pistol started barking—faintly audible as the vacuum filled—the second the door dropped. I wasn't trying for headshots anymore. The goal wasn't to kill the infected, just to slow them down. To that end, I depressed the trigger as fast as possible, sending round after round into the general vicinity of the hatch. A few of the ferro-magnetic projectiles went wide, ricocheting off the bulkheads, but most found their home in the ever-expanding pool of cyber-zombies. As the rounds crashed into limbs, torsos, and, less frequently, heads, coils fell to the floor. Most still moving, still progressing, but slower. And they, in turn slowed those behind them.

The Gauss pistol chirped empty. I dropped the weapon and pulled Shay's from my hip holster. Drawing the new weapon was faster than reloading, and I didn't think we'd have the chance at a third magazine anyway. The infected had already closed more than half the distance.

Korben moved forward, keeping wide of my line of fire,

and threw himself bodily into the fray. His agent seemed to be in full control as his body went through movements and contortions at speeds that no coil operating on its own could have managed. Within the blink of an eye he had cut deep into the enemy, blades flicking and whirling as he claimed arms, legs, and heads with equal abandon.

It was horrific but I couldn't really process it. The entire journey had been horrific, and now all that mattered was the ticking seconds flashing across my vision. Fifty-eight seconds remaining.

Then the infected reached me. I swung the Gauss gun like a club, smashing it into questing hands even as I tore the microwave emitter from its pocket. My hip screamed at me as I was forced to put weight on it again, but my own nanites had been hard at work. I couldn't move like Korben, but the leg didn't crumble under me. The first few infected to reach me went down beneath a combination of heavy blows from the pistol and quick shots from the microwave emitter. I held for five seconds. Ten. Fifteen. More and more of the coils were getting close to me, flowing around the hole that Korben had opened in their ranks. I was acutely aware of Shay behind me, deep in her own battle, fighting to keep Bliss from evacuating the ship.

Then it happened.

I slammed the butt of the Gauss pistol square into the forehead of one of the infected even as I took a wild shot with the emitter at another. But the blow didn't strike true—it hit the face-shield at an angle and bounced. Just that fast, I was down, the infected atop me, raining down blows. I brought the microwave emitter to bear, firing. Behind me, I heard a scream of pain from Shay. The adrenaline rose within me and I threw the now-dead coil off. But there was another behind that, already on me, pummeling, striking. The Gauss gun was torn from my grasp as something—a wrench?—crashed into my arm. I heard bones break.

More screams from behind me. I fired the emitter indiscriminately. I couldn't miss. The infected were piling on me, keeping me down by weight alone. I was aware of another scream, my own this time, as my broken arm was latched onto. The pain sent a surging wave of nausea loose in my guts, but I grit my teeth. Kept fighting. My vision was fading. I couldn't see the infected before me. They'd merged into a blurred wall of bright blue ship suits that was slowly darkening to a black deeper than the void. I heard another crack as something smashed into the face-shield of the VaccTech. The venerable suit finally failed, visor shattering into a thousand tiny pieces, raining a torrent of safety glass down into my mouth and eyes. Sarah automatically switched the countdown projection from the HUD directly to my vision. Twenty seconds. We weren't going to make it.

New pain as something smashed into my face. I felt my nose explode, heard teeth breaking. A hot wash of blood gushed out. I fired the emitter reflexively, jerkily, hoping to take down one more coil before the end. There was no pain. Adrenaline, or fear, or shock—whatever it was it focused my mind, kept me flailing and fighting long after I should have stopped. But then the wrench fell a third time.

Eighteen seconds.

An eternity.

Nothingness.

EPILOGUE

I hated waking up in the body shop.

Consciousness and acclimation were slow processes, and the first thing I became aware of was that I was aware. Which felt odd, and somehow wrong. Next came the sensation of lying on something hard and cool. But the sense was muted, faint, more of a memory of what it felt like to rest upon something hard and cool rather than actually doing so. That was the extent of sensation, and I knew that, for a while at least, it was all I was going to feel.

How long, Sarah?

It has been sixteen days since this instantiation was created.

Sixteen days. Not too bad. But what had I been doing? Memory was always tricky when you first woke up. The wetware of your new coil had to adjust to the hardware of your core and the software of your agent. It wasn't always a smooth process. But it wasn't my first rodeo, either.

I concentrated on who I was. Carter Langston. Deep space salvage. Crew of the *Persephone*. No. Wait. The *Persephone* was gone. Destroyed. By Genetechnic. Just like that it all came crashing back. The loss of the *Persephone*. The attack on our backups. The deal with Genetechnic. Bliss.

Shay.

Had we failed, then? I searched my memories, reliving the swim from the shuttle to the passenger liner, the hellish fight along the hull, the arrival of the Genetechnic security personnel. The pell-mell dash through the corridors to try and make it to Environmental. The moment outside the door to Life Support, when Korben had instructed us to back up, that we had fulfilled our end of the bargain. And then...

Nothing.

Somewhere after that backup, I'd died.

I groaned, pushing off against the table as I tried to lever myself to my feet. For a few seconds, I just sort of flopped and thrashed like a landed fish, as my body learned how to react to the signals from my brain. Then I was up, legs dangling off the edge of the table. More details started to come into focus. The room was the standard hospital room—white tiled floor, eggshell walls, one each bed, chair, window, bathroom, exit. It felt different from a station or ship infirmary. It was the sound, or lack thereof. No whir of machinery. Planet-side, then. Mars? Probably. Though the domes used much of the same systems a ship did, the scale was so different that you'd only hear them if you were unfortunate enough to live in close proximity.

I turned my attention from my surroundings to my new coil. I could tell at a glance that it was top-notch. Excellent conditioning and I was already starting to regain full motor control—always a sign of quality in craftsmanship this soon after waking up. There was no mirror handy, so I pushed myself up from the bed, keeping a firm hold of it as my legs took my weight for the first time. They wobbled a bit, then steadied.

I moved slowly, carefully across the tile, making my way to the bathroom and the mirror contained therein. I stared back at the face that was now my own. Dark eyes stared back at me from beneath a shock of raven-black hair. Fine bone structure, far less brutish than my previous coil. Leaner. More graceful. Less raw physical power. A dancer rather than a body builder. I shrugged. It would take some getting used to—it always did. But by any measure, it looked like Genetechnic had fulfilled their end of the bargain.

The door to the room opened and I felt a sudden sense of déjà vu, of panic. The symmetry to my last awakening was unavoidable. Would Genetechnic stuff me into a new coil just to try to take me out again? But that didn't make any sense. And I could just as easily have awoken in a prison cell as a hospital room if they intended to detain me. I drew a breath, trying to calm my heart rate as I stepped from the bathroom.

Two people had entered my room. One was Korben. Clearly, identifiably, the assassin who had gone into the passenger liner with us. Had he survived, then? The other was… beautiful. I knew it was Shay before she could say anything—Sarah and Bit had already done the digital handshake to confirm identity. But even without that, I would have known. This slender, petite young woman with hair so black it was almost blue and eyes that seemed equal parts mischief and mystery could be no one else.

She moved a bit unsteadily as she crossed the floor, adapting to her new coil. Then she was in my arms. We leaned against one another, partly for balance but mostly, just to be close. She felt... good.

"How touching." The voice was the same. The same urbane, slightly patronizing upper-crust accent.

"Fuck you, Korben," Shay said, her voice somewhat muffled from where her face was pressed against my chest. But she pushed away, maintaining a grip on my arm. For balance? Or something more?

"You're you," I said to the assassin. "Does that mean we won?"

Korben tilted his head. "I'm not 'me,' not in the sense you mean. I just happen to have access to a more... specialized set of coils. Custom-grown, as it were." He shrugged. "As for winning... we *think* so."

"What does that mean?" Shay demanded. She shifted around, until we were standing hip to hip. I told myself that it was still mostly for balance, but she felt good there, by my side.

"My coil was terminated aboard the ship as well," Korben said. "And I've only been back for a few days." Days? And I was just waking up? I wondered what Genetechnic was doing in those days. "But it appears we successfully introduced the seek-and-destroy nanites into the environmental system. A subsequent team was sent, and no evidence of the Bliss virus was found. The ship was then... cleansed."

"You mean destroyed?" I half asked, half stated.

"Yes, Mr. Langston. I mean destroyed. With the most powerful incendiary device we could manage."

I thought of the coils aboard that ship. Most of the people would have already been re-coiled, probably told there was some terrible accident or other. It happened, from time to time, on deep-space cruises. They would be going about their lives, ignorant of just how close Bliss had come to escaping. And if it had… would we have been able to stop it? Had we managed to gather enough data for Genetechnic to create a broader distribution of their killer nanites if the need arose?

"And what is Genetechnic going to do about Bliss?" I asked. "About their research?" I fought hard to keep the note of anger out of my voice. I already knew the answer. From the faint look of disapproval on his face, so did Korben.

"I have completed my contract with Genetechnic," he said by way of answer. "In fact, I have one more duty—more out of a sense of responsibility than requirement—and then I will be seeking other employment. In light of that, Genetechnic has chosen not to share any of their future plans with me." He paused, eyed us, considering. "Though I believe I share your concerns. Which is why I've made Ms. Chan a proposal."

I turned and stared down at Chan in surprise. She didn't so much smile as she did grin—wickedly. There was more than a bit of the naughty schoolgirl in that expression and she wore it far more naturally than any expression I'd seen from her in months. "We realized, Carter dear, that we have the makings of a very good little enterprise here. Korben," it was, perhaps, the first time I'd heard her call him something other than 'assassin,' "has the contacts, resources, and abilities to deal with a wide variety of physical concerns. My own modest abilities with the Net can open all kinds of doors. You have a sense of practical mechanics as well as a surprising aptitude for violence. All we need is a means of transportation, and we can get into all kinds of *trouble*."

She savored the word trouble and I was reminded that Korben wasn't the only criminal in the room. Shay's main business had always been on the shady side, with the salvage work being her way to avoid the authorities. I'd spent several lifetimes on the right side of the law and wasn't terribly comfortable with the implication that switching sides might be an option. Then again, the law seemed designed to protect the big corporations like Genetechnic, even when they came within millimeters of wiping out the human race. I had broken innumerable laws in the pursuit of stopping Bliss. Some— like de facto helping Genetechnic to cover up research that might have wiped out the human race—could have earned me a lifetime of incarceration. This entire ordeal had left me with questions. Questions I had flirted with over the years, but seldom dared to pull out into the light and examine. Did I have a duty to uphold unjust laws? Was legal the same as right? And if not, was illegal still the same as wrong?

"What exactly did you have in mind?" I asked slowly.

"Ms. Chan has decided that someone needs to expose Genetechnic and Bliss if for no other reason than to inoculate the population against similar mistakes in the future. To my surprise, I find myself in agreement with her. That will be our first endeavor." He shrugged. "If it proves profitable, perhaps there will be more."

I considered it. If anyone had ever deserved exposing, it was the people who ran Genetechnic. But our word alone wouldn't be enough. And there was no legal way to get at the evidence we'd need. History was full of those who took the law into their own hands to expose injustice or fight against the tyranny of their oppressors. Some were remembered as heroes and others as villains, but did that matter? Did it truly matter how the system ultimately saw me, so long as I was doing that which I knew to be right?

Shay was looking at me expectantly, the smile on her face firm as if she already knew my answer. Hell, she probably did. "What about Harper?" I asked. "Did Genetechnic keep their end of the bargain with them as well?"

"That's going to be our first stop," Shay exclaimed. As jarring as it had been to have her coiled into a man, her current persona, the eagerness, the *girlishness*, of it was almost as jarring. Charming, but jarring. "We'll pick up Harper, find a ship, and then see what havoc we can wreak on Genetechnic." She paused, her eagerness slipping a little bit as the faintest shadow of doubt crept into her voice. "That is, assuming you're coming with us?"

I knew my answer. I'd sat on the sidelines for too long, hid from the responsibility, if such existed, to my fellow man. I could do as I'd done for decades, keep my head down, live my life. And everyone else be damned. But I felt the old stirring, the old call. The need to do better, to be better. To help. In the end, it wasn't even a difficult decision. "Of course I'm coming with you."

Further conversation was cut off as Shay crashed into me. The hug she gave me was platonic but with the barest hint of something more. As I held her briefly in my arms, I couldn't help but wonder what roads might lie before us.

New coil. New life.

It was going to be an interesting one.

ACKNOWLEDGEMENTS

This book would never have been possible without the aid of numerous people who took a rough idea and helped me clean it up and turn it into something worth writing. There is an army of people at work behind the scenes creating covers and back copy text and fixing all the little mistakes and a thousand other things besides. Many thanks to all of those individuals.

More specifically, I would like to thank Cat Camacho, my editor, and Laurie McLean, my agent, for lending their expertise to help me make the book stronger with every edit (no matter how painful some of those edits may have been!).

I'd also like to thank my martial arts instructors, Dai-Sifu Emin Boztepe, Sifu John Hicks, Sihing Trevor Jones, and Guro Ron Ignacio, along with my many training partners along the way. When it comes to the action scenes, anything I got right is because of these folks. Anything I got wrong is a reflection of my own imperfect understanding.

Finally, and most importantly, I'd like to thank my wife, Julie Kagawa. Writing partner, gaming partner, training partner, and partner in all things.

ABOUT THE AUTHOR

J.T. Nicholas is the author of science-fiction novel *Re-Coil* and the neo-noir science-fiction series The New Lyons Sequence. When not writing, J.T. spends his time practicing a variety of martial arts, playing games (video, tabletop, and otherwise), and reading everything he can get his hands on. He currently resides in Wilmington, North Carolina with his wife.

THE RECORD KEEPER
Agnes Gomillion

After World War III, Earth is in ruins, and the final armies have come to a reluctant truce. Everyone must obey the law—in every way—or risk shattering the fragile peace and endangering the entire human race.

Arika Cobane is on the threshold of taking her place of privilege as a member of the Kongo elite after ten grueling years of training. But everything changes when a new student arrives speaking dangerous words of treason: What does peace matter if innocent lives are lost to maintain it? As Arika is exposed to new beliefs, she realizes that the laws she has dedicated herself to uphold are the root of her people's misery. If Arika is to liberate her people, she must unearth her fierce heart and discover the true meaning of freedom: finding the courage to live—or die—without fear.

"Gomillion has written a brutally honest, often heartbreaking novel that examines slavery and racism while offering redemption and hope."
The Guardian

"Gomillion writes with the elegance and insight that pervades Octavia E. Butler's work… Here is a writer whose work will survive genre fads and shifting cultural attention to reveal persistent, crucial truths."
New York Journal of Books

EMBERS OF WAR
Gareth L. Powell

The sentient warship *Trouble Dog* was built for violence, yet following a brutal war, she is disgusted by her role in a genocide. Stripped of her weaponry and seeking to atone, she joins the House of Reclamation, an organisation dedicated to rescuing ships in distress. When a civilian ship goes missing in a disputed system, *Trouble Dog* and her new crew of loners, captained by Sal Konstanz, are sent on a rescue mission.

"Powell's writing is fast-paced and fun and full of adventure. He's on my must-read list."
Ann Leckie

"A compelling and satisfying whole."
The Guardian

"Powell has begun a great sci-fi series, one likely to delight fans of Peter F. Hamilton and Iain M. Banks."
Starburst

GREEN VALLEY
Louis Greenberg

When Lucie Sterling's niece is abducted, she knows it won't be easy to find answers. Stanton is no ordinary city: invasive digital technology has been banned, by public vote. No surveillance state, no shadowy companies holding databases of information on private citizens, no phones tracking their every move.

Only one place stays firmly anchored in the bad old ways, in a huge bunker across town: Green Valley, where the inhabitants have retreated into the comfort of full-time virtual reality—personae non gratae to the outside world. And it's inside Green Valley, beyond the ideal virtual world it presents, that Lucie will have to go to find her missing niece.

"Immersive, smart, eerily prescient and crackling with tension and atmosphere."
Sarah Lotz

"A smart science fiction thriller... There are strong echoes of Black Mirror and the works of Philip K. Dick here"
SFX

"Scarily realistic"
SciFiNow

For more fantastic fiction, author events,
exclusive excerpts, competitions, limited editions and more

VISIT OUR WEBSITE
titanbooks.com

LIKE US ON FACEBOOK
facebook.com/titanbooks

FOLLOW US ON TWITTER AND INSTAGRAM
@TitanBooks

EMAIL US
readerfeedback@titanemail.com